THE PRINCE'S GAMBIT

(THE EMPIRE'S CORPS—BOOK XX)

CHRISTOPHER G. NUTTALL

The characters and events portrayed in this book are fictitious. Any similarity to real persons, living or dead, is coincidental and not intended by the author.

Text copyright © 2021 Christopher G. Nuttall

All rights reserved.

Printed in the United States of America.

ISBN: 9798414887812

Independently published

No part of this book may be reproduced, or stored in a retrieval system, or transmitted in any form or by any means, electronic, mechanical, photocopying, recording, or other-wise, without express written permission of the publisher.

Cover By Tan Ho Sim

https://www.artstation.com/alientan

Book One: The Empire's Corps
Book Two: No Worse Enemy
Book Three: When The Bough Breaks
Book Four: Semper Fi
Book Five: The Outcast
Book Six: To The Shores
Book Seven: Reality Check
Book Eight: Retreat Hell
Book Nine: The Thin Blue Line
Book Ten: Never Surrender
Book Eleven: First To Fight
Book Twelve: They Shall Not Pass
Book Thirteen: Culture Shock
Book Fourteen: Wolf's Bane
Book Fifteen: Cry Wolf
Book Sixteen: Favour The Bold
Book Seventeen: Knife Edge
Book Eighteen: The Halls of Montezuma
Book Nineteen: The Prince's War
Book Twenty: The Prince's Gambit
http://www.chrishanger.net
http://chrishanger.wordpress.com/
http://www.facebook.com/ChristopherGNuttall
ALL COMMENTS WELCOME!

CONTENTS

HISTORIAN'S NOTE vii
PROLOGUE I ix
PROLOGUE II xiii

Chapter One 1
Chapter Two 9
Chapter Three 18
Chapter Four 26
Chapter Five 35
Chapter Six 44
Chapter Seven 53
Chapter Eight 62
Chapter Nine 71
Chapter Ten 80
Chapter Eleven 89
Chapter Twelve 98
Chapter Thirteen 107
Chapter Fourteen 116
Chapter Fifteen 125
Chapter Sixteen 134
Chapter Seventeen 143
Chapter Eighteen 152
Chapter Nineteen 161
Chapter Twenty 170
Chapter Twenty-One 179
Chapter Twenty-Two 188
Chapter Twenty-Three 197
Chapter Twenty-Four 206

Chapter Twenty-Five 215
Chapter Twenty-Six 224
Chapter Twenty-Seven 233
Chapter Twenty-Eight 242
Chapter Twenty-Nine 251
Chapter Thirty 260
Chapter Thirty-One 269
Chapter Thirty-Two 278
Chapter Thirty-Three 287
Chapter Thirty-Four 296
Chapter Thirty-Five 305
Chapter Thirty-Six 314
Chapter Thirty-Seven 323
Chapter Thirty-Eight 332
Chapter Thirty-Nine 341
Chapter Forty 350

EPILOGUE 355
AFTERWORD 359
HOW TO FOLLOW 365

HISTORIAN'S NOTE

The Prince's Gambit is a direct sequel to *The Prince's War*, which is written to be as self-contained as possible but refers to events within *When the Bough Breaks (The Empire's Corps III)* which are summarised in the prologue. It takes place roughly a year after *When the Bough Breaks* and a month after *The Halls of Montezuma*.
CGN.

PROLOGUE I

FROM: *An Unbiased History of the Imperial Royal Family.* Professor Leo Caesius. Avalon. 206PE.

AS WE HAVE SEEN IN PREVIOUS BOOKS, Prince Roland—the last surviving member of the Imperial Family—was extremely lucky to escape Earth before Earthfall. The Childe Roland—as he was known—was a spoilt brat, permanently on the verge of descending into a sybaritic madness that would have suited the *real* rulers of the empire quite well. It was only through the intervention of a Marine Pathfinder, Belinda Lawson, that Prince Roland started to climb out of the pit his minders had dug for him. Indeed, it is quite possible—if Earthfall had been somehow delayed—that the prince would have grown into a fine young man.

But it was not to be. Roland fled Earth and found himself in the custody of the Terran Marine Corps. This posed a serious problem. Legally, Roland was the ruler of the empire; practically, the empire was gone and hardly anyone would be willing to recognise Roland as the master of anything. Even the Marine Corps had its doubts. Roland's reputation preceded him, to the point it was unlikely anyone who hadn't met him would offer any support. His value as a rallying cry for loyalists was very limited. The corps finessed the problem by arranging for Roland to attend Boot Camp, under an assumed name. It would either make a man out of him and give him a solid grounding in military and civil realities, or prove beyond a reasonable doubt he was unsuited for any major role in the post-Earthfall universe.

Results were decidedly mixed. Roland had definite natural talent. At the same time, he still bore the scars of his earlier life. The corps was unsure if he should receive advanced training, with the aim of turning him into a full-fledged Marine, or quietly sidelining him into a less significant role. It was decided, after much consideration, to offer Roland a chance to take command of a military training and assistance team, which would be assigned to New Doncaster. The risk appeared minimal. New Doncaster was a volatile planet, and long-term projections indicated the world would either fall into civil war or be invaded by one of its neighbours, but—in the short-term—Roland should be able to prove himself without any real risk. Just in case, Specialist Rachel Green—a Pathfinder—was assigned to serve as a covert bodyguard.

It rapidly became clear that events on New Doncaster were not following the expected timeline. The situation was degenerating rapidly. Roland's training mission worked hard to build up the local military, despite opposition from government factions, but it was barely enough to stabilise the situation. It seemed unlikely, despite Roland's best efforts, that that planet could remain stable long enough for the government to start addressing the deep-rooted structural issues underlying the conflict. Indeed, there were plenty of factions that saw no *need* to address the issues.

Roland showed both the strengths and weaknesses of a young officer with little practical experience. He devised a scheme to mount an airmobile raid on a rebel base, which worked surprisingly well; he also drew up a plan to establish defence lines and blockhouses throughout the threatened islands in a bid to curtail rebel activities, a plan that might have worked if he'd had more resources at his disposal. On the other hand, he also put his life at risk—sometimes to show the troops he was sharing the risks, sometimes for his own selfish reasons—and it could easily have ended in disaster. However, he had good reason to think his plan would slow the rebel advance, giving the government a chance to at least *try* to hammer out a political solution.

He was wrong. The rebels had long been planning a major offensive. Roland's army camp and the capital island came under heavy attack. The spaceport, and the understrength Marine contingent providing protection, was destroyed in a single cataclysmic bombing. It seemed likely, as Roland led his troops in defence of the government, that the rebels had dealt them a fatal blow. Perhaps, if Roland had not acted so quickly, they would have won. Instead, through heavy fighting and a great deal of luck, Roland was able to drive the rebels away from Kingston and save the government.

However, the remainder of the rebel plans went off without a hitch. The government's authority across the outlying plantation islands, long hotbeds of insurgent activity, fell to rebel forces with terrifying speed. It rapidly became apparent that, far from being beaten, the rebels had preserved much of their strength and were working to build up their forces as quickly as possible.

And, as Roland assumed command of the planetary military, it became clear the war was far from over.

PROLOGUE II

LUDLOW ESTATE, NEW DONCASTER

IT FELT ODD, LORD HAMISH LUDLOW REFLECTED, to hold a party in the middle of a war. His estate—and the island—was as secure as his personal armsmen could make it, but he had few illusions about what would happen if the rebels dispatched a small army to take his mansion and lands. The seas were choppy, and the only *safe* way to reach the island was by aircraft, yet the rebels were master sailors and it was quite possible his household included some rebel sympathizers. They were supposed to be trustworthy—they'd worked for his family for generations—but who could tell these days? Hamish had cracked down hard, using the war situation as an excuse to keep his clients and servants under tight control, yet he feared the worst. If the spaceport hadn't been destroyed, he would have been very tempted to send his wife and daughters into orbit for their own safety.

Because the rebels made it clear they consider women and children to be legitimate targets, Hamish thought, coldly. He'd seen the images from the first uprisings, the handful of video files that had been transmitted across the globe. *If they storm the island, they'll show no mercy to anyone.*

The thought pained him as he swept through the dance hall, quietly directing a handful of his fellows towards the meeting room. His wife had arranged the ball with her usual skill, inviting everyone who was anyone; he had to admit, as he passed a pair of young debutantes being chaperoned by their mothers, that she'd done a wonderful job. It was important to keep up the pretence that all was normal, as well as reminding the young men what they were fighting for. He smiled, inwardly, as he spied a handful of men in fancy uniforms. They looked ready and able to fight for the planet. He just hoped they did as well on the battlefield as they did on the dance floor.

Hamish nodded politely to a maid as he left the hall, making his way down to the secure conference room. It looked like a comfortable sitting room, complete with armchairs, a well-stocked drinks cabinet and a fire burning merrily in the fireplace, but his family had invested millions of credits in making the chamber as secure as possible. They weren't *exactly* going to discuss treason, but…he shook his head. The lower orders—and those who'd thrown their lot in with them—wouldn't understand, if they knew what he was doing. They'd assume he was merely being a selfish bastard, rather than a true son of New Doncaster. His lips thinned. Once, he could have spoken his mind and all would have listened. Now…speaking one's mind risked social death. It was just a matter of time until it meant *literal* death.

He poured himself a drink, then waited for the remaining three men to arrive. They were older aristocrats, all descendants of the founders themselves…all so deeply rooted in the planet's history that the mere thought of pulling up roots and moving elsewhere was unthinkable. There were no women, nor any young and foolish men. Hamish's mouth twisted in distaste. It was hard to know who could be trusted, these days. The war had sorted the men from the boys, true, but it had also made it hard to oppose the government. And yet, government policy threatened to lead the planet to ruin…

"Hamish," Lord Prestwick said. He was older than Hamish, with grey hair and cold blue eyes, but his mind was as sharp as ever. "I assume there's a reason you called us here?"

"Yes." Hamish looked from face to face. "The first offensive will begin tomorrow."

None of the men, he noted sourly, showed any hint of surprise. They'd owned the government, at least until the Prime Minister had made peace with the townspeople, and they still possessed a considerable degree of influence. The aristocracy had scattered its clients throughout the government structure; some openly patronised—in all senses of the word—some under strict orders to keep their true allegiances concealed. It would have been more surprising if they *hadn't* been aware the offensive was about to begin. The media might have been muzzled, but word had been spreading anyway.

"That is good, is it not?" Lord Doncaster was the oldest man in the room and the only one who could claim descent from *the* Doncaster. He never let anyone forget it. "The rebels are about to be crushed, freeing the islands from their iron grip. Is that not good news?"

"Perhaps," Hamish said. It *was* good news. The aristocracy *owned* the rebel islands. Losing them had been painful. Some families had gone bankrupt when their ability to pay their debts had been called into question, because they'd lost control of their lands and plantations. "And yet, what does it mean for the future if the army emerges victorious?"

The question hung in the air. It wasn't enough to beat the rebels. They had to restore the founding families to their former position of absolute mastery over the planet and *that* wasn't going to be easy. Hamish wasn't blind to the implications of letting the townspeople have a share in government, certainly not after studying the history of Earth. His distant ancestors had lost much of their power, after they'd widened the franchise to the point *anyone* could vote. Earthfall was clear proof of what could happen if there was too *much* democracy. He had no intention of letting it happen to *his* homeworld. New Doncaster had once been a shining beacon of civilisation. God willing, it would be again.

"The army is under our control," Lord Doncaster pointed out. "Their victories are our victories."

"Except we don't control the army," Lord Prestwick countered. "General Roland Windsor controls the army."

He looked at Lord Windsor. "Is he not one of yours?"

"No," Lord Windsor said, flatly. "When Roland Windsor arrived, we did a search of the archives. There are quite a few people with the same name, as you can imagine, but none of them are *our* Roland Windsor. If there is a family connection, it is a *long* way back in time. We may share a name, but we have nothing else in common."

"Even so," Lord Prestwick said. "He should support you."

Hamish kept his face under tight control. The age-old tradition was very simple. The family supported its children—it birthed, educated and employed them—and, in exchange, the children supported the family. Lord Oakley, the Prime Minister, had betrayed his family, as well as the rest of the aristocracy. And Roland Windsor...it was not clear if there was any connection between the imprudent young man and the Windsors of New Doncaster, but it provided a handy tool to hack away at the soldier's reputation. It would be easy, with a word or two in the right ear, to brand Roland Windsor a traitor. He would never see it coming.

He tapped his glass, drawing their attention back to him. "We have spent the last six months building up the army," he said. "The rebels are tougher than we thought"—it cost him to admit it—"but our victory is inevitable. And what will happen then?"

Hamish didn't give them time to react.

"Our forefathers were the ones who realised this world could become more than *just* a settlement, a refuge from the political storms battering the homeworld," he said. "They saw profit. They invested vast sums in turning the planet into a going concern. They made it work! And are we going to step aside, to surrender to rebels and traitors and short-sighted fools and give up everything we've built?"

Lord Doncaster frowned. "The government *has* agreed to limited political reform."

"If there was no further reform, I might be less concerned," Hamish told him. "But it is unfortunately clear that each reform, each change in the rules, will lead to more demands and more changes and, eventually, we'll surrender everything to keep the peace. It has happened before, time and time again, on hundreds of worlds. Once you get on the slippery slope, you cannot keep yourself from sliding down to disaster. And if you try to say no, to uphold your old rights, you will be branded a reactionary fool if not an outright monster. Do we want it to happen here?"

He watched their faces, hoping they'd understand and agree. He had contingency plans, if one of the little party decided to go straight to the government, but putting them into practice would be difficult. The old freedoms were gone. The government's emergency laws left little room for the old rights. The days he was the absolute lord and master of his estate were gone. It was up to him to bring them back.

"The army is largely townie," he pointed out. "What will it do, if it emerges victorious?"

"General Windsor is a Marine," Lord Doncaster said. "Will he not be recalled, and moved to another trouble spot?"

"We cannot count on it," Hamish said. "And there are townie officers making their way up the ladder."

"They won't reach the top," Lord Prestwick argued.

"They'll be in position to mount a coup," Hamish disagreed. "The rebels did it. Why can't they?"

Lord Windsor leaned forward. "Your point is taken," he said. "I assume you have something in mind?"

"This is our world," Hamish said. He needed to remind them of it, time and time again. They *had* to keep their eyes on the prize. "And we need to defend it."

He took a breath, then started to outline his plan.

CHAPTER ONE

MOUNTEBANK ISLAND, NEW DONCASTER

FROM ABOVE, SPECIALIST RACHEL GREEN NOTED, New Doncaster was a surprisingly beautiful planet.

The hang glider—a flimsy device that would be torn to shreds if the weather changed before she reached her destination—seemed to shift slightly as she glided towards Mountebank Island. Her passive sensor array picked up a handful of radar pulses, but not—thankfully—any active sensors that might pick her out against the charged atmosphere before it was too late. The glider was so fragile that most sensors wouldn't have a hope of spotting it, although she had no illusions about what would happen if the rebel defences *did*. She wasn't anything *like* high enough to see a missile coming towards her before it reached its target, nor would she have any hope of survival if it did. Stealth was her only real defence and she knew it might not be enough.

It will have to be, she told herself. *We cannot afford to fail now.*

She took a breath, waiting patiently as the island slowly came into view. It looked tiny from overhead, a postage stamp of greenery set in an endless blue sea, falling slowly into darkness as the sun sank behind the horizon. The sole city was a mass of dark buildings, the plantations beyond a haze of greenery and the burnt-out remains of manor houses and indent barracks. Rachel's lips twisted in disgust. It wasn't the first time she'd found herself, and the corps as a whole, supporting a government that didn't deserve to exist, but it had never sat well. *She* would have preferred to land an entire division, then thrash both the government and the rebels before dictating terms that might *just* keep the planet from exploding again when the division was pulled out and sent to the next trouble spot. But it was not to be. The government was the only hope of maintaining any sort of stability and *that* meant supporting it to the hilt.

For what it's worth, when we have so little to offer, she thought. *New Doncaster just isn't that important.*

The thought mocked her. She'd had reservations about the mission when she'd first been briefed, although she'd had to concede it was better than either being reassigned to another special ops team or being sent into deep cover somewhere in the former core worlds. The Commandant had even suggested it would be a milk run, a chance to ease herself back into service after losing most of her former team. It would hardly be the first time she'd handled close-protection duty, with orders to watch her charge while watching his back. And yet, *Prince Roland?* Everything she'd heard about the young prince had suggested he was a degenerate, a fop lost in pursuit of pleasure…the idea he might make a Civil Guardsman, let alone a Marine, was absurd. She'd half-expected disaster, right from the start.

And yet, he's done better than I thought he would, she admitted, in the privacy of her own mind. *He has his flaws, and weaknesses, but he's done well.*

She twisted her head slightly, looking up. The handful of government-owned satellites had been zapped when the rebels had started their offensive, although between their outdated technology and New Doncaster's weather they'd been practically useless. The government had made overtures to the spacers, in hopes they'd replace the lost satellites, but the spacers had been reluctant. Rachel suspected half of them supported the rebels or simply wanted to wait and see who won before openly choosing a side. The remainder wanted independence. She had the feeling they would do what they could to stir the pot, making sure the war on the surface lasted long enough to ensure the winner inherited a ruined planet. And there was nothing she could do about it.

And there's no way I can send a message to Safehouse, either, she thought. *I don't even know what happened to the messages I sent to the dead drop.*

She cursed under her breath. New Doncaster had been largely isolated since Earthfall, with only a handful of starships passing through the system before the simmering discontent had exploded into open war. She'd sent a handful of messages on passing starships, in hopes of forwarding updates to her superiors, but she knew it would be months—at best—before there was any reply. It was unlikely the corps would divert a starship to investigate what had happened, not unless the Commandant decided to reassign Captain Allen or Roland himself. And then...Rachel shook her head as a gust of wind carried her over the island. Captain Allen was dead, killed by treacherous attack. Roland probably wouldn't want to leave.

Rachel put the thought out of her mind as she rechecked the sensor array. The rebels didn't appear to be using radio, let alone microburst transmitters, although the latter were difficult to detect, let alone pin down, before it was too late. They'd probably be relying on landlines, if the island's primitive communications infrastructure remained intact, or simply using couriers to take messages from place to place. It was what she would have done, if she had been on the other side. She knew from grim experience that anyone radiating a signal in the middle of a war zone was practically *asking* to get killed.

Her terminal vibrated, once. It was time.

She braced herself. The darkness was inching forward. Her eyes had been heavily enhanced, allowing her to see in the dark, but she knew not to count on it. She was too high up to be seen by the naked—unenhanced— eye, yet...she took a breath as she unhooked herself from the glider, then allowed herself to plummet down. The glider itself would be swept up by the wind and blown well out to sea before it came down, or so she'd been assured. She hated the idea of leaving anything to chance but trying to land the glider or destroying it both raised the odds of detection. She'd been careful to ensure the glider was as clean as possible, with nothing that suggested it was anything other than a civilian model flown by a dangerous sports club. By the time it was found, if it ever was, it would be too late.

The air snapped at her as she fell, a silent reminder of her first parachute jump. It had been fun and terrifying...here, she ran the risk of falling straight into an enemy camp. The intelligence staff had done their best to pin down the rebel positions, but their best wasn't anything like good enough. The rebels knew how to conceal their camps, how to keep their forces safe from prying eyes. Rachel trusted the odds—they were in her favour—but mentally prepared herself for the worst. If she did land in an enemy camp, she'd have to fight her way out before they recovered and brought her down. Roland would never know what had happened to her.

She counted down the seconds, one hand on the parachute cord. It was never easy to be sure when one should deploy the parachute, not on a high- altitude low-opening drop. Opening the chute too early could get her killed, either by the weather throwing her right across the island and into the sea, or an enemy sniper spotting her and trying to do something about it; opening it too late could see her plunging into the ground hard enough to kill her, even with the chute slowing her fall. She kept counting, using her altimeter to pick the right moment to pull the cord. The chute blossomed above, jerking violently as the ground came up and hit her. Rachel grunted as she landed, drawing her pistol as she ducked down and swept the chute aside. She was alone. The half-assed road was as still and quiet as the grave.

Bad thought, Rachel told herself, as she swept up the remains of the chute and hurried into the jungle. *Very bad thought.*

She paused, listening with her enhanced ears. The jungle was never quiet—she heard birds and insects moving through the trees, heedless of her presence—but she couldn't make out any signs of rebel activity. She reminded herself, sharply, that that was meaningless. The rebels had good jungle tradecraft. The ones who hadn't developed such skills, in the years before the insurgency had turned into an outright war, had been killed long ago. She turned slowly, listening carefully, then knelt and dug a small hole with her multitool. The chute needed to be buried, before someone spotted it and started to ask the wrong—or rather the right—questions. It wouldn't be the first time a mission had been compromised by a local spotting something out of place, then passing a warning up the chain to higher authorities.

And we have no friends on this island, she reflected, as she kicked dirt into the hole before moving away. *No one here will give the government a friendly word, let alone any actual support.*

She took a breath as she checked her compass, then went north, remaining within the jungle while following the road. It would rain soon, concealing the few traces of her presence. She kept her eyes on the rough road, reminding herself the lack of paving wasn't proof it had fallen into disuse. The planetary government—and the aristocracy—hadn't been interested in investing in transport infrastructure, not this far from the coast. And besides, even if they'd tried, the rebels would have tried to stop them. A working road network would have made it easier for the militia to move troops from place to place.

The air grew warmer as she walked, faint flashes of light from the dark clouds suggesting a thunderstorm was on the way. Rachel kept moving as the road widened, leading onto the remains of a plantation. The rebels had burned the manor and the surrounding houses to the ground, then tore up the alien plants to ensure it would be years—at best—before the plantation could be made profitable again. She felt a flicker of sympathy for the former workers, men and women who'd been told they could earn their way out of debt slavery...only to discover, when they crunched the numbers, that the system was carefully rigged to make escape impossible. She cursed the government under her breath. If they'd *wanted* an insurgency, they could hardly have done a better job.

No bodies, she thought, as she circumvented the plantation. *Perhaps that's a good sign.*

She dismissed the thought as she resumed her walk. There were hundreds of refugees from the rebel-held islands, people who'd fled the wrath of rebels with nothing to lose but their chains, yet there should have been more. There'd been a middle class, small yet not insignificant; there'd been aristocrats and overseers and trusties who...she shook her head. It had been six months. Anyone who hadn't made it out, in the first chaotic week, was either behind enemy lines or dead. The rebel leadership, to its credit, had *tried* to put a lid on the violence, but the hatred was just too great. Rachel knew what might have happened to any of the former masters caught behind the lines. They'd be lucky if they were *only* killed by their former slaves.

The ground rose under her feet. The skies rumbled, the first smatterings of rain falling around her. Rachel almost welcomed it as she saw lights in the distance, heard the sound of roaring engines. She ducked, careful to choose a vantage point that would let her watch the road without being seen. A line of vehicles came into view, driving down the dirt road. Rachel eyed them warily. The rebel soldiers on guard looked antsy, their weapons shifting from side to side as if they expected to be attacked. She wondered, idly, if there were loyalists or criminals within the jungle. It wasn't impossible. Mountebank was not a penal island, nor one of the hellish colonies where criminals were sent to work themselves to death, but it was quite possible some of the indents were guilty of more than just being in the wrong place at the wrong time. They might not have found themselves welcomed by the rebels...

Her eyes narrowed. The vehicles looked like technicals—civilian vehicles hastily outfitted with makeshift armour and weapons—but there was something about them that had her instincts sounding the alarm. Purpose-built military vehicles? The design was odd, but she couldn't deny the practicality. Would the rebels prefer to build such vehicles, rather than tanks or IFVs? There was no way to know. They might be better off relying on designs they understood, rather than expending resources on vehicles that might prove to be nothing more than expensive white elephants.

She waited for the convoy to vanish into the darkness, then resumed her walk towards the enemy installation. Intelligence had sworn blind the rebels had set up their HQ near the centre of the island, well away from either Mountebank City or most of the plantations. Rachel hadn't expected the spooks to get it right, but—as she closed on the installation—she realised the rebels definitely had *something* in the right location. Her sensor array picked up a couple of microbursts, compressed and encrypted to the point even *modern* computers would take weeks to decrypt the signals. She frowned as she slowed her advance, careful to keep watching for enemy spies. A regular military base would have cut the foliage back, in hopes of keeping someone from creeping up on the fence. The rebels hadn't had that option—it would have revealed their base's presence—but they were doing their best to compensate. Their patrols were alarmingly random.

Someone's been studying the right books, she thought. The patrol would have caught her, if she hadn't stayed back to watch and study their movements, in hopes a pattern would emerge. They appeared to be completely random. *There's no way to predict when a patrol will be passing by.*

Rachel slipped back, then studied the rebel base from a distance. It was half-hidden in the foliage, like the base they'd attacked before the insurgency had kicked into high gear, to the point it was hard to be sure how big it really was. There were no vehicles within view, nothing to suggest the base was anything more than a jungle resort or hidden settlement. If there hadn't been regular patrols, and microburst transmissions, she would have wondered if the spooks had made a mistake. Hell, it was quite possible the real HQ was somewhere nearby…but not too close. The rebels would be foolish to assume that their microbursts couldn't be detected, then pinned down. A single prowling drone could drop a missile on the transmitter before the crew could escape.

She kept inching back, then started to make her way around the edge of the base. The patrols were too solid for her to risk trying to sneak into the base itself, not without setting off the alarms. She thought she could get through, particularly if the rebels were distracted, but it was hard to be sure. Better to wait until the offensive began, then go to work.

Dawn glimmered in the distance as she swept through the surrounding area, looking for hints of a secondary base. There was nothing, but that was meaningless. The rebels knew how to survive in the jungle, knew what was safe to eat, knew where to find water…in their shoes, she might set up a tent, or even a very basic shelter. The rain wouldn't make that easy, but better to be damp and free then dry and in a POW camp. Rachel knew Roland had worked hard to convince the government to treat prisoners well, yet she was all too aware hardly anyone believed it would keep its word. It was hard to take prisoners when the prisoners feared they'd either be worked to death or simply shot out of hand.

She glanced at her terminal, then tapped a code into the touchscreen. The microburst transmitter sent two wordless bursts, before shutting down completely. Rachel was already moving. It was unlikely the rebels could track her signals, even if they had modern sensor arrays, but she dared not rule it out. The rebels had some support from off-world factions, factions that had remained carefully anonymous. It was quite possible they might have been sent modern gear. Better to be safe than sorry.

There was no hint she'd been detected, as she put some distance between herself and her former position. She breathed a sigh of relief, then found a place to hide and settled down to wait. There wasn't long to go, not before all hell broke loose. She checked her stimulant reserve, preparing for the coming chaos. She'd pay for using the boost later, when all was said and done, but there was no choice. She dared not let herself be captured or killed. If Roland hadn't figured out what she really was, she would have been standing beside him, watching his back. Instead, she'd been pressed into service.

He had no choice, she reminded herself. Roland had been persuasive—and right. The political situation was a ramshackle nightmare. The only reason he'd been put in overall command was to ensure the blame didn't fall on any of the locals, if the coming engagement ended in disaster. And she knew what was at stake. *The army must not lose the first battle or it will lose the war.*

But she knew, even as she waited, that there were no guarantees in war.

CHAPTER TWO

NEAR MOUNTEBANK ISLAND, NEW DONCASTER

ROLAND—CROWN PRINCE OF THE EMPIRE, Marine Auxiliary Captain of the Terran Marine Corps—stood on the command deck and tried to look as if he were doing nothing more significant than ordering tea.

He clasped his hands behind his back, keeping his face under tight control as the reports started to come in from the makeshift fleet. Six months of hard work, of backbreaking labour and endless training and desperate preparation for war, all boiled down to the fleet of semi-warships making their way through the choppy waters towards the island. It was remarkable, how much they'd produced in such a short time, yet he was all too aware of the gaps in his order of battle. New Doncaster's stocks of modern technology were limited, forcing them to rely on weapons and equipment that would have been familiar to Roland's distant ancestors, the ones who had lived and died before humanity started its expansion into space. A lone starship with kinetic bombardment projectiles could sink his entire fleet within seconds, if it inched into orbit. Roland was uneasily aware that whoever was backing the rebels could take a more active hand at any moment, secure in the knowledge there was no one left who could hold them accountable for their crimes.

The ship—a makeshift assault carrier, if that wasn't too grand a term for a converted freighter armed with missiles and propeller-powered aircraft—shifted under his feet as it turned into the wind. New Doncaster had no shortage of water-borne ships and sailors, thankfully, but very few of them were trained to serve on warships. There was something amateurish about the fleet, and the army within the landing craft, that haunted him, even though he knew he should be glad of what he had. He could overlook an absence of protocol, and manners that would result in severe non-judicial punishment within the corps, if the sailors did their jobs and did them well. They didn't have time to smooth down *all* the rough edges.

But the rebels had spent the last six months preparing, too.

Roland turned away from the windows and studied the tactical display. It was a joke. The force trackers were makeshift, where they existed at all. He hadn't dared outfit his forces with local-built force trackers, all too aware they would reveal their positions to the enemy as well as himself. The operators had worked hard to develop techniques for coordinating the fleet, and the landing force, but the fog of war lingered over the battlefield like a bad smell, making it difficult for Roland to direct operations with any confidence. He felt a twinge of guilt as he stared at the display, wishing he was on the first wave of landing craft. If his career had followed a regular path, he would have been midway through the Slaughterhouse by now—or dead. Instead, he was a brevet general in an army that had been thrown together in a tearing hurry.

There was no choice, he told himself. *The planet teeters on the brink of chaos or tyranny.*

Admiral Forest caught his eye. "General," he said. "The fleet is entering the combat zone now."

As if I didn't already know, Roland thought. Admiral Forest had commanded a patrol boat, six short months ago. Now...he'd been jumped up several ranks, like hundreds of others, to meet a demand for commanding officers no one had expected to face. New Doncaster had never had a real navy, until now. *Tell me something I don't know.*

He turned to face the older man. Admiral Forest was an aristocrat, by local standards; the second son of a powerful lord who'd made sure his son got the posting he wanted. Roland supposed it spoke well of Forest that he'd demanded a command post, rather than a shore office with little real responsibility. But…Roland suspected the older man was also the target of a great deal of resentment. What was the point of working hard and getting your name mentioned in the dispatches, if someone could be promoted over you just by having the right social connections? Roland had been told a number of Coast Guard personnel had deserted to the rebels, when the insurgency had turned into open war. He believed it. Even now, six months after the government had reluctantly made some concessions to fight the war, it was still hard for the former townies to trust things had changed.

"Very good, Admiral," he said. "Are we ready to begin the bombardment?"

"We'll be in optimum firing position in five minutes," Admiral Forest informed him. "Do you want to give the command personally?"

Roland nodded. The responsibility was his, even though part of him quailed at the thought of unleashing such makeshift missiles in combat. They weren't *that* inaccurate, he had been assured, but he wasn't convinced. There was no way New Doncaster could produce smart warheads, even laser-guided seeker-heads. He was all too aware there was a very good chance he was about to sentence hundreds of civilians to death. It would be accidental, but he wouldn't feel any better afterwards. The only upside, as far as he could tell, was that the rebels were supposed to have evacuated the shore of non-essential personnel.

Or so we've been told, Roland thought. There'd been some contacts between the two sides, over the last six months, but most of them had consisted of little more than unrealistic demands. *They could have turned their own people into human shields.*

He felt his mood darken as he turned his attention to the map. The government's intelligence network, it was clear, had been hopelessly compromised for years. The deep-cover agents they'd inserted into the insurgent cells had insisted, time and time again, that the rebels were nothing more than disorganised thugs lashing out desperately as their inevitable doom grew closer and closer. There had been very little warning, and none of it particularly useful, before the insurgents had mounted a desperate all-or-nothing bid for Kingston. They'd come very close to complete success. Roland hated to admit it, but whoever was in command of the other side had a fine tactical mind. He'd realised the battle was lost and cut his losses with a speed and ruthlessness Roland could only admire, preserving as much of his forces as he could for the next engagement. The enemy commander had shaken the government to the core.

And he knows we're coming, Roland thought. *He can't have missed the fleet heading towards the island.*

He stroked his chin as he contemplated the fleet's position. In theory, they were well clear of any enemy missile batteries. In practice, Roland wasn't so sure. A modern hypersonic missile would be more than enough to sink any of his ships, including the flagship. There were no signs the rebels *had* such missiles, but they were smart enough to keep them under wraps until his ships were in the killing zone. And even if their missiles were no better than Roland's own, they could blanket his rough location in firepower until they wiped out most of his fleet. It would be a disaster.

Admiral Forest caught his eye. "General?"

"Inform your gunners to open fire on my command," Roland said. "Once we start launching missiles, the first assault boats can make their approach."

"Aye, sir."

Roland sighed, inwardly, as Admiral Forest strode away. He liked the older man, but he was no trusted confidante. The only person he could unburden himself to was Rachel and *she* was somewhere on the nearby island, carrying out her part of the plan. He cursed under his breath. He'd wanted to keep her nearby, as a sounding board rather than a bodyguard, but he'd needed to put someone on the island to take out the enemy command structure before it could react to his offensive. And yet, sending her had been risky. HALO drops always were, even on planets with more predictable weather. Roland had feared, even as he wished her luck, that he was sending her to her death.

The timer bleeped. One minute to go.

And then we will see, Roland thought. They'd laid their plans, they'd wargamed each and every variable they'd been able to imagine…soon, they'd see how well their plans worked when confronted by reality. *The rebels know we're coming. But are they ready for us?*

• • •

Captain Richard Collier had grown to dislike the makeshift landing craft intensely, in the hours since they'd cut loose from the transport ship and started their voyage to Mountebank Island. He was no stranger to small boats—he'd spent his summers as part of a fisherman's crew, before he'd joined the militia—and yet, the way the boxy craft rolled under his feet disconcerted him. The crew seemed unfazed, but Richard was all too aware that the entire company was doomed if the boat capsized. His men could swim—he'd made sure of it -yet getting out of an upside-down boat would be difficult even at the best of times. And there had been no time to even *think* of carrying out escape drills.

He felt cold, despite the growing heat, as he sat at the head of the line and watched the island slowly coming into view. Mountebank looked a piece of paradise, a green blur shrouded by haze set within an endless blue, but…somewhere to the north, the rebels were waiting for them. The new recruits might have been bragging the war would be over by Christmas, that the rebels would raise the white flag and surrender the moment they saw the troops landing on the beach; Richard knew better. It wasn't going to be easy. The government had made noises about amnesty for rebels who gave up the fight and surrendered, but it would be a foolish rebel who trusted in such promises. The atrocities the rebels had committed, as decades of pent-up anger and hatred finally broke loose, made it very hard to offer them any kind of forgiveness. He'd heard rumours there were people in government who wanted to drop enhanced radiation weapons on the rebel-held islands, wiping them out without risking a single soldier or militiaman. The only reason Richard doubted the rumour was the simple fact that enhanced radiation weapons were beyond the planet's limited industrial capability to produce. There had certainly been quite enough chatter about weed-killer, defoliants and even nerve gas.

Richard shivered as he looked at his men. The days when the army and the militia had been two separate forces were gone, now that the planet was fighting for its life. His men—and a handful of women—were a mixture of old and new, soldiers he'd led into battle before the insurgency and recruits who'd joined up after the townies had been invited to take part in government. There were even some former indents, trading military service for debt relief and enfranchisement. Richard had worked hard to train them, all too aware that failure would throw the entire enterprise into doubt, but he had no idea how the newcomers would perform when they saw the elephant for the first time. If they failed...

We'll just have to make sure we don't, he thought. *We must not fail.*

He turned his gaze away, wishing he'd had more time to see his family before boarding the ships and setting out to sea. Roland was a more considerate commander than many—the days Richard had doubted his intentions, if not his experience, were also gone—but there'd just been too much to do. Richard wore at least three hats - it rankled, at times, that his father had refused to allow him to accept a formal promotion—but Roland wore even more. The handful of experienced officers—soldiers, militia and training staff—had worked themselves to the bone, trying to get the army into shape before the rebels mounted a second invasion or an outside power intervened. In a way, it was almost a relief to be going back into combat. The world was about to become a great deal simpler. The army wanted to take the island. The rebels wanted to stop them. And everything would depend on who came out ahead.

The boat officer—Richard had never learnt his name—waved for his attention. "Sir, the bombardment is about to begin."

Richard nodded, stiffly. The rebels would have to be blind to miss the fleet advancing on the island. There were so many smaller islands with tiny settlements of their own—to say nothing of entire fleets of fishing vessels—that he would sooner expect the aristos to surrender their wealth and power than the rebels somehow failing to spot the oncoming fleet. Roland had long since given up the thought of achieving strategic surprise, although there was at least a *possibility* they could keep the rebels from guessing where they intended to land. The moment the missiles started to hammer their targets, the landing force would alter course and make a rush for the beach. Richard had planned on the assumption the enemy wouldn't be fooled, but he hoped for the best. There were already too many voices whispering the army was unreliable, that it couldn't be expected to produce victories. The invasion could not be allowed to fail.

"Good," he said. He turned to face his men. "Prepare to alter course."

• • •

Private Angeline Porter had no time to feel nervousness, or anticipation, or anything beyond a burning hatred for the rebels. Hatred had kept her alive, when she'd been gang-raped and nearly killed by her family's former servants. She'd been lucky to be taken off the island, to a facility on Kingston, before the uprising had shattered what remained of the government's authority, but it didn't feel that way. The doctors had done what they could, yet...there was no way they could restore what she'd lost. She'd been expected to take what remained of her family's money—she was the sole survivor—and step out of polite society. Instead, she'd joined the army.

Her hands tightened around her rifle. It hadn't been easy. New Doncaster had never been known for female emancipation, even before the war. She'd been expected to marry well, to someone chosen by her family, and spend the rest of her life with him. The army hadn't quite known what to make of her, although they'd had to admit she could shoot. She'd declined all offers of a non-combat posting, demanding to be sent to the front. And her hatred had kept her going when her fellow recruits had taunted her for being a woman in a man's world.

The surge of hatred threatened to overwhelm her. She'd come very close to killing a recruit with wandering hands...hell, she *had* intended to kill him. The moment she'd felt his touch, she'd yanked the knife from her belt and slashed at him. The bastard had been very lucky to jump back, an instant before her blade sliced through his chest. Perversely, the near-fatal incident had done wonders for her reputation. The days in which she'd been expected to grin and bear it were long gone.

And we're about to meet the rebels, she thought, as the landing craft altered course. *We'll teach them a lesson they'll never forget.*

She composed herself with an effort, drawing on the training that had been hammered into her over the last four months. The goal was to secure Mountebank, to make it impossible for the rebels to use it as a staging base for further attacks on Kingston...she told herself, as the landing craft picked up speed, that it was just a matter of time before the army returned to Baraka. The servants who'd betrayed her family and raped her—she shuddered, caught in the memory—were waiting. She'd hunt them down personally, making damn sure they didn't have a chance to rape anyone else. And then...she didn't care. It wasn't as if she had any hope of resuming her former position. The rebels had made sure of that, too.

We're coming to get you, she silently promised the waiting enemy. *And you won't like it when we do.*

• • •

"General," Admiral Forest said. "The fleet is in position."

So hurry up and give the order to fire, Roland finished, silently. He didn't blame the admiral for wanting to move faster, even though they'd be committed the moment they started shooting missiles at the island. No, that was foolish. They'd been committed from the moment the rebels had kicked the insurgency into high gear. It took two to end a war, but only one to start it. *It's time.*

He took a breath. His distant ancestors had led fleets into battle, back when they'd built the empire, but his parents and grandparents and many others had done nothing more demanding than sitting in the Imperial Palace and waiting to hear what had happened, hundreds of light years away. They hadn't been gambling everything on one throw of the dice... hell, they hadn't even been anything more than puppets. The smarter ones had known it. Roland still hated himself for not realising the truth until Belinda Lawson had opened his eyes, too late for him to do anything but run. Not, he supposed, that it would have mattered. In theory, he was—he'd been—the ruler of the entire galaxy. In practice, he'd had no power at all. If he'd stayed where he'd been, he would be one more dead body amongst billions.

But this is different, he reflected. *An entire army is about to go into battle, on my command.*

The thought tormented him. Hundreds, perhaps thousands, of his men were about to die, along with thousands of rebels. And all of those deaths would be on him. He was the one giving the order to launch the invasion. He could still call it off...no, he couldn't. It was time to emulate his ancestors, the ones who'd won martial glory, and fight.

He took a breath. "Signal the fleet," he ordered. "Begin the bombardment."

"Aye, General."

CHAPTER THREE

MOUNTEBANK ISLAND, NEW DONCASTER

THE REBELS, SPECIALIST RACHEL GREEN NOTED sourly, were shifting to a more alert posture.

She kept her distance, keeping her passive sensor array online. Some brief signals flickered through the air, too short to convey much in the way of actionable information. Not, she knew, that it meant they were meaningless. The mere fact someone had sent the signal could easily convey information, if the rebels had set up a signalling scheme ahead of time. Rachel had spent enough time away from the regular forces to understand how easy it was to spoof listening ears, if one put a little thought into it. There was no way to decrypt a signal with a predetermined meaning, unless one knew what the signal meant ahead of time. And that was vanishingly rare.

The sounds of the jungle grew louder as the rebel troops expanded their patrols, heedless of the wildlife they were disturbing. Rachel tracked their positions through the sound, constantly reminding herself that the rebels she could hear might easily be beaters trying to drive her into the arms of their quieter comrades. Did they know she was there? Had they caught a sniff of her presence? Or were they simply tightening their security, now that Roland's fleet was coming into view? They might have doubted the precise target—Roland had spread hundreds of rumours, from training exercises to a strike directly at Baraka itself—but there could be no doubt now. The fleet was just too close. Mountebank was the only logical target.

She stayed low as a pair of rebels crashed through the undergrowth, tensing as she readied herself to act if they spotted her. They weren't making a beeline for her, but that proved nothing. The loud men, stamping around as if they didn't know the meaning of the word *stealth*, weren't the problem. It was the ones lurking in the silence who might be the real killers…if, of course, they were there. The rebels didn't seem *that* alert. They certainly weren't *acting* as if they were walking towards a possible sniper…she shook her head, mentally. She would have preferred to back off, to make her escape without contact in hopes they'd assume they were panicking over nothing so she could sneak back later, but that wasn't possible now. The offensive was about to begin.

Her ears pricked up as she heard the missiles, an instant before the first explosions began. She ducked instinctively, even though the rebel CP wasn't one of the primary targets. The missiles were dangerously inaccurate and she was all too aware that *some* of them were being fired right over the island, raising the very real spectre of one crashing too close for comfort. She didn't fear death, but the thought of being killed by friendly fire—as if there was such a thing—was maddening. The ground shook a moment later, flashes of light and fireballs rising in the distance. Rachel had no time to try and determine if any of the targets had actually been hit. Roland was smart enough to assume none of them had been hit and destroyed.

She put the thought out of her head as she triggered her enhancements, the booster drug running through her system. Time itself seemed to slow as she lanced forward, darting through the undergrowth and into the rebels before they could register her presence. Rachel killed one of them with a blow, then threw the other into a tree. The body lay still. There was no time to check if she'd killed him. Instead, she turned and raced towards the rebel camp. It didn't sound as if anyone had realised what had happened, but it was just a matter of time. She had to get inside and complete her mission before the boost started to wear off.

The camp came into view, a handful of buildings built within the jungle. Rachel didn't try to go for the doors. There were too many guards. Instead, she scrambled up a tree—snapping off shots at the guards as she moved—and threw a grenade ahead of her, blasting a hole in the wooden roof. She dropped through into a barracks, a pair of sleeping men looking up blearily as she landed between them. She cracked their skulls before they could react, then hurried down the hatch and into the lower levels. A young woman appeared out of nowhere, hastily trying to draw a pistol. Rachel punched her in the stomach, then kicked her in the head. She collapsed and hit the ground, completely out of it. Rachel hoped she'd stay unconscious long enough for her reinforcements to arrive. She didn't want to kill a woman if she could help it.

Which is foolish, she told herself. *She would have killed you, given a chance.*

She plunged through a mess hall, empty and abandoned, and found her way to a staircase. There was something oddly charming about the rebel base, although there was no time to appreciate it. Her sensor array bleeped an alert as she rocketed down the stairs, cautioning her someone was sending radio messages. Rachel darted through the door and straight into a trap, four men charging her with neural whips. Good thinking, she acknowledged. They probably wanted to take her alive, relying on the non-lethal weapons to put her down long enough to secure her. It would have worked too, if she hadn't been heavily enhanced. She grabbed hold of the first whip, yanked the rebel behind it towards her and threw him into a second rebel, knocking both of them to the ground. The sound of breaking bones told her they'd stay down, long enough for her to deal with the other two. A third man grabbed for his pistol, too late; a fourth turned and ran. Rachel knocked the third out, then threw him at the fourth. He had no time to get up before she kicked him in the head...

Bullets crackled through the air. Rachel threw herself down, then crawled forward. Someone was actually shooting *through* the door...either they were panicking, which was very possible, or they were trying to buy time. She didn't think any of the rebels were enhanced to the point they could determine her exact position. None of the shots were anywhere near her. She grabbed one of the stunned men and threw him at the door, the impact smashing the wooden barrier and revealing a small office beyond. A man stared at her, trying to bring his pistol to bear. He was moving fast, but with the boost pouring through her system he might as well have been *trying* to give her a free shot at him. She shot his weapon out of his hand, then plunged into the chamber and knocked him out with a single blow. A pair of computer terminals sat on the desk, dark and silent. Rachel cursed under her breath as she saw the puff of smoke drifting into the air. The operator had set them to self-destruct, then fought to buy time. She had to concede he'd succeeded. The only way to ensure nothing was recovered from computer terminals was to destroy them completely. He'd done it.

She glanced around, noting the map on the walls. It was largely unmarked, save for a handful of locations within the city. She frowned—there was no way to tell what the marks signified—then searched the rest of the chamber. The rebels had practiced good operational discipline, certainly better than many terrorist and insurgent groups she'd fought over the years. The datafiles had been destroyed with the computers, along with the microburst transmitter; there were, as far as she could determine, no paper files to be recovered and studied. She glanced up as she heard someone crashing down the stairs and hurried back into the antechamber, concealing herself within the shadows. She'd hoped the confusion outside would last a little longer, the missiles adding to the chaos as the fleet pounded its targets, but it seemed it was not to be. Rachel lifted her pistol as two armed men ran past, clearly assuming she was still in the command room itself. She hesitated, then let them go and hurried back up the stairs. The sound of distant explosions was growing louder. If the timetable was being followed, as they'd hoped, the invasion force would be landing.

A guard swung around, his eyes going wide as he saw her. Rachel shot him—no time to slow down now—and ran past him, into the open. The camp looked surprisingly deserted, as if half the occupants had run for their lives. Somehow, she doubted it. The rebels weren't cowards, nor were they terrorist bullies who cringed and begged for mercy when they encountered someone willing and able to fight back. They had a cause… and, presumably, contingency plans. The camp was compromised beyond recovery. If she'd been in command of the rebel force, she would have ordered the remainder of the camp's population to make their way to the city or fallback positions within the jungle, ready to continue the fight.

Clever bastards, she thought, as she ran across the camp and out into the jungle. *They know we landed on top of one of their camps. They had to have come up with plans to react, if we tried it again.*

She slowed as soon as she was concealed within the foliage, then keyed her terminal to record. "General. Enemy CP neutralised. No data recovered. All communications equipment destroyed. Proceeding with stage two."

Her fingers pressed a second command as her implants signalled a warning. The boost was wearing off. She dared not linger. She'd trained to fight while in withdrawal, but it was never pleasant and always dangerous. There was a *reason* most soldiers never even *heard* about the boost, let alone were considered for enhancement. Her lips quirked as the terminal compressed the message, then sent it. The cost of a single enhanced soldier was staggeringly high. She put the thought out of her mind as she hurried through the jungle, trying to keep away from enemy contacts. Her limbs ached, but she had to keep moving. It was unlikely the enemy had modern passive sensor arrays, the kind of technology that would pick up her signal, yet she couldn't take it for granted. A single mortar round, dropped on her position, would really ruin her day.

The sounds from behind her dwindled away as she kept moving, overshadowed by the endless thunder from the coast. Roland's plan called for dumping a *lot* of missiles and shells on enemy targets, softening the rebel positions as much as possible before landing troops and moving in for the kill. Rachel hoped the rebels would see sense and surrender, once the main force was ashore. The city would rapidly become indefensible. And yet, she feared the worst. Roland—and the government—needed a quick victory. He might have to try storming the city, which would cost him badly.

She kept the thought churning through her mind, trying to distract herself as her body started to shake. She'd been told she was one of the lucky ones, that her reaction was surprisingly mundane compared to some of the others, but she didn't believe it. Her temperature soared, sweat beading on the palms of her hands; her legs felt wobbly, as if some passing sorcerer had turned her bones to noodles. She snickered at the thought, the withdrawal messing with her mind to the point the joke was almost *funny*. Somehow, Rachel kept moving. She didn't dare slow down, even to catch her breath. The withdrawal would overwhelm her completely.

There is a reason we use the boost so rarely, she recalled. The thought sounded like her old instructor, a man who'd outlined—in great detail—*precisely* what would happen if they overused the boost. It was dangerously addictive, to the point that even a hardened special ops soldier might find himself enslaved by his implants. *And there's no one who can help me, not here, if I go too far.*

The path started to incline up again, taking her up the old volcano that—a long time ago—had given birth to the island. The geologists had sworn blind the volcano was dead, unlike some of the active volcanoes outside the habitable zone, but the fanciful part of her mind wondered what would happen if a missile happened to crack the rock between the lava and the open air. It wasn't likely, yet…she shook her head, dismissing the thought as another relic of the withdrawal as she kept climbing. Given time, she would recover; given time, she would be fit to return to duty. She grimaced. She just wasn't used to being unfit for combat.

She heard the sound of aircraft high overhead and looked up. The three planes were a glorified recon flight, rather than a modern precision bombing or close-air support force. She hoped the latter wouldn't be needed, not when there was a shortage of modern technology to ensure the CAS aircraft hit the right targets. Rachel had been in battles where, even with complete communications superiority, air support had pounded the wrong side. Here, it was anyone's guess how accurate the CAS aircraft would be. She feared the worst.

No antiaircraft fire, she noted. *Why not?*

It was a puzzling thought. The rebels *did* have some modern air defence weapons. They could also have produced a handful of older designs, including some that did double duty as antitank weapons. Were they holding them in reserve? Or…or what? She wanted to believe the rebels had fewer modern weapons than they'd thought, but she knew better than to allow wishful thinking to override common sense. Perhaps the rebels were unwilling to make a major commitment to the island's defence. Roland had assembled such a powerful force that the rebels might prefer to stay out of its way, to slip back into the shadows and wait for a chance to resume the offensive. It was what she would have done, if she'd been in charge.

She paused as the trees parted, allowing her to look over the ocean. The fleet was clearly visible, the larger warships hanging back while the landing craft made their way towards the shore. The advance teams would already be hitting the beach, she was sure. There was no such thing as a perfect offensive—she'd been cautioned that a smoothly unfolding plan was a sign of imminent defeat—but they'd worked hard to keep friction as low as possible. The troops would be ashore shortly and then…

If we take the island, we prove we can win battles, she thought. *And then, if all goes well, we can start chipping away at the rest of the rebel islands.*

• • •

Abdul Al-Singh stared at the enemy fleet and felt his heart sink into his boots.

He'd thought, when he'd been given his final assignment, that the task would be simplicity itself. The mountain cabin was primitive, to the point there was nothing that would draw enemy attention unless they stumbled into the clearing. Abdul didn't mind the lack of electronic devices. The previous owner had stocked his retreat with books—real *paper* books—and Abdul had been reading them, one by one. All he'd really had to do was keep an eye on events from a safe distance. He'd never quite understood what his superiors had meant, when they'd given him his assignment. His job was to pass on a warning when—if—the CP was unable to do it.

He reached for his notebook and started to compose a message, cursing his ignorance. There were thirty-seven ships within eyesight, but how many were actual *warships*? Some were clearly converted freighters, yet he could see guns and missile batteries mounted on their decks. Others...he swallowed, hard, as he spotted a line of landing craft making their way to the beach. The first wave might already have landed. His vantage point wasn't as all-seeing as he might have wished. But there was no time to try to get a better view. His superiors had to be informed.

Taking the notebook with him, he opened the hidden compartment under the cabin and found the terminal. It was completely powered down, to the point—he'd been assured—even the most advanced sensors couldn't detect its presence. Abdul pressed the switch, half-expecting to hear a missile rocketing towards him. Silly, he knew. The missile would probably arrive before he had any warning, let alone a chance to take cover or run. His fingers darted over the keyboard, composing the message before it could be compressed and transmitted to the rebel HQ. And then...

He sucked in his breath. His orders were clear. The cabin was to be abandoned. He'd considered burning it to the ground, but it would simply draw unwanted attention if prowling eyes spotted the fire before it was too late. Instead, he keyed the transmit switch, waited for the bleep that told him the message had been sent, then switched off the terminal and ran for the door. His bug-out bag was already waiting for him, where he'd hidden it weeks ago. He had enough, he'd calculated, to survive in the jungle for at least a month. Plenty of time for the island to calm down, before he slipped away.

For you, the war is over, he reflected, as he ran. He had strict orders to avoid enemy contact, if possible. His superiors wanted intelligence, not dead heroes. *For everyone else, the war has only just begun.*

CHAPTER FOUR

MOUNTEBANK ISLAND, NEW DONCASTER

"BRACE YOURSELVES," the pilot yelled. "We'll hit the beach in a moment!"

Richard nodded, gritting his teeth as the landing craft picked up speed. The island had been hammered by the invasion force—smoke was rising in the distance, turning the sky black—but it was quite possible the enemy had already anticipated their destination and set a trap. There weren't *that* many places they could land even a small force, not without mobile jetties and harbours and dozens of other requirements that would push the invasion timetable months—if not years—into the future. And yet, it looked as if they'd gotten away with it. If there was any enemy force nearby, it was keeping itself well hidden.

He smiled, coldly, as the last seconds ticked away. The harbour was small, by the standards of Mountebank City or Kingsport, but it was large enough to handle a couple of midsized freighters at a time. The file stated it had been constructed by an aristocrat who'd hoped to cut down on shipping costs—the island's transport infrastructure was poor, barely worth the name—only to be abandoned shortly afterwards when the insurgency had kicked itself into high gear. He hoped the rebels had overlooked the tiny harbour, after burning the plantation and driving the owner into flight. It was possible. The harbour had never made any real impact on the island.

His radio bleeped. "Firing sequence one..."

Richard resisted the urge to duck as shells whistled over his head and crashed down in the jungle beyond. The shelling was random, but—hopefully—it would cover the landing force when it hit the beach. If there was an enemy force within the jungle, it had to suspect it had been spotted even if it was dug in deeply enough not to be harmed by the shelling. Richard watched the blasts for a moment, then raised his rifle as the landing craft grounded on the beach. Water splashed around the ramp as it fell to the ground, allowing the soldiers to leave the craft. It was time.

"Follow me," Richard ordered. "Now!"

He jumped into the water and splashed through the surf, heading for the beach. It was risky to expose himself to enemy fire, but he had to set a good example. Besides, if the enemy already had guns zeroed in on the beach, he would be in deep shit the moment they opened fire. He ran onto the beach, hearing the noise as his troops followed him along the sand and on to the harbour. It was deserted. The old harbourmaster's station—more of a hut, Richard noted—had been torn to shreds, but the remainder of the harbour was intact. The bigger transports should have no difficulty landing and unloading their cargo.

"Harbour team, prepare for landing operations," he shouted. The enemy couldn't have any doubt, now, where the troops were landing. They might have lost their radio network—there was no way to be sure—but they would have couriers racing all over the island in hopes of preparing a counterattack. "The rest of you, follow me!"

He glanced at the beach—the remainder of the landing craft were unloading now, waves of green-clad soldiers making their way onto the sand—and then led the way to the plantation itself. The mansion was a burned-out shell, but the barracks and sheds appeared to have been abandoned at very short notice. A nasty flicker of suspicion shot through his mind as the troops swept through the buildings, checking for everything from ambushes and sniper nests to IEDs and other unpleasant surprises. Standard doctrine—and the rebels clearly agreed with the military on this point—was to have small units deployed to slow an advancing army as much as possible, while massing the remainder of one's forces to man a defence line or mount a counterattack. The rebels *had* to be on their way. And he needed to push his own forces out as much as possible before they arrived.

The heat slapped at him as they pressed through the remains of the fields. The water gullies were nightmarish, clogged with the remnants of the planet's native biology in the wake of the uprising. Richard understood, although he had no idea how the rebels intended to finance the planet's economy after they won the war. The crops were useless in the short term—humans couldn't eat them—but in the long term, they *were* what brought in the cash. He shook his head. It wasn't as if the plantation owners had ever shared the wealth with their indentured slaves. No wonder the rebels had done so much damage. Even if they lost the war, it would be years before the planet recovered.

He paused, recalling the map he'd memorised as they reached the edge of the plantation. The road led around the island and down to the city, giving them a chance to surround the major settlement and secure the airport. The rebels would know it too. They might have assumed the landings would take place closer to the city—Richard knew Roland had considered it—but that assumption no longer held true. He directed a team of antitank gunners into position, backed up by riflemen. If the rebels didn't show themselves before the transports were unloaded, and the first tanks were on their way down the road, he had an excellent chance of pushing all the way to the city before he ran into something he couldn't handle.

Don't count on it, he reminded himself. *The rebels know where we are now. They'll be coming for us.*

• • •

"General," Lieutenant Tricia Bear said. "The harbour has been secured. The transports are landing now."

Roland nodded, stiffly. He'd feared the worst, when he'd drawn up the plans, but it looked as if the bombardment—and Rachel—had crippled the enemy's ability to coordinate their forces. It wouldn't stop them—Roland had no doubt the insurgent cells wouldn't sit down and wait for orders, not when his troops were bearing down on their positions—but hopefully they'd have problems trying to bring their power to bear. Given time, he'd land enough troops and armour to force the rebels to either stand and fight or flee into the jungle.

Which isn't quite what I want, he reminded himself, as the next set of reports started to come in. His staff updated the display, careful to add reminders the positions were all approximate and increasingly outdated. *We need to trap as many of them as possible.*

He shook his head. He wanted to be on the island himself, setting up a command post on the landing zone or leading his men towards the city. He owed it to himself to take some risks, particularly as it was *his* plan. His staff might have worked out the details, and turned his vague concepts into operational orders, but the responsibility was his and his alone. And yet, he knew he didn't dare put himself in the firing line. Not yet. There was no one who could take his place, no one who both knew what he was doing *and* was politically acceptable. It burned at him, more than he could say. But he'd given Rachel his word he'd stay out of danger, and he'd meant it.

There will be time later, when the island has been secured, he told himself. *For now, concentrate on your job and trust Richard to do his.*

•••

"Well," Private French commented. "Is this where you used to live?"

Angeline shook her head, biting down on her anger as the squad made its way through the remains of the plantation. It wasn't hers—it was on the wrong island, for starters—and yet, she had no trouble reading the land. The owner had built a productive plantation, only to lose it when his ungrateful indents rose up and killed him. She wondered, as bitter anger churned in her gut, if the owner's family had made it out. She was the only survivor of *hers*, save for a few distant relatives who'd expressed no interest in her, and she knew she wasn't the only one who'd lost everything. The rebels had been utterly murderous. Anyone who didn't drop everything and run would die, when the rebels caught them. Angeline just hoped it had been quick.

She kept her eyes open, looking for bodies, but saw none. It had been six months, she reminded herself. The rebels might be bastards, but they weren't *stupid*. They would have buried the bodies, perhaps, rather than risk disease outbreaks or wild animals developing a taste for human flesh. The nasty part of her mind whispered the rebels might have developed a taste for human flesh themselves, but cold logic suggested it wasn't true. They might be able to overcome the taboo on cannibalism—they might be desperate enough to force themselves—yet disease would carry them off. Angeline had had a limited amount of survival training. She *knew* how dangerous it could be.

The squad continued to advance, leapfrogging down the road to the city. Angeline heard engines and tensed, before realising they were coming from behind her. The landing force was already unloading the light tanks. Angeline had declined the chance to become a tanker—she wanted to get face-to-face with the rebels—but she'd trained with them and it was good to know their firepower was behind her. The rebels *had* to be on their way. She wanted to believe that they were quivering in fear, that that were unable to move for fear of facing punishment for their crimes, but it seemed unlikely. The government had promised to treat surrendering captives well. Angeline hated the idea of offering any sort of amnesty to the bastards who'd destroyed her life. If she met them, she had no intention of taking them alive.

She felt sweat prickling down her back as the road seemed to narrow. The squad flitted from tree to tree, trying to conceal their movements as much as possible even though it was probably futile. Angeline knew there'd been rebels near her plantation who'd taken to jungle like ducks to water. She'd spent some time there herself, before her father had put a stop to it, and she knew how easy it was to get through the jungle undergrowth if you knew what you were doing. The rebels…she froze as she saw small animals and birds, fleeing from the jungle ahead of the squad. There was no time to think.

"Get down," she snapped, throwing herself to the ground. "Hurry…"

The rebels opened fire, bullets snapping through the air over her head. Angeline sucked in her breath, feeling a surge of naked hatred as she returned fire. A few more seconds and the rebels would have had them bang to rights, probably wiping them out of existence with a single burst of machine gun fire. She snapped off shots at the enemy positions but couldn't tell if she hit anything. It smacked of a pre-planned ambush. The enemy had had more than enough time to dig in. Moments later, she heard the CRUMP-CRUMP-CRUMP of a mortar as it hurled shells towards them.

Lieutenant Ellis caught her eye. "Fall back!"

Angeline nodded, launching a pair of grenades into the enemy position as she crawled back as fast as she could. The enemy shells fell short, but she still felt a piece of shrapnel passing through the air bare millimetres above her head. She shouted at Private Tzu to move his ass, then realised—too late—that he'd been hit. There was no point in screaming for a medic, not now. His head had been cracked like an eggshell. She gritted her teeth—she'd liked him, though she'd never allowed herself to show it—as she joined the rest of the squad. The enemy fire was intensifying, bullets tearing through the foliage as if the rebels just wanted to force them to keep their heads down. She suspected they were trying to slow the invasion force long enough for a *real* defence line to be thrown into place, perhaps even a solid thrust that would push the invaders back into the sea. Raw hatred surged through her as an aircraft rocketed overhead, spraying machine gun fire onto the enemy position. Trees shattered, their trunks disintegrated by the strafing. For the first time, the rebel fire slackened.

Ellis lifted his hand, signalling the advance. Angeline pushed herself up and ran forward, the rest of the squad joining her a moment later. They darted from tree to tree, trying to close on the enemy position. A rebel stumbled to his feet, blood pouring from a gash in his arm; Angeline shot him through the head and ran on, heedless of the risk of her own safety. She heard the mortar firing again, the ground shaking as the shells crashed down; she saw the enemy mortar team and opened fire, spraying them and their mortar with bullets. Four men fell, a fifth started to raise his arms. Angeline shot him down without thinking. She was in no mood to take prisoners.

The first of the tanks rumbled into view, machine gun turrets traversing menacingly as they sought targets. Angeline was too stunned, coming off her first taste of *real* combat, to feel fear as the tanks roared past. The tankers *might* mistake them for rebels...she gritted her teeth as she sensed, more than felt, a sniper bullet whipping through the air. A tank returned fire, hosing down the distant nest. Angeline rallied with the remains of the squad, feeling unaccountably guilty as she realised Private Lopez was dead, too. He'd been one of her critics, back during training; he'd been a constant thorn in her side, needling her about being a woman in a man's world. And now he was dead...she watched as the body was hastily slipped into a body-bag and marked for later attention. It bothered her, despite everything, that she hadn't seen him die.

She put the thought out of her mind as they resumed the advance. The rebels seemed determined to slow them down, rather than standing and fighting. There were brief patches of silence, broken by IED explosions or shooting from the jungle that faded away as the rebel fighters withdrew rather than push their luck. Angeline cursed under her breath as they overran another antitank position, *after* the rebel gunners had turned two tanks into flaming coffins. The tankers hadn't been able to escape before death came for them. She kept going, feeling as if she was being pushed to the limits of her endurance. The entire world seemed to have narrowed to the road and the rebels lying in wait.

It will be over soon, she promised herself, as the sniping resumed. The tanks returned fire with savage intensity. *And then we can move on to the next target.*

THE PRINCE'S GAMBIT

...

Carlos Sanchez hadn't *expected* to find himself in command of the island's defences. The plan had called for the defence to be coordinated by his superior, while he controlled the forces based around Mountebank City and Airport himself. But a courier had told him, only a few short hours ago, that the command post had been hit and effectively destroyed...and, while he'd been trying to come to terms with the fact he was now in command, he'd heard the government's forces were landing on the island.

He cursed savagely as he studied the map. The government planners had surprised him. Really, he hadn't expected actual *imagination* from the bastards. Landing at the isolated harbour made it harder for them to get troops to the city, and there would be hard limits on how much they could land before the fighting came to an end, but it also let them outflank the defences the rebels had thrown up around the nearer harbours and docks. Carlos had been hopeful, when it became apparent the missile bombardment had looked impressive yet done relatively little damage. He wasn't so hopeful now.

A courier appeared at the door. "Sir, the invaders have reached Point Nine."

Carlos scowled, although he'd expected as much. He'd only had light forces between the tiny harbour and the city and, despite his best efforts, it wasn't proving easy to get forces into position to block the enemy. They'd have a harder time of it when they reached the outskirts, assuming they wanted to seize a larger harbour or storm the city itself. And yet...the more he looked at it, the more he admired the enemy move. He was going to have real problems if he wanted to evacuate the city before the enemy arrived.

"Order Pablo's Division to move into blocking position," he said. It wasn't a *real* division, more like an oversized company, but hopefully it would confuse any listening ears. "And then order Khan and his command to break contact and head into the jungle."

"Yes, sir."

The courier hurried away. Carlos turned back to the map. The enemy advance was slowing, but it wouldn't stop, not until it reached the city. He didn't have much time to decide what to do. His communications were already fraying. Even if he ordered a general retreat, the orders might not reach everyone in time and *that* would be even worse. And he hadn't received any orders from his distant superiors. The enemy jamming was strong enough to ensure he probably never would.

He summoned another courier. When the young woman arrived, he gave her a handful of messages before ordering her to leave at once. There wasn't time any longer. They had to force the enemy to commit themselves to a meatgrinder or a long siege. Either way, there was a very real chance the cause might come out ahead. Their deaths would not be meaningless after all.

It wasn't much, he reflected as he checked his rifle, but it was all he had.

CHAPTER FIVE

BARAKA ISLAND, NEW DONCASTER

IT HAD BEEN A RISK, Sarah Wilde considered, to set up her headquarters—and the core of a new government—in a mansion that had once belonged to the island's largest landowner. Certainly, she'd had second thoughts when the idea had been proposed to her. The original owner might be dead—he'd been lynched by his own workers, when the uprising had begun—but she had no doubt his heirs knew everything about the building, from the location of the bed and conference rooms to the underground tunnels leading to the outbuildings where the owner had kept his mistresses. It simply didn't feel secure. Sarah would have preferred to direct operations from a base camp deep within the jungle, or perhaps an anonymous building somewhere within a city, but it was vitally important for the provisional government to take the reins of power. Or so she'd been told.

She scowled as she studied the paperwork in front of her. She'd never dared write more than the bare minimum down, when she'd been just another rebel leader, and even after she'd been elected overall commander she had been reluctant to use anything from paper records to electronic files. There was just too great a chance of the government's troops overwhelming a camp before the records could be destroyed, handing them an intelligence windfall that might lead to dozens of spies, deep-cover agents and waverers who were hedging their bets by backing both sides. And yet, the provisional government needed good records in order to function. The ones they'd captured during the uprising were practically worthless.

Except as toilet paper, she reflected sourly. *And propaganda.*

It was hard not to feel a twinge of annoyance. The rebels had long suspected the government had done everything from debt manipulation to outright falsification of records in a bid to keep the planet under control. Hell, they hadn't really hidden what they'd been doing. But the rot had clearly been far deeper than anyone, save the most paranoid, had ever suspected. She understood, now, why the planet was both rich and desperately poor. And why so many landowners had cheated on their taxes.

Which might be more useful if the aristos hadn't brought the townies into government, Sarah reflected. The townies had never been *that* fond of the government, but—unlike most of the rebels—they'd had something to lose. They'd done their level best to stay on the sidelines as much as possible, although the more far-sighted had realised the balancing act was unlikely to endure indefinitely. *There's little to gain by exposing wide-ranging tax fraud now.*

She put the thought out of her head and raised her gaze, meeting Colonel Bryce Ambrose's eyes. He'd had a checkered career, and Sarah was all too aware he wasn't entirely trustworthy, but there were few rebels with any proper military experience. They knew how to wage a guerrilla war, how to choose their targets carefully and hit them hard, then withdraw before the enemy managed to muster a counterattack. They didn't know how to organise men to stand and fight, how to turn a rag-tag force into a tough and professional military that could take and hold ground. She'd read the books and manuals, as had most of her local commanders, but turning the words into reality was beyond her. Ambrose was the only person at her disposal who could do anything about it, at least before all hell broke loose. It was just a matter of time.

"Colonel," she said. It hadn't been easy to give *anyone* a rank, when they'd worked hard to ensure everyone was treated as an equal. The commanders had never enjoyed total authority over their cells, to the point that anyone who tried to boss his men around was likely to be fragged the moment he turned his back. "How's it going?"

"Better than I hoped," Ambrose said. They'd become close, at least partly because their fates were bound together, but he was professional while they were on duty. "There's still a lot of resistance, from people who think they learnt everything there is to know before the war turned hot, but we're making good progress by combining old and new tactics. We should be able to launch the invasion of Kingston soon."

Sarah nodded, curtly. She'd gambled on overwhelming the government before it could muster a response, when the insurgency had turned into open warfare, but the bastards had been lucky. They'd managed to clear most of the insurgents out of their capital city, then launch a thrust at Kingsport that had threatened to break her grip on the port before she could bring in more troops and equipment to continue the offensive. Sarah hadn't been wedded to the plan—she'd been honest enough to admit it had failed and signal the retreat before it became impossible—but it was still frustrating. The government had been gravely weakened, to the point the rebels had secured the rest of their targets without serious fighting, yet the war was far from over. Neither side could afford to let the stalemate continue indefinitely and that meant...

She glanced at the map, gritting her teeth. It had grown harder to stay in touch with her spies on the government-held islands—their navy had become adept at intercepting and searching fishing boats heading into deep waters, where they could slip messages to their contacts—but the government hadn't been able to hide their makeshift fleet. It had slipped out of Kingsport and gone...gone where? The mere fact she'd lost track of it was worrying, although she had little doubt the fleet would be spotted if it approached the core islands. The government had told everyone it was a training exercise, but she didn't believe it. They'd pulled *that* trick before. Besides, they'd put far too much effort into the deployment for it to be anything so minor.

Ambrose tapped the map. "We've got the crews training on the boats now," he added. "We may not have as much modern tech as we might like, but we'll give them a very hard time when they come for us. They can't take many defeats."

Sarah wasn't so sure. There weren't *that* many aristos, but the government had been recruiting amongst the townies. Whoever had come up with *that* idea—and she suspected General Roland Windsor, on the grounds the aristos weren't that imaginative—had done well. She was sure the government wouldn't keep its promises—she had a feeling many of the townies feared the same—but it was unlikely to matter. The strange alliance wouldn't collapse until the government won the war, or—at the very least—drove the rebels back into the shadows.

"We shall see," she said, finally.

She looked at the wooden table, remembering how *easy* life had been when she'd been just a local commander. Then, all that mattered was keeping her group intact while finding ways to strike at the enemy. Now, she was in charge of the entire war effort. She had to train her troops, many of whom had only signed up after the uprising had overwhelmed the island, while arranging for supplies of everything from food and vehicles to weapons and armoured vehicles. The islands had more industrial capacity than she'd realised—she'd been amused to discover one of the factories concealed a galactic-level fabber, a device on the import blacklist—but setting priorities and finding war materiel was incredibly difficult. It didn't help they couldn't rely on imports from distant allies. She had a nasty feeling they'd come with a price tag attached, now that the rebels had become a provisional government.

And those bills will come due, when we occupy Kingston, she thought. *We may have to pay through the nose for what little they send us.*

She stood, brushing down her pants as she looked around the chamber. The room had once been a garden of sybaritic delights, the walls covered in paintings that had been so erotic they'd shocked even her. She'd grown up on Earth, where—in the planet's final years—all taboos had been thrown aside, but the original owner had crossed so many lines she couldn't understand how his fellows had tolerated him. Even aristos had *some* standards. She'd had the paintings torn out and burnt, the gold and silver artwork melted down to pay her troops and everything else stripped out and replaced with cruder furniture, but the office still felt unwelcoming. She supposed that was a good thing. If she stayed in such a room indefinitely, what would it do to her? Would she become used to luxury? Would she allow it to corrupt her? Or simply turn her into a lazy brat?

The thought nagged at her as she walked to the window and peered over the square below. A handful of bodies hung from makeshift gallows, twisting slowly in the wind. Sarah grimaced. Two of the men had been aristos, who'd been hiding out in the jungle until they'd made a bid to steal a boat and flee; the others were looters, men and women she'd had to order executed to set an example. She regretted their deaths, if only because she understood why they'd turned to crime. Food wasn't precisely in short supply, thanks to the algae-farms they'd captured, but the best of the grub was reserved for fighting units. She would have preferred to send the thieves to a work gang, where they could slave beside the former aristos who hadn't been killed during the uprising, but too many people had wanted them dead. The mob needed to be placated. God knew the uprising, with all the pent-up savagery that had been unleashed on the island, hadn't been enough to satisfy the mob's demand for bloody revenge. How could it?

Her eyes wandered over the nearby streets. They were bustling with life, from newspaper sellers advertising their wares to merchants inviting passers-by to come into their shops. The old rules and regulations were gone, allowing anyone who wanted to open a shop to do it without splashing out thousands of credits in bribes, then paying more in punitive taxes. The people below knew the war was far from over, that there was more struggle to come, yet…they were doing their best to enjoy the freedom and safety while it lasted. Her lips quirked into a smile as she saw a line of teenage girls walking past the square, assault rifles slung over their shoulders. A year ago, owning weapons without special permits had been utterly illegal. Now, everyone was armed and the streets had never been safer.

And if we'd been allowed to own pistols on Earth, she reflected, *would the megacities have been safer for women?*

There was a sharp knock at the door. Her hand dropped to her pistol as she turned, bracing herself. The mansion was heavily guarded, but she was uneasily aware an intruder might manage to get through the defences, either by tricking the guards or simply sneaking through a tunnel they didn't know existed. Sarah knew, without false modesty, that she was far from irreplaceable, but it would be difficult for the rebel leadership to appoint someone to take her place. Her origins had made it easier, perversely, for them to accept her as their warlord and provisional president. Her successor might not have that advantage.

"Come," she said.

The door opened. A young woman poked her head into the room, her eyes nervous. "Ah…"

Bad news, Sarah thought. She'd done her best to convince her expanded staff that she wasn't in the habit of killing the messenger, unlike some of the aristos, but only a handful actually believed her. Too many of the newcomers had clerked for aristocrats who'd had a habit of using their fists to express their displeasure. *Whatever she wants to say, it isn't good.*

She made a show of relaxing, keeping her hand away from her pistol. "Spit it out," she ordered, as gently as possible. "What's happened?"

The young woman looked as if she expected to be struck at any moment. "Ah…we just picked up a radio message from Mountebank," she said, cringing. "The island is under heavy attack. They think they are about to be invaded."

Sarah turned to look at the map, pinned to the wall. "Details?"

"Very little," the young woman said. "I...ah...the message cut off abruptly."

"I see." Sarah wasn't too surprised. The planet's atmosphere played merry hell with radio signals. The government didn't really *need* to jam transmissions or bomb transmitters to keep word from spreading—effectively instantly—from island to island, although she was sure they would do it anyway. Their off-world commander wouldn't miss *that* trick. "Go back to your station, order them to keep listening for updates. If there are any, bring them to me."

The woman bowed low, then retreated as quickly as she could without openly running. Sarah scowled as the door closed. She couldn't blame someone for doing whatever she had to do to survive—she felt sick, sometimes, when she thought of the things she'd had to do—but the woman's former master was gone. Dead, perhaps, or simply fled. His servant could afford to be more of a free woman now, couldn't she? But it wasn't so easy to get rid of habits that had made the difference between life and death. Sarah wondered, perversely, if her descendants would think of her as a weakling, for getting on her knees—literally—when confronted by superior force. If everything went as planned, her offspring would know freedom. The ever-present fear that had governed her early years as an involuntary colonist would be alien to them.

"That's an odd target," Ambrose mused, studying the map. "They can take the island, perhaps, but it won't get them any closer to us."

Sarah was inclined to agree. Mountebank had never been considered particularly important. The island was too far from the core islands for her to risk improving its defences, for fear the government would simply bypass the island and leave the garrison to wither on the vine. She was tempted to wonder if the invasion was nothing more than a raid, perhaps an operation intended to test the government's forces while giving them the chance to withdraw if the defenders proved too stubborn to be easily overcome. The government's expanded forces were as green as her own, although she knew they had a solid core of military veterans to stiffen their spine. They might see value in a probing attack they could convert into a full-scale invasion if victory seemed assured.

"We can't get anyone out there to help," Ambrose commented, grimly. "The gunboats would be operating without support, right at the edge of their range."

"Yeah." Sarah let out a breath. There was nothing she could do. The defenders had to win or lose on their own. She suspected there'd be a result quickly. Mountebank wasn't a big island, not compared to Baraka, Rolleston or Winchester. "If they convert the island into a base, how much does it hurt us?"

"Very little, unless they've built long-range aircraft," Ambrose assured her. "They'd be too isolated to have any real effect on the rest of the war."

Sarah hoped he was right. Ambrose had had only a few months of military life when the balloon had gone up, more than she did or many others, but far less than their opponent. He was, at best, a gifted amateur. General Windsor was young, or at least he *looked* young, but he'd spent years in the military. And he lacked the short-sightedness of the aristocrats who'd tried to lead the militia into battle. He was a dangerous—and sometimes reckless—foe. She dared not assume the invasion wouldn't weaken her position...

The mere fact they pulled it off, if they win the engagement, will do wonders for their morale, she thought, crossly. *And our morale will go down at the same time.*

"They'll have to fight as long as they can," she said. There was no point in trying to direct operations personally. Even if it had been possible, from such a distance, it would have been worse than useless. The local commander would hardly surrender his authority to someone he barely knew, nor would his troops follow orders from the radio. "And then slip back into the jungle."

"Unless there's an opportunity to counterattack," Ambrose said. "They might have a chance."

Sarah let her eyes wander over the map, before shaking her head and stepping back. It might be hours, or days, before she knew what was happening...no, what *had* happened. By the time she found out, it would be too late to issue any meaningful orders. The local commander did have standing orders, but...who knew how seriously he'd take them? He might decline to fall back, if confronted by superior force, or...she bit her lip. The insurgency had suffered defeats in the past, but none of them had been fatal. Now they were out in the open, a defeat might be far more significant.

"Contact the boats," she said. "We need to expand our warning network. If they get a fleet close to the core without being detected..."

"It's unlikely," Ambrose assured her. "They probably took a very evasive course to Mountebank, letting them get close without being spotted. Here...there are a lot more inhabited islands and shipping between them and us."

"Better to be careful." Sarah knew he was right, at least on paper, but she hadn't survived so long without taking basic precautions. "If they force a landing here, we may have trouble driving them back into the sea."

CHAPTER SIX

MOUNTEBANK ISLAND, NEW DONCASTER

"GENERAL, WE JUST PICKED UP A SIGNAL from Unit Are," Lieutenant Church said. "They're ready to head to the coast."

Roland nodded, curtly. Unit Are was *Rachel's* designation. He hadn't been sure if she'd be able to continue her mission, let alone make it back to the coast under her own power; he'd been careful to devise plans that didn't rely on her presence, just in case the worst happened. She'd given him a whole string of dire warnings about what might happen if she overused the boost. But if she'd signalled the fleet, it was clear she was alive and reasonably well.

"Good," Roland said. "Inform me when they signals again."

He turned his attention to the display. His men were landing more troops, vehicles and equipment all the time. The tiny harbour was rapidly being turned into a stronghold, tanks and AFVs taking up blocking positions while antiaircraft and antimissile batteries swept the skies for incoming threats. He didn't have anything like as much of the latter as he would have liked, but—thankfully—the rebels didn't seem to have any long-range missiles in their arsenal. Their forces had largely been caught out of place, although—he had to admit—not as badly as he would have liked. The city was teeming with enemy fighters, while the larger harbours were heavily fortified. Some enemy troops were trying to flee to the jungle, but the remainder seemed determined to dig in and fight to the last. And in an urban environment, Roland's advantages would be minimised.

We need to keep pushing, he thought. He would have preferred to ensure his men had a chance to rest, rather than marching forward with a dangerous recklessness, but he needed to trap as many fighters within the city as possible. Taking the city would be costly, and a siege would be time-consuming, yet better that than the rebels getting into the jungle and resuming the insurgency. *If we can cut them off and trap them, perhaps they'll see sense and surrender.*

He looked at Admiral Forest. "I'll move my command post to the island," he said. "Have the gear transported at once."

Admiral Forest looked caught between relief and concern. Roland understood. It couldn't be easy for the admiral to have Roland on his command deck, not when the makeshift navy had yet to sort out matters like command precedence under fire. A smart commander *had* to worry about confusion, when missiles were blazing towards his ships. And yet, he also had orders to keep Roland safe. His death would be more than *just* a personal disaster. There were no candidates who enjoyed bipartisan approval waiting in the wings.

"Yes, sir," Admiral Forest said, finally. "Good luck."

Roland nodded, curtly. It was unlikely he'd be in any real danger. The invasion force had secured the lodgement within moments of landing, then spread out. There were no major rebel forces within two miles and individuals were unlikely to get through the perimeter, not unless they were as capable as Rachel or Belinda. He doubted it, although he'd been cautioned the rebels knew how to use the jungle to best advantage. And besides, he needed to get a feel for the island. Issuing orders from a safe distance, without any real awareness of the island's realities, was asking for trouble.

Rachel will tell me off later, he reflected as he headed for his boat. *But she'll understand what I had to do.*

The town didn't look *that* threatening, as the AFV nosed down the dirt road towards the settlement, but Richard's instincts sounded the alarm even before the first bullet *pinged* off the vehicle's armour. He was morbidly pleased to have proof the enemy awaited them, although it hadn't been unexpected. The town sat on the road leading up to the jungle, ensuring that whoever controlled it could also control the road. Richard suspected that the town had been emplaced with malice aforethought, even though neither the rebels nor the government could have expected Mountebank to become a warzone. There'd been plenty of indents and *de facto* slaves within the city and keeping them from running away had been a priority for years. His heart twisted. He knew the rebels couldn't be trusted. He knew they would tear down the good, as well as the bad, if they won the war. His own family would be destroyed...

...And yet, part of him wondered if he was on the wrong side.

He forced himself to study the town's defences as the AFVs opened fire, forcing the rebels to keep their heads down. Most of the buildings were sturdy enough to stand up to machine gun fire, although a handful of missiles would be more than enough to destroy the town. The rebels had adapted well, he noted, as a handful of mortar shells flew up from behind the buildings and fell towards his forces. They obviously knew how to take best advantage of the terrain...he reached for his communicator, ordering the lead elements to return fire. The rebels might not be aware of it, but he needed to take the town intact. Any delay in clearing the rubble would slow the timetable still further, giving the rebels time to set up more booby traps while pulling as many men as they could out of the trap.

"Unit One, provide covering fire," he ordered, curtly. There was no point in taking the AFVs closer, not when the rebels had makeshift anti-tank weapons as well as IEDs. "Squad One, flank the town, then clear it."

His fingers itched. He wanted to disembark and join the flanking attack, even though he was in overall command of the offensive. He cursed under his breath as he glanced at the tracker, reminding himself—once again—that everything was slightly out of date. The offensive had been slowed, the rebels buying time with their lives, but the main thrust was still on target to reach its destination. And then...

Once we break up their positions, we can force them to surrender or simply starve them out, he reflected. *And then we can try to put an end to the war.*

...

"Keep your fucking heads down," Ellis snarled as the new recruits stumbled into the jungle. "If they can see you, they can kill you!"

Angeline nodded, feeling sweat running down her back and pooling in her boots as the makeshift squad pushed through the foliage. She'd never thought of herself as a hardened veteran, and it had only been six months since she'd gotten out of hospital and joined the army, but she'd learnt fast. It helped that she'd watched others make tiny mistakes and die. The newcomers, the young men who'd landed with the second wave, hadn't had the chance to learn yet. She hoped, as she stayed low, that they'd last long enough to make it.

The sound of shooting grew louder as they tried to flank the town. Angeline stayed alert, watching for prying eyes or booby traps. The jungle might look impassable, on a map, but anyone who'd actually *lived* in or near a jungle knew better. The rebels couldn't move heavy vehicles through the foliage, thankfully, yet there was nothing stopping them from abandoning their positions and retreating. Angeline was mildly surprised they hadn't started to run already. The bastards were brave enough, when confronted by unarmed men and defenceless women, but they turned into cowards when they fought someone willing and able to fight back.

Ellis held up a hand, signalling for the squad to get down and crawl. Angeline obeyed without hesitation. To hell with dignity. Better to stay in the mud than get shot. She followed her commander, bracing herself as the first of the buildings came into view. Her heart twisted in outrage. It was a barracks, just like the ones on her family's plantation. The men who'd lived there had turned on her family...

Get ready, she told herself. Her hands felt sweaty, slippery, as her commander counted down the final seconds. *Fuck this up and get fucked.*

She darted forward on command, reaching the door as Ellis hurled a grenade through the window and into the barracks. Angeline felt the building shake as the grenade detonated, heard someone scream. She shoved the door open and threw a noisemaker into the barracks, then followed it in. The wooden bunks were shattered ruins, a handful of wounded men on the floor. Angeline felt sick as she saw the carnage, then forced the sensation out of her mind as a pair of men ran towards her. They didn't have any visible weapons, but she didn't dare take that for granted. Besides, she wasn't inclined to accept surrender. She shot them both down, then pressed onwards. The tunnel at the rear of the barracks looked new. She heard voices at the far end and drew a grenade from her belt, hurling it into the darkness. Angeline hoped, vindictively, that some of the rebels had been buried alive. They deserved it and worse.

There was no time to rest on their laurels. She ran outside, keeping her head down as the rebel position started to crumble. A wave of heat, hot even by the planet's standards, washed through the air and she looked up, just in time to see a man with a makeshift flamethrower. She almost froze as the flames billowed towards her, an instant before Ellis shot the man, sending him and his weapon crashing to the ground. Flames leapt up, the stench of roasting flesh permeating the air. Angeline heard someone throwing up behind her and rolled her eyes in disgust. She'd smelt worse, when the insurgency had begun. The newbies behind her would do so too, given time. They probably thought their training barracks smelt so bad it simply *couldn't* get any worse.

She forced herself to keep going, heedless of her own personal safety. The infantry spread out, clearing buildings with cold determination. The flames spread behind them, threatening to burn much of the town to the ground. Angeline didn't care. Her superiors could worry about keeping the town intact, if they wanted. She just wanted to kill rebels. She crashed into a small house and looked around, spotting a man leaning against the far wall. A gun sat by his feet. He had to be a rebel. She shot him, then swept the rest of the tiny building. It was very clearly an observation point. She made a mental note of the radio's location—the spooks might want to see it, afterwards—then rejoined the squad outside. The enemy position was collapsing. She breathed a sigh of relief as the AFVs rumbled into the town, despite the risk of accidentally being shot by her own side. The drivers were good—she'd trained with them—but, for most of the crews, the invasion was their first taste of combat.

The shooting stopped, so abruptly she half-thought someone had flipped a switch. The remaining rebels, if any had survived, were on the run. She hoped they were wounded, that they'd bleed out and die in the jungle before they reached safety. Her lips twisted. No, they wouldn't reach safety because there was none to be found. They might have a slight edge in jungle craft, but it wouldn't last. Angeline and her comrades would search the entire island, quartering it piece by piece until they found and slaughtered the rebel forces. There would be nowhere to hide.

She sagged, taking a moment to catch her breath as the squad reformed. A handful of faces were missing…she hoped that meant the newbies were wounded, rather than dead. Or simply ordered to join other squads. The unit had never been that coherent, even before it had been sent into combat for the first time. Their training officers had insisted they learn to form new units at the drop of a hat. She was starting to understand why. They'd learnt a great deal, since they'd volunteered to fight, but some lessons could only be learnt by doing. And that could get someone killed…

Ellis clapped her shoulder. "You did well, Private."

Angeline tried not to flinch. She'd had a great deal of experience in concealing her real feelings from authority figures—her father would not have been amused if he'd known what she was feeling—but her defences had been shattered. Once, she wouldn't have been too concerned about a clap on the shoulder; now, it felt like a threat, like the promise of worse to come. A person invading her personal space…she turned away, trying not to vomit as her memories threatened to overwhelm her. It would be a long time before she felt safe again, even when she was alone. She'd found it near-impossible to share a barracks with the rest of the squad. Only the desire for revenge had kept her going.

She nodded as she turned back to him, unhooking her canteen from her belt and taking a swig. They had a few moments to rest, before they pressed onwards. The follow-up units, looking disgustingly fresh and untested, marched past, securing the town and setting up blocking positions. The rebels could still escape through the jungle, although that would be a great deal harder once the army started to patrol the roads, but they'd have problems getting their heavy equipment out of the city. They'd have to abandon the gear, perhaps spiking the guns to keep their enemies from using them, or stand and fight. Angeline hoped they'd make a stand. She wanted to crush them like bugs.

"Grab a ration bar," Ellis ordered his men. "We'll be moving again shortly."

Angeline nodded. She was tired, her entire body aching, but she wanted to be in at the death. She wanted to be *there* when the rebels were crushed... she wanted to do it herself. She wanted to watch them scream...she looked up as a trio of aircraft roared overhead, flying towards the burning city. There was nothing keeping them from bombing the hell out of the rebel defences, weakening them so the groundpounders could overwhelm their positions and wipe them out. Angeline hoped they wouldn't surrender, no matter what the brass said. She wanted them all to die.

• • •

Rachel felt almost *normal* again as she made her way down the dirt road, keeping her eyes open for possible ambushes. Mountebank wasn't *that* big, on a planetary scale, but the island was still large enough for the rebels to regroup in the aftermath of the invasion. The sound of shooting was easily audible—she doubted there were any rebels who didn't know what was happening—but it would be a long time before Roland and his commanders got a patrol up here. She was all too aware she'd stand out, if someone got a good look at her. Her ghillie suit was designed to camouflage her as much as possible, but there were limits. If nothing else, the suit was unique. As far as she knew, there were no other top of the line ghillie suits on New Doncaster.

She tensed as she heard engines further up the road. It was hard to be sure—her enhanced ears could pick up aircraft as well as ground-based vehicles—but it sounded like a motorbike. Rachel briefly considered concealing herself within the jungle, then stopped and waited. If the reports were accurate, the rebels had commandeered every vehicle on the island. Whoever was riding the bike was almost certainly a rebel.

And I can steal the bike for myself, she thought. *I need to get back…*

The motorbike came into view. It looked primitive, burning hydrocarbons for fuel rather than using power cells, although it was at the peak of what the planet could produce without off-world help. The rider, a young man wearing makeshift camouflage, gaped at her, then tried to gun the engine and zoom past. Rachel darted forward, *without* using the boost, and knocked him off the bike, landing on top of him as he hit the ground. He tried to struggle, but she was far stronger. The shock, and fear, in his eyes didn't surprise her. If he knew what she was, or even guessed at her mission, he had to assume she'd torture him for information and snap his neck once he'd finished talking.

"Where are you going?" Rachel deepened her voice, trying to sound masculine. She didn't look very feminine in the ghillie suit—he might not have realised she was a woman—and if he assumed she was a man, he might be happier about surrendering. "Answer me!"

The man stared at her. "The airport," he managed, finally. "I…they told me to take a package there."

"Now?" Rachel found it hard to believe, but the courier was too scared to think of a lie. She could smell the urine as his bladder gave way. "Why the airport?"

The courier didn't move. He'd fainted. Rachel checked, just to be sure he wasn't faking it, then rolled off him and searched him quickly. He wasn't carrying much, just a primitive pistol and a sealed datachip box. The package, she guessed. The rebels wouldn't have sent it to the airport unless they'd thought the datachips could be flown out, before the airport fell. It was a priority target...she played with the box for a moment, then stood as a thought occurred to her. The man's shirt and trousers were stained, but his overcoat was still wearable. If she took his place...

They'll defend the airport to the death, she thought. It wasn't *impossible* they'd get a flight out. The locals made good pilots, their aircraft designed for the planet's cursed weather. If the pilot stayed low, and well away from the fleet, there was a good chance of escape. *But if I can get inside, we can put the brakes on before they get away.*

CHAPTER SEVEN

MOUNTEBANK ISLAND, NEW DONCASTER

BLAIR SMITH HAD NEVER BEEN SO SCARED.

He'd thought himself a brave man, when he'd fled the plantation bare inches ahead of the overseer who'd intended to beat him to death. He'd joined the insurgents shortly before the uprising, fighting beside them as they destroyed the plantations and stormed the city, executing the aristos too stupid to run before their time ran out. And he'd danced and sang with the rest of his people, when they'd thought they were free. But now...

He stood at the guardpost and tried not to show fear. The aristos had returned and they'd brought an army. The rumours were insane—*billions* of men, *millions of tanks*—but it was clear the rebels were rapidly losing control of the lowlands. Blair had heard the radio messages, before they'd been brutally silenced; he'd seen the aircraft flying overhead, dropping their bombs without interference. There could be no doubt. The aristos had landed and they could not be dislodged. And that meant the lowlands would have to be abandoned before the defenders were trapped and killed.

It was hard not to give into the temptation to turn away and run. The airport had seemed a nice safe billet, when he'd accepted the assignment. He'd never seriously considered it might come under heavy attack, certainly not without a week's warning. He had to admire the nerve the aristos had shown, landing well clear of the main defences and practically outflanking them rather than trying to drive into rebel fire and clear them out pillbox by pillbox. Now...the reports were vaguer, and some observers had stopped transmitting completely, but Blair was no fool. He could tell the aristos were driving on the airport. It wouldn't be long before they came into view.

Something moved, down the road. He lifted his rifle, unsure if there was any point in trying to make a stand. The airport had never been designed to serve as a strongpoint and what few additions had been made, when the insurgency had started to bite, weren't anything like enough to stand off an armoured division. He was tempted to run himself, or to try to surrender...no, that wasn't an option. The man who'd owned Blair and his family might be dead—it was hard to be sure—but he had heirs. They'd insist Blair was their property. The best he could hope for, if they took custody of him, was a quick return to the plantation. He couldn't stand the thought.

He breathed a sigh of relief as the motorbike came into view. They'd been told to watch for a courier, someone bringing something to the airport...he hoped, as fear twisted in his gut, that the rider wasn't a senior rebel trying to escape before it was too late. The rider was a young man wearing a black trench coat and a cap that concealed his hair and most of his face. It was a disguise...Blair's eyes sharpened, then relaxed as he spotted hints the rider was decidedly feminine. He supposed that accounted for the disguise. Women—his sisters amongst them—had been wearing male clothes for years, even though it had been officially forbidden until the rebellion, in hopes of avoiding harassment by the militia and plantation overseers. His stomach clenched at the thought. He couldn't go back there. He just couldn't.

"I have a package for the boss," the courier said. She didn't sound very feminine, but there was definitely something in the tone that convinced Blair it was an act. "Can I take it through?"

"He's in the tower," Blair said. He knew he should pat her down, at the very least, but he was too nervous to bother. "Good luck."

The courier nodded politely, then rode past. Blair wondered, idly, if she'd be on one of the last flights out of the airport, before the enemy closed it down. He wasn't sure it was possible to get an aircraft out safely, although—from the boasting he'd overheard—the pilots thought they could fly through mountains without scattering their atoms over the island. He was pretty sure they were bullshitting. The technology to fly through solid matter simply didn't exist.

He flinched as the sound of shooting grew louder, followed by the rumble of engines. There was nothing between the invaders and the airport now, nothing save for Blair and a handful of guards. They couldn't stand up to the enemy for more than a few seconds, if that. He wondered, suddenly, if he could beg his way onto one of the aircraft, perhaps make his escape with the others. It was quite possible they could escape the tightening noose and get back to the jungle, even if they didn't get to another island. And then...he gritted his teeth. No. It wasn't going to happen. If he didn't run now, he was doomed.

And if I do run, I'll be shot in the back, he thought. *There's no way out.*

...

It was a given, Rachel had learned years before she'd been invited to train as a Pathfinder, that war was chaotic, as well as dangerously unpredictable. Proper security relied upon the guards knowing what was normal, and having a good idea of who might be allowed to walk through the checkpoints even without checking the paperwork or calling for superior officers, but there was no normal in war. She'd feared, even as she'd checked in with Roland and arranged for the army to rush the airport to support her, that the guards would insist on checking her identity. It had been quite possible, at least in her view, that the guards would know the couriers by sight. Rachel had bluffed her way onto military bases before, but that had been wearing the right uniforms and generally acting like an entitled asshole who *did* have the right papers, even if they'd been temporally misplaced. Here...

And I would have gleefully reported anyone who let me through without checking, she thought, without a twinge of guilt. The guards should never have let themselves be browbeaten into allowing her to enter, even if she'd threatened them with permanent KP or something even worse. *That was the whole point of the exercise.*

Rachel kept her face under tight control as she parked the motorbike with a bunch of others—there were no moving vehicles within the perimeter—concealing a small charge under the saddle before she looked around. The airport was bigger than she'd expected, with a handful of concrete hangars and a single large control tower.... much bigger, she thought, than the island really needed. Mountebank wasn't really close enough to any of the major islands to serve as a refuelling point, although she supposed the excess capability might have come in handy for something. Or maybe it had been built in a bid to boost the island's economy. The government was reluctant to invest in long-haul aircraft, when the weather made flying difficult much of the time, but private investors might have been willing to take the risk.

Her eyes narrowed. There were dozens, perhaps hundreds, of people within eyeshot, most running around as if they had no idea where they should go. She thought she knew how they were feeling. The airport might have been reasonably secure during the insurgency, but there was a small army bearing down on the defences. The refugees had made the wrong call, coming to the airport instead of trying to run to the jungle, and now they were trapped. She glanced into one of the hangars and saw dozens of youngsters gathered around a mid-sized aircraft. The ground crew were doing what they could, but it wasn't easy to get it ready to fly. There were just too many people waiting to get onboard.

She kept moving, careful to look as if she had a perfect right to be in the middle of operations. The airport was in chaos, with so many strangers running around it was unlikely anyone would notice her, but there was no point in taking chances. The trick to not being challenged, she'd learnt over the years, was to avoid giving anyone the slightest hint you *should* be challenged. It was a difficult trick to master, but the confusion made it a great deal easier. If she'd been in command of the airport's security, she would have ordered everyone out before it was too late.

Even without an intruder, the people are making it impossible to get the aircraft out, she mused, as she walked to the control tower. A handful of guards were on duty, eyeing the crowds nervously. There were no aircraft inside the tower, nor were there any other ways out—assuming the plans she'd downloaded were complete—but crowds were rarely rational. One spark would be more than enough to start a riot, tearing the airport apart from the inside. *One little spark...*

She pasted a nervous expression on her face as the distant shooting grew louder. Roland had promised he'd do what he could and it sounded as if he'd made it happen, directing the advance elements to race down the road and reach the airport as quickly as possible. The guards looked nervous too, exchanging glances as she approached. She had no trouble recognising men who were slowly coming to realise, no matter how much they tried to fight it, that they were trapped and doomed. The rebel propaganda worked against them, she noted wryly. They'd tried so hard to convince their people that POWs faced an unspeakable fate that many rebels, given a chance to run, might take it rather than risk standing and fighting to the death.

"I have a package for the boss," she said, again. It didn't help she had little idea of just *who* was expecting the courier. The rebel command network was a mystery, save for a handful of codenames that could easily be nothing more than disinformation. It was what *she* would have done. The local spooks were doing what they could, but they'd yet to match any of the codenames to real people. "I need to deliver it now."

The guards hesitated. Rachel realised, in a flash, she'd been caught out. Either they knew the courier by sight or they'd simply expected a young man, rather than a woman. She briefly considered trying to bluff, to lie her way out of the mess, but she didn't know enough to make the story convincing. If there were no women working as couriers, which wasn't impossible given how few rights women had on New Doncaster, lying would only make things worse. Instead, she used her implants to send a signal back to the motorbike. The charge she'd hidden under the saddle, in preparation for a diversion if she needed it, detonated. For a moment, all was chaos. The guards jumped in shock, staring at the blast; the crowd fled in panic, shouting and screaming. The explosion had triggered a chain reaction, destroying the remaining vehicles. It gave her a moment of complete surprise.

She used it ruthlessly, punching out one of the guards and hitting the other in the throat before shoving open the door. The interior was surprisingly warm—she guessed the rebels hadn't bothered to keep the air conditioning on—and welcoming. She drew her gun as she raced through the empty room, heading up the stairs. The tower had looked, from the outside, relatively standardised, although built from concrete instead of prefabricated colonist crap. She hoped they hadn't made any non-standard alterations, as she ran up the stairs. There wasn't time to search the building from top to bottom. If the sound outside was any indication, the first scouts had arrived.

The door at the top of the stairs was firmly closed. She tested it gingerly, first to make sure it was actually locked and then to determine if she could either pick the lock or break down the door. Neither seemed possible. She did a quick scan for control circuitry, in hopes of finding a command circuit she could hack, but the door seemed too primitive for anything other than brute force. She wondered if she could break the door down, then kicked herself—mentally—for overlooking the simple solution. She knocked. A moment later, the door started to open.

Rachel didn't hesitate. She shoved the door open, boosting as she darted into the control room itself. A man stumbled back, hitting the floor in front of her; she stamped on his chest, too lightly to kill but hard enough to keep him down long enough for her to deal with the others. Her gaze swept the room. There were five other people within eyesight, two men and three women. She was surprised to see the latter. She'd bet good money they weren't airport staff. Unless they'd been cleaners, spying on their former masters…

"Hands in the air," she ordered. The boost made it harder to do something as subtle as take prisoners. She was stronger and faster than them, but she knew from bitter experience it was easy to get overwhelmed and then blindsided. "Hands in the air, now!"

The staff obeyed. Rachel motioned them into a corner, looking around for something—anything—she could use to restrain them. There was no way she could trust them not to do something stupid, not when she was coming off the boost and shaking so badly she was clearly in no state for a fight. She briefly considered breaking a few of their bones when nothing came to hand, then found a roll of duct tape in a storage locker. She had to smile as she tossed it to one of the women and ordered her to tape up the others, rather than risk doing it herself. Duct tape was so useful, she reflected, that she should have expected to find it somewhere it could be easily reached.

She bound the last woman herself, once the others were helpless, then checked the communications console. It was strikingly primitive, to the point she doubted it would be easy to spoof. The sound of shooting from outside was growing louder, shouts and screams echoing through the open windows. She heard engines powering up and cursed under her breath. The pilots were likely to squash a bunch of innocent victims under their wheels as they made their way onto the runway and took off, without waiting for orders. She keyed the radio and ordered the planes to stay on the ground, without any real expectation the orders would be obeyed. It was worth a try.

A prisoner—one of the men—made a coughing sound. "What…what'll happen to us?"

"If you behave yourselves, you'll go into a POW camp where you'll be held until the end of the war," Rachel said, as she searched the room for anything else that might be useful or informative. The rebels practiced good operational security, but it was possible they might have turned the tower into a command post once they'd secured the island. It was very easy to lose good habits when they no longer seemed necessary. "If not..."

She let her words hang in the air as she completed the search. The government hadn't been *that* keen on taking prisoners, let alone treating them as POWs rather than insurgents and terrorists who could be legally interrogated then shot without trial. Roland had burned up a lot of his political capital, when he'd insisted the government agree to treat prisoners well, and Rachel had no idea what would happen after the war was won. Normally, POWs were exchanged with the enemy government, but...unless the two sides agreed to split the planet between them, there wouldn't *be* an enemy government. And *the* government regarded many of the POWs as property, rather than people in their own right. She hoped Roland could find a way to deal with the problem, without laying the groundwork for *another* civil war a decade or two down the line. New Doncaster's odds of surviving the first war were not as high as she might have liked.

The sounds from outside grew louder. Rachel glanced through the window—it looked as if the defence line was crumpling—then ducked as bullets smashed the glass, sending fragments flying everywhere. She hit the ground, covering her head with her hands as debris shattered around her. Someone had spotted her and probably thought she was an enemy sniper, although they hadn't reacted very well. Rachel chuckled, despite herself. She shouldn't complain if someone had missed her, but the shooter should get a sharp lecture from their CO for having a clear shot at a suspected sniper and missing. It wasn't really that funny. After all she'd done, to be shot by her own side would have been embarrassing.

No, it wouldn't, she corrected herself. *You'd be too dead to be embarrassed.*

The ground shook. Something had exploded, something big. A fuel tank? Perhaps not, or the entire airport would have exploded. An aircraft? Rachel heard one of her prisoners whimpering and felt a flicker of sympathy, mixed with the grim awareness they probably wouldn't have hesitated to kill her, if things had been reversed. If they'd known what she was, they certainly would...no one in their right mind would risk leaving a fully trained and outfitted special ops soldier in their rear, no matter how heavily they shackled her. A person with the right enhancements could break handcuffs as easily as one might snap a twig.

"Don't worry," she said, as kindly as she could. "It'll all be over soon."

But she knew, even as she spoke, it wasn't remotely true.

CHAPTER EIGHT

MOUNTEBANK ISLAND, NEW DONCASTER

ANGELINE COULDN'T HELP HERSELF. She whooped.

The IFV charged towards the fence, the squad keeping their heads low as bullets cracked through the air and bounced off the IFV's armour. Whoever had designed the airport hadn't taken security very seriously, from what she could see; they'd set up guardposts that *might* have made good strongpoints on the gates, but the remainder of the perimeter was secured by nothing more than rough terrain and a single fence. There weren't any walls, not even solid prefabricated blocks. She was perversely disappointed, even as the IFV crashed over the terrain and slammed into the fence without slowing down. The airport had changed hands at least once, if the briefing notes were accurate, yet neither owner had bothered to set up proper defences. It made a certain degree of sense, she supposed. The aristocrats hadn't expected an uprising and the rebels hadn't figured there'd be a full-scale invasion.

She kept her head low as bullets zipped overhead, a handful of rebels trying to mount a brief and utterly futile resistance. They'd been caught in the open, unable to run or hide. The IFV returned fire, sweeping the enemy positions with its machine guns. Angeline grinned, savagely, as the rebels disintegrated, reduced to little more than blood and gore splattered against the hangar wall. It was no more than they deserved. She checked her rifle automatically as the IFV lurched to a halt, then followed Ellis through the hatch and down to the ground. The airport was burning, flames rising up from near the gates. She hoped that meant the defenders had other things to worry about, something that might keep them from mounting a proper defence before it was too late.

The hangar doors slammed open, revealing a midsized aircraft heading for the runway, heedless of the rebels in its path. Angeline blinked, honestly surprised, as the aircraft kept moving, catching sight of the pilots desperately preparing for takeoff. A moment later, the roar of machine guns almost deafened her, the IFVs hosing the aircraft with bullets. It seemed to stagger, just for a second, then exploded into a colossal fireball. Angeline threw herself to the tarmac without thinking as the flames rose into the sky, then picked herself up and followed her superior into the hangar. A single shot rang out, barely audible over the roar of the flames. Ellis staggered, then fell. He'd been shot in the head. Angeline lifted her rifle, uncaring of her own safety. The shooter—a man in plain clothes—was still trying to draw a bead on her when she shot him in the chest. He crumpled, screaming in agony. It wasn't enough.

She glanced back, trying to determine who was in command. The original squad was effectively gone. Too many soldiers had been killed in the fighting, to be replaced by the remnants of other squads that had been even less lucky. Ellis had been in undisputed command, but now…she didn't have *time* to try to parse out the new chain of command. It should have been settled during the race to the airport…she snapped orders, knowing she'd be in deep shit if it turned out she wasn't the senior survivor. She told herself it didn't matter as the squad swept the remnants of the hangar, then moved to the next. It was teeming with people, refugees… now, rebels. She clenched her teeth as they stared at her, their eyes dull and hopeless. They'd rebelled against the government, they'd committed hundreds of atrocities like the one perpetrated against *her*, and now they thought they could just get away with it? A surge of hatred shot through her. Her CO, a man who'd accepted her as one of the boys, was dead. Her family was dead. And the people in front of her had fought for the monsters who'd torn her world apart.

"Hands in the air," she barked. The shooting outside was dying down. The guardposts had either been taken out by antitank missiles or forced to surrender. The plan had been thrown together at very short notice, the assault more like a barroom brawl than a precise and perfect offensive, but it had worked. "Stand up, then get your fucking hands in the fucking air."

The rebels stared at her numbly, then moved to obey. Angeline glared at them, her eyes scanning for possible threats. A handful of men…cowards, like all rebels, for not fighting on the front lines. Women and children; the former no doubt cursing themselves for supporting the rebels, the latter unaware their lives were over before they'd even reached the age of maturity. She met the eyes of a girl who couldn't have been more than a year younger than she was and glared, hating the bitch for daring to fight for the rebels. There was no way to know, but Angeline was *sure* the stupid girl had whored for them. Everyone knew the rebels tormented their own people as much as their enemies. The silly bitch hadn't had the slightest idea what was being done in her name until it had been far too late to say *stop*.

And now it's too late for her, Angeline thought, as she directed the prisoners out of the hangar and onto the tarmac. *She'll go into a POW camp, then spend the rest of her miserable life on a penal island.*

Her hands tightened on the rifle as she saw the gold and jewels some of the women were wearing. There was no way they'd come by them legitimately, not when they couldn't have afforded even the simplest of jewellery. No, they'd stolen it from a looted mansion, just as Angeline's own jewels and family heirlooms had been taken during the first uprisings that had left her a broken woman. There'd been over a dozen mansions on Mountebank, all now nothing more than burned-out rubble surrounded by ruined cropland. Either the women had been looters themselves or they'd traded sex to the looters for fine jewels…jewels they were completely unable to appreciate. It was too much. A woman met her eyes and smirked, as if she was somehow the victor despite being nothing more than a prisoner. Angeline saw red.

She lifted her rifle, clicked the setting to automatic and opened fire.

・・・

Rachel had stayed low as the incoming forces stormed the gates and swept into the airport, doing her best to follow the action as government forces moved from hangar to hangar, rapidly and brutally quashing all resistance. She'd kept her hands in the air as the soldiers had crashed into the control tower, all too aware she wasn't wearing a uniform. There was a very real chance, in the confusion, someone would take her for an enemy combatant and open fire before she could react. It wasn't until a senior officer arrived to take custody of her prisoners that she relaxed, a little. There was still much to be done as the invasion force reorientated itself on the city, readying itself to storm the defences if the rebels refused to surrender.

She spoke briefly to the senior officer, directing him to keep the tower as secure as possible until the spooks had a chance to sweep the building for actionable intelligence, then donned a combat jacket and made her way down to the tarmac. The shooting had come to an end, the remaining rebels dead or captured. A line of prisoners lay on the ground, outside the command tower, their hands bound with plastic ties. They'd be moved to a POW camp as quickly as possible, once the invasion force set one up. It would take longer, she reflected, than a civilian might assume. Fencing and prefabricated barracks were low on the invasion force's priority list, while a local building would need to be searched from top to bottom before it could be converted into a makeshift camp. Perhaps it would be better to use the airport's hangars. They could be searched easily, then sealed off from the rest of the complex without particular difficulty.

And then we can see who we've caught, she thought. It was unlikely, to say the least, that they'd captured the core of the rebel leadership—and it might not be a good thing if they had—but it was possible. It was certainly worth taking some time to make sure. *If we captured someone who can order them to surrender...*

She rounded the corner, just as she heard shooting ahead of her. Someone was firing a rifle on automatic...she forced herself to run, instincts screaming at her that something had gone badly wrong. Had a prisoner grabbed a weapon? Or had they stumbled across someone hiding in the hangar, someone intent on selling his life dearly. Or...she swore under her breath as she saw a soldier, one of the *government's* soldiers, gunning down prisoners in cold blood. Rachel was no stranger to terrorists and insurgents claiming to surrender, then lifting their weapons and opening fire as soon as the Marines came into point-blank range, but... she couldn't see any sign the prisoners had done anything. They were women and children...she boosted, picking up speed and hurling herself into the soldier, yanking the weapon out of his hand and throwing him to the ground. No, *her*. Rachel had no time to wonder as she pressed down, holding the shooter still. It might be perfectly legal to shoot enemy combatants who pretended to surrender, but gunning down unarmed prisoners was a war crime. And the other soldiers should have stopped it.

"Medics," she shouted. The shooter twisted underneath her. Rachel upped the pressure, pressing down with her knee as she caught the shooter's hands and wrenched them behind her back. The shooter screamed, but kept struggling. "Get the medics over here!"

She bit down the urge to curse as she looked at the carnage. The shooter had fired on automatic...the bullets had gone through their targets effortlessly, killing or injuring everyone in their path. Blood pooled on the ground. Some of the bodies were so badly mangled it was hard to tell how many people had been caught in the atrocity and slaughtered. Rachel shuddered. She was no stranger to carnage either, but this...she knew mistakes happened, she knew sometimes innocents got swept up and slaughtered in war, yet this was nothing more than an outright war crime. She gritted her teeth, watching sourly as the soldiers finally got to work, helping the medics sort out the mess. They should have done something.

They had a goddamned *obligation* to do something. They should have shot the wretched war criminal in the back, rather than just…let her get on with it. If they'd been Marines…

"Let me go." The shooter was struggling, still. It would have been impressive if she hadn't been a war criminal. Rachel held her down, somehow. "Let me go!"

Rachel snapped her fingers as a squad of fresh soldiers hurried up, a handful recoiling in shock as they saw the carnage. "Give me a plastic tie."

The soldiers obeyed. Rachel hoped that was a good sign. She'd worked with too many military forces that had loose ideas about discipline, or the proper treatment of prisoners taken in war. Here…she wrapped the tie around the shooter's wrists, then searched her roughly, removing everything that could be used as a weapon. The ID tags said ANGELINE PORTER. Rachel vaguely recalled some kind of political stink about the girl, a conflict she hadn't paid too much attention to at the time. There was no proof it was the same person. The name was hardly unique.

She stood, yanking Angeline to her feet. "You are under arrest for committing a war crime, in violation of the Articles of War as approved by your government," she said, flatly. She had to do it by the book. There was going to be one hell of a political explosion when the news reached Kingston. "You will be held in custody until a tribunal can be assembled to hear your case. You have the right to represent yourself or select someone else to represent you. If you make any attempt to escape, I am authorised to do whatever is required to stop you, up to and including the use of lethal force."

Angeline said nothing. Rachel pushed her back to the command tower. Roland would have to be informed, *quickly*. Word was already spreading, or she was a Civil Guardsman with delusions of grandeur. The local government might not take the same view of the atrocity, particularly if Angeline was well-connected. The training mission had explained the laws of war to the new recruits, and Angeline had no excuse, but…Rachel had seen well-connected people get away with rape and murder before, their families refusing to stand in judgement of their own people. And that meant…she shook her head. Right now, it wasn't her problem. She had to get Angeline into custody before something worse happened.

And the rest of her squad will have to be rounded up too, Rachel thought. She'd faced the pressures of combat herself, but…it was no excuse for war crimes. *What the fuck were they thinking?*

Captain Blythe met her at the tower. "What happened?"

Rachel was in no mood to answer his questions. "Private Porter is under arrest," she said, sharply. "She is to be treated as a dangerous prisoner, kept shackled and isolated until she can be transported back to Kingston. She is to be monitored at all times, Captain. I want at least two people in the cell with her, even when she's on the toilet, and recording equipment trained on her and her guards. If anyone wants to see her, they are to go through me. Do I make myself clear?"

Blythe stiffened. He'd been an aristocratic militiaman before the militia had been folded into the regulars and he'd never quite gotten used to the change. Or to Rachel personally. The idea a woman might outrank him…Rachel shook her head. She didn't have time for petty prejudices from idiots too stupid to realise the world had changed. If Blythe screwed the pooch, she'd make damn sure he spent the rest of his career standing guard on an island on the edge of the habitable zone. It would be nice and safe and, best of all, it would keep him out of her hair.

"Yes," he said, biting off the word.

"Good," Rachel said. There was no *time*. She wanted to get help, but who could she trust with the prisoner? Roland was on the other side of the island, the training mission was hundreds of miles away. "I'll take her to the storage room. Have two guards, reliable men, sent down to join me. And then I need to call the general."

• • •

Angeline felt…numb.

She was barely aware of her surroundings as she was pushed down a flight of stairs and into a bare room. Her wrists hurt, but the sensation was somehow…illusionary, as if it wasn't really there at all. She felt strong hands pushing her to the cold stone floor, then a knife cutting away the remnants of her uniform. Once, being forcibly stripped would have terrified her. Now, it was…nothing. Had she been drugged? It was possible. Her memories were a jumbled mess. The fact she couldn't bring herself to be worried about anything, even her own nakedness, hinted she might well be drugged…

"Wow," a male voice said. "Naked and…"

"Be quiet," a female voice snapped. The anger in her voice would have stopped Angeline in her tracks, if she hadn't been so numb. Only her mother had ever spoken to Angeline like that and only rarely. "This room is being monitored. If you show the slightest hint of unprofessionalism, you will be joining her in the brig."

Angeline found it hard to care as icy fingers poked her in delicate places, as if her captor thought she was concealing a weapon in her genitals, then withdrew. She felt someone snapping metal cuffs around her wrists and ankles, before the plastic tie was removed. It wasn't easy to turn over, but—when she did—she found herself staring up at a wiry young woman. Two men stood by the door, watching her with cold eyes. She was in a prison cell…

Her memories fell into some form of order. She'd taken prisoners, she'd been angry at the prisoners, she'd pulled the trigger and then…she'd been knocked down. She was concussed. It was the only explanation and yet… she swallowed, hard, as she remembered what she'd done. The rebels had deserved it, hadn't they? They'd looted and raped and killed their way across the island and…and they thought they were going to just go back to normal? They'd deserved far worse than merely being gunned down by government troops.

"Water," she managed. "Please."

Her captor pressed a small tube to her lips. Angeline sipped, tasting something strange on the tip of her tongue. She wondered, as the tube was withdrawn, what would happen to her. The government would understand, surely. It certainly hadn't been able to decide what to do with the rebel prisoners. There was no hope they could be redeemed, no suggestion they could even go back to the plantations. And then...what was to be done?

They deserved it, she thought, vindictively. She clung to the thought, telling herself—time and time again—that it was true. It had to be true. If it wasn't, she was nothing more than a murderer who was on a short trip to the gallows. No, it had to be true. *They deserved everything I gave them and more.*

CHAPTER NINE

MOUNTEBANK ISLAND, NEW DONCASTER

"JESUS FUCKING CHRIST."

Richard stood by the IFV, shaking his head in dismay. He'd served in the regulars long enough to admit, at least in the privacy of his own mind, that there were some officers—regular and militia—who'd gotten away with murder. Sometimes literally. The militia had never been noted for training or discipline, leading to the creation of units that threw their weight around or were really little more than criminal gangs. He was honest enough to concede, because of his background, that the militia had supplied the rebels with an endless series of rallying cries. God knew, one of the first insurgents he'd fought had claimed he'd taken up arms because his sister had been raped and murdered by a militia officer. And he might well have been telling the truth...

His stomach churned. Twenty-seven women and children dead, nineteen more injured...it was a fucking war crime alright, one committed by his own side. Richard was all too aware civilians could be caught in the crossfire and killed, but this...no, there was no getting around it. There was no excuse. The act was an atrocity, a war crime, a rallying cry for insurgents who might think they had no choice but to fight to the last. Who could blame them? Richard doubted there was any way to make things better, certainly not in time to make a difference. Even putting Angeline Porter in front of a firing squad, without bothering with a trial, wouldn't be enough. He briefly considered suggesting the government hand her over to the rebels, to deal with as they saw fit, but he knew it would never fly. Angeline Porter had become a rallying cry before, when her family had been killed and she'd been gang-raped and left for dead. The government wouldn't want to hand her over to anyone.

Fuck. He kicked a stone as he raised his eyes, looking over the city. *What do we do now?*

The fighting had, briefly, stalemated. The rebels had raised solid defences around the city and the nearest harbours, forcing him to either bleed his men white in a bid to break into the city or set up barricades and lay siege to the rebel force. The latter would work, given time, but it wouldn't be the quick victory the planners wanted. He allowed his eyes to wander along the enemy defences, sourly admiring how they'd woven the factories, warehouses and cheap cookie-cutter houses into a solid line of death and destruction, just waiting for his men to try to storm the city. It wasn't clear how many rebels remained inside the city—the invaders had caught hundreds of rebels trying to reach the jungle before it was too late—but he was morbidly sure there were enough to man the defences and keep him from breaking through in a hurry. Sniper and mortar fire was already being exchanged, up and down the line. He hated to admit it, but all hope of a quick and decisive victory was gone.

He keyed his radio. "Anything from the rebels?"

"No answer, sir," the operator said. "We're signalling on their frequencies."

Richard grinded his teeth. Nothing spread faster than bad news, to the point there were jokes about *starships* powered by bad news. The rebels might already know what had happened at the airport, convincing them that surrender meant certain death. What did they have to lose, if they fought to the last? They might win and, even if they didn't, they'd claw the government's forces badly before they died. Richard wasn't blind to the limits facing the government. If the fighting became too costly, it might have to hold its nose and try for a negotiated solution.

The rebels probably feel the same way too, he thought, crossly. *Right now, they have no reason to take us at our word.*

He turned, watching as the latest forces started to arrive and take up position. The siege lines around the city looked fragile, but without armoured fighting vehicles or heavy antitank weapons the rebels were unlikely be able to break out without getting themselves slaughtered for nothing. It wasn't clear how many modern weapons the rebels had, yet they'd shown none. Roland had suggested the rebels intended to hold them in reserve, for the coming campaigns, and Richard was inclined to agree. Mountebank wasn't *that* important, not in any great sense. Roland had picked the island as their first target because the offensive could be called off at any moment without risking overall defeat.

But a stalemate might be even worse, he reflected. *They can tie up thousands of our men more or less indefinitely.*

His radio bleeped. "Sir, we just picked up a communication from the rebels," the operator said. "They're prepared to meet you at the old church."

Richard frowned as he pulled the map from his belt and unfolded it. The old church had been in ruins for decades, burnt down well before the insurgency had turned into a full-fledged war. It was a good place to meet, he noted; it was roughly midway between the two sides, allowing them to meet without fear of one side doing something stupid. Roland had already cleared him to treat with the enemy, if they agreed to meet. Richard wasn't about to let the chance slip by.

"Inform them we'll be there in two hours," he said, folding up the map. "And then get me a direct link to the general."

He kept his temper under control as he contacted Roland and explained, briefly, what had happened. The original plan had been fairly simple. They could offer to treat the surrendering troops well, after they marched into the camps; now, it was unlikely anyone would be convinced. Richard had no idea what sort of guarantees they could offer and, even if they did, he feared the rebels wouldn't believe them. They could promise the world, only to break their word when the rebels were safely disarmed. He shook his head, sourly, as he arranged for a close-protection detail to accompany him, with snipers on overwatch just in case the rebels were planning something. It was quite possible. Thanks to Angeline Porter, the rebels had nothing to lose.

And quite a few people back home would be relieved if I died in the line of duty, Richard thought, as he prepared for the meeting. *They'd praise me in public, as the son of a councillor, but in private...*

The thought nagged at him as he crossed the lines and made his way down to the old church, his close-protection team keeping their distance. Richard had never been particularly religious, but he couldn't help thinking there was something eerie about the ruined church. The church itself was little more than a shell, the graveyard surrounding it torn and broken...he felt oddly uneasy as he stepped around the graveyard, into what had once been a small playground. The rebels were waiting for him; two middle-aged men, wearing civilian clothes with green armbands. Richard nodded to them, politely. The purists would probably berate him for not getting there first, or for timing matters so both sides arrived at the same time, but it probably didn't matter. He had a nasty feeling the meeting would end up being worse than useless.

"I'm Captain Richard Collier," he said, once they were facing each other. "May I ask your names?"

"You may call me Jericho," one of the men said. "My friend is Heartbreak."

Richard nodded. Jericho was one of the known rebel codenames, although—until now—the spooks hadn't had a face to go with the name. He was in his early forties, if Richard was any judge, his exposed skin bearing the signs of a life in the sun. There was a nasty mark on his arm that suggested he'd been whipped, a few years ago. Richard tried not to feel sick. In theory, there were strict limits on corporal punishment for debtors and indents. In practice, such limits were rarely observed. Who gave a damn about the workers?

Later, he told himself. *Right now, you have work to do,*

"I'm not a diplomat," he said. It was true. "My forces are embedded to the north, blocking your line of escape; the navy can and will keep you from shipping supplies into the city or transporting men out. You are trapped. I can afford to wait long enough for you to starve. If you surrender now…"

"We get slaughtered, as you slaughtered your earlier prisoners?" Heartbreak's voice was cold and hard. He looked younger than Jericho, although it was hard to be sure. Richard suspected he was the child of a debtor, someone born into serfdom rather than the original debtor. The debtors who'd inherited their status tended to be the most resentful—and who could blame them? "Or will you try to deny the slaughter at the airport?"

"No." Richard was sure lies would be worse than useless. The rebels had fabricated a number of atrocity stories out of whole cloth, but this one…they clearly knew there had been a *real* atrocity. It couldn't be a wild coincidence. "The person responsible for the slaughter has been arrested and will be tried for mass murder, as well as whatever other war crimes are uncovered by the investigation. If she is found guilty, she will be executed."

"If," Heartbreak said. "How do we know you won't come up with a pettifogging excuse for her?"

Richard frowned. The honest answer was *you don't*. Angeline Porter's fate would be decided by people *well* above his pay grade. The further they were from the scene of the crime, the easier it would be for them to accept excuses. And yet…he shook his head. They would suspect he was lying, if he offered guarantees. He didn't have the authority to make them.

"I believe she will be tried," Richard said, finally. "However, that isn't the issue here. If you surrender the city, we will take you into custody and treat you as legitimate prisoners of war."

"We have no reason to believe you," Jericho said. "Here is our counteroffer. You let us slip out of the city and back into the jungle. In exchange, we surrender the city largely intact."

Richard shook his head. There was no way either Roland or the War Council would go for it. The rebels would slip into the jungle and continue the insurgency, perhaps even retaking the island when the invasion forces pulled out. Better to keep the rebels penned up, they'd reason, than have them loose in the jungle once again. And besides, the city had been devastated by the rebels. Even if it was recovered without a fight, it would be years before it returned to its former glory.

"No," he said, for the record. "I repeat my earlier offer. Surrender now and you will be treated well."

"We're done here," Jericho said. "Thank you for your time."

He turned and strode away, his partner following. Richard cursed under his breath. It would be one thing if the atrocity had convinced the rebels to surrender, but instead it had only hardened their resolve to fight. He briefly considered handing the other prisoners back to the rebels, in hopes of both convincing them to change their mind *and* draining their supplies, yet…he shook his head as he turned and walked back to his lines. Moments later, he heard a handful of shots as the snipers resumed fire. The truce was already at an end.

"Sir." Sergeant Yu met him as he reached the tanks. "Any luck?"

"No." Richard shook his head. "They won't surrender."

He glanced at his watch. The plan had been ambitious, perhaps a little *too* ambitious. There'd be people back home, he was sure, carping and criticising because the offensive hadn't produced immediate victory. Poor Roland was likely to find himself spending the next few days patting politicians on the head, convincing them the war was not about to end in inglorious defeat. In many ways, it had been very useful—and revealing. They knew more about the strengths and weaknesses of their forces, as well as the rebel tactics and suchlike…and it had all been wasted, because of someone proving unable to control herself. Perhaps she'd had a good reason. Richard conceded the point, although he doubted it. But who cared? By now, the story probably credited her with murdering thousands of people.

"Direct the troops to start tightening the defences," he ordered. Days were long on New Doncaster, but night would fall soon. The rebels would probably start trying to sneak out of the pocket, once darkness provided cover to their schemes. There weren't anything like enough NVGs in the army to keep the rebels from probing the defences. "And move the tanks into blocking position."

"Aye, sir."

Richard nodded as he tapped his radio, sending a brief signal back to Roland at the beachhead. The general had to be informed, although there was very little he could do beyond ordering a suicidal attack. Richard had had commanders who would have thought that was a very good idea indeed. Roland, thankfully, was smart enough to realise the downsides and keep his forces out of the meatgrinder. If nothing else, a few days of being under siege might convince the rebels to rethink their stance on surrender.

And we can drop leaflets into the city, inviting the defenders to give up, he thought, as a pair of aircraft buzzed overhead. The little fighters were primitive, by modern standards, but they were the best the government could produce without off-world imports. *Who knows? Maybe they'll think better of resistance after we tighten our grip.*

He walked up and down the lines, inspecting the hastily dug trenches as shots and primitive missiles echoed in the distance. The government wasn't the only one digging up ancient weapons and putting them into mass production, he noted sourly; the rebels, it seemed, had been doing the same. Their missiles weren't *that* dangerous—they were quite light, even when compared to a simple antitank missile, and their accuracy was terrible—but they were incredibly distracting even when they overshot their targets. Richard had to order the antimissile batteries to ignore them, fearing the rebels hoped to drain his supply of interceptor missiles. It was quite possible. They knew the government couldn't get much of anything from off-world.

Because anyone who has any significant military hardware doesn't really want to part with it for love or money, Richard thought. *And even if they did, it would come with massive strings attached.*

He rubbed his forehead as he returned to the command vehicle and sat down, resting his back against the heavy armour. His government was a mess—and that was being charitable—but he loved his planet. The thought of off-worlders taking the high orbitals and dictating terms was unacceptable. The spooks thought the rebels were working for outsiders, trying to destabilise the planet in hopes of an easy invasion and occupation. Richard suspected that analysis was simplistic—the rebels didn't *need* off-world agitators to hate the government—but it was possible. And yet…really, it struck him as an excuse not to make any significant reforms.

We have a chance to make things better, he thought, as guns boomed in the distance. *But we have to survive the war first.*

...

Private Warner McGonagall tried not to shiver as he was marched into the chamber. He'd been cautioned, in no uncertain terms, not to speak to anyone until he was summoned to face the inquisitors. It wasn't clear if he was in trouble himself—he honestly wasn't sure, despite everything—but he was sure he *would* be if he disobeyed orders. He forced himself to salute as he saw the three people at the table, a young woman and two older men in military uniforms. They looked at him as if he was something they'd scraped off their shoes.

No, he corrected himself. *As if I were something they hired gentlemen's gentlemen to scrape off their shoes.*

The young woman leaned forward. Her voice had a nasal twang that hung in the air. Warner disliked her on sight. "McGonagall. Five hours ago, you were present when Private Angeline Porter opened fire on a group of unarmed prisoners. Is that correct?"

"Yes," Warner said, shortly. He wasn't sure how he should address the woman. Sir? Or madam? "I was there."

"You could have stopped her," the woman said. "Why didn't you?"

Warner hesitated. He honestly wasn't sure how to answer. Prisoners could be dangerous, he knew, and he'd no reason to doubt Angeline's combat instincts. Once he'd gotten used to the revolutionary idea of having a woman in the squad—it helped she didn't *act* like any of the women he'd known—she'd just been one of the boys. He'd trusted her to do the right thing.

"You could have stopped her," the woman repeated. "Why didn't you?"

"You were cautioned, when you went through basic, that violent abuse of prisoners would not be tolerated," one of the men added. "Why didn't you intervene?"

Warner *still* had no idea how to answer. His thoughts were a jumbled mess. It had all happened so quickly. He'd trusted Angeline. He'd…he shook his head, fighting down the urge to scream. It wasn't fair! He hadn't had any reason to expect her to do…to open fire on a bunch of prisoners. And…and…and…

He tried not to scowl as his heart sank. They didn't want answers. They were only interested in covering themselves, when the shit hit the fan. He was going to be blamed, even though it hadn't been his fault. And what could he do about it?

"Why?" The woman held his gaze. "Why?"

Warner looked down. "I don't know," he mumbled. "I just don't know."

CHAPTER TEN

MOUNTEBANK ISLAND, NEW DONCASTER

"THAT'S HER," RACHEL SAID. Her voice was emotionless, but Roland could hear an undertone of disgust. "Angeline Porter."

Roland said nothing as he studied the live feed from the cell. Angeline Porter was a young woman, as naked as the day she was born, cuffed to the chair in a manner that brought back uneasy memories of how he'd treated the maids as a young man. They hadn't said no to him, when he'd proposed the games, but how could they? The thought made him feel a flash of guilt, made worse by the grim awareness there was nothing he could do to make it up to them. His maids had probably died on Earth, during Earthfall. Even if they'd somehow escaped, he didn't have the slightest idea where to find them. All he could do was try to do better in the future.

He dismissed the thought as he stared at the young woman. What *had* she been thinking? There was no indication she'd thought the prisoners were carrying weapons, nor that there was any other threat; there certainly hadn't been the slightest chance, at the time, that the rebels might be on the verge of recapturing the prisoners. Even if there had been, gunning the poor bastards down would *still* have been a monumental war crime. Roland was tempted to walk into the makeshift cell, draw his pistol and blow her brains out. She might have single-handedly cost them the chance for a major victory.

Roland drew a shuddering breath. "What was she *thinking*?"

"The interrogations have been inconclusive," Rachel said, flatly. "There was no sense there was any threat. None of her squadmates said anything to suggest otherwise. She hasn't said much of anything to us, beyond a request to call her distant relatives back on Kingston. It's possible she just flipped out, in the heat of the moment, but…"

"No," Roland said. "That's not an acceptable excuse."

He forced himself to calm down. He was the commanding officer. He was ultimately responsible for the men under his command. And yet… he told himself to worry about his own future later. It wasn't fair that he was likely to face consequences for the war crime, but…it was just a fact of life. He wanted to rage at the universe, to protect the gross unfairness of blaming him for something no one could have predicted, yet there was no point. His enemies would make political capital out of it, no matter the rights and wrongs. What could he do about it?

"No," Rachel agreed. "I scanned her file. She was brutally mistreated by the rebels. In hindsight"—her lips curved in distaste—"there will be people saying we should never have accepted her as a prospective soldier, even though we needed more aristocrats on the front lines. She needed rest and medical care, not a military career."

"They said that about me too," Roland said. He'd never read his file, but he'd heard enough—from Belinda and Rachel as well as the DIs—to guess at the contents. The corps had taken quite a risk, when it had accepted him as a new recruit. "Were they wrong?"

Rachel shrugged. "We have to get ahead of this quick," she said. "What do you want to do?"

"I need to speak to her," Roland said. Rachel lips tightened, as if she wanted to object, but said nothing. "While I'm inside, contact Richard. He's to leave command of the siege lines to his second and report to me here."

"Yes, sir." Rachel's lips thinned. "I must warn you, sir, that the cell is under constant observation. Anything she says will be noted and, perhaps, used in evidence against her."

And me, Roland thought, as he turned to the door. *If the government or the corps tries to blame me for this…*

He sighed as he made his way down the stairs. The interrogation reports had been…odd. It was clear, at least to him, that there'd been nothing premeditated about the atrocity. Angeline Porter's former squadmates seemed more inclined to rally around their comrade, rather than throw her to the wolves. Roland had seen it before—the aristos always backed their fellows, even when their fellows needed to be left to face the consequences of their own actions—but it couldn't be tolerated. They should have stopped Angeline Porter from committing a war crime. He supposed it spoke well of them, although…he shook his head. No, it wasn't a good thing. Right now, the pressing need was to deal with the war criminal before the rebels tried to retaliate. It was just a matter of time until they did.

The cell door opened at his touch. A whiff of urine reached his nose. He grimaced, despite himself. Angeline was being treated as the worst of the worst, kept shackled even when she was on the toilet. Humanity demanded she receive better treatment, even though he knew what would happen if she pulled off an improbable escape. He snorted at the thought. If she got away…it wasn't going to happen. But he dared not take chances.

"Wait outside," he ordered the guards. "I'll call if I need you."

The guards looked at each other, then left the cell. They looked tired and worn, stressed by having to keep a sharp eye on a prisoner who could barely move. Roland made a mental note to have them relieved as quickly as possible after he'd spoken to Angeline. Guard duty was boring at the best of times, to the point a guard might miss something dangerous before it put a knife in him. Roland had done it himself, during training, to know how easy it was to get drowsy or even fall asleep. Being yelled at by the DI wasn't pleasant, but far superior to having one's throat cut by the enemy.

Angeline didn't move. Roland studied her, thoughtfully. She'd been pretty once, but her face and body were now badly scarred. She could have gone for reconstructive surgery, yet had apparently chosen to keep the scars. Roland suspected that wasn't a good sign.

He knelt in front of her. "Hi," he said, lightly. "Do you know who I am?"

"Yeah," Angeline said. She sounded tired, as if she was really too tired to sleep. "General Windsor, of the Windsor Family."

"Yes," Roland said. Roland's superiors had given the planetary government a completely false biography, when he'd been assigned to the posting. It was pretty much impossible to verify, which hadn't kept the Windsor Family from reaching out to him, convinced—or pretending to be—that he was a long-lost relative. Roland had found it irritating, but the alternative was worse. "Close enough, at least."

He took a breath. He'd studied the files. He knew there'd been people who committed mass slaughter for all sorts of reasons, from religious hatred to simple land grabs, but Angeline didn't seem to fit any of them. Nor did she have the profile of the average small-time war criminal. One day of combat shouldn't have been enough to break her...

She didn't get anything like the training she needed, Roland reminded himself. *None of them did.*

"I need to ask," Roland said. "Why did you do it?"

Angeline looked up, meeting his eyes. "Because they were rebels," she said, finally. "Because they deserved it."

"The children, too?" Roland had heard the argument *nits breed lice* used as an excuse for targeting young children, but his superiors had made it clear that anyone who tried that was beyond the pale. "You killed over a dozen children."

"After what they did to me," Angeline said, "what do they deserve?"

Roland kept his voice even. "The people who violated you are on another island," he said, gently. He had no idea if *any* of Angeline's rapists were even still alive. There'd been so much confusion, as the islands fell to the rebels, that it was quite possible they'd been killed, their bodies dumped in the ditch. "You shot innocents."

"They weren't innocents," Angeline protested. "They were rebels!"

"Rebels who had surrendered," Roland said. "Did they have any weapons? Anything, anything at all, that might justify their deaths?"

Angeline's face twisted. "They were wearing their loot!"

Roland sighed, inwardly. He hadn't been hopeful—the report from the medics had made it clear the murdered prisoners had been unarmed—but he'd wondered, when he'd heard the story, if Angeline had thought she'd seen a weapon. It hadn't been impossible. If someone was drawing a gun, their target would have bare seconds to spot the threat and react...he stood, brushing down his uniform. At least she wasn't trying to claim they'd been armed. Nor had someone managed to plant a weapon on the bodies before they were put under guard. It wasn't any real consolation, but...it would have to do.

"You will be flown back to Kingston, where you will stand trial for your crimes," he said, flatly. "They will decide what to do with you."

Angeline said nothing as Roland left the cell. He directed the guards to resume their watch, then made his way back to the office. There was no way to know how the trial would go. He'd prefer a general court-martial, but...the case would turn political very quickly, if it hadn't already. Better to put the hot potato firmly in the government's hands. He tapped his terminal, making the arrangements, as he stepped into the room. Richard and Rachel were studying the maps on the table, talking in low voices. They straightened as he entered.

"Sir," Richard said. "The rebels refused to surrender."

Roland nodded as he studied the map. Mountebank was shaped roughly like a tear, with the city at the pointy end. His forces were deployed in a line between the city and the jungle—and the mountains at the rounded end—blocking the rebels from retreating...stalemate, he feared, unless the rebels did something stupid like attacking the blockade and trying to break out. Or if he attacked them instead.

"I'm not surprised," he said, finally. "Did you get any impression of their strength?"

"No, sir," Richard said. "They were very focused. I'd say they think they can hold the line long enough to hurt us, although it's hard to be sure. They may have been bluffing."

"We can try to slip someone into the city," Rachel said. "Or see what the POWs can tell us."

"We may have no choice," Roland said. He hated the idea of questioning POWs—it was a breach of the Articles of War, at least if they'd surrendered freely—but there might be no alternative. "It might be pointless. The POWs might not have the slightest idea what's happening in the city."

Richard looked up. "Why were they even in the airport in the first place?"

"Apparently, their evacuation planning, such as it was, didn't factor in a full-scale invasion," Rachel said. "Their assumption was that they'd have time to either fly the evacuees out to some other island, which suggests they may have a fallback position somewhere a little closer than we'd like, or simply get them moving into the jungle. Instead, hundreds of them met their deaths instead."

Roland nodded, curtly. The airport had been a chaotic nightmare even before it had turned into the scene of a war crime. The investigators were still finding bodies crushed under planes, left to rot as the pilots tried to escape. There was even one report a small plane had made it out, bodies dropping from the wings as the pilots tried to flee. Roland had no idea if that was true—the radar reports were inconclusive—but he had to admit it was possible. It had certainly happened before.

"Right now, it doesn't matter," he said, tapping the map. "I think we have to conclude the invasion has stalemated. We can't clear them out of their fastness in a hurry, not without taking unacceptable casualties, but they can't drive us back into the water either. Our best bet is to keep the siege lines in place and wait for the rebels to surrender."

Or starve, his thoughts added, sourly. How far would the rebels go, to keep their fighting men healthy? Would they send out everyone who could not fight, in hopes of prolonging their supplies by reducing the number of mouths to feed, or would they kill them? *Or will they even turn into cannibals and start eating human flesh?*

He shuddered. It wasn't impossible. There'd been reports of cannibal gangs in the Undercity of Earth, although he couldn't recall any hard evidence. God knew the underfolk had shredded every other taboo, from incest to things that made even *his* hardened stomach churn. And now... he tried not to think of their final hours, the power going out, leaving them in darkness before the CityBlocks came tumbling down, crushing them flat. The chaos had been beyond imagination. No one, not even the Marine Corps, had a clear picture of the final days of Old Earth.

"The government may press for a quick and decisive strike," he said, putting the dark memories back where they belonged. "I need to dissuade them. We also need to see to Angeline Porter's trial, before the politics get out of hand. Rachel, you'll accompany me back to Kingston. Richard, you'll remain here, in command of the overall operation. I'll inform Admiral Forest he's to take his orders from you."

"Try not to step on his toes *too* much," Rachel added. "The last thing we need right now is a bitter struggle over command."

Richard looked pained. "I'm sure we can work something out," he said. "Did he give you any trouble?"

"No," Roland said. If Richard's father hadn't stood in the way, Richard would have been jumped up several ranks. "But he wouldn't."

He winced as he returned his gaze to the map. The planet's original officer corps had largely been drawn from the aristocracy, with a handful of lower-born officers—such as Richard—filling the gaps and doing the jobs none of the aristos wanted to do. It hadn't been easy for them. The aristos worked together, keeping their counterparts down. Now, with the army rapidly expanding, there were more commoner officers than before, leading to all sorts of culture clashes. Roland himself was the unchallenged overall commander, subordinate to the War Council alone. If Richard had to take his place...

He'd never be accepted, Roland thought. The pressures of war would break down social barriers, given time, but it was a long hard slog. Richard and his peers didn't *just* lack aristocratic connections. They lacked the funds to do everything from order fancy uniforms to order infinite rounds of drinks in the officers club. *Give it time.*

"Keep the pressure on, but don't launch any major attacks unless their defences start to crumble," he ordered. "Keep offering to accept surrender, too. They may change their mind, as hunger starts to bite."

"Yes, sir," Richard said. "What *are* we going to do with the rebels, after the war?"

"That's a matter for the government," Roland said, although he intended to pressure the government into making concessions when it broke the back of the insurgency. "I don't think the matter can be decided right now, while the war is still underway."

Richard didn't look convinced. Roland agreed. The government was caught between two fires, between the need to prevent a second war ten years down the line and the need to placate the aristocrats who considered their workers nothing more than property. Roland himself had been tempted to suggest the Prime Minister and the War Council tell them to go to hell, and agree to a degree of debt forgiveness in hopes of putting the war behind them, but it was politically impossible. As long as the aristos were loyal, their interests could not be overlooked. Roland wondered, idly, if he could get away with a program of assassination. If there'd only been a handful of them...

Probably better not to consider it, he told himself. The corps had no qualms about sniping enemy officers on the battlefield, but it drew the line at assassination. And yet, if killing the aristos would shorten the war...he put temptation out of his mind, before the idea got too deeply embedded. *There are too many for them to be wiped out without questions being raised.*

"We can hold the line for the moment," Richard said. "What about the jungle?"

"Leave it alone," Rachel advised. "The terrain doesn't suit us. If we can deal with the city, and impose a more even order on the former plantations, the jungle rebels will become immaterial."

"If," Richard repeated.

Roland nodded. "I'll speak to Admiral Forest, then fly back tomorrow morning," he said. "That should give us enough time for the command transfer. Angeline can come with us—we'll hand her over to the authorities when we reach Kingston. The council can decide her fate."

"Unless you want to deal with her now, by field court-martial," Rachel said. "The possibility exists."

"It's political," Roland said. He was surprised she hadn't raised the idea earlier. It would be perfectly legal, but...no. He shook his head. It would solve one problem, but create a host of others. The aristos would choose to believe Angeline had been railroaded, denied even the chance to speak for herself. Roland had *been* an aristocrat. He knew how they thought. "We need to prove her guilt, then make it clear we are holding her accountable for her crimes."

"Yes, sir," Rachel said.

"Dismissed," Roland said. He'd speak to Rachel later—she rarely left him alone for long, when she wasn't on a mission—but right now he needed to call the admiral. "I'll see you both in the morning."

"Yes, sir," Richard said. "Good luck on Kingston."

"Thanks," Roland said. "I'm sure it will be dangerous as hell."

CHAPTER ELEVEN

BARAKA ISLAND, NEW DONCASTER

"IT'S MORNING," A MALE VOICE SAID.

Sarah sat upright, too cranky to play any morning games. It had been a long night. She'd known there was no point in loitering around the radio station, hoping to hear good news from Mountebank, but she hadn't been able to keep herself from doing just that until Bryce had convinced her to go to bed. They'd found comfort in each other, a comfort she knew was illusionary. The war had taken a dark turn. And yet, she wasn't the sort of person to simply give up. The atrocity on the distant island, if nothing else, offered a grim warning of just what would happen to anyone who tried to surrender.

She rubbed her eyes, then stood and headed for the shower. The master bedroom had been stripped of almost all of its furnishings, creating the odd impression they were squatting in an abandoned building. She could see faded patches on the walls that had once been hidden by giant pieces of furniture, or paintings of self-satisfied aristocrats that had been torn down and thrown on the bonfire. Her lips twitched in droll amusement as she stepped into the bathroom. The giant bathtub, easily large enough for three or four grown adults, had only been left in place because it was secured to the floor. She was tempted to try it, but it would send the wrong message to her followers. Besides, she didn't have time. She showered quickly, then pulled on her tunic and headed outside. They'd have to go down for breakfast.

It's almost like home, she reflected, although—in truth—Earth hadn't been *home* for over a decade. The giant CityBlocks, where the inhabitants had gathered for meals in huge communal dining halls, had been destroyed, smashed flat by rocks falling from the sky. It was hard to wrap her head around how many people had died, wiped from existence so completely their bodies would never be found. *If my parents made it out...*

She shook her head. Her parents had probably disowned her, when they'd realised she'd been arrested and deported without even a pretence of a trial. They wouldn't have had a choice. They'd worked their asses off to build a decent social credit score. Having a daughter who'd been arrested would ruin it, raising the ghastly spectre of a fall back to the lower levels—and, if they were really unlucky, the Undercity. Sarah shuddered at the thought. Her sister had been twelve, when Sarah had been deported. She'd been young and pretty and she wouldn't have lasted a week in the Undercity, if the family had fallen so far so fast. Sarah liked to think her parents had emigrated, that they'd taken ship to a distant colony world, but she'd never know. Even if they had, she would never see them again. It was unlikely they had even the slightest idea what had happened to her, after she'd been deported...

The thought mocked her as they made their way down to the breakfast hall and took their places in line. Sarah had done what she could to avoid rationing, but supplies of everything beyond the very basics were limited. One could have as much algae-based mush as one wanted—she'd made sure of that, by setting up factories and vats—yet everything else...she shook her head, mentally, as she took a bowl of bacon-flavoured porridge and sat down. If there was anything more than a hint of *real* bacon in the mix, it was a tragic accident.

She kept her mouth closed and listened as rumours swept around the hall. The government forces had won effortlessly. The government's forces had been thrown back into the sea to drown. The government's troops had mutinied and refused to fight the rebels, turning their guns on the aristos and blowing them away. The invasion was nothing more than a major raid and the government would be withdrawing soon, perhaps within the day. Sarah sighed, inwardly, as the stories got wilder and wilder. No one trusted the media, be it government or rebel-controlled. She knew they had a point. And yet…it meant the truth, whatever it was, wouldn't be believed.

Bryce winked at her. "We couldn't possibly be that lucky."

Sarah shrugged. One rumourmonger was insisting a passing starship had intervened in their favour and dropped KEWs on the government's fleet. It wasn't true—and she knew, if it was, it would cause no end of problems. Why would outsiders help the rebels, if they didn't want to gain control of the planet's only source of foreign exchange? They could easily wind up being just as oppressive as the aristos, if not worse. Sarah hated the aristos—she made no bones about it—but even *she* had to admit they were smart enough to view the planet as a long-term investment. Offworlders might not be anything like as careful with a planet that had simply fallen into their hands.

She finished her porridge, then led the way down to the meeting room below the old mansion. There were guards everywhere—one report from Mountebank insisted the government had been able to get into the command post, even though it should have been inaccessible—and they had to pass through two checkpoints before they could get into the room itself. It was irritating, but there was no choice. They still didn't understand how the CP on Mountebank had been infiltrated. She would have expected the government to bomb it, not get someone inside the complex. And who knew how much intelligence had fallen into enemy hands?

They didn't know that much, she thought. She'd worked hard to keep the rebellion as decentralised as possible, even as they'd taken land and started the long process of turning into a rival government. *Even if they were all taken alive*—she was too much of a realist to assume that prisoners couldn't be made to talk—*they can't tell what they don't know.*

She took her chair—there was no point in standing on ceremony—and waited for the room to fill up. Gathering so many leaders in one place was a risk, no matter how many precautions she took, but she feared there was little choice. The island's datanet wasn't worthy of the name—the government hadn't invested in anything beyond a very limited network—and she suspected it was compromised to the point that anything they said online would be immediately relayed to the government's intelligence officers. Radio was even worse. The government would intercept the transmissions, then know where to aim their missiles. She dared not assume the government was stupid. The war had removed a great many blockheads from the enemy chain of command.

And they have an offworlder leading their armies, she reflected. *I wouldn't have expected them to give up so much power, just to please the townies.*

The doors closed, leaving the leaders alone. Sarah cleared her throat. The room was as secure as they could make it, although she feared the offworlders might have tech that would let them eavesdrop on everything the rebels said. There were too many horror stories, everything from nanotech bugs to implants that turned rebel leaders into unwitting spies for the government, for her to know what to take seriously. They'd invested heavily in counter-surveillance tech, but…was it enough? She ground her teeth in frustration. It was easy, all too easy, to second-guess herself into paralysis.

"The rumours are true," she said, without preamble. "The government has established a solid lodgement on Mountebank."

She waved a hand at the map on the wall. It had been updated repeatedly over the last few hours, although she was grimly aware it was almost certainly out of date. The situation was settling down, if the latest reports were accurate, but that could change at any moment. She couldn't hope to exercise any control over the combat zone. The locals were completely isolated. It would be hard, even for experienced sailors or fishermen, to run the blockade and convey supplies to the besieged city.

"So far, the government troops seem unwilling to storm Mountebank City itself," she added, calmly. "Indeed, their offensive was targeted against a weak spot in the island's defences, catching the defenders out of place, and they did their best to avoid challenging the defenders directly. They overran a number of strongpoints in their path, but otherwise chose to isolate rather than smash when they had a choice. Right now, they have the city under siege. It seems unlikely they will risk pressing matters."

She paused, allowing them a moment to take in her words. "The bad news is that we have confirmation. The government's forces *did* gun down surrendered prisoners, including a number of women and children."

There was a sharp intake of breath. "Incredible," Colonel Caroche said. He was an older man, who'd been in the rebellion longer than Sarah had been alive. "Do they *want* us to fight to the last?"

"It would suit them," Colonel Jayne said. Her scarred face bore mute testament to the horrors of life as a plantation wench, before she'd escaped into the jungle and joined the nearest rebel force. "Let's face it. Even if we surrender tomorrow, they will never feel comfortable around us again. They could never trust us not to bide our time, then launch a second rebellion when the aristos forget the lessons of *this* one. Slaughtering us is their only viable option."

"And then, who would work the plantations?" Colonel Bolos snorted, rudely. He was younger than the others, a rare townie in their ranks. "They're not going to work the fields themselves, are they?"

Sarah smiled, despite herself. She'd seen too many aristos—men who liked hunting and shooting, women who swanned around wearing fancy dresses—to imagine them working the fields like common labourers. Bolos had a point, she conceded. The plantations were worthless without workers to tend the crops, then drain the sap and prepare it for processing into something a little more useful. The government might wage and win a genocidal war, only to discover—too late—they'd cut their own throats.

"There's no shortage of new slaves," Jayne growled. "They'll just bring in more from Earth."

"Earth is gone," Sarah reminded them flatly. "I doubt they can get so many slaves from other worlds."

She tapped the table, before the discussion could move any further away from the subject at hand. "The government has yet to put out an official story," she said. "Our spies on Kingston insist the massacre was perpetrated by a rogue soldier, but it seems unlikely."

"We were told that atrocities would not be condoned," Bryce added. "If a rogue really did commit the crime, I'd expect General Windsor to make an example of him."

"Unless it was some aristo fop, who'll get a slap on the wrist and nothing more," Jayne growled. "It isn't as if he gunned down anyone important."

"The point is that surrender is no longer an option, if it ever was," Sarah said. "And that the government has proved it can land an army on our soil and take effective control of our territory."

"Mountebank is very isolated, compared to the other islands," Caroche said, waving a hand at the map. "They'll have a harder time of it elsewhere."

"And they can't storm the city unless they want to be chewed up and spat out," Jayne added, sharply. "How many of their troops will they have to leave there, if they don't want us simply retaking the island when their backs are turned?"

"Fewer than you might think," Bryce cautioned. "They can keep the city cut off from the rest of the island with a relatively small number of troops, at least for the moment. "

"Which means they'll be coming for the rest of us," Sarah said. "We may be on the defensive, at least for the moment, but we are far from helpless. We'll lure them into killing grounds, then smash them."

She spoke in vague terms, outlining the defensive preparations that had been made since the rebels had taken control of their core islands. She'd hoped to have enough time to build an army and land it on Kingston, but the government—thanks to General Windsor—had built up its own forces quickly enough to make it impossible. The rebels had a great many advantages, if her calculations were correct, yet...it might be better, from their point of view, to let the government make the next move. Mountebank really *had* been an isolated target. If the government wanted to win, their next target would be a great deal harder to overwhelm before it was too late.

"We are gambling everything on them walking right into our gunsights," Jayne pointed out, curtly. "Would it not be better to hit them first?"

"Most of their territory is effectively worthless, from a strategic point of view," Bryce countered. "There is nothing to gain by striking aristocratic retreats. It'll annoy them, sure, and probably lead to demands the other retreats are protected, but it won't weaken them overall. We can take steps to slow their operations, including minelaying operations in their waters, but actually invading Kingston is beyond us."

"For the moment," Sarah added. "If we can sink most of their navy, we can take an island near Kingston and develop it into a base for a proper invasion."

"Perhaps, if you'd pushed harder, we would *have* Kingston by now," Jayne snapped. "And the war would be over."

"It wouldn't have worked," Bryce said. "The government refused to let itself be isolated or crushed in the first few moments of the operation. Once the army got underway, any hope of taking the capital quickly enough to prevent the government from decamping and continuing the fight from a safe distance was gone. We came very close to a major disaster, Colonel, and we were very lucky to escape. As it was, we wrecked a sizable percentage of the harbour facilities and delayed any counter-offensive for quite some time."

Sarah sighed, inwardly, as Jayne looked around the table for support. It had been *her* decision to withdraw, rather than risk an engagement the rebels would probably have lost. The plan had been drawn up before the government started hiring offworlders to train and lead its armies...she cursed under her breath, all too aware the offensive's failure had left them in a precarious position. They'd risked picking a fight with offworlders, including whatever remained of the Marine Corps, when they'd blown up the spaceport. Sarah's backers insisted the Marine Corps was dying, along with the empire it had served, but it was hard to be sure. It wasn't as if New Doncaster was strong enough to tell even a minor interstellar power to go pound sand.

"We do not have time to go over this again," she said, calmly. "Right now, our priority becomes meeting and defeating the government when it launches the second invasion."

"Quite," Bryce agreed. "We may not have as many weapons as the government, let alone aircraft, but we do have enough to give them a very hard time. Our small stockpile of off-world weapons and tech will be held in reserve, waiting for the right moment to strike."

"The plans have been laid," Sarah said. "Once we know where they're going, we will be ready for them."

She smiled. She'd made sure that everyone old enough to carry a gun was given one and taught how to use it. The government was going to discover, when it invaded, that every single blade of grass hid a rebel with a gun, a man—or a woman—ready to sell their lives dearly. And the government had played into her hand, when it had allowed the prisoners to be executed. No one would surrender now, whatever promises were made. They'd fight to the last.

"They won't get a moment's peace," Jayne agreed. "Last time, they had the advantage of surprise. This time, we'll see them coming."

Sarah nodded. "It won't be easy," she said. The plans were vague because no one knew precisely where the enemy would strike, although she had a suspicion it would be one of the core islands. The government didn't have enough time to play a waiting game, particularly if it intended to roll back the concessions it had made after the insurgency had turned into a full-scale war. "But we have the time we need."

She paused. "And we will continue to appeal to the townies," she added. "I dare say they'll be as shocked by the atrocity as we are."

"It is their sons who are putting their lives on the line," Caroche agreed. "Can we use it to split them?"

Bolos shrugged. "The government offered them what they wanted, in exchange for their support," he said. "It will be hard to better the offer, unless we find something they want more."

Sarah nodded, coldly. The townies might have been effectively disenfranchised, but they'd been far better off than the debtors and indents. They'd had something to lose. Now...she was entirely sure the aristos planned to cancel the reforms as soon as they were no longer needed, yet how could they convince the townies of that? The smarter ones would be playing a waiting game, quietly making their position unassailable for the moment the first war came to an end. They wouldn't commit themselves completely until they *knew* there was no longer any room for sitting on the fence.

"We can push the news as much as possible," she said. "But we need to know what actually happened first."

She stood. "Good luck to us all," she added. There was a very good chance she wouldn't see them again, at least for a month or two. "Return to your bunkers and prepare for combat."

CHAPTER TWELVE

KINGSTON, NEW DONCASTER

ROLAND HAD TO ADMIT, as the aircraft circled the airport before coming into land, that Kingston was a beautiful island. It lacked the jungles, and the alien biology, of much of the habitable zone—the island had been intensively terraformed, in the first decade after settlement—but there was something about the green fields and blue lakes that appealed to him. Even the ever-present heat wasn't enough to change his mind. He doubted he'd be allowed to stay on New Doncaster indefinitely, not unless he wanted to give up his name, but it wasn't a bad place to spend his military career. It was certainly unlikely the corps would have any pressing need for him elsewhere.

His heart ached as the aircraft touched down and taxied to a halt. He'd expected *something* from Safehouse, in the weeks and months since the spaceport—and an understrength company of Marines—had been blown to atoms. Surely, the corps would react to the death of so many irreplaceable men. And yet, none of his messages—or Rachel's—had received a reply. He was tempted to wonder if they'd gone astray, as if the merchants he'd paid to take the messages to the dead drops had forgotten them, or fallen prey to pirates, but it was hard to believe they'd *all* been lost. They were alone, even though...

He shook his head as he unstrapped his belt, then headed for the hatch. New Doncaster might be important to the locals, for obvious reasons, but it was a very minor colony world to most interstellar powers. The Marine Corps might have wanted to commit a division to teach the rebels a lesson, yet there were just too many other demands on its limited resources. Roland knew he'd done well, but he had few illusions about his capabilities. He wouldn't have been assigned to the planet, let alone been put in command of the training mission, if there'd been any better options.

Rachel caught his eye. "I'll take our prisoner to town," she said. "Good luck."

Roland nodded as the hatch opened. A wave of heat struck him in the face, carrying with it the promise of a tropical thunderstorm. Roland took a breath, seeing the clouds growing over the distant mountains. The planet's weather was dangerously unpredictable, as far as the meteorologists were concerned, but the locals seemed able to sense what was coming. Roland had learnt to respect their insights, over the last few months. They were certainly far more accurate.

He checked his pistol, automatically, as he jumped to the ground and hurried towards the security checkpoint at the edge of the airfield. The training base had mushroomed in the last six months, turning from a relatively small compound to a giant complex that would give a Marine Corps boot camp a run for its money. Rachel had pointed out, with each successive expansion, that security was turning into a minor nightmare. No one, not even the guards, knew *everyone* authorised to enter or leave the base. Roland had done what he could to ensure visitors were checked, before they were allowed inside the fence, but he feared it was just a matter of time until an insurgent managed to get through. Hell, the odds one or more of the recruits were rebels were alarmingly high. Roland was uncomfortably aware vetting of prospective soldiers was little more than a joke.

We're short of manpower, he reminded himself. *And we don't have time to vet everyone.*

The guards checked his ID, then waved him through. Roland nodded as he made his way to the command barracks, passing parade grounds and shooting ranges and recruit barracks, carefully avoiding lines of young men—and a handful of women—jogging from place to place. The drill instructors—many with little more experience than their charges—led the way, shouting orders in a manner designed to draw attention and command obedience without crossing the line into open bullying. Roland wished there'd been more time to season the DIs, before they'd been pressed into service. Marine DIs normally had years of service under their belts, to the point that—whatever their official ranks—they were actually quite senior. It was a rare CO who'd ignore advice from an experienced NCO. Here…Roland gritted his teeth. There had been incidents, incidents that he'd had to deal with, that stemmed from simple inexperience. It would have been easier, he thought, if the men he'd busted had been malicious instead. He could have kicked them out and felt no remorse afterwards.

He paused by a shooting range and watched as the instructors put the men through their paces. They were expending thousands of rounds, and the penny-pinchers in the nearby city had been complaining about it, but Roland found it hard to care. Better they learnt how their weapons worked now, rather than trying to pick up lessons under enemy fire. Bullets were cheaper than soldiers. He recalled the horror stories about military bureaucracy in the old army days and shuddered. Making training officers fill out a stack of paperwork to obtain even a single case of ammunition was pretty much *asking* for a shortage of training, which meant the poor trainees would get their asses kicked when they went up against a real enemy. He had no intention of letting that happen here.

The command barracks loomed up in front of him. Roland allowed the guards to check his ID—again—and then stepped inside, breathing a sigh of relief as the cool air washed over him. The handful of staff—all middle-aged women trying to do something for the war effort—glanced at him, then went back to work. Roland hid his amusement as he made his way to the CO's office, knowing they hadn't recognised him. His combat battledress was unmarked. The rebels had good snipers. Wearing his rank badges in a combat zone was asking to be shot.

He tapped on the door, then waited. "Come!"

Roland smiled and stepped into the office. Master Sergeant (Auxiliary) Brian Wimer—*de facto* base CO—looked up from his desk, then smiled and stood. "Sir!"

"Sergeant," Roland said. He wasn't sure if Wimer knew who he *really* was. Rachel had been vague, when he'd asked her, and he didn't want to risk asking Wimer himself. "I take it you heard the news?"

Wimer nodded, waving Roland to a folding chair as he poured them both some coffee. "It's never easy to tell how someone will react to combat," he said. "I've seen braggarts turn to cowards when the bullets start flying, and wimpy fops stand their ground even when I feared they'd turn and run, but shooting prisoners…"

He grimaced. "She went through utter hell, sir," he added. "Under normal circumstances, we wouldn't have recruited her at all."

Roland frowned. The Marine Corps believed *anyone* could become a Marine, if they were prepared to work their way through a training course designed to weed out the ones unable to take the pressure, making them quit rather than kicking them out. It was a point of honour the Corps never forced anyone to leave, allowing them to pass or fail on their own. And yet…he grimaced as he sipped his coffee. The Corps certainly had had second thoughts about taking *him* on, when he'd recovered from Earthfall. It hadn't let him proceed to the second stage of his training.

"We may be asked to account for it," Roland said. "Were there any warning signs?"

"According to her file, very few," Wimer said. "She was traumatised, but the shrinks thought the fact she wanted to join the military was a good sign, rather than curling up in a ball and refusing to move. She was still fighting, they said. Her DIs noted she was a good recruit. A handful of minor problems with the others, back when they weren't used to having a young woman amongst them, but she coped well. She was on the list for accelerated promotion when she was shipped out. Now, of course…"

"She'll be lucky not to be hanged," Roland said, curtly. "Do we have any other problem children?"

"It depends on what you mean," Wimer countered. "We have too many recruits who want a little revenge, sir, and no way to screen them out."

"And no way to ensure a slower transit into military life," Roland added. "We can't put the brakes on now."

He sighed. The government should have started building a proper army years ago. Right now, there weren't enough warm bodies in the pipeline to let him pick and choose the recruits at will. Hell, turning some of them down would provoke a political crisis the wartime government was ill equipped to handle. But it meant training was scanty, with worrying gaps at practically all levels, and a lack of specialists in dozens of different fields. Roland knew Wimer and his team were doing their best, yet… he shook his head. There was nothing to be gained by harping about it. They knew the problem and were trying to fix it.

"We will revise the training course to ensure everyone knows what not to do," Wimer said, grimly. "But we already *told* them, including Porter, not to commit anything resembling a war crime."

"Tell them again," Roland said. "And make it clear."

He stared at his empty mug. Accidents happened in war. Civilians died all the time, from being used as human shields by terrorists to making the mistake of driving towards a checkpoint manned by jumpy soldiers unwilling to risk letting a potential IED any closer to them than strictly necessary. They were horrific accidents, but they were accidents. The mass slaughter of prisoners, on the other hand, was deliberate. It could not be allowed to go unpunished.

Wimer's terminal bleeped. "Excuse me, sir."

"Sir, Lady Oakley has arrived," his secretary said. "She requests an audience with General Windsor."

Roland blinked. "Sandra?"

"Yes, sir," Wimer said. He smiled, although there was an edge to his expression that reminded Roland he didn't approve of Sandra Oakley. "I dare say she heard you were coming from her father."

"I'll speak to her," Roland said. He'd hoped to get a shower before heading into the capital for the appointment with the war cabinet, but… he was torn between being pleased to see Sandra again and concern about why she might have come to greet him. "Once I've talked to the cabinet, we can discuss the next stage of the plan."

Wimer raised his hand in salute. "Yes, sir."

Roland smiled, then made his way to his office. Sandra was already there, sitting on a chair wearing a short skirt that showed off her perfect legs. Roland felt his heart begin to race, reminding him of just how long it had been since they'd slept together. He was no fool—he knew Sandra's father had *encouraged* her to get close to him, something he'd seen on Earth before Earthfall—but he *was* a young man. It was all he could do to close the door behind him, instead of running to her.

Sandra smiled, as if she knew what he'd been thinking. "Dad wants me to drive you to the city," she said. "Are you ready?"

"I suppose." Roland took a breath, calming himself. Their relationship was…odd, although—in all honesty—he'd never had a normal relationship. He'd been the Childe Roland, surrounded by aristocratic women who said they wanted him and commoner women who couldn't say no. He felt sick, every time he thought about his past self. He wanted to go back and slap himself silly. "I take it you've heard the news?"

"About Angeline?" Sandra stood, brushing down her dress in a manner that drew the eye to her breasts. "Yes, we have. And we don't know how to handle it."

Roland met her eyes. "She committed a war crime," he said. "We cannot allow it to stand."

"I agree," Sandra said. She looked back at him, evenly. "But others do not."

Tell me, Angeline thought. *Are you really that scared of me?*

She'd been shackled for the brief walk to the plane, then manacled to the chair and forced to sit there, for hours, before the plane had finally landed somewhere on Kingston. There was no point in arguing, she'd discovered. Her escort, an unsmiling woman who was clearly an offworlder no matter what uniform she wore, had told her—flatly—that everything she said would be recorded and might—Angeline suspected she'd meant *would*—be used against her, when she faced a court. Angeline found it hard not to be bitter. After everything she'd gone through, *she* was the bad guy?

She kept the thought to herself as she was half-carried off the plane—her legs were too stiff for her to walk—and into a car, which rumbled towards the distant city. It was hard to so much as move her head, but she managed to spot some familiar buildings from the training base before her escort ordered her to keep her eyes to herself. Angeline resisted the urge to make a snide remark as the car picked up speed, crossing the ring road and only slowing when it reached the first checkpoint. She couldn't hear what her escort and the driver said to the guards, but it was clearly enough to get them waved through without the vehicle being searched. It gnawed at her. The DIs had promised that anyone who just *let* an unsearched vehicle into the compound would be lucky if they were *just* yelled at by their superiors. An insurgent with bad intentions could cram a shitload of explosives into a car, they'd pointed out, and the driver might not even know he'd been turned into a suicide bomber.

The car slowed, then went down a ramp and finally came to a halt. Her escort opened the door and dragged Angeline out into an underground garage. Two men in black uniforms took custody of Angeline, searching her quickly before marching her into an elevator that went even further below the ground. Angeline felt her heart sink. She'd heard rumours of underground prisons, owned and operated by the secret police, but none of them had ever been substantiated. Now…her gut churned with outrage. She was a prisoner in a complex hardly anyone knew existed, a prisoner who had been denied her rights as well as everything else. It just wasn't fair.

She grunted as she was shoved into a cell and manacled to a bench, then told to wait. Tears prickled in her eyes as she looked around. The room was bare, nothing more than concrete walls and a solid metal door. The air stank faintly of piss and shit and hopelessness…she wondered, suddenly, how she was meant to answer the call of nature. Did they expect her to wet herself, to soak her clothes as well as the cell? Or…

The door opened. Angeline looked up. A figure stood in the light, staring at her. It was too bright for her to make out his face, but…

"I need answers," the figure said. The voice was unfamiliar, but the accent was very definitely aristocratic. No one, even a townie who married into the aristocracy, could fake it well enough to fool a *real* aristocrat. Angeline's mother had been very clear on that point, when she'd been insisting Angeline had to master the accent herself or risk seeming countrified when she came out. "What actually happened?"

Angeline swallowed, hard. Her mouth was dry. "Water."

"Fetch her water," the figure called, then turned back to her. "What happened?"

"I…" Angeline forced herself to think. Her feelings were a tangled mess. The rebels had been thieves, as well as rapists and murderers. They'd worn the evidence of their crimes right in front of her eyes. They'd deserved to die. The sheer hatred that washed through her was overpoweringly strong. They'd deserved to die and yet she was the one in jail? It just wasn't even remotely fair. "I killed looters."

The figure took a glass of water from someone and held it to her lips, letting her drink her fill. "Start at the beginning," he said. "What happened?"

Angeline wet her lips, then started to recount the entire story. The invasion. The landing. The march to the airport. The victory. The thieves. And…she clenched her teeth as she tried to put her feelings into words. The rebels had deserved it. They'd killed hundreds of people and forced thousands more to flee to safety, as if there was *any* safety. The only thing they understood was force. They deserved to die. She had no doubt of it.

"Very good," the figure said, when she finally finished. "You will be taken to a more…*pleasant* prison cell, where you can shower and sleep without shackles. As long as you behave yourself, you will be treated well. Quite what will happen to you is still in the air, but you're not alone. Do you understand me?"

"Yes," Angeline said. It occurred to her, too late, that the figure might have been gentle with her to get her to talk, that she might have made a full confession for anyone who cared to listen, but so what? She'd done the right thing. Anything else was unimaginable. "I thank you."

"You're welcome," the figure said. "Do you have anything else you wish to say?"

"No." Angeline tried to shake her head, but the shackles made it hard. She wanted to know who he was, yet she was sure she wouldn't get an answer. "I'm just…I'm just tired."

"Rest now," the figure said. "I'll see you in the morning."

CHAPTER THIRTEEN

KINGSTON, NEW DONCASTER

THE CAPITAL OF NEW DONCASTER, Roland noted, had changed a great deal since the insurgency had turned into a full-scale war. There were police checkpoints everywhere, backed up by SWAT teams and army infantry patrolling the streets. The shops were either boarded up, in the vain hope of keeping the next round of fighting from causing real damage, or closed altogether. There were only a handful of civilians in plain view, almost all of them aristos or townies. The city's population of debtors and indents were keeping their heads down.

Roland brooded as Sandra drove them into the underground garage, then led the way past a pair of checkpoints and up into the council chamber. The war council had been thrown together in a tearing hurry, drawing councillors from both the aristos and the townies. Roland hadn't had anything like enough time to monitor the political squabbles, but he was uneasily aware there were people on both sides who regarded the war council as nothing more than a placeholder, a temporary measure rather than a permanent part of the planetary government. Roland hoped—prayed—no one would try to reshape matters before the war was brought to an end, let alone go back on the power-sharing agreements everyone had made after the first insurgency had exploded into life. It would be utterly disastrous to the war effort.

The rebels must be praying we'll fall out amongst ourselves, he thought. *If we start fighting amongst ourselves, their ultimate victory is assured.*

He saluted the Prime Minister—Sandra's father—then looked around the table. There were nine members in all, but only two others had been invited to attend. Lord Hamish Ludlow sat on one side of the Prime Minister, his face unreadable; Daniel Collier, Richard's father, sat at the other. Roland suspected the decision to exclude the other five members boded ill, particularly as *his* vote was only meant to be used to break a tie. Or maybe the others simply hadn't been able to attend. No, that was unlikely. Roland himself had travelled further than any of them to attend the meeting.

"General," Lord William Oakley said. The Prime Minister seemed to have aged a decade in the last six months. He'd only become PM, from what Roland had heard, because he'd been seen as a safe pair of hands. The insurgency had seemed containable. There'd been no reason, not at the time, to look for a more active war leader. Now…"We must put formality aside, when we are discussing Lady Porter."

"Yes, sir," Roland said. "There is little dispute about the facts. Private Angeline Porter murdered prisoners in cold blood. Word is already out and spreading. We have to get ahead of it by putting her in front of a court-martial, then—at the very least—sentencing her to a lifetime on a penal island. Ideally, she should be executed. There is no way we can tolerate her actions."

"I protest," Lord Ludlow said. "It is a point of law that aristocrats are spared capital punishment."

Roland met his eyes. "She is a murderer whose actions have almost certainly prolonged the war," he said, flatly. "We must throw the book at her."

"We committed ourselves to fighting a reasonably civilised war," Collier agreed. "Her actions have thrown our commitment into question. If we fail to discipline her, to make an example if nothing else, we will be seen as condoning an atrocity. The rebels may well retaliate against our own people, either the prisoners in their hands or our civilian populations."

Roland nodded. The rebels had dozens, perhaps hundreds, of prisoners. It was an open secret that there were thousands of people in Kingsport—and the outlying islands—who had never been accounted for, even when the investigative teams started digging up the graves to check the bodies. Many would be dead, he was sure, but a number might well have been kept prisoner. Hell, the smarter rebels wouldn't have let their men kill *all* the aristos. They'd make good human shields, as well as field workers.

"The rebels themselves have not fought a civilised war," Ludlow countered. "How many mansions have been destroyed? How many men have been killed? How many women have been raped and *then* killed? Why should we fight a civilised war when they are manifestly committed to an uncivilised war?"

Roland chose his words carefully. "It is easy to fall into the trap of believing that one side ignoring the laws of war is an excuse for the other side, your side, to do the same," he said. It had been discussed at Boot Camp, the DI explaining how the perception of unfairness could wear away at military discipline until the urge to retaliate in kind became overwhelming. "In the short term, it might be satisfying. In the long term, we must convince the vast majority of rebels that they have a future with us or commit ourselves to a war that will be disastrous, even if we win. People who feel they have nothing to lose will not surrender. They will keep fighting and do their best to claw us, even as they go down."

He took a breath. "We must reach out to the uncommitted and try to convince them to join us," he stated. "And that means we must admit what she did, and make it clear she has been punished for her crimes."

"Agreed," Collier said.

"There are political issues that have to be addressed," Ludlow said, smoothly. "First, she went through utter hell. Her servants betrayed her family. She was raped repeatedly, by at least six different men. The rest of her close family was apparently killed, if they weren't taken prisoner, and she was expected to die herself. The only reason she survived was sheer luck."

Roland scowled. "That is not an excuse."

Ludlow ignored him. "There was a great deal of sympathy for her, when the story broke," Ludlow continued. "Her life, and all hope of being a wife and a mother, were destroyed through no fault of her own. She was even seen as a heroine, of sorts, for not letting everything that happened destroy what little she had left. There is no way any of her supporters, her admirers, will condone her imprisonment or exile."

"And will they be happier," Roland demanded, "when the rebels strike back by blowing up the next debutante ball?"

He went on before Ludlow could muster a response. "It is a simple fact, as much as the civilised universe may try to deny it, that the only thing preventing war crimes is the promise of bloody revenge. We don't do it to them because they'd do it to us; they don't do it to us because we'd do it to them. Right now, the rebels have all the excuse they need to commit an atrocity of their own, an atrocity that will slip through our defences and take lives. We need to punish her for her crimes, to make it clear we do not support them, before the rebels kick off a series of atrocities, and retaliations, and more atrocities!"

Ludlow glared. "The rebels have committed thousands of atrocities," he said. "They have killed and raped and looted and destroyed homes and crops that took centuries to build. What makes hers so special?"

"It was committed by one of us, by someone under my command," Roland snapped. "And we cannot afford to condone it."

"I would take rebel protests more seriously if they hadn't committed atrocities of their own," Ludlow said. "Why shouldn't we strike back?"

"Because the goal is to win the war without tearing the planet apart," Roland said. He wanted to point out – to scream – that Angeline Porter had killed children! "If the rebels think they cannot surrender, *they will not surrender!*"

Collier leaned forward. "I think it is fairly true to say that support for her is concentrated amongst the aristocracy," he said. "Us townies are largely indifferent to her."

"She was treated..." Ludlow made a visible attempt to calm himself. "Those vile *animals* destroyed her life! How can you be indifferent to the atrocity they perpetrated against her?"

Collier started to speak, but Roland overrode him. "I understand what she went through, as much as anyone can," he said. "However, that does not excuse her crimes. She was cautioned not to slaughter prisoners, or indeed commit any of a number of war crimes, and she did it anyway. She needs to go to a penal island, at the very least."

"And if you try to bring charges against her, there will be political uproar," Ludlow said. "Right now, the story is breaking. Many news reporters, sick to death of rebel atrocities, are taking her side. The remainder will still not condemn her. Do you really want to tear the government apart over a minor incident, no better or worse than what the rebels did to *their* victims? Why don't we just paint her actions a retaliation for *their* crimes?"

"Because they *weren't*," Roland said. "She killed children, sir, and people who had nothing to do with how she was treated. The problem with eye-for-an-eye reasoning is that you eventually run out of eyes!"

"Her conduct was disgraceful," Collier said. "We can agree on that, if nothing else."

The PM held up his hand. "There are good reasons to move ahead with a formal trial," he said, calmly. "At the same time, the trial *will* prove divisive at the worst possible moment. Her defenders are already getting organised. They will paint the trial as a witch hunt, and insist she is being unfairly blamed for her actions."

Roland snorted. "Nonsense."

"People will believe anything, when they want to," Collier said. "Or even when it is convenient for them to believe it."

"It doesn't matter," the PM said. "What matters is that her supporters will believe it. There is a *lot* of anger over the devastation the rebels wrought, from the destroyed mansions and fields to the raped and murdered aristocrats. Her supporters will try to argue that she did the right thing and enough people will agree with them, or pretend to do so, to make putting her on trial very difficult. And there's..."

He paused. "There's also the issue of the hell she went through, and what it might have done to her," he added. "They may even claim diminished capacity, on the grounds she was traumatised by her experiences. No matter the result, no matter what happens to her, there will be absolute chaos. We simply cannot afford it."

Roland felt a hot flash of anger. "The rebels will retaliate," he said. "Can we afford *that*?"

Ludlow scoffed. "You don't know they'll retaliate."

"I do." Roland clenched his fists. "I told you. The law cannot, just by existing, prevent atrocities. They can only be stopped by the threat of punishment or retaliation. If we fail to punish her, the rebels will assume we decided to condone her actions, or that we planned them in advance, and they will conclude the only way to keep us from doing it again is to carry out an atrocity of their own. They must, because if they don't they'll only encourage us to do it again and again. Turning the other cheek after you've been struck is not a good idea, in a world without enforced laws. It merely encourages the aggressor to *strike* the other cheek too."

"It's a valid point," Collier said. "Perhaps we should hand her over to the rebels."

"That will not go down well," Ludlow stated. "The government will fall."

"I suggest a compromise," the PM said. "We will not put her on trial, because that would trigger a major faction fight at the worst possible time. However, she cannot be allowed anywhere near a military operation ever again. We will, therefore, assign her to a guardpost in the middle of nowhere, perhaps somewhere along the edge of the habitable zone, and leave her there. She can stay there for the rest of her miserable life."

Roland shook his head. "Compared to what she deserves, that's letting her off with a slap on the wrist. No, without even a slap on the wrist!"

"It has its advantages," Ludlow said. "On paper, she will have been sent into *de facto* exile, somewhere so far away she might as well have been sent to a penal island. She will be punished without actually undergoing a trial. And she'll never return to aristocratic society."

"It isn't enough," Roland said, although he suspected he'd already lost. The PM had suggested the compromise and Ludlow had agreed to it, leaving Collier as the sole holdout. Roland's own vote was worthless if there wasn't a tie…he tried, hard, not to show his frustration. There was no point in even lodging a protest vote. "We cannot afford to be seen as condoning the atrocity."

"We won't be," Ludlow said. "That's the beauty of it. We'll be sending her into exile without ever quite making it permanent, without ever charging her with something she can appeal against. She will know she is being punished, as well everyone else, but it will never be formally recorded. She'll…just remain in exile for the rest of her life."

Roland tried not to snap at him. "Do you think the rebels will be impressed?"

"We do have some low-key communications channels," the PM reminded him. "We can let them know."

"We'll see," Roland said. "But I think this will end badly."

He sighed. On the face of it, Ludlow's idea of sending Angeline Porter into exile without ever quite making it formal had a lot to recommend it. Angeline had some survival training—she'd been a soldier, as well as a plantation resident—but it was unlikely she'd last very long. Her exile might be more of a death sentence than anything else. He supposed the government would play that up as much as possible, when they communicated with the rebels. They hadn't sentenced Angeline Porter to death, but…they'd sentenced her to death. Roland tried not to groan openly. There was something mealy-mouthed about the whole affair that didn't sit well with him. Surely, it would be better to hold a formal trial and let the chips fall where they may?

And what can you do, he asked himself, *to change their minds?*

It was a galling thought. There was nothing. Even threatening to resign wouldn't have the effect he'd hoped. The days the government had hung on his every word as gospel were gone. There weren't that many officers better than he was, not on the planet, but…he wasn't irreplaceable. Trying to fight would be utterly disastrous, both to the war effort and to his career. He dreaded to think what his superiors would say, if they knew how badly he'd fucked up. And the only thing he could do was step back and let a war criminal effectively get away with it.

She's going into exile, he reminded himself. *It's a fucking death sentence wrapped up in pretty words and pathetic excuses.*

He tried to keep his face under tight control. The hell of it was that, a couple of years ago, he would have done the same thing. The spoilt brat he'd been, too wrapped up in himself to acknowledge the humanity of his peers, wouldn't have spent any time thinking about the issue. Angeline Porter was an aristocrat, the heir to her family's titles and monies, while her victims were nothing more than filthy commoners. Who gave a damn, his old self would have asked, what she did to them? They were just… *things*. If Belinda hadn't sorted him out…

You would be dead, his thoughts pointed out. There was no doubt of it. No one, save for Belinda, had considered him worth saving. Who could blame them? He'd been a little brat in an adult body. *You'd have died during Earthfall.*

"Then we seem to have agreement," Collier said. He made a show of looking at his watch. "I think it is too late to continue the rest of our planned discussion. We can meet again tomorrow to discuss the war, and our future operations?"

"I think that will be suitable," the PM said. "I'll have the police make arrangements to transport Angeline Porter to a holding cell, then prepare her supplies for her exile. Once she's ready, she can be dumped on an island and she'll no longer be our problem."

But even if she dies within the week, her ghost will haunt us, Roland thought, sardonically. *There's no way the rebels will let this pass. They'll strike at us, at a soft target, and we'll be left holding the bag.*

"Good," Ludlow said. He clapped his hands together. "I agree. We should resume tomorrow."

Roland nodded, curtly. He had the oddest feeling he'd been played... and yet, he couldn't put the sensation into words. Had Ludlow wanted him to demand Angeline Porter's execution? Or...or what? Perhaps he was just overthinking it. Ludlow had good reason to stand up for the young woman, even if she was a war criminal. And the solution might just work...

"With your permission, I'll see you tomorrow," Roland said. He'd already arranged to meet Rachel afterwards, then go back to base with her. If nothing else, talking through the matter with her would clarify things. "And I hope this won't come back to bite us."

"There is no way we will not be bitten, whatever we do," Ludlow said. He shot Roland a smile that looked as if it were intended to be reassuring but failed miserably. "We just have to choose what bites us and when."

And you are prepared to risk the rebels retaliating against your civilians—our civilians—rather than start a fight over her future, Roland thought, as he stood. It galled him, more than he cared to admit, that he understood Ludlow's thinking. *You may be right, in the long term, but the effects are still going to be bad.*

CHAPTER FOURTEEN

KINGSTON, NEW DONCASTER

"FUCK IT," ROLAND SAID.

He forced himself to calm down as the car drove away from the government building. Rachel wouldn't be impressed by a temper tantrum. No one would be. And yet...he clenched his fists, feeling a wave of unaccustomed frustration and anger. He didn't know how to deal with it. As a spoilt brat of a prince, he'd been able to get almost anything he wanted as soon as he wanted it; as a recruit, he'd always had a clear path to work towards anything he wanted. But this...he honestly didn't know what to do. Perhaps it would have been better, all along, if he'd shot Private Porter himself, when he'd heard the news. The government could then have quietly blamed everything on him.

"Fuck it," he repeated. "What are they thinking?"

Rachel considered it. "Probably that putting her on trial would be an unacceptable risk," she said, finally. Roland had filled her in, when he'd left the council chamber. "And that sending her away is the best of a set of bad options."

"It would be better to put her in front of a firing squad," Roland growled. He'd spent his time at Boot Camp being lectured about war crimes, with the DIs explaining what a war crime actually *was*, then explaining what he had to do if he uncovered one. He had an *obligation* to report it, even if it was committed by his squadmates. "We need to send a message to the troops that such behaviour won't be tolerated."

"She's not going to have an easy time, playing Robinson Crusoe on a desert island," Rachel pointed out. "She'll be alone for the rest of her life."

Roland scowled. It was true, he supposed, but it was hardly as salutary an example as he would have preferred. A skilled survivalist could live off the land for quite some time…although, he decided, it wasn't clear if that was true on New Doncaster. The planet's native biology grew stronger, the closer one went to the edge of the habitable zone. It was quite possible Angeline Porter would eat the wrong thing and die or get caught up in a storm and perish without a proper shelter. And yet…he suspected her supporters would make sure she was well equipped before she was sent into exile. It wasn't as if she was going to be stripped naked, then thrown ashore to live or die alone.

"I suppose," he said. "It doesn't sit well with me, though."

"Nor should it," Rachel agreed. "Even if we make a big song and dance about it, the rebels will claim we let her get away with it."

"I said as much," Roland told her. "They'll seek to strike us in retaliation."

Rachel nodded. "There are plenty of planets trapped in vicious cycles of attack and counterattack, each atrocity carried out in payment for the last…each one birthing more and more people with newer grudges, even as the old ones fall into the ashtray of history. The empire used to try to stop them, but rarely succeeded. There was always one last atrocity which needed to be repaid, leading to the cycle kicking off all over again."

Roland rubbed his forehead. "Is there anything we can do about it?"

Rachel said nothing for a long moment. "Not unless you want to take over the government yourself," she said. "And that would upset your superiors."

"I suppose." Roland laughed, humourlessly. "How far would I get, if I tried?"

Rachel shrugged. Roland looked away. He'd grown used to consulting her, when he'd realised she was more than just an administrative assistant, but he suspected she had secret orders to do more than just watch his back. Her superiors probably wanted her to keep a close eye on him, to determine his progress towards becoming either a Marine or... or what? Roland was the legitimate ruler of the known universe, but he had no illusions about the outcome if he tried to press his claim. He'd be lucky if the galaxy's new rulers *only* laughed at him.

And even if I had the corps backing me, it wouldn't be enough to reclaim what was left of the core worlds, he thought. *The rest of the settled galaxy would reject me immediately.*

He rubbed his forehead as the car drove out of the city and back to the training camp. It was clear, in hindsight, how much had been kept from the bratty prince. He'd never met anyone outside his bubble, never heard so much as a single dissenting voice. His minders had kept him so isolated he'd believed all sorts of nonsense, from people singing his praises in the streets to the empire ruling from one end of the galaxy to the other. Now... he shook his head in disbelief. Why hadn't he realised the problem and done something—anything—about it? But even if he had, so what? His minders would have put him back in his box pretty much effortlessly. They wouldn't even have needed to threaten to replace him with someone else.

The thought mocked him. He hadn't known, until it was far too late, how much the empire had been hated in its final years. There was no way any of the new warlords would subordinate themselves to *him*, not when they could build their vest-pocket empires or even try to reunite the galaxy under their banners. Why would they give a shit about him? He was nothing more than a liability. Sure, they could try to force him into marriage—to link their bloodlines to his—but it wouldn't work in their favour. The galaxy was sick of his family.

"Call Richard," he said, finally. "I want him to hand command over to his second, then report back here as quickly as possible. Then arrange for everyone under my command, and I mean *everyone*, to be given a quick refresher course on war crimes. If someone else does the same, they'll be shot out of hand."

Rachel glanced at him. "Is that a good idea?"

Roland felt a hot flash of anger. "Is it?"

"On one hand, we have to make it clear atrocities will not be condoned," Rachel said. "On the other, we don't want to force our troops into conspiracies of silence if they think there's no hope of mercy."

"If they gun down unarmed civilians, or surrendering troops, there really *will* be no hope of mercy," Roland said, curtly. "But if there's ambiguity about what actually happened…"

He groaned. Soldiers were loyal to their squadmates, more than they'd ever be to their superior officers. Betraying their squadmates was never easy—and they'd never be trusted again, even if they'd done the right thing. It was a paradox, one he didn't know how to solve. On one hand, he needed men willing and able to fight for their comrades; on the other, he needed them to be prepared to stop, or report, their comrades if they went too far. It would be a great deal worse if their superiors appeared to be out of touch, to the point their orders were impractical, impossible, or downright suicidal. Roland had glanced at the files, during the flight back to the capital. The atrocity-prone units of the Imperial Army, nothing more than a dead letter after Earthfall, had all been the playthings of superior officers who'd been ignorant of their own ignorance. Roland could understand their feelings, but it wasn't an excuse. How could it be?

Rachel shot him a reassuring look. "The world is a messy place," she said. "The rebels know it too."

"And now they know what'll happen if they surrender," Roland said. "How many people are going to die, because they *can't* surrender? How many of our men will be killed reducing rebel strongpoints, because the rebels feel they must fight to the death?"

"Don't obsess about it," Rachel advised. "Concentrate on your planning. Let the DIs do their job, explaining what happened and how it cannot be allowed to happen again. And then, fight the war, trying to bring it to a close before the rebels can rebalance themselves and counterattack."

Roland nodded, staring out the window. The shanty towns around the capital had grown larger, in the month since he'd last visited the island. There were hundreds of thousands of refugees; some ready and able to work, others seemingly convinced the government would take care of them until they could return home. He dreaded to think how many rebels might be amongst them, after studying how some of the trustees had been very untrustworthy indeed. Angeline Porter might not have reacted so badly, if she hadn't been betrayed by servants she'd trusted. And yet, why *should* she have trusted them? They'd been treated like slaves. Of *course* they'd looked for a chance to get their own back.

And are we talking about her here, his own thoughts mocked him, *or you?*

"We probably can't eradicate the rebels completely," he said, tiredly. "But we can reduce the violence, through military action and political settlements."

He sighed. He'd have to raise *that* issue with the PM too, now the fighting was beginning in earnest. What *would* they do with captured rebels? Roland had no intention of letting them be enslaved, once again; the rebels would fight to the last if they thought they'd just go straight back into chains. Perhaps they could be shipped to unsettled islands—there wasn't exactly a shortage—and given a chance to live there, without interference. Or…who knew? If the workers were paid a reasonable wage, and given a chance to actually earn their way out of debt, the plantations might improve in short order. But it would be a political nightmare.

They're going to have to come to grips with it, sooner or later, he reflected. *Or the rebels will just keep fighting to the end.*

• • •

"On your feet," a voice ordered. "Now."

Angeline rolled over and stood, cursing both her nakedness and the constant dim light within the cell. She'd lost track of time, to the point she wasn't sure *just* how long she'd been imprisoned. The guards had fed her mush and given her water to drink, but otherwise left her strictly alone. Angeline suspected her solitude was at least partly an illusion. She was probably under constant surveillance, her every utterance recorded for later analysis. A year ago, it would have horrified her. Now, after months in barracks, it was almost homey.

The door clattered open. Two figures stood there, wearing black suits and masks. Angeline said nothing, offering no resistance as they searched her roughly, as if they feared something had been smuggled into the cell. They marched her out as soon as they were sure she wasn't carrying anything, pushing her into another room. A set of clothes—very plain—sat on a chair, waiting for her. Angeline resisted the urge to ask the guards to turn their backs as she dressed quickly, then ran her hands through her hair. The guards looked her up and down, then cuffed her and marched her further down the corridor, into an underground garage. She was lifted into a van, shackled to a bench and left alone. Angeline tried to get comfortable as the vehicle roared into life. She might be alone now, but that was about to change. And yet...

She frowned, despite herself, as the seconds turned into minutes and then hours. Where was she? Where were they going? It was possible, she supposed, the driver was trying to confuse her by doing several laps around the ring road, before heading back into the city, but what was the point? Besides, it didn't *feel* that way. She thought they were driving further and further away with every passing second. Why...?

The vehicle lurched to a halt. Angeline started, uncomfortably aware she'd been on the verge of sleep. How long had it been? She'd learnt to sleep anywhere, during training, but this...her arms and legs ached as the doors were thrown open, revealing yet another underground garage. A pair of men in drab tunics studied her for a long moment, their faces tightening slightly—very slightly. Aristocrats, Angeline decided. The not-expression of distaste was all too familiar.

"Unchain her," one ordered. "And then take her upstairs."

Angeline eyed them both as she was freed, rubbing her wrists where the handcuffs had dug into her skin. Perhaps she could overwhelm them... no, it would be unwise. They might underestimate her, because they were aristocrats and she was a young woman, but if they were household retainers they probably had *some* combat training. Besides, she was hungry and aching and she had no idea where she was or where they were taking her. Better to wait and see, rather than do something that would land her in worse trouble. She followed the leader docilely, all too aware of the man behind her, as he led her into an elevator. The upper levels were so finely furnished she *knew* she was in an aristocratic mansion.

A twinge of hope ran through her. They wouldn't have taken so much trouble, if they'd merely wanted to put her in front of a firing squad. Instead...she tried to look around without making it obvious, in hopes of spotting something useful. There was nothing. The paintings on the wall, *de rigueur* for an aristocratic family, were unfamiliar. She supposed it shouldn't have been so surprising. Her family had been the masters of their island, but they were quite low-ranked compared to some of the older families on the capital. And they'd never been allowed to doubt it.

The escort stopped in front of a door, then opened it and stepped aside, motioning for Angeline to enter. Angeline did as she was told, bracing herself for...she didn't know. The study—it was clearly a study—was perfectly decorated, showing off the owner's wealth and taste without being gaudy or ostentatious. It was a quiet statement, one all the more important for being so subtle. A person who didn't pick up on it was a person, in the eyes of the aristocracy, with no sense at all.

Her eyes widened as she spotted the man behind the desk. She knew him. "Lord Ludlow!"

"Lady Porter," Ludlow said. His voice was calm and polite – and familiar. He'd been the one who'd spoken to her in the cell. "Thank you for coming."

Angeline felt her legs wobble. She'd been presented to Lord Ludlow once, when he'd visited her island two years ago. Since then...if her family had had any contacts with him, she didn't know about it. Her heart clenched in frustration. Politics were a male preserve, as far as her father had been concerned. Angeline's job was to look pretty and attract a good husband, not assist either her father or her future husband in running the plantation or *anything*. If her father had survived, he would have forbidden her to join the army. She wondered, sourly, if his death was the price she'd paid for her freedom.

"Thank you, My Lord," she managed. She was too unsteady to risk a curtsey. "I..."

"Please, be seated," Ludlow said. "Would you like something to eat? Or drink?"

Angeline felt her stomach churn. This wasn't a polite meeting, no matter how he acted. She'd been plucked from a prison cell and driven to the mansion and...and what? It wasn't as if she had anything to offer, not really. Her patrimony was in rebel hands and even if she regained it tomorrow, it would be worthless without a small army of workers to get it back into shape. And...she laughed at herself. They'd told her she'd committed a war crime. For all she knew, she was about to be executed.

She cleared her throat. "I'd like to know why you brought me here."

It was unforgivable rudeness. Her mother would have slapped Angeline for even *daring* to use that tone with her. Her father would have whipped her. God alone knew what Ludlow would do. She was completely at his mercy...and he was smiling? For a moment, she was sure he was laughing at her, as an adult might laugh at a child's foolishness, then she realised he was honestly amused. The world seemed to shift around her. It just wasn't...it just wasn't *right*.

"Direct, and straight to the point," Ludlow said. "I like it."

His smile shifted, turning cold. "They wanted to execute you, even though you were perfectly justified in what you did. I convinced them to change the sentence to exile. As far as anyone knows, you are being shipped to a distant island, never to be seen again. If anyone follows up on it, later, they'll find no trace of you. It will be assumed you tried to swim to another island and died, your body lost below the waves."

Angeline tensed. "And why did you go to so much effort for me?"

"The coalition government cannot last," Ludlow said, simply. "The townies want more than we can reasonably give them. General Windsor is too focused on dealing with the rebels to consider the long-term impact of his actions. And, as the army is majority-townie, we cannot rely on it if push comes to shove."

"Quite," Angeline agreed. "And what do you want to do about it?"

"You have already proven you can be trusted to handle the situation decisively," Ludlow said, simply. "I want you to join my forces. Agreed?"

Angeline considered it, briefly. She doubted she had a choice. Ludlow wouldn't hesitate to either make her exile real, or simply have her executed and her body cremated, if she refused to go along with him. And...she *did* want to join him. The government had betrayed her and her family. The thought of setting matters to rights...

"Agreed," she said. "When do we begin?"

CHAPTER FIFTEEN

KINGSTON, NEW DONCASTER

ROLAND AWOKE, SLOWLY.

He felt...rested, for the first time in months. His body was completely relaxed and yet...he tensed, very slightly, as he realised he wasn't alone. Someone was in his bed, cuddled up to him...he braced himself, half-expecting the worst, then remembered Sandra had joined him on the base the previous night. It had seemed *right* they'd go to bed together...she shifted against him as he rolled over, her bare breasts brushing against his chest. He felt a sudden surge of lust as he opened his eyes to meet hers, her blue eyes shining with mischief...

Afterwards, they went for a shower together. Roland felt guilty for sleeping with his girlfriend, when so many of the men under his command wouldn't have a chance to meet theirs—or even visit the brothels—for weeks, if not months. And yet, he'd been so tense last night, so worked up over everything that had happened that her touch had been the only thing that had let him sleep. He hadn't felt so well-rested in months, ever since he'd discovered Belinda hadn't saved his life at the cost of her own. It was funny, he reflected, that she'd been the first one to teach him to care about others, instead of just himself. If his selfishness had gotten her killed...

"I took the liberty of arranging for breakfast to be sent up for us," Sandra said. "Do you want it now?"

Roland shrugged as he pulled on his tunic, then nodded. It was 0800. They had to be back in the council chamber at 1000, where he'd be briefing the war council on the Mountebank landings and his planned next steps towards winning the war. And then…he wondered, wryly, if there was anything to do in the city. Perhaps they could go dancing…Rachel would slap him senseless for exposing himself to possible harm, but he wanted to do something—anything—other than military service for a few hours. Maybe they could just find a hotel room, if there was one that wasn't crammed with refugee aristocrats trying to pressure the government to help them. Perhaps…

Sandra keyed her terminal, sending the message. "They sent Lady Porter into exile last night," she said. "It was done very quickly."

Roland grimaced. He would have preferred to supervise, just to make sure her supporters didn't slip her something she could use to get off the island. The exact location was supposed to be a secret, but Roland suspected word was already out and spreading. And if someone decided to rescue her…he shook his head. Where could she go, where she wouldn't be noticed? It wasn't as if she could reclaim her lands without being arrested and sent straight back into exile. He'd just have to hope her exile was enough to convince the rebels she'd been severely punished for her crimes.

Perhaps we can let them know where to find her, he reflected, as someone knocked on the door. *It might give the rebels a chance to punish her themselves.*

Sandra took the tray, then placed it on the table. "You're brooding again."

"I can't help it," Roland said. "Besides, I've been told women like men who brood."

Sandra stuck out her tongue. "Five credits says whoever told you that wasn't a brooder himself."

Roland grinned, then sobered. "Did you know her? Angeline Porter?"

"Not in the sense you mean." Sandra paused, taking a moment to put scrambled egg on her toast. "We aren't—weren't—social equals. Her family was well below mine, even though they're both aristocrats. I don't believe we ever met, not until she was brought here after the uprising on Baraka. We certainly didn't spend any real time together."

"And she joined the army," Roland said. "What did you make of that?"

Sandra shrugged. "If her family had remained alive, they would have been utterly horrified," she said. "The idea of one of their daughters joining the military...oh, horror of horrors. Her father would have flatly forbidden it, while her mother...it wouldn't have worked out. And after her family died...no one really knew what to make of it. Polite society pretended to simply ignore the whole affair."

Roland smiled. "It's the empire in miniature, isn't it?"

Sandra gave him an odd look. "Did you ever meet the empire's aristocracy?"

"No, but I heard the stories," Roland lied, cursing himself for the mistake. "What do you think will happen now?"

"I think they'll be satisfied with exile, rather than execution," Sandra said. "It's just a little difficult for them to wrap their heads around everything that happened."

"The fact their servants and slaves had thoughts of their own?" Roland scowled, remembering how he hadn't given much of a damn about his old servants either. "Or what she did when she had a gun in her hand and rebels in her sights?"

"Both. Neither." Sandra sighed. "And, of course, they'd have an obligation to defend her regardless."

Roland said nothing as he started to eat his breakfast. The cooks had done a surprisingly good job...he smiled, wryly, as he recalled explaining to the pre-war staff that the recruits needed good food, not the cheapest mass-produced inedible crap the military bureaucracy could find. They had to believe, deep inside, that senior officers and NCOs really *were* invested in taking care of their men, or their willingness to follow seemingly insane or even suicidal orders would drop to nothing. And yet... he wondered, idly, if Sandra had talked the staff into making something special. It wasn't impossible. She had enough entitlement in her little finger to push through almost any objections, if she wanted something badly enough.

"But no matter," Sandra said. "Do you feel the offensive was a success?"

And if I answer that question, Roland thought, *will you share it with your father?*

He considered his answer for a long moment. "I think we achieved all our primary goals," he said. It was a weaselly answer, but it would suffice. "I hoped to capture the city and take the rebels into custody, but after the atrocity it was impossible. We'll just have to rotate troops through the siege lines until the rebels do something to break the stalemate."

Sandra nodded. "So you think you can continue the war as planned?"

"Yeah." Roland smiled to himself. "I certainly hope so."

He felt his smile grow wider. To him, her questions were clearly designed to extract information she could share with her father. To the average male aristocrat on New Doncaster, they were nothing more than invitations to talk freely to someone who couldn't *possibly* have the wit to understand what she was hearing. Roland found it absurd—both Belinda and Rachel were clever and insightful—but he supposed it made a certain kind of sense. If women were excluded from politics, who'd expect them to understand?

Idiots, he thought. *How many of them talk freely in front of a pretty face?*

He finished his breakfast, then winked at her. "Have you been keeping busy here?"

"Father has me working as his assistant, as you know," Sandra said. "I've also been assisting the older women in setting up balls to raise funds for the war, or tend to the wounded when they return from the field, or…"

Roland had to smile, again. The projects seemed more than a little useless, not comparable to the work they could be doing. They could help turn the refugee camps into decent places to live, or simply arrange for the refugees to live and work on the estates…if, of course, the aristocrats were prepared to share space with the commoners. He sighed, feeling his heart sink as she babbled about her work. The aristocratic women were doing their best, as much as their society allowed them to do, but it wasn't enough. And it was unlikely it would change in a hurry.

"I'm glad to hear you've been keeping yourself busy," he said, when she'd finished. "And I hope it will lead to more soon."

Sandra looked downcast. "If we're allowed," she said. "It isn't easy to get permission to do much of anything, not unless our parents or husbands are particularly liberal."

"I understand," Roland said. He did—he'd grown up on Earth, where he'd been locked into a gilded cage. "But the war effort comes first."

• • •

"Richard," Daniel Collier said. "It's been a long time."

Richard nodded as he embraced his father. Being an MP, and then a War Councillor, hadn't changed the older man that much. He still held court in a dingy office, on the edge of the townie part of the city, rather than moving into a compound nearer to the centre of government. It made his father unique, in Richard's experience. The townies had a handful of MPs, but most of them preferred to be closer to the government. And then they lost touch with their roots.

"Dad," he said. "It's good to see you again."

"I'll put the kettle on," Daniel Collier said. "You take a seat."

Richard hid his amusement. It was commonly believed aristos had a servant who put the tea leaves in the pot and another who poured the water and a third who stirred the liquid before making room for the fourth and fifth, who poured the milk and then the tea respectively, although he was fairly sure that was so implausible it was silly. And yet, they'd faint in shock at the sight of an MP making his own tea, even if he was sharing it with his son rather than an honoured guest. Richard was privately relieved his father hadn't allowed power to corrupt him, to give him a taste for fine living that could only be satisfied by the aristocracy. His father hadn't lost touch with his voters. Richard hoped it would stay that way.

He accepted a mug, smiling at how...*common*...the whole setup was. His father disdained fine bone china, let alone tealeaves. He used tea bags, and bottles of milk, and mugs that had clearly seen better days. Richard suspected it was a test, of sorts. The visitor who sneered at the ceremony was someone who couldn't be trusted, not completely, because he looked down on commoners. Who knew what he'd talk himself into doing, because it was being done to a commoner? Richard feared the worst.

"Your mother is looking forward to seeing you," Daniel Collier said, as he sat on the ancient armchair and rested his mug on his lap. "And your sister is continuing her medical work."

Richard frowned, inwardly. His sister had decided she wanted to be a nurse on the front lines, although—after much argument—she'd finally accepted a posting to a medical camp in the capital instead. It bothered him—he'd seen how cruel the rebels could be—even though he had to admit she was making something of herself. The family couldn't afford to keep their daughters at home, unlike the aristocracy. And the skills she'd learned as a nurse would help her attract a decent husband...

He leaned forward. "I heard Lady Porter was sent into exile."

"It was done very quickly," Daniel Collier confirmed. "Not an ideal situation, not for anyone, but better than we feared."

Richard wasn't so sure. "Would they really have tried to defend her?"

"Probably." Daniel Collier snorted. "The defence team would have had a field day. They'd have talked up her experiences, how her family was killed and she was raped and left for dead. They'd have blamed the rebels for triggering her, then General Windsor for putting her in the line of battle...they'd have blamed everyone, save for the silly girl herself. I don't know if it would have worked, as the evidence against her was pretty damning, but it would have snarled up the government for months. Sending her into exile lets everyone tell themselves they came out ahead."

"Typical," Richard said. "Does it work?"

"She wasn't given a medal, or patted on the back and told to get back to work," his father pointed out. "I suspect it was the best we could have expected."

"I see." Richard sipped his tea. "How is the power-sharing agreement working out?"

His father said nothing for a long moment. "It's hard to say," he admitted, finally. "There are times when everything is working smoothly, when the PM seems committed to making it work, and times when I have the impression some of the aristocrats are just waiting for a victory to start rolling back the reforms. The emergency powers have let us cut through a lot of red tape, and we've been able to cut the aristocracy out of much of our sphere of influence, but it may not last. They see us as paring down their age-old rights."

"We may not have helped fund the original settlement," Richard said flatly, "but we didn't go into debt just to settle here."

"No," his father agreed. "But the devil is in the details, as always."

He sighed, looking older than ever before. "Who owns the land outside the city? The aristocracy. Who compensates the original owners, when the land is turned over to us? Good question. It hasn't been properly settled, not yet. We may wind up paying higher taxes, just to pay for the land. I wanted to seize land owned by families that got wiped out, during the rebellion, but the aristocracy refused to even consider it. I can see their point—it would set a terrible precedent—but it is still a pain in the ass. And then we have to decide what we do about debtors. Trading military service for debt forgiveness is great on paper…"

"It is," Richard injected.

"…But it means someone else has to pick up the tab," his father finished. "And whoever owns the damnable debt wants compensation. I've got people haggling—we'll pay off the original debt, not the interest—but it's going slow. A large tranche of money is about to simply vanish, and—when the money didn't really exist in the first place—it's not easy to figure out if someone should be compensated, let alone how much they should be offered."

Richard stared into his cup. "I hate economics."

"They made the system as confusing as possible," his father agreed. "Right now, we are faced with paying compensation to people who bought the debt from the original owners or...hell, the debt passed through several sets of hands before reaching the *current* owners. I suspect it was intentional, either to confuse the debtors or to hide the fact the debts would never be repaid anyway. If that becomes public...anyone who owns such a debt is going to find themselves holding worthless pieces of paper. I think it won't be long before it dawns on the owners that it has really already happened."

"I hate economics," Richard repeated. "What can we do about it?"

"I don't know," Daniel Collier admitted. "We have considered simply offering a small amount of money for the worthless pieces of paper, more than they're actually worth whatever they may say. A penny or two would be moot if the value is effectively nothing. But once we start down that road, the owners will try to demand more and more..."

He shook his head as he caught himself. "If we try to do something about it now, the crisis will explode; if we don't, sooner or later we'll get the explosion anyway. And then the whole system comes tumbling down."

Richard met his eyes. "Is that a bad thing?"

"On the face of it, no," Daniel Collier said. "However, the effects will be utterly disastrous. It has happened before, according to my staff. If we go by the pre-Earthfall pattern...large sums of money will effectively vanish. The banks will find themselves short of cash. They'll respond by calling in all their debts, which will set off a chain of business failures that will throw hundreds of thousands of people out of work, smashing the tax base beyond hope of repair. The government cannot seize money that isn't actually there."

"They could confiscate the aristocracy's bank accounts," Richard pointed out. "They have billions salted away, just waiting for the taking."

"It would take a long time to convince them to do it," his father countered. "By the time they did, half the money would be hidden, or invested in things that couldn't be taken so easily. If that failed…it would work once, then utterly destroy confidence in the economy and make further investment impossible. And then…I don't know. Pre-Earthfall, the Imperial Bank stepped in and tried to provide a degree of stability. Now, the Imperial Bank no longer exists."

He shrugged. "It won't be a complete disaster," he added, as if he felt he'd gone a little too far. "We'd still be able to feed ourselves, unlike the Theta Sigma Banking Crash, which ended with starvation and civil war. But it would be a long time before we could recover."

Richard nodded, slowly. "So what do we do?"

"We treat the economy as an unexploded bomb and disarm it, very gingerly," his father said, quietly. He didn't sound hopeful. "And we hope for the best."

His terminal bleeped. "It's time to go back to work."

"I'll walk you there," Richard said, putting the empty mug aside and standing. "General Windsor expects all hands on deck, later this afternoon."

"Good," his father said. He clapped Richard on the shoulder. "Take care of him. If he gets killed, there'll be one hell of a struggle to decide who takes his place."

Richard nodded, as if the thought had never crossed his mind. "I will."

CHAPTER SIXTEEN

KINGSTON, NEW DONCASTER

ROLAND SMILED, INWARDLY, as he stepped into the council chambers and looked around. All nine councillors had been assembled, along with a handful of aristocratic and bureaucratic staffers, advisors, and general minions. Sandra herself was sitting in the corner of the chamber, a writing pad perched on her knees. Roland wondered, idly, if anyone was actually fooled by her pose. There was no need to have her, or anyone, transcribe the meeting. It was being recorded for posterity. But it was an excuse to have her in the room without anyone making an issue of it.

She isn't the worst problem, he thought, as he took his place. *It's the others who worry me.*

He sighed, inwardly. The government had tightened up security—there was nothing like a major insurgency in one's capital to convince a government it needed to be tougher—but he was convinced the rebel spies and informers hadn't been rooted out. The councillors might be above suspicion—personally, he doubted it—yet what about their aides, mistresses and even their maintenance staff? The young woman who brought the drinks might be listening to every word they said, relying on a low-cut dress and general sexism to keep her master from realising what she was doing. Roland ground his teeth in frustration. If it had been up to him, the council would be serving their own bloody drinks. The security risk was just too great.

The PM cleared his throat as the doors closed. "We are gathered here today to discuss the fighting on Mountebank and the implications it holds for the future," he said. "By prior agreement"—Roland wondered who'd made the agreement—"the matter of Lady Porter will not be discussed, not here. Our priority is the war."

Roland kept his face blank as he studied the councillors. They'd been deliberately excluded from yesterday's meeting and they knew it. Roland was sure they weren't happy, even though it gave them a cast-iron excuse to evade the blame if the whole affair blew up in their council's collective face. Having the decision made by the three senior councillors—realistically, the PM and Lord Ludlow—would not sit well with them. And yet, they could blame any blowback on their seniors too.

The PM looked at him. "General Windsor, the floor is yours."

"Thank you, Prime Minister," Roland said. He picked up the remote and keyed a switch, dimming the lights and activating the display. "Three days ago, the combined fleet—wet-navy fleet—launched a major invasion of Mountebank Island. The invasion, preceded by a major missile bombardment which disabled the enemy communications network, was successful in establishing a beachhead, then cutting the island in half and laying siege to Mountebank City itself. The rebel positions have been effectively neutralised."

He paused. "Thanks to the actions of She Who Must Not Be Mentioned"—he heard a handful of chuckles—"it has proven impossible, so far, to convince the rebels to surrender the city and march into POW camps. However, we have set up siege lines that will keep the rebels penned up until they starve or surrender. They do, we assume, have forces remaining within the jungle, but it will take some time for them to regroup and launch further offensives against our troops. Although it does look like a stalemate, unless we throw our troops at the city's defences, we have succeeded in our primary goals. We have tested our troops, as well as our ships and aircraft; we have proven we can fight and win an engagement on rebel-held territory. They cannot fail but take note of what we have done. The gulf between our positions and theirs is no longer an impassable barrier."

"Very good," the PM said. "I believe we owe you a vote of thanks."

There was a rumble of agreement. Roland hid his annoyance as the motion was proposed, then passed. A vote of thanks was effectively meaningless. It didn't bring him more troops, or more equipment, or even more freedom in determining his next moves. And the moment he fucked up, the vote of thanks would be swept off the record so quickly future readers would never know it had been there at all.

He cleared his throat. "The rebels still possess a considerable number of ships, as well as aircraft and armoured vehicles," he said. "Now we have given them a bloody nose, the rebel leadership will feel the urge to give us one in return. They can mount a spoiling attack of their own, or even try to land on Kingston for the second time. I believe we need to push ahead as quickly as possible."

Lord Ludlow leaned forward. "I was under the impression Kingston was heavily defended," he said. "Is that not true?"

"The more forces we commit to defending our rear areas, the less we have on hand to continue the offensive into enemy territory," Roland pointed out. Kingston was a *big* island. The idea he could afford to line the coastline with armoured divisions was absurd. "Our plans are to slow an invasion force, then pocket and destroy it. It should suffice."

"We need more forces to defend our rear," Ludlow insisted. "They could land anywhere they like, whenever they want."

Roland had to admit he had a point. New Doncaster's orbital surveillance network had been a joke even *before* the rebels had started shooting down the satellites. A wet-navy fleet that maintained perfect radio silence could sail from the rebel islands to Kingston and, as long as it was careful, wouldn't be detected until it got too close for comfort. Roland had deployed a handful of picket boats around the more important islands, and promised vast rewards to any fishermen who spotted an enemy fleet, but he had to admit the odds weren't good. The planet's weather was just too unpredictable. An enemy fleet would have plenty of cover if the rebels were prepared to take the risk.

"Perhaps we can spend more on the militia," the PM said. "Or working up newer armoured units on this island, rather than sending them elsewhere."

He tapped his table. "General?"

Roland adjusted the display. "There are hundreds of rebel-held islands," he said, as the display switched to a planetary map. There were hundreds of red islands scattered across the ocean, either overwhelmed by insurgents or simply snatched by rebels while the government's attention was diverted by events on Kingston. "However, most of them are of little immediate value. They have no industrial base, no way to influence events on the wrong side of the ocean. We can afford to leave them alone, for the moment. Given time, they may well be developed into threats, but we will do our best to ensure the rebels don't have the time."

He kept his face blank, wishing he didn't have to tell them so much. His words would probably reach the rebel leadership before too long, which meant...perhaps they wouldn't believe their ears. Perhaps they'd wonder if they were being conned. Perhaps...he told himself, sharply, that it was wishful thinking. The rebels had to be aware of their own weaknesses, as well as their advantages. They'd hear his words and see the sense behind them.

"There are three major *immediate* threats," Roland continued. "Baraka, Rolleston and Winchester. All three have sizable populations, respectable industrial bases and—in Baraka's case—probably the rebel leadership. Given time, the rebels can build up their position and eventually try to overwhelm us. I propose we capitalise on our brief advantage and invade one of the three islands. I submit Winchester would make the best target."

"You just told us the rebel leadership was on Baraka," Councillor Tiega said. "Would it not make a better target?"

"Baraka will be harder to reach, particularly if the nearby islands haven't been suppressed by the time the fleet arrives," Roland said. "We can overcome that problem, given time, but it leads neatly to a second one. If we kill or capture the rebel leaders, there will be no hope of organising an overall surrender. We will have to either overrun each of the other islands or commit ourselves to a permanent counterinsurgency campaign."

"Which would leave us back where we started," Ludlow said. "Why Winchester?"

Roland frowned. Ludlow was showing himself to be a better thinker than Roland had expected, which meant…what? "Winchester has a bigger industrial base than either of the other two islands. Capturing or destroying the factories would put a severe crimp in the rebel plans, even if we fail to defeat the island's defenders decisively. It also allows for us to withdraw, if the invasion fails, without risking total defeat. Neither of the other islands are anything so well-placed, from our point of view."

He paused. "Finally, if we turn the island into a base, the gulf between us and the remaining two islands will become a great deal shorter," he concluded. "Our logistics will be simpler, making it easier to deal with the other islands."

"Assuming you take the industrial base intact," Ludlow pointed out.

"I'm not assuming we will," Roland said, simply. He wanted to retake the factories, if only to keep the aristocrats from complaining they'd been smashed deliberately, but he wasn't optimistic. The rebels would be fools not to prepare the installations for destruction, in case the government forces came close to recovering them. "If we do, we do. If not…our plans will not need any adjustment."

He tapped the remote. "Assuming the plan works, we'll be in position to move on to Baraka before the rebels can react," he added. "If it doesn't work as quickly as we hope, we will still be in an advantageous position. Time will be on our side."

"Which is important," Daniel Collier said. "The rebels have off-world allies."

Roland nodded. *Someone* had given the rebels a great deal of modern weapons, someone who'd steadfastly refused to be identified. Secessionists? Warlords? Or merely interstellar traders? It wasn't impossible. Roland had little doubt merchants would sell their own mothers to make a buck—why *not* sell weapons to rebels on poor little New Doncaster? And yet...he suspected the worst. The off-worlders could have easily made contact with the government, if they'd wished. Instead, by dealing with the rebels... they might intend to support the rebels, if they won the war, or simply take over once the rebels had done the hard part.

"We need to move fast," he said. "Their allies may take a more active hand in events if we don't recover control quickly."

He winced, inwardly, at their grim expressions. New Doncaster had once been protected by the empire. Now...there was nothing stopping the nearest warlord from sending a cruiser, mounting a handful of demonstration KEW strikes, and then declaring New Doncaster the latest part of his empire. The planet's defences were so flimsy a lone pirate ship would have no trouble taking the high orbitals, then raining death on anyone who stood in their way. And if the rebels were prepared to make concessions to off-worlders...

I wonder if the off-worlders are playing both sides, Roland thought, suddenly. *It isn't as if half the government would hesitate to sell out the rest, if they thought they'd come out ahead.*

He dismissed the thought. "It will take upwards of four weeks, perhaps five, to lay the groundwork for the invasion," he continued. "Winchester is a far larger island than Mountebank, with far more powerful defences, and will require a considerably larger degree of effort from us. I believe we can launch the first stage of the operation within seven to eight weeks, assuming the timetable doesn't slip and force us to delay our departure. That will give the rebels more time than I would like to ready themselves—they will not expect us to rest on our laurels—but it can't be helped."

"We have the fleet," Ludlow said. "Why can't we move *now*?"

"Professionals study logistics," Roland said. He was tempted to add the observation about amateurs studying tactics. "We have the shipping, sir, but we expended a considerable amount of ammunition as well as equipment, both of which will need to be replaced. We will also have to pull some of the more experienced units off Mountebank, give the men some leave and use their experience to stiffen the less experienced units. We still have, very much, an army of amateurs. We need to learn lessons, particularly when they've been paid for in blood."

"Or we'll just have to learn them again," Daniel Collier said.

Roland nodded. The army was bigger than he'd dared hope, but it was still little more than a blunt instrument. It would take time, time he wasn't sure they had, to turn out special forces operators and specialists and everything else he'd need to tip the balance against the rebels. He wished, not for the first time, that he'd thought to request a bigger training team, perhaps even recruit ex-Imperial Army soldiers. It wasn't as if there was a shortage.

"The men need leave," he said, flatly. "And we need to learn our lessons, before we go back into war."

Ludlow nodded, stiffly. "It seems a workable plan."

"Thank you." Roland took a breath. "There is, also, a political issue that must be addressed."

He paused, letting his words hang in the air. "She Who Must Not Be Mentioned"—he ignored the PM's sharp look—"did a great deal of damage to our moral authority. We need to determine how we are going to treat prisoners quickly, before we start taking more of them. Frankly, we have to determine a long-term solution. There is no way we can send them off-world, councillors, or keep them in POW camps for the rest of their lives. We need a solution."

"I seem to recall we have discussed this before," Ludlow said. "You have raised the issue repeatedly, time and time again."

"Yes." Roland felt a hot flash of irritation. Ludlow was right. He had raised the issue many times. "It is no longer an academic issue, sir. We took nearly seven hundred prisoners on Mountebank, most of whom—as far as can be determined—are not guilty of being long-term rebels. They are former debt-slaves, either runaways or liberated by the rebels during the insurgency. What are we going to do with them? We need an answer now."

"They are debtors or indents," Ludlow said. "Let them be put back to work."

"If they think they will be put back to work, as you say, they will not surrender," Roland said, curtly. "With all due respect, conditions in the plantations are—were—awful and the debts were managed to ensure the poor bastards couldn't hope to get free. They know it as well as we do, if not better. They'll have no reason to surrender if they think they'll just be going back there."

"They do owe us money," Councillor Yang pointed out. "Or they were convicted of serious crimes."

Roland snorted. He'd checked the records. It was hard to be sure, unsurprisingly, but the majority of indentured settlers—slaves, in all but name—had been minor criminals or protesters at best. New Doncaster hadn't been interested in accepting major criminals—Roland didn't blame them—and Earth hadn't pressed the issue. The really major criminals would have been sent to hellish mining camps, where they would have been worked to death to pay for their crimes. Roland found it hard to be sorry for them. They deserved to suffer and die.

"So what?" Daniel Collier smiled as the rest of the councillors stared at him. "Is there any hope they'll ever be able to repay the money?"

He looked at Roland. "What do you suggest?"

"I'd suggest," Roland said, "letting them have a few islands to develop as they see fit."

"Out of the question," Ludlow said. "They need to pay."

"We cannot make them pay," Daniel Collier countered, sarcastically. "What are we going to do to them? Put them in the fields and make them work at gunpoint? Or tell them all will be forgiven if they put in a year or two..."

"Perhaps that might work," Roland said. "A year—a single year—helping to repair the plantations, then they're free to go. No games with their debts, no fiddling the figures...just make them serve one year, then let them go. Some of them might even stay, if paid a fair wage."

The PM tapped the table. "I believe we must discuss this in private."

"We need an answer soon," Roland said. It wasn't clear if the rebel leadership knew about the atrocity, but he wouldn't have cared to bet against it. "We need a policy, one we're prepared to put into place when we start the first major invasion, and we need to stick to it to encourage surrenders. Or else we'll be refighting the war ten years from now, with the rebels even more determined to win and even less inclined to trust us."

"A good argument," the PM said. "We will discuss it."

Roland stood back, recognising the dismissal. "It is vitally important the rebels don't learn we're coming," he said. He feared his words would land on deaf ears, but he had to try. "Do not share the target, or the planned timescale, or anything with anyone outside the council. If the rebels have time to get ready for us, the invasion will end badly."

"We'll take your words under advisement," the PM said. He was already inclining towards Ludlow, who seemed to have something to say. "And thank you for your time."

Roland saluted, then turned and left.

CHAPTER SEVENTEEN

KINGSTON, NEW DONCASTER

MARILYNN LOOKED AROUND the private room and tried not to be sick.

It looked like a high-class apartment. The furnishings were real. The long dress she'd donned, after a shower, was real. The dinner on the table, cooked to perfection by a trained chef, was real. And yet, the whole affair was as fake as a treasure starchart pointing to a world of ancient aliens, or long-lost tech that would turn its new owners into the wealthiest men who ever lived. It was hard, sometimes, to let herself slip into the role, not when she was all too aware she was little more than an actor on a stage. She would never have the life before her for herself and she knew it. She wondered, sometimes, how easily her clients forgot it wasn't real.

Because they're getting what they want, she told herself, as the timer bleeped. *And they don't want to question it, because questioning would destroy the illusion they want so desperately.*

She glanced at the timer—five minutes to go—and then inspected herself in the mirror. She was tall, but not too tall; her long brown hair and dark dress designed to give an impression of demure womanhood and domestic bliss, rather than a whore or even a mistress. It baffled her why her clients couldn't get the real thing—she wasn't *that* expensive—but perhaps they didn't really want a loving and caring wife, just someone they could rent for a few hours. She twisted slightly, her experienced eyes running over every last detail. The slightest flaw could undo the illusion, then bring her world crashing down around her. Bad for her, naturally, but worse for her clients.

The timer bleeped, again. She lit the candles and dimmed the lights, then headed to the door as someone pressed the bell. She checked the viewer before opening the door—the government's security forces had been more active lately, although she had enough friends in high places to ensure she remained off whatever suspect list they'd compiled—and then beckoned Samuel Vernon into the apartment, giving him an affectionate kiss on the cheek as he placed a gift-wrapped box on the table beside the door. It was all part of the illusion, all designed to convince her clients they really *weren't* buying her companionship for a few short hours. She felt sorry for them, sometimes. She would have felt sorrier if they hadn't been part of a machine that had ground her parents into the dirt, then threatened to do the same to her. Outwitting men too desperate to think clearly was her only means of revenge.

"Let me take your coat," she said, gently. "Long day at the office?"

"Yes," Vernon said. He would have been handsome, if he'd bothered to take the time to exercise before his six-pack had become a keg. He wasn't precisely ugly, Marilynn had thought, but he'd find it hard to get a woman's attention. "They're keeping us busy all day."

Marilynn nodded as she took his coat, then steered him to the table. The trick to getting a man to open up was not to press too hard, nor to look too disinterested. Men disliked being forced to talk, to the point that demanding answers made them clam up—or lie—instead. Marilynn had never understood why so many *real* wives failed to grasp the point, although she had a feeling it had something to do with them being secure in their position. She wasn't a real wife, someone who couldn't be discarded in a hurry. She couldn't afford to become complacent, let alone make him resent her, or he'd dump her so quickly her head would spin.

"I made your favourite," she said, pulling out a chair for him. "Lamb shanks, cooked in stew, with mash and peas."

Vernon nodded, waiting for her to pour the wine and then take her own seat facing him. She'd been amused to discover his tastes were so plebeian—he could easily have afforded something a little more expensive—but perhaps his mother had cooked something similar, when he'd been a child. It wouldn't have surprised her. The previous generation of townies hadn't needed to send both parents out to work, ensuring the mother could stay at home and look after the kids. Now…Vernon would be lucky if he married at all, let alone found a wife who could afford to stay home. She felt a twinge of sympathy, which she ruthlessly suppressed. Vernon was a source, nothing more. She could no more afford sympathy than guilt.

She sat and ate, listening quietly as Vernon slowly unburdened himself. The bureaucracy, hastily expanded along with the army, the navy, the security services and everything else, was working desperately to prepare for the coming invasion. They were going to be striking Rolleston, Vernon told her; they were going to take the war deep into the heart of rebel territory. Marilynn memorised everything, keeping a subtle eye on Vernon to make sure he wasn't trying to mislead her. She found it hard to believe the invasion target had been openly discussed, even amongst bureaucrats and civil servants who firmly believed security laws and regulations didn't apply to them. She'd hated their arrogance, their conviction they were always in the right even when they were in the wrong, when she'd been a young girl. Now, she had to admit it had its uses. Vernon told her everything and he didn't seem to think there was anything wrong with it.

"I'll be joining the fleet," Vernon boasted. "We're due to leave in four weeks."

Marilynn did her best to look fearful for his safety, as an ideal wife should. She didn't think he was lying, but she was fairly sure he wasn't going to sail into danger either. Vernon was no fighter. He wasn't *that* bad, certainly not compared to some of her more perverse clients, but no one in their right mind would put a gun in his hand, let alone point him at the enemy and tell him to charge. Perhaps he had enemies amongst his superiors...no, that wasn't too likely. The planet was under martial law. If someone wanted to get rid of him, it would be as simple as assigning him to an isolated posting in the middle of nowhere or simply firing his fat ass.

"You will be careful, won't you?" She kept her voice low. "I don't want to see you hurt."

Vernon smiled, as if she'd touched his heart, then started to tell her all about the fleet's security precautions. Marilynn listened, comparing his words to what she'd learnt from her other clients. It was hard to put together a precise picture—there were limits to how much she could ask them, without raising their suspicions—but the details were steadily coming together. The government was raising more troops, as well as expanding both the regular army and the militia. Vernon seemed to think a great deal of effort was being duplicated, for reasons beyond his understanding. Marilynn didn't pretend to understand it either.

She finished the dinner with a simple chocolate pudding, then waited. Her clients didn't *just* want sex, something that had baffled her when she'd become a courtesan. They wanted her companionship, her presence...Vernon would signal, she knew, if he wanted to take her to bed. Sometimes, he just wanted to linger in her presence before going back to his real home, an apartment near the government complex. He lived alone...she sighed, inwardly, as she recalled the signals he'd been making about turning their arrangement into something more permanent. He wanted a real wife and...

Don't feel sorry for him, she told herself, sharply. *Without him and his peers, the government simply couldn't function.*

Vernon stood, then took her arm and led her into the bedroom. Marilynn put her doubts aside and forced herself to play the game, even though Vernon was...bland. He wasn't into really kinky stuff, nor was he the type of person to ever threaten to hurt her if she didn't submit to him... there was something pathetic about him, something she regretted even as she took full advantage of it. He was no different, she reflected, than someone playing a VR game where they had an unlimited bank account and could purchase whatever they wanted, because money was no object. She played her role to perfection, despite her strange combination of guilt and boredom. Vernon was getting too clingy, too deeply invested in the pretence. She might have to break it off soon, for her own safety as well as his. Who knew what would happen if he had a breakdown at work?

"I should go," Vernon said, after a quick shower and a change into fresh clothes. He wanted her to tell him to stay, but she couldn't. "I'll see you in a couple of days?"

"Just email me," Marilynn said. She gave him a deep kiss, then walked him to the door. "Be careful out there."

She didn't let herself weaken until the door was firmly closed, then sat on the sofa and took great heaving breaths to calm herself. It was hard not to feel guilt. It was hard…she clenched her teeth, then stood and forced herself to clean up the mess. The apartment block had cleaning staff on hand, but she didn't dare let them into her apartment for fear of what they'd find. She rinsed the plates, then stacked them in the dishwasher as she recalled everything he'd told her. The invasion was a month off… perhaps. She wished, once again, that she could ask him directly. But it would be far too revealing.

Her terminal bleeped, a reminder she had an appointment tomorrow at the delicatessen. It would pass unnoticed, if the security services had their eye on her. She dared not assume she was completely safe. No one would be surprised if she visited a high-class shop, where she could purchase the very finest of foods, before wandering down to the clothes shop and trading whatever Vernon had given her for cold hard cash. Her lips twitched. It was…pathetic. Vernon was buying the services of a whore, not a wife. Did he know she had other clients? Or did he delude himself that she was his mistress?

She went to the bathroom, showered quickly and clambered into bed. Her alarm woke her the following morning, snapping her out of an uncomfortable sleep. She dressed, ate a small breakfast, then hurried out of the apartment and down the stairs to the giant shopping complex underneath. Policemen were everywhere, watching warily for threats to the upper-class townies and civil servants who lived and worked nearby. Marilynn wasn't too impressed. They might not be as corrupt as the policemen who worked the docks—she'd been told they could be bribed very cheaply—but they knew when to pretend they hadn't seen something. They ignored her clients, even though they should pay close attention to them. She felt an odd little thrill as she walked past a pair of policemen, their eyes following her. They didn't see anything but the mask she wore when she was out and about.

It was early morning, but the deli was already busy. A handful of wealthy women were clustered in front of the display, displaying their expensive fur coats and handbags as they competed for the last of the rare and expensive foodstuffs. Marilynn hid her amusement with an effort as she signalled the youngest shopgirl, who led her into the office behind the shop. There was little difference between her and the women, she thought, although the women no longer had to work at keeping their husband's attention. She could spot a social climber a mile away. They'd been born upper-class townies and, somehow, they thought they could clamber into the aristocracy itself.

Poor Vernon, she reflected, wryly. *Even if he did get married to someone of his class, she'd be constantly looking for someone above him.*

The manager—and her contact—rose to greet her. "It's good to see you again," he said, as he picked a scanner off the desk and swept it over her. "I trust you're ready for the next shipment?"

"Of course," Marilynn said, keeping her voice light, with just a hint of aristocracy. She couldn't afford to relax, not now. Better to be taken as just another social climber than a spy. "The last batch of sliced ham was just perfection."

"Good, good," the manager said. His voice grew more authoritative as the scanner revealed Marilynn was clean. "Did you learn anything useful?"

"Perhaps," Marilynn said. "If my guests are to be believed, the target is Rolleston."

The manager—she'd been careful never to learn his name, for more reasons than the obvious—frowned. "Do you believe him?"

"I believe he thinks he's telling the truth," Marilynn said. "But it's quite possible someone lied to him."

"I've heard it from a couple of other people," the manager confirmed. "It isn't something anyone would *want* to get out."

Marilynn nodded. The government leaked like a sieve. There was no way anyone in the lower bureaucracy could keep a secret, not when they saw it as a chance to impress their families or friends or...or people like her. And if she knew it, chances were that the government's officials knew it too. They could have told their people a lie, in the certain knowledge the lie would be spread right to the rebel leadership. No one would know the truth until it was far too late.

She shrugged—it wasn't her problem—then outlined the rest of what she'd heard. The production figures. The enlistment numbers. The ever-expanding bureaucratic infrastructure to govern the planet. She hadn't been surprised to hear tax revenues were falling. Between the loss of so many plantations, and townies joining the army, the tax base was actually shrinking. Vernon hadn't said as much, but—sooner or later—the government was going to start running out of money. What would it do about the problem? It wasn't as if it could take money that simply didn't exist.

Not my problem, she told herself. She'd salted away quite a bit of money, as well as concealing caches of supplies and gifts she'd been given over the years. *If they raise taxes, I should be fine.*

She finished, taking the papers he offered her and signing her name with a flourish. She *was* a valued customer, as far as the deli was concerned. The manager had every incentive to keep her sweet, providing a perfect excuse for a private meeting. She scanned the papers, then stood. She didn't know how he'd smuggle her report out of the city, although she had some theories. The war hadn't been allowed to interfere with the fishing industry, where fishermen from both sides shared fishing grounds. They even helped each other out, much to the fury of both government and rebel leaders. She guessed it provided a channel for covert communication, ensuring messages could be passed from place to place without being intercepted. She knew better than to ask. It had been made clear to her, when she'd been recruited, that *anyone* could be forced to talk. She couldn't tell what she didn't know.

The manager escorted her to the door, then waved her goodbye as she strolled down the street towards the clothes shops. There were more policemen visible outside the more expensive places, although she wasn't sure why. The mall was incredibly secure. No one could hope to snatch a bag and run, not without being caught as they tried to go outside. She overheard a pair of older women talking about rumours and scandal within the aristocracy, turning the details over and over again as they searched for advantage. Marilynn couldn't help thinking it was stupid. So what if Lord Someone cheated on Lady Someone? Lord Someone would remain a lord and his lady would have no choice but to tolerate his adultery. It wouldn't clear room for a pair of social climbers to clamber up a couple of rungs, then make their way to the top.

Everyone needs their illusions, she reflected, as she stepped into the shop. *Even I need mine.*

Marilynn scowled, causing the shopgirl to flinch. Marilynn cursed inwardly, then tried to look apologetic even though most women of quality—or women who thought they were quality—wouldn't apologise to a mere servant even if they were completely in the wrong. The shopgirl didn't look relieved. Marilynn slipped her a tip, then took her bag to the manager. He'd take a look, then refund the money Vernon had paid…she wondered, wryly, if he knew what they were really doing. Marilynn would hardly be the first wife to return her husband's gifts time and time again, trading them for something she *really* wanted. Or maybe he thought it was just a money laundering scheme. The plans to create a wholly electronic currency had proved unworkable. New Doncaster simply didn't have the infrastructure.

It doesn't matter, she told herself. There was a certain safety in concealing a major crime behind a minor one. *If anyone looks at me, they'll see nothing but a high-class courtesan to a bunch of desperate men. They won't see the truth.*

She smiled, coldly, despite the guilt. She'd watched her parents get crushed under the weight of official indifference. She'd do more, she'd do a hell of a lot more, just to ensure the government was brought down. She would have her revenge, for herself and for her long-dead parents. And, in the end, that was all that really mattered.

CHAPTER EIGHTEEN

KINGSTON, NEW DONCASTER

ANGELINE HAD NOT, IN ANY PRACTICAL SENSE, been given any training in how to run an estate. She'd been told it was something for the men, something she shouldn't worry her pretty little head about. She should leave it to them, while concentrating on attracting and keeping a good husband who'd take care of such things for her. It had been Angeline's mother who had quietly—very quietly—showed her the books and taught her how to read them, pointing out she couldn't be a good helpmate if she didn't know how to help. Angeline suspected, in hindsight, her mother had been trying to teach her something very important. She just wished she'd spent more time studying, despite her father's opposition. But she'd been a very different person back then.

She sighed, inwardly, as she surveyed the records in front of her. She'd wondered, as she'd eaten the first of many good meals, why Lord Ludlow had gone to so much trouble to secure her services. She didn't have anywhere to go, she supposed, but her mere presence was a dangerous liability. It hadn't made any sense, until she'd looked at the records and realised that anyone with any *real* military experience had been called into service. Lord Ludlow's private retainers and guardsmen had been gravely weakened. It hadn't been easy to put together more than a handful of men, let alone arm them with modern weapons without sending up red flags. Angeline suspected, reading between the lines, that the books had been thoroughly cooked. The men she would be joining, the men she would be *leading*, had all been reported dead, or granted official exemptions, or—in some other way—excluded from the draft. She feared it wasn't good news. The only reason the draft board had overlooked the men was because they had no experience at all.

Neither did you, she reflected, as she stood. *And you did well, didn't you?*

The thought haunted her as she made her way out of the hunting lodge and into the clearing beyond. Lord Ludlow's estate was huge, easily large enough to conceal thousands of trainees. It was a little crude, compared to the facilities near the capital, but it would suffice for the moment. They'd have to bring in more men over the next few months, rapidly multiplying their forces…she glanced up into the cloudy sky, hoping there was enough cover to keep the government—or the rebels—from spying on the estate. Lord Ludlow had seemed convinced they were safe, that his contacts would inform him if the estate came under investigation, but Angeline wasn't so sure. The moment someone spotted her, the entire edifice would come tumbling down.

They'd have to recognise you first, she reminded herself. *And you look nothing like the pictures in your file.*

She smiled, despite herself. She'd cut her hair short, when she'd joined the army; now, she'd shaved it completely and treated her scalp to ensure her hair wouldn't grow back in a hurry. The estate's autodoc—a piece of equipment that was technically illegal, as it should have been handed over to the military—had erased the scars on her body, changed her eye colour and altered her fingerprints beyond easy recognition. She couldn't fool a DNA test, but one wouldn't be carried out unless the government was already suspicious. And…she smiled, again, as she stepped into the clearing. If that happened, she was fucked anyway. Again.

Her eyes swept the small gathering of young men. They weren't precisely the dregs she'd feared—gamekeepers and estate workers had been granted exemptions, as well as doctors and nurses and government bureaucrats—and they were fitter than she'd dared hope, but it wasn't going to be easy to assert her authority. Some of them were aristos, others…were young men who hadn't had any real military experience. She hid her annoyance with an effort. They'd just have to get used to her.

"We are here to train, to prepare to do the tasks the government is unwilling to do," she said, without preamble. Lord Ludlow—and his recruiting officers—would have hired them, paid them, and explained *precisely* what would happen if they breathed a word out of turn. "If any of you have a problem with me in command, this is your one chance to say so. Afterwards, you'll go straight into the pits."

She waited, bracing herself. It was an open secret there were cells—the pits—under aristocratic mansions. The aristos were the only source of law and order on the estates, the authority rarely questioned even by their peers. If they decided to defy her…she almost hoped they'd do it now, when she'd challenged them. Later, if she was backed by threats and naked force, they'd find it harder to respect her personally. Angeline scowled, inwardly. The men in front of her had *not* been raised to consider women as anything other than mothers, sisters or wives.

A young man leered at her, then stepped forward, right into her personal space. "And you expect us to take orders from you…?"

Angeline punched him, hard enough to send him tumbling backwards. She darted forward and placed her foot on his chest before he could rise, pinning him down. He was probably stronger than her, if he'd spent his life in the fields, but she knew what she was doing. And…she had to be seen to beat him fairly. It was the only way they'd come to respect her.

"I know what I'm doing," she said, simply. She held his eyes for a moment, then made a show of removing her foot and turning away. "Anyone else?"

No one spoke. Angeline hid her relief. The first challenger had underestimated her…odd, when his mother and sisters probably worked the fields too. Perhaps he'd thought she was just another aristo girl who never lifted anything heavier than her pet cat. Angeline looked about as un-aristocratic as it was possible to be, yet…would she even have been *here*, on the estate, if she didn't have ties to the aristocracy? She shrugged, inwardly, as she turned to face them. She'd done as much as she could to ensure they thought of her as a soldier, rather than a young woman. And if they didn't listen…

"We will be going into combat soon," she said. Ludlow hadn't been clear on *precisely* when they'd be turning their plans into reality, but she feared they had months at most. "If you listen to me, to someone who has actually been there, you will have a decent chance at surviving. If not, the odds are good you will be killed when the bullets start flying. If we lose…"

She paused. "The rebels destroy lives and burn crops, to the point their islands are starving because they wiped out their own food supplies. They kill men and rape women and kidnap children, adding them to their ranks. Anyone who refuses to support them, for any reason at all, gets the same treatment. They may claim they are fighting for the people, but they are really fighting for themselves. Their cause is just an excuse to impose their own order."

Her voice hardened, although she knew it wasn't really necessary. Lord Ludlow had picked his men well. They were all loyalists, the kind of men who would help their master bury the body and provide alibis when—if—someone came asking questions. Angeline's own father had had his own loyalists…she wondered, in a flicker of grim insight, what had happened to them. Had they betrayed him? Or had they merely been the first to die, that grim night?

"We are all that stands between our way of life and monsters," she said. "And we have no choice, but to do whatever we must to save our people."

She barked orders, carefully not giving them time to think. Their military bearing was non-existent—she kicked herself, mentally, for being surprised—but at least they knew how to listen. She led them in route marches, then runs, then back to the firing range to learn how to handle military weapons. They were already experienced with firearms, somewhat to her relief. They didn't have anything like as far to go as her former comrades.

Keep them busy, she told herself, as the day wore on. *Make them work to impress you.*

It was almost a relief, despite everything, when the day finally came to an end. Angeline sent the men to their barracks, where they would be fed and watered and told to sleep before resuming in the morning, then made her way back to her office. Lord Ludlow was waiting for her, sitting in a comfortable armchair. She was too tired to hide her surprise. She'd been in good condition, after six months of intensive training, but the trainees had pushed her to the limit. They'd grown up in the countryside, spending most of their days outside. They might lack discipline, but the raw material was there.

"My Lord," she managed. She couldn't even curtsey. "I beg your pardon. It has been a long day."

"So I gather," Lord Ludlow said. His tone suggested he'd been watching the proceedings for a while. Angeline wondered when he'd arrived, then dismissed the question as pointless. "When do you think they'll be ready?"

Angeline hesitated. "At best, three months," she said. "I learned the basics myself in two months, sir, but I had instructors who knew what they were doing. Realistically, that may be insanely optimistic."

"I defer to your experience," Lord Ludlow said. "We have been informed that the military will be launching the next invasion in a few short weeks, unless the timetable is thrown off by unforeseen events. I'd like to have our forces ready to act if the government fails in its duty."

"It may not be possible," Angeline cautioned. "The more newcomers we add, the harder it will be to avoid...accidents."

"Or attract attention," Lord Ludlow said. His eyes sharpened, suddenly. "Your men will also need to be blooded, won't they?"

"Yes, sir," Angeline said. "But we need to deal with the basics first."

"Quite." Lord Ludlow stood. "I have to be back in the city for tomorrow. You know the code key, but only use it if there's a genuine emergency. The staff should be able to provide anything you could reasonably request."

"We need more training gear," Angeline said. "Can we arrange for some to fall off the back of a lorry somewhere?"

Lord Ludlow didn't smile. "We'll see what we can find," he said. "But these days, it is a great deal harder to fiddle with the books."

Angeline nodded. "Yes, sir."

• • •

Richard shivered, despite the heat.

He was a city boy, born and bred, and the watery darkness terrified him at a very primal level. The freighter was nothing more than a dark hulk, drifting on a dark sea, with nary a light to mark its presence as the speedboat roared towards it. Richard was *sure* the watcher in the crow's nest could hear the boats, even if he couldn't see them. In his place, Richard would be raising the alarm right now, screaming for all hands on deck. A stiff resistance might just be enough to keep the soldiers from gaining a foothold, let alone seizing the ship.

"Cut the engines," he ordered, as the speedboat came alongside. "Follow me."

He lifted the grappling gun, aimed it at the vessel's superstructure and pulled the trigger. The grapple shot out, striking the vessel with an audible *clang*. Richard braced himself as he was yanked forward, lifting his legs so he could walk up the side of the hull. His head spun, his perspective shifting, as he reached the railing and clambered over the rails, letting go of the grappling gun as he landed on the deck. A sailor grabbed for a gun, too late. Richard knocked him down as the rest of the boarding party landed around him, then led the way to the bridge. Two more sailors tried to block their way. They got knocked down too.

A dull rumble echoed through the ship as the engines came online. Richard gritted his teeth as the deck shifted below his feet, then pushed onwards into the bridge. The ship's captain made a show of staring at him, then lifted his hands as Richard pointed his rifle at the man's chest. The rest of the crew followed suit, allowing the boarding party to take control and shut the engines down again. Ten minutes later, with the entire crew prisoner, it was all over.

Richard keyed his radio. "ENDEX," he said. "I say again, ENDEX. The exercise is now terminated."

"We could have kept you from boarding, if we'd been allowed to notice you a little sooner," the captain growled. He didn't sound happy about his ship being used for an exercise, or—Richard suspected—the threat of having his ship impounded if he didn't play fair. "You got lucky."

"We'll be trying it again under harder conditions," Richard assured him. He would have preferred to use jetpacks to land on the freighter, but there were only a handful on the entire planet. "Next time, you get to greet us with a hail of fire."

The captain didn't seem pleased, as he resumed his post. Richard understood. There weren't *many* independent freighter captains and most of them had sided with the rebels, after years of struggling with government bureaucracy and corporate harassment. *This* captain had been unlucky, his vessel laid up for repairs when open war broke out. He'd had no choice but to pledge allegiance to the reformed government. Richard suspected the captain would have preferred to join the rebels instead, if things had been different. The man needed to be watched.

"Take us back into harbour," Richard ordered. The speedboats were already casting off, readying themselves to return to their base. "We'll meet the rest of the force there."

He mentally composed his report as the ship came to life, coming about and heading for Kingsport. Roland would need to know what had worked and what hadn't, particularly anything that might cause problems against an enemy armed and ready to repel borders. This time, their target had been a sitting duck; the next, the freighter might be moving at high speed, adding yet another variable to an exercise already plagued by them. He spoke briefly to the rest of his team, then forced himself to explore the rest of the freighter. It was small, compared to some of the bigger corporate vessels, but still easily large enough to carry hundreds of soldiers.

The rebels had proved it, when they'd launched the invasion of Kingston. They'd sent dozens of freighters into Kingsport, each one crammed to the gunwales with armed men. And they'd come very close to success.

They'll be expecting us to do the same, he reflected. The reports suggested the rebels were searching each and every ship that tried to enter their ports, a precaution that irritated shipping officers yet made perfect sense. *And that means we need to find a new way to get onto the island.*

He was still considering it as dawn broke, revealing the port of Kingsport in all its glory. The harbour city had been badly battered by the fighting—the old skyline was gone, never to return—but the people were slowly bringing it back to life. Fishing boats headed out to sea, followed by warships and converted freighters. Richard felt a stab of sympathy for the soldiers on the latter, knowing they were being encouraged to develop their sea legs before the next invasion formally began. It wasn't going to be an easy time for anyone. There were no island bases near the target, nowhere they could amass their forces before going into combat. But they'd just have to cope.

We need more time, he thought, numbly.

The smell of decaying fish drifted through the air as the freighter tied up at its assigned dock. A handful of militiamen stood ready to search the vessel, backed up by a pair of makeshift tanks and a single IFV. They weren't the real threat, Richard recalled. The army maintained several companies on permanent readiness; half stationed at the gates, the other half just outside Kingsport. The rebels wouldn't get a second chance to storm the city, not now. They'd come far too close to winning the war outright, six months ago.

"Good luck," the captain said. He sounded about as welcoming as a husband greeting his wife's lover. Richard had met friendlier people when he'd applied for military service. "We'll be here when you need us."

Richard nodded, trying not to yawn. It was early morning, but he hadn't slept all night. Perhaps he could go to the barracks and get some sleep before reporting to his superior or visit one of the brothels that had been reopened, after the fighting had died down six months ago. Or...he shook his head. He had to report in first, then find his bed. It wasn't *that* long a drive to the training base.

"I'll see you next time," he said. It might not be *him*—Roland had told Richard not to put his life in danger—but he'd wanted to know what he was asking his subordinates to do, before they did it. "And thank you for the use of your vessel."

The captain snorted. "Thank me by paying my bill," he said. "Or giving me priority for resupply."

"I'll do what I can," Richard promised. He understood the older man's feelings, really he did. "But right now, I have to go report in."

CHAPTER NINETEEN

KINGSTON, NEW DONCASTER

"TELL ME SOMETHING," Roland said, as he stared down at the map. "How does the Commandant handle all the details himself?"

"He doesn't." Rachel looked up at him and smiled. "He has a staff. He has people who take his vague concepts—invade that planet, defeat that enemy—and turn them into workable, practical, plans. Most of them have served themselves, certainly long enough to understand the realities on the ground. The Commandant doesn't have to let himself get bogged down in detail, or spend his time micromanaging his subordinates."

"He has people to do it for him," Roland muttered. "I need a bigger staff, don't I?"

"Yes," Rachel agreed. "But you don't have the people you need."

Roland couldn't disagree. The last six weeks—the timetable had slipped, then slipped again—had been hectic. He'd brought units back from Mountebank, giving his soldiers leave before preparing them to return to the fray; he'd watched newer soldiers graduate, then get assigned to units that would—hopefully—teach them what the DIs hadn't before they learnt the hard way. He'd inspected tanks and aircraft, rolling off the production lines, and watched drivers and pilots as they put their vehicles through their paces. And he'd checked and rechecked the growing wet-navy fleet, preparing itself for the next offensive.

And I don't have enough people capable of handling the planning, he reminded himself, sourly. *We need to build up a bigger logistics staff.*

They'd spent the last two weeks running drills, the first turning into a disaster so great that—if the bullets had been *real*—the defeat would have been near-total. It was galling to realise the only thing standing between him and total defeat was his own shortage of shipping, but… the only upside, as far as he could tell, was that the shock had convinced his people they needed to work harder too. They'd studied the results carefully, determined what had gone wrong and done their best to fix it, although they wouldn't *know* how well they'd done until they went into battle. The rebels knew they were coming. Roland would bet his title, whatever it was worth now, that they were already laying their plans to defeat him.

"We won't have the advantage of surprise this time," he said, sourly. "They'll see us coming well before we reach our target."

"Perhaps not," Rachel agreed. "But we can keep them guessing about our final destination."

Roland eyed her suspiciously, wondering if she was trying to cheer him up. The rebels weren't stupid. They'd have no trouble at all narrowing down the list of possible targets, and the forces to defend all three of them. He'd done his best to spread rumours about his plans to hit Rolleston, a lie which had the great advantage of being plausible, but he feared the rebels wouldn't buy it. Even if they did, they might try to defend other possible targets too. His plans assumed they'd have no advantage of surprise whatsoever.

"If we can get ashore in force, we should be able to secure the industrial facilities," he said, tiredly. He'd said the same to the war council, time and time again. "And then we can start putting an end to the war."

"Perhaps," Rachel agreed. She looked concerned. "Do you still intend to hold the command conference this afternoon?"

Roland hesitated, then nodded. New Doncaster's wet navy lacked both holoconference projectors and the secure datanet required to use them. The command conference would be his last chance to meet his subordinates in person, before the fleet set sail for rebel territory and destiny. It would be the last time he could shake their hands, gauge their true feelings and—in confidence—address any concerns they might have, concerns they wouldn't want to put on the record. The PM had wanted to hold a farewell ceremony, but Roland—and Lord Ludlow, oddly—had objected. There was no point in letting the rebels know they were coming any sooner than strictly necessary.

Don't delude yourself, he told himself. *You may have staggered the departure times, so it looks like a number of ships leaving alone rather than in convoy, but you're not going to fool anyone for long.*

"Get some rest now." Rachel met his eyes. "You've done all you can do, given the limitations you're facing. Go back to your bedroom, spend some time in bed—with Sandra, if she's around. And awake fresh and rested for the conference."

Roland nodded, tiredly. It was easy to forget, at times, that Rachel was a far more experienced soldier than he was. And at other times…he sighed as he stumbled to his feet, his body crying out for coffee or sleep. There were just too many things to do, too many glitches in the supply lines that required his personal attention, too many problems that could only be sorted out by himself. He scowled as he recalled the discovery, too late, that an underpaid bureaucrat had sold a crate of weapons and training supplies to the rebels, a crate that had never been recovered. It wasn't a major loss, but it had undermined his position at the worst possible time.

He forced himself to keep going until he was back in his bedroom, staring at his bed as if it represented paradise. It was just a camp bed, rough and primitive compared to the four-poster bed he recalled from his childhood, but it was infinitively superior to conditions in the field. He'd made sure no one, neither army officers nor naval captains, received anything beyond the basics. Giving superior officers luxuries denied to the men was just asking for trouble.

Roland heard someone behind him and turned. Sandra stood there, looking wary. Roland guessed Rachel had called her and wondered, wryly, what she'd said. Rachel had never approved of Sandra, pointing out her seduction had been too corny to be real and that she was probably reporting back to her father. Roland didn't doubt it, but still...he had to look bad, he supposed, if Rachel was calling Sandra to take care of him. He could barely keep his eyes open.

"Bed," Sandra said, closing the door behind her. "Now."

Roland muttered something—he wasn't sure what he'd said—and collapsed into the sheets, the bed shifting underneath him. There had been times when he'd had trouble sleeping, when he'd been a little prince, but now...darkness swept over him, sending him plunging down into dreams. He was vaguely aware of her presence, yet...it felt like hours before a pinging sound yanked him out of sleep. Sandra was lying next to him, reading a datapad. Roland was so dazed it took him a moment to realise it was his terminal that was bleeping.

His fingers mashed the buttons. "Yes?"

"I've postponed the command conference for two hours, as Admiral Forest has orders to report to the war council," Rachel said. "Have a shower, eat something, then report to the briefing room at 1900."

Roland had to smile. "Yes, boss."

Sandra blinked at him. "You let her talk to you like that?"

"She's right," Roland said, although he knew it wasn't anything like enough of an explanation. As far as anyone on the base knew, Rachel was just his aide. Richard was the only person who knew more and he'd been cautioned not to discuss it. "And we have served together long enough for her to tease me a little."

He stood, then hastily removed his uniform. His fingers still felt numb, forcing him to concentrate on doing something he could normally have done automatically. He didn't want her to try to help him, not now. Instead, she started to undress herself. Roland watched, feeling oddly conflicted, as she stripped. It felt wonderful and yet...it felt as if she was just playing a role. Normally, it wouldn't have bothered him. Now...

"You will come back, won't you?" Sandra kissed him as he mounted her, wrapping her arms around him. "Won't you?"

"I'll do my best," Roland promised. "I should be fine."

Sandra didn't seem convinced as she pulled him to her. Roland tried to lose himself in her, to forget his woes as he moved inside her. He'd learnt to be a little cold about sex, after discovering there was nothing like being the heir to the throne to make you attractive to women, but... he thought, for the first time, that Sandra was giving her all to him. The cynical part of his mind wondered if she thought she'd gone too far. Did she have feelings for him? Or did she think she'd be in deep shit, after he left? It wasn't impossible. Roland wasn't sure if she'd been a virgin, when they'd made love for the first time, but she sure as hell wasn't now.

Forget about it, he told himself. *She knew what she was doing when she seduced you.*

A flash of pleasure ran through him, followed by a strange surge of energy. He kissed her lightly, his mind already returning to everything he had to do. Sandra didn't seem to notice. Roland forced himself to stand, then headed for the shower. He'd wash and dress and eat, then attend the conference before flying out to the fleet. And then...

"Hang on," Sandra said. "I'm coming."

Roland felt a flicker of affection as she joined him in the shower, her bare breasts glistening under the water. He stepped back to let her wash, wondering if he was developing feelings for her. How would he know, if he was? It wasn't as if he'd ever had a real partner before, not when he'd been in the gilded cage. They'd been his servants, unable to say no, or people who wanted something from him. Belinda...he'd had a crush on Belinda, he admitted to himself, but she'd never been interested. Why should she be?

He scrubbed her back, then turned to allow her to return the favour. What was she thinking? Did she hope he'd stay, permanently? Or did she hope he'd take her with him, when he was finally recalled? It wasn't impossible. The DIs had warned their young recruits that there was never any shortage of young women willing to do anything, anything at all, in exchange for getting off stage-one colony worlds. And yet, Sandra didn't fall into the standard type. She had a place on the world, if one that was a little restrictive.

Ask her, his thoughts mocked. They sounded like Rachel. *Or wait and see if she tells you.*

He put the thought out of his head as he clambered out of the shower, dried himself and poured two mugs of military-grade coffee. It tasted foul, compared to the coffee he'd drunk as a young princeling, but it woke him up. He allowed himself a moment of relief, then dressed hastily and ordered food. Rachel must have already given instructions to the kitchen staff. Sandra barely had time to dress before it arrived,

"Take care of yourself," Sandra said, after they'd eaten. "Come back to me."

"I will," Roland said, fearing he was storing up trouble for himself. "If I can, I will."

He was still fretting about it when he walked into the conference room and looked around, silently noting who was in attendance and who'd yet to arrive. The naval officers were almost all aristocrats, drawn from the former coast guard and corporate shipping lines and promoted—heavily—as the makeshift fleet grew larger. They were reasonably competent, he'd been assured. They'd spent most of their time at sea, rather than flying desks in offices hundreds of miles inland. The army officers were something of a mixed bag. Some of them had been promoted for competence, but the majority—both aristo and townie—had been selected through political interference. Roland told himself he'd managed to get rid of much of the dead wood. The war had been a harsher teacher than any DI.

"Gentlemen," he said. The only woman in the room was Rachel, sitting in the far corner ignored by everyone. She had a remarkable talent for blending into the background, he'd discovered. "If you want a drink"—he waved a hand at the dispenser—"take one now, then be seated. Time is pressing."

He paused, waiting for the officers to sit down. His old DI would have cried—or exploded with rage—if he'd seen them, calling the officers out for everything from limited discipline to a complete lack of military protocol. Roland would be happy, as long as they had the competence to go with their rank. Eight months of training, preparation and limited military operations had done what they could, but he was uneasily aware it took time to build the cohesion the military required to operate and win. One solid enemy blow would be enough to shake his force to its foundations, perhaps break it up into fragmented units trying to escape the oncoming storm. If they broke...

"You should all have had a chance to study the plan," he continued. "It is a little rough and ready, and parts of it will have to be adapted on the fly, but there is no way to tighten it up until we actually go to war. With that in mind"—he paused—"do you have any points you wish to raise?"

His words hung in the air. He'd done his best to convince his subordinates that he wouldn't bite off their heads for questioning him, even if they were wrong. And yet...too many of them had grown up in environments where speaking freely was asking to have one's career blighted, if not destroyed. Roland understood how they felt, but it was important to have them involved in discussions. If something happened to him, and it might, they'd be the ones charged with continuing the offensive.

"I have one," General Hangchow said. "Can we land enough troops on the island before the rebels counterattack?"

"Our exercises say yes," Admiral Forest said. "Realistically, they will assume our first priority is to secure a port. They are unlikely to draw their troops out of protective cover just to hammer us on the beach, when our guns will batter their men into dust. By the time they realise they're wrong, it will be too late."

We hope, Roland added, silently. He'd reviewed past engagements, from minor colonial skirmishes to maritime combat before humanity had expanded into the galaxy, and he was all too aware the rebels could have done the same. There were supposed to be copies of the Imperial Library on Baraka and Winchester, although it wasn't clear if they had survived the uprising. Or if the rebels even knew they were there. *They may have researched the past too.*

He leaned forward. "We must not fail," he said. "Once we have a secure lodgement, and the special units are in place, we will advance as quickly as possible to our final targets. They have to know where we're heading, so they will do everything in their power to stop us. If you see a chance to hurt them, take it. Don't wait for orders."

The room seemed to hang on his every word. "This will be our first really big operation, so I want to make two points very clear. First, I expect each and every one of you to work as a team. I know we have had our differences. I know we have had disagreements and fights and…but, right now, we have to work together. This is a team effort, not a bout between individual champions. If any of you, and I mean any of you, does anything to imperil our ability to work as a team, I will break you. Is that clear?"

He paused, long enough for a rumble of assent to sweep across the room. He'd hoped the lesson would sink in, without him needing to hammer it home, but…better to make it clear now rather than risk disaster later down the line. He meant it, too. If anyone, no matter their connections, tried to slow things down, he'd send them home in disgrace.

"Second, I want you to remind your subordinates, all of them, that atrocities will not be permitted nor tolerated," he said. "Surrendering prisoners are to be treated with respect, if a healthy degree of paranoia. We will take care to make sure they don't have the opportunity to harm us. However, we will not slaughter unarmed enemy POWs or civilians or anyone else. I do not expect you to tell me that no civilians will be harmed, because that isn't likely to happen, but if anyone commits a war crime they will be put in front of a firing squad and shot. This time, there will be no exile. They. Will. Be. Shot."

He looked from face to face, silently gauging their feelings. "We're leaving tonight," he said, changing the subject. "The fleet will unite tomorrow, then set course for our target. If you want to say your goodbyes, or write your last letters, do so now, but be mindful of security precautions. We can at least *try* to keep them in the dark."

Roland hoped they'd listen. He doubted the deception would last, and he'd planned on the assumption it wouldn't, but he'd take what he could get. The coming engagement would be costly, even if everything went according to plan. He knew, without waiting for the fighting to begin, that it wouldn't. The rebels would have plans of their own. Roland had spent hours asking himself what he'd do, in their place. The answers hadn't been reassuring.

"Good luck to us all," he said. "Dismissed."

CHAPTER TWENTY

BARAKA ISLAND/WINCHESTER ISLAND, NEW DONCASTER

"BRYCE," SARAH SAID. "What do you make of it?"

Bryce said nothing for a long moment, thinking hard. The reports from the spies on Kingston were clear—General Windsor intended to invade Rolleston—and yet, he didn't believe them. The government had tightened security considerably since his days on the capital island and they certainly *should* be able to keep the military's target off everyone's lips. The idea that everyone knew the secret didn't sit well, because General Windsor was hardly a fool. Hitting the island everyone expected him to hit was asking for trouble.

Unless he's confident he has enough firepower to make resistance futile, Bryce considered, then dismissed. General Windsor knew better. The islands were difficult to reach, let alone attack, at the best of times. Giving the enemy any warning at all would make invasion far more costly, if not impossible. *No, he's not planning to go anywhere near Rolleston.*

"It's a lie," he said, as he studied the map thoughtfully. "They're trying to trick us."

Sarah gave him a thoughtful look. "You think our spy networks have been compromised?"

Bryce shrugged. He'd *been* a spy. He knew, as well as anyone else, that it wouldn't be *that* hard for counterintelligence officers to start unravelling the network, even though there were hundreds of cut-outs and dead drops scattered throughout the web. He'd never been told the identity of his contacts, not until there'd been no choice, but a dedicated foe with enough manpower to cover all the bases could steadily dismantle the network, convincing mid-level agents and sources to switch sides and start reporting back nonsense to their superiors. And yet, the network wouldn't *need* to be compromised for the government to start slipping the rebels disinformation. They'd just need to make sure their people bought into the lie. How many of them would be able to point to Rolleston on a map, let alone take a look at the logistics and figure out it was a terrible choice of target?

"I think they're using our own network against us," Bryce said. "If they told everyone their target was Rolleston, I think we can take it for granted they're going somewhere else."

"Precisely my thought," Sarah said. "Where do you think they're going?"

Bryce hesitated. "Doesn't the council have any thoughts on the affair?"

"There's a great deal of dispute," Sarah told him. "I'm interested in *your* input."

"In more ways than one," Bryce said, dryly. Sarah didn't show any visible reaction. He'd never seen her shocked by anything, although he supposed she'd spent most of her life either on a plantation or in the jungle. He'd never realised just how bad the plantations truly were until he'd visited one, after fleeing Kingston. "Don't they trust you? Or me?"

Sarah shrugged. Bryce understood. The rebels would never admit it, not even if someone put a gun to their heads, but they had more in common with the government than either side cared to know. The government had appointed General Windsor to command the war effort, using him to paper over the cracks in their edifice; the rebels had done the same, appointing Sarah the Earther as their leader, rather than risk their unity being shattered by a faction fight at the worst possible moment. Bryce wondered, absently, if Sarah knew she'd likely be shoved aside when the war was over, then decided she probably wouldn't mind. He'd come to know her well, over the last six months. She wanted to tear down the government and piss on the ruins. Building a better world could be left in someone else's hands.

Sarah nodded to the map. "Thoughts?"

"There aren't many targets worth the effort," Bryce said. The government needed to end the war quickly, before their coalition fragmented or an off-world power intervened. Bryce was entirely sure offworlders would find the government surplus to requirements, when—if—they took control of the high orbitals. What was the use of a government that couldn't even pay tribute? "The only realistic choices are here, Baraka itself, or Winchester."

"Quite." Sarah looked unconcerned, but Bryce knew her well enough to tell she was deeply worried. "If you were in command of the enemy fleet, where would you go?"

"Winchester," Bryce said. He didn't really need to think about it. "It offers the greatest reward, if they take the island or even establish a major presence on the land, while also allowing them the opportunity to withdraw if things go badly. The island is just too big for any sort of static defence, at least until we know where the enemy is landing. They'll know it too."

"It's also very well developed, unlike the other possible targets," Sarah said. "The Winchesters invested a *lot* of money in infrastructure."

Bryce nodded, curtly. The Winchesters were gone—either dead or fled—but their legacy remained. Reading between the lines, he was tempted to wonder if they'd planned to dominate the planet themselves in the next century, given just how *much* effort they'd invested in building up a private industrial base. There were more factories on Kingston, he knew, but none quite so productive. As interstellar trade routes continued to collapse, the Winchesters would have found themselves in a very strong position indeed. It was just a shame—for them—that they hadn't anticipated the uprisings. The factories had fallen into rebel hands largely intact.

THE PRINCE'S GAMBIT

"Yes." Bryce drew a finger down the map. "The government needs to capture or destroy the factories themselves. That won't be easy, which means..."

He scowled, wishing he had more military education. The insurgents knew how to set traps, how to ambush isolated convoys or conceal IEDs along the roads, but they'd always shied away from stand-up battles. The government forces had been tough enough to make open engagements costly, particularly when they'd been able to call on the Marines for fire support. Now...he sucked in his breath. They were learning their lessons on the job, readying themselves to face a foe with far more experience. He was the best the rebels had, when it came to commanding a modern army, and he was achingly aware of how much he didn't know. General Windsor was so far ahead of him, Bryce suspected, that the gulf was too great to be traversed in a hurry.

"We'll be moving troops and equipment to Winchester, to back up the forces that are already there," Sarah said, quietly. "I want you to take command."

Bryce frowned. "The local commanders won't like it."

"There isn't a single local commander for the entire island," Sarah said, grimly. "The command committee has all the disadvantages of a committee, with none of the advantages we might normally expect. All the petty little disagreements they buried during the insurgency are now getting in their way, making it hard to coordinate anything. You'll have overall command and they'll go along with you. We don't know how much time we have to prepare before the government starts to land."

"Two weeks, perhaps three," Bryce said. He'd run the calculations. The government's fleet would need to stay out of the regular shipping lanes and fishing grounds, which suggested it would take a very circular course around the islands before turning and heading straight to Winchester. They'd be spotted then, if not earlier, but the island would only have a few days of warning before the troops started to land. "That isn't much time."

"No," Sarah agreed. "You'll be leaving this afternoon. Good luck."

Bryce hugged her, feeling her stiffen against him an instant before relaxing into his arms. She was an odd duck and no mistake. Everything he'd heard about Earthers suggested they'd do it with anyone, that they resided in degeneracy that—on a civilised world—would be regarded with utter horror. And yet, Sarah was nothing like that. He wasn't even sure why she'd invited him into her bed, the first time. She'd made no attempt to manipulate him, let alone control him. Perhaps she just hadn't wanted to sleep alone. There weren't that many people she could invite into bed, not without all sorts of unfortunate implications. It might even undermine her authority.

The thought bothered him as he returned to his room, grabbed his knapsack and headed for the airfield. He didn't need much, beyond a change of clothes and ammunition for his pistols. A lifetime of being a spy, before becoming a soldier, had taught him not to carry anything that could be turned against his comrades, if he fell into enemy hands. He silently blessed his teachers for helping him develop his mind, even though they'd hate what he was doing with it. He'd taken a good look at the map and committed it to memory. He could consider his options during the flight, then arrive—the cynical part of his mind added—to discover half of what he'd seen on the map was inaccurate. The map was not the terrain and, if he forgot it, he was likely to run into something that wasn't shown on paper.

Like a mountain, he thought, as he boarded the tiny aircraft. *That would be embarrassing.*

The pilot grinned at him. "It's going to be a bumpy ride," he called. "Make sure you're strapped in."

Bryce shuddered. The tiny aircraft were little more than couriers, although both the government and the rebels had been outfitting them with guns and bombs. No matter how skilled the pilot, the flight really was going to be bumpy. He made sure to check the location of his sick bag, as well as the ejector cord. He didn't want to dive out of the plane over water—he wasn't even sure the parachutes were reliable—but there might be no choice. The whine of the engines distracted him from his thoughts, as the aircraft taxied down the airstrip and hurled itself into the air. The turbulence started moments later.

"We'll be there in a handful of hours," the pilot assured him, as they picked up speed. "Just sit back and enjoy the flight."

Bryce scowled, then closed his eyes as the tiny airframe shook again. The aircraft had a surprisingly long range, something to do with solar-powered cells within the wings, but the planet wasn't exactly *small*. The buffeting got worse, making it harder and harder to think about his plans. There was no point in doing anything but trying to sleep. And yet, even that was impossible. Bryce knew he was no coward—he'd been in combat, time and time again -but there was something about the tiny aircraft that made him feel helpless. He was trapped, in a metal airframe that could easily become a flying coffin if they ran into a storm. He'd die and no one, not even his nearest and dearest, would ever know what had become of him.

They don't know anything, Bryce told himself. His family on Kingston had never known about his double life. He'd been careful to make sure there was no hint he was anything other than MIA, just another soldier who'd been killed during the march to Kingsport, although he had no idea if the counterintelligence services had bought it. They might well think he'd simply deserted. *And they can't know anything, not until the war comes to an end.*

He sighed as he drifted off to sleep. He loved his family...and yet, if the counterintelligence service ever figured out what he'd done, his family would be in deep shit. They'd never be trusted again, for starters; it was quite possible their debts would be called in and, when they couldn't pay, they'd be turned into *de facto* slaves. He shuddered at the thought. He'd thought it was bad on Kingston, but it was far worse on the plantations. His mother and father would be worked to death, while his siblings...he didn't want to think about it. The sooner they won the war, the better.

The aircraft bounced, jerking him out of an uncomfortable sleep. There were trees around him...for a horrible moment, he thought they'd crashed before his mind caught up and realised they'd reached their destination. Winchester had two airports, including the second-largest on the planet, but the island's leaders had decided to rely on airstrips in the jungle rather than places they *knew* would be targeted by enemy aircraft. Bryce had to admire their thinking, although he suspected it would be a long time before the government could risk landing an airborne force in the middle of rebel positions. General Windsor *had* launched an airborne assault on a rebel camp, but it had been a complete surprise. If he'd tried it again, it would have turned into a bloodbath.

"Here we are," the pilot said. "Did you sleep well, sir?"

Bryce swallowed a sharp response as he stood and clambered out of the aircraft. His body felt stiff and unresponsive, a grim reminder he wasn't *designed* to sleep in an aircraft chair. It was all he could do to get down to the ground without losing his balance and tumbling down the steps. He gritted his teeth in pain as he looked around, noting how well the airstrip had been concealed within the jungle. The landing strip was little more than a dirt road; the handful of buildings hidden within the foliage so carefully that only an experienced eye could spot them and only then from very close range. Bryce smiled as he spotted a pair of men waving to him. They looked like jungle dwellers but held themselves like men of authority. He nodded to the pilot, then hurried to join the men. They beckoned him inside the nearest building. Inside, it was surprisingly cool.

"I'm not happy to see you," the leader said, curtly. He waved a hand at a map, hanging from the wall. "We can handle our own defence."

Bryce bit down the angry response that came to mind as he studied the map. It shouldn't have been there at all. If the buildings were raided, the map would tell the government everything it needed to know about the defence lines. Or…he scowled as he studied the details. A lot had been left off, or mentioned only in very vague terms, but still…he turned back to the leaders, trying to choose his words carefully. Sarah wouldn't be happy if he got into a real fight with the locals. It would risk a fracture within the rebel force at the worst possible time.

"So far, you haven't faced any real offensive," Bryce said. "No offence, but the government never deployed any of its more modern units here. The idiots thought the militia would be enough to keep the island under control."

"Idiots," the leader agreed.

Bryce smiled. The militia, from what he'd heard, had been very much a mixed bag. Some units had been tough and capable, others had been little more than aristos playing at being soldiers. The latter had scattered, the moment the uprisings had begun in earnest. Bryce had heard some of them had been so poorly commanded the militiamen had actually tried to defect to the rebels. It was very hard to blame them.

"This time, they'll be taking you seriously," Bryce cautioned. "Most of the bad commanders have been killed or sidelined. The beancounting supply officers have been sent to count trees on deserted islands, while corrupt supply officers have been shot without trial. The government's troops are now led by men who know what they're doing, with all the ammunition, air support and long-range artillery they need to give you a good kicking. Yeah, sure, you can fall back into the jungles and come out when they're looking the other way, but that's not going to secure the island. Rather the opposite."

He traced a line on the map. "You're going to be fighting a very different battle," he added, calmly. "And I'm here to help you do it."

"We have plans," the leader said, curtly. "There's no way they'll secure an intact port."

"I hope you're right," Bryce agreed. The map suggested heavy rebel forces were dug in around the ports. They'd have plans to destroy the facilities, if they couldn't be defended. "But they will have contingency plans for that too."

He met the leader's eyes. "The truth is, you're probably not going to be able to keep them from landing," he cautioned. "But you can trap them on the beaches, pin them down and either drive them back into the waters or keep them penned up long enough to ready a blow that will shatter them in a single decisive battle."

"And then...what?"

Bryce smiled. "There are limits to their manpower," he said. The government had offered the townies what they wanted, in exchange for their support, but Bryce wasn't blind to the implications. He was sure there were already townies muttering about the government being willing to fight to the very last townie. "If we can stop the invasion, they'll have to come to terms with us or risk trouble in their rear."

"And you think we can rely on it?" The leader shook his head. "It seems chancy."

"It is," Bryce agreed. Sarah and he had discussed it, endlessly. How much could the government lose before it ran into problems? How many casualties? How many sunken ships? "They've done well, to build up as much as they have. But they are starting to run up against some hard limits. If we kill thousands of men and sink dozens of ships, they're going to have real problems pressing the war against us. And that will shatter their unity and—hopefully—bring them to the table."

He paused, dramatically. "And if it doesn't, we can launch an invasion of our own. And this time, we will not fail."

CHAPTER TWENTY-ONE

NEAR WINCHESTER ISLAND, NEW DONCASTER

"YOU'RE UP LATE," RACHEL SAID. "Or are you up too early?"

Roland shrugged. He hadn't been able to sleep, even though he knew *he* wouldn't be going into combat in a few hours. Not really, not in the sense bullets would be cracking through the air and past his ears...he felt a twinge of guilt as he peered into the darkness, hearing water lapping against the ship's hull. The rebels probably knew they were coming. He would be astonished if they *didn't* know. The fleet had altered course two days ago, picking up speed as it headed straight for Winchester. They'd spotted enough fishing boats to be fairly sure they'd been spotted in return.

"I couldn't sleep," he admitted, looking up at her. He wouldn't have confessed as much to anyone else. "If this goes wrong..."

Rachel met his eyes. "Do you have any reason to think things will go wrong?"

"No." Roland shook his head, then turned back to stare into the darkness. "We've done everything we can to ensure success, but..."

He felt his heart twist in pain. He'd staked everything on the operation. If it failed...it seemed unfair, somehow, that the worst that could happen, if he came back to the mainland when so many others didn't come home at all, was that he'd be told to wait for the next interstellar freighter to arrive before he was sent straight back to Boot Camp in disgrace. Assuming, of course, he survived his own failure. The rebels would do everything in their power to sink the fleet and, despite everything, there was a very real chance they'd get lucky. Ships would be sunk, Roland knew, and one of them could be *his* ship. And then...he'd practiced evacuating the ship in an emergency, but the emergency drills had always left out the *emergency*. He might die in the next few hours, even though he wouldn't be going ashore until it was secure. Rachel had threatened to cuff him to his chair if he even thought about it.

Rachel patted his shoulder. "You've done everything you could," she said. "Now, all you can do is wait."

"I know," Roland said. "It doesn't help."

"Think about something else," Rachel advised. "Anything else."

Roland snorted. "Do you have any better advice?"

"No." Rachel grinned. "You could always spend the next few hours thinking about Sandra."

"You're not helping," Roland told her, stiffly. "Are you ready for your part of the operation?"

"Yeah." Rachel met his eyes, again. "You take care of yourself, sir, and don't put yourself in danger."

Roland nodded, then checked his terminal. It was 0630. They should be in position to attack Winchester—and land the first troops—by 0900, assuming everything went according to plan. They'd worked hard to gather all the intelligence they could, but he was uneasily aware there were too many question marks hanging over the enemy defences. They were leaping in blind and, although he'd devised plans to withdraw if the enemy proved too strong, the risks were higher than he wanted to admit. The plan looked good on paper, but so too had many of the truly disastrous blunders of the last thousand years. There were no shortage of examples of detailed plans failing because of something—anything—the planners failed to take into account. Roland had been forced to study them all.

War is a democracy, he reminded himself. The very first Terran Marine had said as much, when he'd compiled his book of hard-earned military wisdom. *The enemy, that dirty dog, gets a vote.*

Rachel straightened and walked away. Roland lifted his head to watch her go, marvelling at how she walked. There was nothing feminine about her movements, nothing to draw the eye, and yet…he clamped down hard on that train of thought before it led to utter disaster. He was both her superior officer and her junior and even if they'd been equals, she would hardly give him the time of day. And…he snorted, remembering something his tutors had drilled into him. His body knew he might be about to die, that he might not have any further chances to sow his seed…of *course* it was trying to tell him to copulate one final time. He rolled his eyes as he turned away, silently reviewing the plan one final time. It wasn't as if he'd have acknowledged heirs, not when they'd technically be heirs to a throne and an empire that no longer existed. It would only complicate his life… as if it wasn't already complicated beyond belief.

He spotted a faint glimmer in the distance and nodded. The sun was slowly, very slowly, starting to rise. The darkness was lifting, revealing distant islands wreathed in early-morning mist. Roland shivered, despite the heat. Anything could be out there, anything at all. He turned, heading to the CIC as the deck quivered under his feet. The bridge crew was already sounding the alert, bringing the crew to action stations. It was only a matter of time before the rebels came for them. And then…

Admiral Forest saluted as Roland entered the compartment. "Sir," he said. "Long-range sensors picked up radio chatter only a few short miles from here."

Roland nodded, curtly. "About us?"

"We're unsure," Admiral Forest said. "The messages were very short. But that is suspicious in and of itself."

"Yes." Roland frowned as he glanced at the map. The commonplace radio transmitters had no encryption systems, but it wasn't hard to establish a selection of codewords for anticipated events. A spotter could transmit a short message, nothing more than a word or two, alerting the rebels to the fleet's presence. "Are we ready to repel attack?"

"We're as ready as we'll ever be," Admiral Forest said. "If we'd had more time..."

"There's a lot of that going about," Roland told him. "Luckily for us, the rebels have the same problem."

...

Kathy was naked.

She felt oddly exposed as she peered into the distance, although it was hardly the first time she'd been naked while sailing the friendly seas. She normally wore little more than a belt and bra, or bikini if she felt there was a better than even chance of slipping and falling into the water. It had never bothered her, not when everyone else was just as naked. It had seemed normal and yet...this time, she wasn't naked for any practical reason, but to distract watching eyes.

The message had been short, but clear. The government fleet was on the way and she could expect to see it in a few minutes or so. It could have altered course, if it had picked up the message and divined the meaning behind it, but there were so *many* ships in the fleet—if the reports were to be believed—that changing course wasn't something they could do in a hurry. Kathy had been a sailor since birth and *she* knew how hard it could be to sail in formation, even with tiny fishing boats. The giant freighters the government had converted into warships and military transports had to wallow like pigs in the mud, unable to change course or even slow down in time to avoid her. And that meant she'd get one free shot...

Her heart started to race as she spotted the fleet, advancing from the north. She lifted her binoculars and peered towards the ships, silently counting them as she planned her attack. The warships—crude designs, from what she'd heard—weren't the real targets, although she felt they needed to be taken out first. It was the transports that needed to be killed, sending hundreds—perhaps thousands—of young men to watery graves.

Kathy hesitated, struck by the sheer enormity of what she was about to do, then took the steering rod in her hand and gunned the engine. The speedboat jumped to life, the engine roaring as she guided the craft onto the waters. It felt a little rough, as if the designers hadn't gotten the weight just right, but Kathy was experienced enough to compensate. She reached up and undid her hair, allowing it to fan out behind her. Normally, she kept it tied up, but this time...she smiled, despite the situation. The enemy wouldn't be distracted for long, yet if it bought her a few more seconds it would be worth it. It would let her take her revenge.

The range closed rapidly, the enemy vessels moving rapidly from distant shapes on the water to looming monsters, towering over the sea. Kathy heard shouts, then shots, as she swung the speedboat from side to side, trying to get as close as possible before bailing out. The escort vessels were moving rapidly to block her way, trying to keep her away from the bigger and slower transports. A bullet zinged past her head, passing so close she was sure it grazed her skin. Her lips twisted. Clearly, they weren't distracted by her bare breasts any longer, if indeed it had worked at all. A speedboat charging straight at the transports was about as subtle as a punch to the head.

She palmed her breather and locked the steering rod into place, then hurled herself backwards in a practiced move that threw her straight into the water. She twisted the moment she hit the waves, diving deeper and deeper as she pressed her breather to her mouth. The compressed air wouldn't last long, but she should have enough to remain underwater until she managed to get well away from the enemy fleet. If she survived the next few moments...the water vibrated, a shockwave passing through the waves as the speedboat exploded. She hoped it had struck its target, although there was no way to be sure without surfacing. The enemy might have sprayed the boat with machine gun fire, setting off the explosives. She didn't know.

Not that it matters, she told herself, as she kept swimming. *There are more speedboats on the way.*

Roland had to bite his tongue to keep from demanding a report, as more and more enemy speedboats appeared out of the islands and launched themselves towards his fleet. The first had exploded just short of its target, but it had still managed to do considerable damage; the others, engaged the moment they'd come into view, had kept his men on alert without getting close enough to strike his ships. He had to admire the tactic, he noted, as another speedboat sprayed his escort ships with machine gun fire, before ramming the nearest warship and blowing both ships out of the water. There were literally millions of such craft on the planet and if even a small percentage were aimed at his forces...

Another explosion shook the hull. Roland lifted his eyes, looking at the live feed from the cameras outside. A ship was burning, the flames rapidly spreading out of control. He saw men jumping from the deck, trying to swim away before the fires reached the ammunition or fuel tanks or...Roland looked away as the ship exploded into a giant fireball, the bow and stern breaking into two pieces before crashing back into the water. How many men had just died? He wasn't sure he wanted to know.

Admiral Forest turned to face him. "Sir," he said. "The lead patrollers report encountering mines."

Roland sucked in his breath. Mines. He'd never thought of mines... clearly, the enemy, less used to thinking about interstellar warfare, had been bright enough to realise mines were actually *useful* in wet-navy combat. He cursed mentally, wondering how the enemy had worked out where to lay mines. Had the secret been out all along? Or had they had enough mines to turn all the approaches into death traps? Or...he shook his head in annoyance as he put the pieces together. The rebels hadn't done anything of the sort. They'd seen the fleet coming, then laid the mines while the speedboats distracted his fleet. He should have seen it coming.

"Launch the aircraft," he ordered. He'd hoped to hold the aircraft in reserve, particularly the ones designed to fly off ships, but they had to be deployed ahead of time. "Get them sweeping the space between us and the landing zone for minelayers."

"Yes, sir," Admiral Forest said.

Roland nodded, trying to project an air of calm. The invasion was barely underway and he'd already taken losses. He checked the timetable, assessing when the missile bombardment was due to begin. The enemy would be ready for them, after the missiles had proven their worth on Mountebank, but there were limits to how much they could do to prepare. The first missiles had been little more than crude projectiles. The second generation were much more accurate.

"If you pick up more enemy transmissions, direct a missile at them," he ordered. It would be costly, and probably wasteful, but anything that kept the enemy from making more transmissions to coordinate their attacks would be worthwhile. "Don't give them time to recover."

"Aye, sir."

Roland braced himself as the timer ticked down. Once they were in position, they could sweep most of the southern side of the island with missiles. The enemy would have real problems…if nothing else, they'd have to duck and cover, giving his troops a chance to land without interference. How many other speedboats and minelayers were waiting for him? Roland didn't know…

"Incoming fire," an officer snapped. A rustle of alarm, near-panic, ran through the compartment. "Missiles incoming! I say again, missiles incoming!"

Shit, Roland thought. The enemy had set up missile batteries on the outlying islands, giving them a chance to drench his ships in fire. He doubted their missiles were any more accurate than his own, but there were a hell of a lot of them. The close-in weapons systems started to chatter, hurling lead at the missiles in hopes of downing them before they got too close, yet…Roland braced himself. *This could get nasty.*

"How many did we hit?"

Bryce wished, not for the first time, that General Windsor had seen fit to give him more time. He'd done well, given what he'd had on hand, but it probably wasn't enough to do more than slow the invasion force for a few short hours. It was still impossible to determine where it intended to land, ensuring he couldn't move his reserves forward until their target became unmistakable. The coastline was just too long for his peace of mind.

Be glad of it, he told himself. *If the island was a little smaller, we'd lose the moment they got a solid foothold.*

He scowled, crossly. The bunker was completely off the books, the dark and dingy complex put together hastily after it had become clear just how much the government knew about the island. He doubted it would survive, if the enemy bombed it, although the landlines made it hard—if not impossible—for someone to find the bunker except through sheer luck. The enemy could waste their time bombing the remote transmitters, if they wished. There were plenty more, just waiting to be put into service. He'd planned on the assumption the enemy knew everything and gone on from there.

"It's hard to be sure, sir," the reporter said. "The messages say seven ships were sunk, and nine more heavily damaged, but we lost contact shortly afterwards. We just don't know."

"And some of the kill-claims may have been exaggerated," Bryce agreed. It was probably harder to be mistaken about how many ships had been sunk, but it was quite possible several kills had been counted twice. He'd given up hope of being able to maintain any control over the battlefield as soon as he realised just how chaotic the speedboat offensive was likely to be. The fishermen were skilled sailors, no one could dispute it, but they weren't exactly military officers. "We'll just have to hope for the best..."

"Missiles!" Another operator jumped to her feet. "They're firing missiles!"

"Sit down," Bryce said, calmly. There was no point in panic. If a missile was going to kill them, it would have done so by now. "Don't send any radio transmissions. Use the landlines to determine what got hit."

Which might be complicated, because their missiles aren't any more accurate than ours, his thoughts added. *They may not have hit their actual targets.*

He frowned as the reports started to come in. The government had spread their targeting pattern wide, denying him any insight into their thinking…he felt his frown deepen as he mentally placed the targets on a map. He might be wrong about the latter. The missiles had hammered lots of targets, but a handful of bridges and roads seemed to have come in for special attention. On the map, it suggested the enemy was trying to isolate a particular beach from the rest of the island.

"Contact Group Four," Bryce ordered. It looked as though the enemy was isolating their landing zone. "They are to prepare to repel attack."

"Yes, sir," the operator said.

"And then inform Groups Nine and Ten that they are to be ready to move up in support," Bryce added. The landing zone was a good one, on paper, but the harbour facilities were very limited. They'd have to take the city's ports if they wanted to bring in more supplies and that would be difficult, if not impossible. "Group Five is to remain in place, but prepare to repel attack too, either from the sea or from the west."

"Yes, sir."

Bryce smiled, despite the incoming army. "And then send a message to the relay station," he added. "The invasion has begun."

CHAPTER TWENTY-TWO

WINCHESTER ISLAND, NEW DONCASTER

RACHEL HAD ALWAYS LOVED TO SWIM, even before she'd joined the Marines and perfected the skill a long time before she'd been invited to try out for the Pathfinders. She didn't need much, beyond a breather and a skinsuit, the latter carefully designed to help her blend in to her surroundings. In the early-morning light, she should have been invisible as she swam up to the river and made her way up to the ruined plantation. Compared to some of the missions she'd undertaken, it was a piece of cake. She kept her head low anyway, just in case, as she slipped into position behind enemy lines. The beach was too obvious a target for the enemy to risk leaving it undefended. She wasn't remotely surprised to spot the bunkers and trenches concealed within the foliage, then dug deep into the undergrowth. The rebels hadn't had time to make the beach completely impregnable, but they'd done very well with what they'd had.

And we can't allow them to slow us down, she thought, as she carefully evaded an enemy patrol. Whoever was in command was taking nothing for granted. It looked as if the patrols were deployed randomly, without a pattern an observer could discern and exploit. *We have to get ashore quickly, before they manage to muster a counterattack.*

She slipped to the rear of the beach, carefully noting all the enemy positions. The beach would have been lovely, if it hadn't been turned into a warzone. The white sand, blue waters and green trees contrasted oddly with the metal debris dumped along the shoreline, probably backed up by mines and other unpleasant surprises. A skilled team could use the wreckage to channel an attacking force into a predetermined location, then zero their mortars and machine guns on the target and cut the attackers to ribbons. The enemy would probably have more forces in reserve too, if they had any common sense. Roland's plan called for the bridges to be smashed by missiles, slowing any major counterattack, but she hoped he wasn't counting on it. The missiles were too inaccurate to be relied upon. Only a handful of missiles had modern targeting warheads and *they* were needed elsewhere.

A distant rumble of thunder split the air. She checked her terminal, just to ensure the mission hadn't been terminated at the worst possible moment, then took the targeting beacon from her belt, linked to it with her implants and uploaded the location data. The first wave of missiles—already inbound, if everything had gone according to plan—were aimed at more distant targets. The second, using her targeting data, would hammer the local defences. She braced herself as the first missiles swept overhead, then put the beacon on the ground and set the timer. She'd have just enough time to get well clear before the beacon started pulsing, sending the targeting data to the missiles. If the enemy had a signals unit nearby, and if it happened to be on the ball, they might just have time to realise what she was doing—and cut her off—before it was too late.

She drew her pistol as she ran, silently counting down the seconds. There was no longer any point in stealth. The targeting beacon was a dead giveaway, if anyone was listening. Dull distant explosions shook the air, the first missiles coming down on their targets…she hoped they were effective, even though she feared they wouldn't be enough. The rebels had had plenty of time to plan their countermeasures…her terminal bleeped once, a five-second warning. She hurled herself to the ground, covering her ears an instant before the ground shook violently. This time, the thunder was so close it nearly deafened her. Rachel gritted her teeth as the remaining missiles slammed home, coming down right on top of the enemy positions. It was probably overkill—she was fairly sure there was no *probably* about it—but they didn't dare let the enemy slow them down. She rolled over, just in time to see the last fireball rising into the air, casting a baleful light over the beach. If there were any survivors, they were hopefully too stunned to offer any resistance when the landing craft started to disgorge their troops.

Don't take it for granted, she told herself, sternly. *The rebels are tough.*

...

Richard watched in awe and terror as the distant beach seemed to explode in fire, the shockwave passing over the landing craft seconds later and rushing on into the distance. He'd heard stories of vast landing operations, spearheaded by bombardments that turned beaches to glass and burnt trees, but coming face to face with the reality was shocking. The trees had once been pretty; now, they were burning rapidly, flames leaping from place to place as if they were permanently on the verge of running out of fuel. He was tempted to wonder, despite everything he'd learnt during the planning sessions, if the entire island was on the verge of being burnt to the ground.

Don't be silly, he told himself, as he surveyed the beach. *The fires will burn out quickly.*

He issues orders as the landing craft headed to its destination, picking its way amongst the rows of debris and makeshift barricades. It looked as if the rebels had taken every damaged or ruined vehicle from the island and laid them along the beach, in hopes they'd delay the invasion for a few additional seconds. Richard lifted his binoculars to his eyes and swept the shores, looking for hints the rebels might have survived long enough to mount a defence. It seemed unlikely—the fires had burned so hotly they'd probably suffocated anyone lucky enough to survive the flames—but he knew better than to rule it out completely. The rebels probably didn't have any kind of powered combat armour, yet…who knew what their mystery backers had given them? It could be almost anything…

The landing craft grounded, hitting the beach with surprising force. Richard raised his rifle as the hatch swung down, jumping into the water and splashing through the surf until he reached the blackened beach. Something exploded behind him and he glanced back, just in time to see one of the landing craft picked up and thrown away by a mine that had survived the missile bombardment. There was no time to go back and help the wounded, if indeed anyone had survived the crash. He forced himself to keep going instead, heading into the remains of the enemy defences. The bombardment made it look like the dark side of the moon.

Shit, he thought, as he crashed through a trench. A handful of bodies, barely recognisable, lay at the bottom. *How many people did we kill?*

He snapped orders as the rest of the squads caught up with him, fanning out as they sifted through the remains of the defences and thrust the perimeter out as far as they could. The rebels knew they'd landed—they couldn't have missed the bombardment—and they'd be doing everything in their power to mount a counterattack as soon as possible. There was no post-strike assessment, no way to know how much damage the missiles had done to the bridges. The enemy had had more than enough time to produce tanks of their own. They might already be mounting an armoured counterattack to trap the invaders on the beaches.

His communicator bleeped. "Landing zone clear, sir."

Richard nodded. "Bring in the second units, now."

A line of men, armed with assault rifles and antitank missiles, ran past him as he turned to face the waters. The two heavy transports—his heart twisted as he recalled it should have been three, but one had been sunk by the rebel speedboats—were heading right for the beach, ploughing their way through the waves at top speed as if they were in the middle of the ocean. Richard braced himself, half-expecting the exercise to end in complete disaster even though they'd practiced repeatedly until they'd gotten the whole thing down to a fine art. The transports were old, bound for the scrapyard before they'd been pressed into service for one last mission. The planet could afford to lose them...

He watched, unable to keep from taking a step back, as the two vessels grounded themselves hard, their hulls creaking in agony as they forced their way up the beach. The crews sprang to work, laying down cables and pushing the superstructures forward to turn the freighters into makeshift jetties. They wouldn't last long, Richard thought, but they'd last long enough to get the first units ashore without a proper harbour. The engineers were already opening the rear of the grounded ships, deploying more and more pontoons. The next transports wouldn't have to ground themselves. They'd simply have to dock at the jetties so the crews could unload them.

Get moving, Richard told himself. *The enemy already knows we're here.*

He keyed his communicator as he broke into a run, demanding updates from the lead squads as shooting broke out in the distance. The enemy seemed scattered, more than a little uncoordinated, but that would change very quickly. He'd worked with Roland and the others in hopes of calculating what, precisely, the enemy could actually *do* about the invasion. Their only real choice was to either drive the invaders back into the sea, which would be tricky, or rely on a long, drawn-out defence to slow the advance. Richard knew which one he'd prefer. The enemy were probably already on their way.

...

"It's confirmed, sir," the operator said. "They landed at Pallas Beach, after a heavy missile bombardment. I've been unable to establish any contact with the local defenders."

"Which probably means they're dead," Bryce said, coldly. He wanted to think the defenders had merely suffered a communications breakdown, but he didn't dare let himself believe anything of the sort. Better to assume the worst and be pleasantly surprised than think the best and get a nasty shock when reality intruded on his plans. "What contact do we have?"

"I have a link to an OP near Torne," the operator said. "She says the enemy have landed and are currently solidifying their beachhead."

Bryce nodded, curtly. He'd hoped the beach defences could slow the enemy long enough for his reserves to reinforce the defenders, then mount a counterattack. Clearly, that was no longer possible. And that meant… he mentally drew lines on the map, muttering orders to the operators as he moved from one set of contingency plans to another. If the beachhead could no longer be secured…

"Order the aircraft to give them hell," he said, finally. "Remind them to concentrate on the transports. We want to slow the enemy as much as possible."

"Yes, sir."

...

"Hey," Garvin Winter said. "When I come back, will you date me?"

The engineer gave him the finger, then swung the propeller. Garvin smirked as he ran through a hasty set of pre-flight checks, feeling oddly calm as he ticked off every last item on the list. He was a brave man—cowards didn't fly aircraft on New Doncaster—and yet, it was the first time he'd actually taken his tiny aircraft into combat. Part of him was looking forward to the chance to show what airpower could do, the rest wanted to fly beyond the sunset and vanish until the war came to an end. He was no coward and yet…

He put the thought out of his mind as he guided the aircraft out of the concealed hangar, then powered down the bumpy runaway and into the air. The aircraft was designed to land on a dime—a saying that dated back to pre-space days, when everyone knew what a dime actually was—but it was the first time he'd ever flown in such crowded airspace. There were nine other aircraft right behind him, as well as whatever aircraft the invaders had brought with them. The reports from the front suggested the invaders had quite a few aircraft, although Garvin had no idea if they were accurate. Some of the reports were definitely absurd. Naked women on speedboats charging into the teeth of enemy fire? What idiot expected him to believe such crap?

His lips twisted into a smile, which slowly faded as the squadron flew toward the distant beachhead. He knew the island well—he'd flown all over in happier times—but the plumes of dark smoke were enough to tell him precisely where he was going. He stayed low, all too aware the enemy might see or hear him coming. There were all sorts of horror stories about what happened to pilots who flew too high, too close to enemy antiaircraft systems. He wondered, idly, if his superiors expected them to fly into the teeth of enemy sensors. It was the sort of dumb thing he'd expect, from superiors who wouldn't know which end of a plane was which if you paid them. The rebel leaders weren't fools—and they were the only game in town—but none of them were pilots. They didn't understand flying, let alone aerial combat. How could they?

You don't know that much either, his thoughts reminded him. *Don't start thinking you know everything until you do.*

He sucked in his breath as he rose above the treeline and peered down on a scene of utter devastation. Pallas Beach had been a favoured destination for the wealthy and powerful, once upon a time. It had been unspoilt, save for the plantation lurking balefully at the edge...the plantation that had been torn to shreds, when the workers had risen and taken what their masters had refused to grant. Garvin felt no sympathy for the aristos. They'd been demanding enough to him, when he'd owned his own aircraft. How would they have treated people who they literally *owned*?

Poorly, he thought, coldly.

He dismissed the thought as he swooped over the beach. The enemy seemed to have grounded two ships, crashing them so hard into the sand it looked as though even high tide would not be enough to free them. They were being unloaded rapidly, small tanks and wheeled vehicles motoring down a heavy metal ramp while large crates were being lowered to the beach by a crane and picked up by workers...he sucked in his breath, then pulled the switch to drop the bombs. His aircraft jerked as they fell, exploding below him as a burst of tracer fire shot past his aircraft. He jinked automatically, spotting—too late—the antiaircraft vehicle below. His fingers itched to retaliate, but he knew he didn't dare. The aircraft was no hypersonic fighter jet, no assault shuttle designed to land troops in a hot zone. A single hit in a delicate place would be enough to send him cartwheeling into the ground. All he could do was stay low, so low he was practically touching the water, and get away as fast as he could. Behind him, he saw explosions billowing into the sky. He hoped that was a good sign.

The enemy fleet lay ahead of him, launching a handful of missiles into the air. He couldn't tell if they were shooting at him or not, but it didn't matter. The aircraft rose slightly, allowing him to circle around the battlefield and head straight back to the airfield. The onboard cameras would be able to determine, hopefully, if he'd hit anything important, anything that might slow the invaders down for a few short moments. Even if not… the intelligence they'd gathered might prove helpful to someone. He just hoped it was worth the risk.

He reached for his radio switch, then stopped himself. They'd been cautioned against using radios, or anything else that might attract enemy attention. He glanced back and cursed. There were only seven aircraft following him home. He tried not to think about what that meant, although it was impossible. The enemy had killed two of his fellow pilots, killed or captured. He hoped they'd be safe, if they'd been taken alive…he shuddered, remembering how government troops had slaughtered unarmed prisoners. The pilots might already be dead. He hoped their deaths had been worth it.

I guess we'll find out, when we get home, he thought. *And then we'll rearm and go right out again.*

• • •

Richard picked himself off the ground, cursing under his breath. They'd been luckier than they'd deserved, under the circumstances. He'd never really expected the rebels to mount an aerial offensive so quickly, although it shouldn't really have surprised him. They had enough aircraft to risk a handful on a strike mission, one that had come far too close to outright success. If the bombs had been released a second or two later, they might have exploded within the grounded ships and triggered a chain reaction...

No, he told himself. *Worry about it later.*

"Get more antiaircraft defences into position," he ordered. The rebels would learn from their own mistakes, then launch another attack. He was sure of it. "Don't let them get close again."

He keyed his radio, sending a quick report to Roland. Hopefully, the fleet's radar would have tracked the aircraft taking off, telling them where to aim their missiles. Even if not...the rebel airfields couldn't remain hidden for long. They'd be found and destroyed and their aircraft taken out with them...

They probably have contingency plans, Richard thought, tiredly. *They can land those workhorses on any piece of road, no matter how bumpy.*

He shook his head, sourly. The invasion was only a few hours old...

...And, no matter how he looked at it, he couldn't deny it was already slowing down.

CHAPTER TWENTY-THREE

WINCHESTER ISLAND, NEW DONCASTER

"CLEVER OF THEM," BRYCE MUTTERED, as he studied the images from the aircraft as they buzzed over the enemy beachhead. "Very clever indeed."

He frowned as he considered the implications. He'd assumed the government wouldn't be able to land much in the way of supplies, at least until they captured a port. There were limits to how many troops and men could be landed without one, certainly with aircraft and speedboats slipping in to strike the enemy position and get out again before they could be mercilessly sunk. But grounding a couple of freighters, crammed to the gunwales with troops, armoured vehicles and supplies? He had to admit it was a workable tactic, all the more so as sinking the transports was no longer possible. They'd have to blow up the entire ship to deprive the enemy of their supplies and that wasn't going to happen. The aircraft bomblets weren't anything like powerful enough to take out the entire ship.

And they presumably have plans to do it again, if they see no other choice, he thought. *How many freighters are they prepared to sacrifice, just to get a solid beachhead on Winchester?*

He silently saluted his opponent, then turned his attention to the map. The counterattack plans had stalled. The combination of destroyed bridges and missile strikes had slowed the attack so badly he doubted it could reach the beach without being stopped in its tracks. The enemy were deploying artillery as well as antitank weapons and infantry patrols, making it impossible for his men to get into striking distance without being pummelled. Bryce had expected as much, although he'd hoped otherwise. General Windsor was hardly the type of person to be slow and methodical, particularly when he might hope to keep the enemy off balance by a thrust deep into their interior. But Bryce had already planned for it.

"Contact Pallas City," he ordered. "The defenders are to hold the line as long as possible, then retreat as planned."

"Yes, sir," the operator said. "Do you want them to blow the docks?"

"Not yet," Bryce said. It was a risk—a shell falling in the wrong place might cut the wires, leaving the docks intact long enough for the enemy to take control and remove the demolition charges—but as long as General Windsor saw a chance of taking the docks, he'd be forced to divert his troops into the city. "They're to leave the docks alone until the enemy is within striking distance."

"Yes, sir."

"And get the aircraft rearmed and back out there," Bryce added. "We need to slow them down as much as possible."

"Yes, sir."

...

If Rachel sees you, she'll throw a fit, Roland's thoughts reminded him. *You're meant to stay on the flagship, nice and safe while your subordinates go into battle on your behalf.*

Roland shook his head, dismissing the thought as the landing craft powered towards the blackened beach. Rachel had a point—his death would cause all sorts of command issues, at the worst possible time—but he owed it to himself, as well as the men under his command, to take some risks. They had to see him sharing the danger or they'd lose respect for him, which would weaken their willingness to take orders that might seem crazy or, worse, lead straight to their deaths. He'd felt the same way too, when he'd been at Boot Camp. The best leaders had always been those who led from the front.

Or as close to the front as is possible, in the modern age, Roland reminded himself. *Rachel really would blow a fuse if I went any closer.*

He frowned as his eyes swept the beach. A nasty scar marred the stern of one of the grounded freighters, but it wasn't enough to keep the crew from hastily unloading their vessel and setting up positions further inland. The freighters were flanked by automated antiaircraft vehicles, radars combing the air for enemy aircraft gliding in to bomb or strafe the invasion force. Roland silently gave the enemy pilots credit for daring, if not for accuracy, although he had to concede they probably hadn't had the training or resources they needed to be really dangerous. If they had control of the airspace over the combat zone, the invasion would have been defeated by now.

Guns boomed in the distance, flashes of light flickering and fading beyond the treeline as shells fell on enemy positions. Roland felt cold, despite the heat. Rachel was out there somewhere, calling in strikes on every enemy force she encountered. The beancounters would moan about the cost, Roland was sure, but shells were cheaper than infantry and less likely to cause political trouble if too many of them got expended. Besides, slowing down the enemy counteroffensive was vitally important. Intelligence hadn't been entirely sure what awaited the invasion force, but anyone who'd studied military history would know the best way to win was to destroy the beachhead as quickly as possible. The rebels were probably already on their way.

The landing craft grounded hard, the shockwave nearly sending him to his knees. He caught himself and headed for the hatch, following the reinforcements as they jogged through the surf and onto the beach. MPs greeted them, directing them to jump-off points on the far side of the ruined trees and plantations. They blinked at Roland, then gestured him to the CP hidden within the ruins. Roland hid his amusement at their stunned expressions.

They might respect him more, for entering the battlefield before it was truly secure, but they couldn't be unaware of the tidal wave of shit that would land on their heads if a prowling enemy sniper put a bullet through their CO's brains. Roland's lips twitched at the thought. He was probably in no danger. Given how brainless he'd been as a young princely brat...

Don't be fucking stupid, he told himself, as he ducked into the CP. *A bullet through your head will kill you, as surely as it would kill anyone else.*

He tensed as the door closed behind him, even though he knew the CP was as safe as reasonably possible. The prefabricated bunker was tough. It could take anything, save for a direct hit...unless the enemy got very lucky, it wasn't going to happen. The CP still felt oddly confining, the semi-darkness casting an eerie gloom over the screen. The operators sat at folding tables, working laptop terminals and speaking into headsets that relayed their words to a distant transmitter before sending them into the airwaves. Roland expected to lose quite a few transmitters, when all was said and done. There was no way to hide their radio transmissions from the enemy. They'd start hurling missiles at the transmitter as long as they got a solid bead on its exact location.

Which is why standard doctrine calls for us to keep moving the transmitter, Roland reminded himself. *Or use microburst systems, which are much harder to track.*

"Sir." Lieutenant O'Neal stood and saluted. "The invasion is proceeding as planned."

"Good." Roland resisted, barely, the temptation to roll his eyes. His operations staff was too used to briefing politicians, who wanted platitudes rather than anything detailed. Idiots. The devil was in the details, as all soldiers knew. "Details?"

Lieutenant O'Neal flushed. "The lead units are ashore and pushing forward as we speak. Their reinforcements are landing now and moving up in support. The enemy has made only limited attempts to stop us, mainly a handful of isolated positions or air raids. We think the pre-landing bombardment tore their defence plans to shreds."

"Don't count on it," Roland growled. "Winchester is a big island. They couldn't have known where we'd be landing."

"Yes, sir." Lieutenant O'Neal pointed to the map. "We have scouts making their way towards Pallas City, probing the enemy defences. We think their defence lines around the city remain intact, as do the ports. However, attempts to confirm the latter have been futile. We lost two drones before I called off the recon flights."

Roland nodded, curtly. Basic drones were easy to produce, but also easy to blow out of the sky. He'd allocated five of the more advanced military drones to the operation, tiny craft that should have been damn near impossible to shoot down without modern tech. Two drones lost... that boded ill. He'd known the rebels had *some* modern tech, but still...

An operator updated the map. Roland cursed under his breath. The standard force trackers he'd used in boot camp simply didn't exist here. It wasn't a bad thing—the illusion of omniscience they created had ruined better officers than him—but it was still deeply frustrating. He didn't even have a network of remote sensors and high-altitude drones, monitoring the battlefield and providing constant updates. Sure, he had reports coming in from his men, but they were delayed or incomplete...he understood now, all too well, what the old sweats had meant when they'd talked about the fog of war. There were large swathes of the map that might as well be *terra incognita*, even though his lead elements had already passed through them. For all he knew, the enemy were already slipping commandos into his rear area.

He shook his head. "Did we capture any prisoners?"

"No, sir," Lieutenant O'Neal informed him. "We shot down two aircraft, but they were both so lightweight the pilots were almost certainly killed when their planes were hit, not when they crashed. So far, we haven't recovered any living prisoners from the advance. I think they were either killed in the first bombardment, or decided they wanted to sell their lives dearly."

Roland nodded, curtly. "Inform me if that changes," he said. He was the commander and yet, now the invasion had begun, he was helpless to steer events. The war rested in the hands of Rachel, Richard and their fellow officers, as they probed forward to find the enemy positions. By the time they reacted to their reports and issued new orders, they'd already be outdated. "And keep a close eye on the unloading."

"Aye, sir."

"Good." Roland tried to resist the urge to start pacing. He wanted to snatch up a rifle and join the advance, but it would be worse than useless. "All we can do now is wait."

...

Jasper—his surname had been taken from him, when he'd arrived on New Doncaster—lay in the tangled foliage and watched the road, waiting for the first enemy troops to come into view. He'd hoped, when he and his fellows had risen and burned the plantation to the ground, that their independence would be respected. How could the aristos work the plantation without a workforce? It wasn't as if paying a decent wage and treating the workers a little better was impossible, even for snobs who thought they were important because their ancestors really *had* been important. But... if rumour were to be believed, the aristos intended to kill all the former workers and bring in new slaves. Jasper had no idea where they intended to find them, but it wasn't his problem. If they were doomed anyway, he might as well to take some of the enemy down with them.

He felt sweat on his back as the sun beat down, every passing minute feeling like an hour. The ever-present insects were silent, their constant buzzing replaced by the sound of shooting and shelling. Jasper felt alone, yet surrounded by an enemy presence that was all the more ominous for being unseen. His scalp itched. He'd spent most of his adult life sneaking through the jungle, crawling past militia checkpoints without giving the rapist scumbags any clue he was there. The government troops might have learnt to do the same, since the uprising had begun. He'd been cautioned the bad militia officers—and their troops—had been slaughtered. Their replacements would be far superior. They could hardly be *worse*.

The sound of engines echoed through the air. Jasper tensed, his sweaty hands clutching the makeshift weapon as the noise grew louder. He had a sudden absurd urge to run, although there was nowhere to go. The government intended to burn down the jungle, he'd been told; the government wouldn't rest until every last person on the island, from debtors to indents like Jasper himself, had been hunted down and killed. They'd probably exhume the mass graves, just to be sure they knew who'd been slaughtered during the first uprising. It was almost a shame they hadn't cremated the bodies, Jasper reflected. It would have made it far harder for the government to account for each and every former slave on Winchester.

He put the thought out of his mind as the enemy vehicles advanced into view. Tanks...maybe not the giant mechanical monsters he'd seen in countless flicks, before he'd been sent into exile without trial, but nasty enough to men without antitank weapons. They advanced slowly down the road, machine guns constantly traversing as their gunners searched for threats. The main guns looked intimidating as hell, although Jasper wasn't too impressed. They'd have to find a target before they blew it away first. The machine guns posed a far greater threat to him.

Probably overcompensating for something, he thought, as he spotted the commander. His head was poking out of the turret, his eyes sweeping for threats as the tanks rumbled down the road. *And what are you doing, you bastard?*

He can't see very well inside the turret, his thoughts reminded him. *And as long as no one is actively shooting at him, he'll be able to keep the tank from driving straight into a tree.*

He put the thought out of his head as he picked up the antitank rocket launcher and carefully took aim, then keyed the transmitter. The signal would be easy to detect, he'd been cautioned, even though it was programmed to last only a couple of seconds. The enemy would know he was there...Jasper had no idea how long it would take for word to reach the tankers, but it didn't matter. He squeezed the trigger, launching the rocket directly towards the lead tank, then turned and crawled away as quickly as he could. The enemy reacted quickly—a stream of bullets crashed through the undergrowth, slashing through trees and narrowly missing him. He heard an explosion behind him as he found the old gully and tumbled into it, then picked himself up and started to run. Behind him, more shells started to whistle through the air. The gunners had only a few seconds, before the government troops started firing back, but they planned to make full use of them. Jasper's signal had told them the enemy troops were in the kill box.

The ground shook violently, time and time again. Jasper stayed low, even as the bombardment sent insects and animals bursting from their burrows and running for their lives. He thought he heard someone shouting behind him, but the noise was too deeply buried within the racket for him to be sure. His back itched, painfully, as he picked up speed. He had to get back to the lines, before the rest of the force pulled out. He wasn't sure what would happen, if the enemy caught him, but he doubted it would be anything good. The government had promised to treat prisoners fairly, yet everyone knew what had happened on Mountebank. The rumours about the island's entire population being marked for death suddenly seemed very reasonable.

Keep moving, he told himself. If he could link up with the rest of his comrades, he could get a new weapon and set up another ambush. *Don't give them a chance to catch up with you.*

Behind him, the sound of shooting grew louder.

• • •

Rachel tensed, despite herself, as she spotted the tiny twitch in the foliage.

It was the sort of movement most people would have dismissed. Even experienced soldiers might have missed it. But *she'd* been taught how to set ambushes, how to go behind enemy lines and slow them down while the regular forces prepared for counterattacks and the movement was precisely where *she* would have hidden herself, if she'd been lying in wait, hoping to snipe an enemy officer. She held herself very still for a long moment, enhanced senses probing the greenery. There was another twitch, then another. Rachel nodded to herself and crawled forward, circumventing the sniper nest and slipping up behind the position. It looked as if there was only one person ahead of her, but it was hard to be sure. The enemy fieldcraft was pretty good...

She palmed a shockrod, then lunged into the nest. A figure in makeshift camouflage rolled over, too late, as Rachel crashed down on him and rammed the shockrod into his back. He jerked, their entire body twitching violently. Rachel felt a twinge of sympathy. Their clothes wouldn't have provided much, if any, protection from the shock. She looked around and nodded to herself. The sniper was alone. And he was...

No, *she*.

Rachel frowned, inwardly, as she secured her prisoner. A woman, armed with a hunting rifle clearly taken from a plantation? It was odd. Rachel had heard hunting and shooting were male preserves, on New Doncaster. And her captive was clearly no aristo. Why had she been allowed to keep the rifle? Where had she even gotten it?

The woman struggled, mightily, as Rachel pressed down on her. She was terrified. Rachel understood, all too well. Angeline Porter had made it difficult to convince the rebels they could surrender, not without being put in front of a wall and shot. The poor girl probably thought she was going to be raped, then murdered. She might not even realise she'd been captured by another woman. Rachel didn't come close to fitting the local ideal for womanhood. But then, who did?

"If you behave, you'll be safe," she promised. "Now, come with me."

CHAPTER TWENTY-FOUR

WINCHESTER ISLAND, NEW DONCASTER

"AIRCRAFT!"

Richard ducked, instinctively, as the enemy aircraft came into view. The pilots were good, good enough to follow the road as if they were driving cars rather than flying aircraft. It made it incredibly difficult to spot the aircraft before they started shooting, let alone blowing them out of the air. The aircraft spat fire towards the squad, bullets lashing into the road, bouncing off tanks and tearing into men who hadn't taken cover in time. Richard gritted his teeth as the lead tanks returned fire, their machine guns filling the air with lead. The aircraft seemed to hang in the air for a long chilling second, then exploded into a fireball, fragments of debris falling to the ground. Richard directed a squad forward, although he had no real expectations of finding a living pilot or even an intact body. The explosion suggested the aircraft had been carrying bomblets, ready to drop on their heads.

And it might be for the best, he told himself, as the scouts reported back. *The pilot might not survive being taken into captivity.*

He cursed under his breath as the force resumed its advance, heading down the road to Pallas City. The soldiers had been given clear orders to accept surrenders and take prisoners, unless it was obvious the enemy troops were only pretending to surrender long enough to lure the soldiers into a trap, but the men were reluctant to take snipers and pilots prisoner. Richard had heard one report of a sniper being shot down as he tried to surrender and two more shot while trying to escape. Roland had ordered the culprits returned to the beachhead, but Richard had a feeling it would be difficult to prove anything. Soldiers reserved a special hatred for snipers and pilots. The evidence would be gone, and everyone would have their stories straight, before a court-martial could be held.

The tanks rumbled down the road, machine guns constantly searching for targets. Richard stayed alert, even as the foliage started to thin before giving way to overgrown fields and the city beyond. Pallas City wasn't *that* big, not by the standards of Kingston, but it was still a major port as well as residential area. Richard frowned as he saw smoke rising from the distance, near the harbour. Something was burning, but what? Shots darted through the air, a bullet pinging off the tank nearest him. The nearest side of the city was a collection of soulless residential blocks, put together from diagrams that had been outdated long before the planet had been settled, reserved for merchants and the handful of townies who'd settled on Winchester. The locals had hated them, if the spooks were to be believed. Now, they'd turned them into sniper nests.

Richard keyed his radio. "Snipers, if you get a clear shot at the enemy, take it."

"Yes, sir."

"Good," Richard said. "The heavy guns are not to engage. I say again, the heavy guns are not to engage."

He saw a pair of infantrymen looking dubious as they started to harden the new position and smiled, grimly. They probably didn't realise it, but the residential blocks were notoriously flimsy even on Kingston. The designers hadn't seen the importance of preparing their blocks for heavy weather, which meant some of the earlier buildings had simply been blown down, and—when they'd learnt to compensate for high winds—they still hadn't been prepared for constant rainfall. Richard had grown up in a well-maintained apartment block—the locals had been willing to take care of their environment—and even *they* had had trouble dealing with leaky roofs, water dripping inside the walls and mould growing everywhere. It said a great deal about the wretched buildings that even his father, an elected official, couldn't do anything about them. The buildings in his gunsights were so fragile, he feared, that blasting them with the machine guns would send them tumbling to the ground. Richard understood it might be impossible to take the city intact—they couldn't let the buildings be turned into sniper nests or worse—but the rubble would make excellent barricades, blocking his men as they tried to advance. It was going to be hard enough to take the city without it.

Richard changed channels, giving Roland a quick update as more and more troops flowed down the road to lay siege to the city, then started to survey its defences. The loss of the drones was a dangerous inconvenience, suggesting there were some modern weapons within the city. Richard wanted to believe it was just an electronic distorter, something capable of blowing an unarmed drone out of the sky, but he feared it was something worse. A plasma cannon could turn his tanks into flaming coffins, burning through their armour and incinerating the crews before they had a chance to escape. Hell, a skilled gunner could probably take out several of his tanks with a single shot.

He lifted his binoculars and peered towards the city. The enemy had taken every damaged or destroyed vehicle they could find and turned them into barricades, welding them together and then pouring concrete over the mess to make them impossible to remove in a hurry. The warehouses on the far side looked normal to the naked eye, but he could see the murder holes through the binoculars. The enemy had gunmen in there, waiting for them, or he was a monkey's uncle. He cursed under his breath. It would be simple enough to reduce the city to rubble, but taking the facilities intact would be a great deal harder. He mentally updated the vague assault plans they'd sketched out, before they'd known anything about the enemy defences. The basic outline remained suitable, barely, but they still knew very little about what to expect. Ideally, he would have preferred to surround the city and wait for the defenders to starve. But that wasn't an option.

"Prepare the lead assault units," he ordered, as he turned away from the city. "We'll move as soon as we're ready."

. . .

"We still don't know much of anything about the enemy positions," Lieutenant O'Neal cautioned, as the operators sketched out more details on the map. "They could have anything beyond the outer lines, anything at all."

Roland nodded, curtly. It was never easy to assault a city. The defenders had so many advantages, as he'd learnt in boot camp, that the attackers were very firmly on the back foot. They might have better weapons, better training and the ability to choose when and where the attack would begin, but all those advantages would be minimised when the shooting actually began. Too many of his men were about to die. Roland wished, not for the first time, that some of the promised advances in robotics had actually come off the drawing board and into reality. It was strange to realise that one could purchase a sexbot, but not an expendable robotic infantryman.

The cost is just too high, he reminded himself. *A top-of-the-range sexbot used to cost almost as much as a navy frigate.*

His heart sank. Taking a city, and clearing it of enemy forces, was a long and nightmarish job. Any hopes he'd entertained of bouncing the enemy out of Pallas without a real fight had died long ago. He'd deployed his forces to isolate the city, to keep the enemy from launching a counterattack, but...Roland knew, all too well, that the offensive might turn into a bloody disaster. They were trying to take a city, even a relatively small city, within a day. It might not end well...he sighed, hoping the enemy had the sense to surrender. Richard had orders to invite the enemy to surrender, before the shooting started again. If they refused...

"Inform Collier that he is in tactical command," Roland said. He would have preferred to go himself, but he couldn't leave the CP. "And that he is cleared to begin the offensive when he is ready."

"Yes, sir."

...

Tamara White sat in her chair and studied the live feed from the sensors she'd concealed on top of the apartment block, peering down on the enemy forces. They were doing their best to conceal their movements but they hadn't realised—or simply didn't care—that they could be observed from the buildings. They had swept the rooftops, picking off snipers with disturbing accuracy. Tamara suspected they didn't realise the sensors were there.

Which wouldn't be a bad guess, normally, she thought. She'd needed weeks to convince the rebel leadership she could be useful as something more than just another grunt. Half the people she'd known were either carrying guns on the front lines or helping to move supplies from one place to another. Coolies, they called them. Tamara wanted to be something more, even if it meant admitting to skills no indent was supposed to possess. *The planet's tech base is pathetic. Why would they go looking for near-modern tech sensors?*

She frowned as the enemy tanks came into view, their main guns swinging around to point at the city. They'd been reluctant to open fire into the city itself, something that puzzled her. It wasn't as if the government had ever given a damn about public safety. Tamara had seen grown men and women whipped to death, their children taken away to be raised by loyalists or servants. Why would they hesitate to reduce the city to rubble? Did they think they could take the port intact?

"Sir," she said, quietly. "They're moving in for the kill."

The rebel leader shot her a distrustful look. He'd been born on New Doncaster and had very little time for an indent from Earth, pointing out—the one time she'd asked—that she had no real loyalty to her new world. The only reason he put up with her, she suspected, was because his superiors had overruled him. He wasn't stupid, but he was short-sighted. It wasn't enough to trigger an uprising, kill the aristos and burn the plantations to the ground. They had to win the war or...

"Alert the troops," the leader ordered, stiffly. "Then get your ass out of here. They know what to do."

The enemy tanks seemed to explode. Tamara stared, convinced—just for a second—that they'd blown themselves up. Her mind spun in circles. There'd been talk of a wonder-weapon that could sweep the enemy from the field...she wondered, numbly, if it was actually true before the truth dawned on her. The enemy had opened fire, shelling the barricades...the ground shook, violently. Pieces of plaster and dust fell from the ceiling, drifting down to land in her hair. They weren't just shelling the barricades. They were shelling the city itself.

"Get out of here," the rebel leader ordered, curtly. "Go."

Tamara hesitated, then deactivated the terminal, folded it up and stuck the device under her arm. It wasn't *hers*—her personal terminal had been left behind on Earth, if it hadn't been confiscated in hopes of using her contacts to uncover the remainder of the hacking underground—but it would suffice. God knew the aristo brat who'd owned the terminal hadn't had the slightest idea what to *do* with it. One of the most advanced terminals one could get, as a private citizen, and he'd stuffed it with porn that would have shocked even a hardened explorer of Earth's datanet. She'd made it her own very quickly, after wiping it down with bleach.

The ground shook again. The bombardment was growing stronger. The leader didn't look at her as he snapped orders into the primitive telephone, ordering his men to fight to the last while he prepared to destroy the docks. Tamara was tempted to stay, despite orders, but she knew better. She'd always been on thin ice, as an Earther with a skill few of the locals could evaluate. If she disobeyed orders now, she might be put in front of a wall and shot.

"Goodbye, sir," she said. "Good luck."

Richard heard shots cracking through the air as he crawled towards the remains of the barricade in front of him, now little more than a burning ruin. The tanks had hammered it hard, first with armour-piercing shells and then with high explosives. If there'd been any enemy soldiers lying in wait behind the barricades, they were dead now or wishing they were. Richard slowed as he reached the ruins, then unhooked a pair of grenades from his belt and hurled them over the rubble. There was no point in taking chances. He was on his feet the moment the grenades detonated, leading his squad into the enemy position. There were no rebels to be seen. The encampment had been so completely devastated he couldn't tell how many, if any, there'd been.

He cursed as he heard mortar shells dropping to the ground, far too close for comfort. The enemy presumably hadn't expected the barricades to last for long, certainly not when the attackers had had plenty of time to lay their guns as they pleased. Instead of trying to waste their time making the barricades even tougher, they'd zeroed their mortars on the position they'd known they'd lose very quickly. He darted forward, tapping his communicator to call in artillery strikes. They had to take out the mortar teams before they managed to slow his men.

The ground shook, again and again, as the squad pressed on towards a warehouse. Richard saw tongues of fire blasting from the murder holes and ducked again, summoning an antitank team to put a HE rocket through the holes. The warehouse was solid—the merchants hadn't been shy about demanding better accommodation for their wares—but the walls had already been weakened by the rebels. Richard saw the rocket slam into the wall, blowing it open and—hopefully—killing or wounding the rebels inside. There was no time to wait. He led his squad forward, his rifle sweeping for targets. A pair of rebels stumbled to their feet, weapons in hand. Richard shot them both down, then ducked as more bullets started cracking through the air. The rebels had a team in the office, right at the front of the warehouse...they'd broken a window and turned it into a shooting position. Richard nodded to two of his men, who launched a pair of RPGs towards the enemy troops. The explosions took them both and nearly wrecked the warehouse.

Richard's lips twitched. *I wonder if they stole the goods before they turned the warehouse into a firing position.*

He shook his head, dismissing the thought as more mortar rounds hurtled overhead. His reinforcements were coming under fire, while his gunners were clearly not doing their bloody job. He felt a hot flash of anger, mingled with a grim awareness mortars were designed to be set up, launch a few shells and then torn down again, the team well away before the enemy's return fire crashed down on their former position. Their shooting would be much less accurate, as they moved from place to place, but it wasn't as useful as he might have hoped. As long as the shells fell within the right general location, it would slow the offensive down.

His radio crackled. "Bravo and Delta Company are entering the combat zone now."

Richard keyed the radio. "Understood," he said. "Caution them to keep their heads down."

He took a breath, then led his men onwards, the fighting blurring into an endless series of tiny skirmishes that seemed to be part of a greater whole. The enemy had surveyed the city well over the last few months, carefully choosing fighting positions that could be abandoned in a hurry when he brought his forces to bear on it. He broke into building after building; sometimes running into ambushes, sometimes crashing his way through an abandoned house or office, only to discover—too late—that the enemy were already raining mortar shells on his head. There were fewer rigged buildings than he'd feared—the enemy clearly hadn't had the time to turn more than a handful of former homes into oversized IEDS—but the ones they discovered cost them dearly. He resorted to calling in artillery strikes on a handful of targets, knowing they didn't have time to disarm the IEDs themselves. The rubble made it harder to advance, but there was no choice. His body ached, as if he'd gone beyond exhaustion and into a twilight world in which there was nothing left, but the war.

"Watch it, sir," a voice snapped.

Richard looked up, just in time to see an enemy gunman point his rifle in his general direction and open fire. He threw himself aside as bullets cracked through the air, bouncing off metal walls and flying in all directions. His saviour snapped off a shot, sending the gunman tumbling to the ground. Richard silently saluted the enemy's bravery. If he'd fired a moment or two earlier, Richard would probably have been hit and killed. He had no illusions. The body armour was good, but not *that* good.

"Fuck," he muttered, suddenly too tired to keep going. "Bring up the rear units, then hold position here."

He sagged against the wall. He'd been told urban combat was rough, but he hadn't really believed it. Kingsport had been bad, yet…it had been a walk in the park compared to the nightmare all around him. The ground heaved, something crashing in the distance so loudly it seemed to wash away all other sounds. Pallas was a small city. What would happen, he asked himself numbly, if the rebels turned a bigger city into a death trap?

We've already lost at least fifty men, he thought, although he had a nasty feeling the real number was a great deal higher. *What'll happen if this goes on?*

CHAPTER TWENTY-FIVE

WINCHESTER ISLAND, NEW DONCASTER

RACHEL COULDN'T HELP FEELING a *little* guilty as she slipped through the streets of Pallas.

It wasn't that she was an infiltrator. She'd done the job before, time and time again, often fooling people who really *should* have paid close attention to their surroundings. It wasn't *that* easy to pretend to be someone she wasn't, certainly when meeting someone who *knew* the person she was pretending to be. The concept of a perfect disguise, and a perfect impersonation, was something straight out of science-fantasy, not the real world. An enemy force that took even a handful of relatively small precautions could save itself from someone like her...

She shook her head, mentally. She'd stripped the sniper, taking her shirt and trousers before handing her over to the advancing troops. Rachel had made it clear she'd castrate any man who took advantage of the poor girl—she'd been careful not to tell them what the girl had been doing when she'd been captured—but the prisoner had been utterly terrified, all the more so because Rachel couldn't tell her *why* she wanted the clothes. Her being female—if the sniper had even noticed—wasn't a guarantee of anything. Rachel had met female pirates who'd actually been worse than the men, something she'd thought impossible until she'd seen the human wreckage they'd left in their path. The poor girl had probably thought Rachel wanted to *watch*.

Rachel shuddered, keeping her head down as she hurried down the streets. Pallas was in chaos. If there was anyone in command, it wasn't evident even to her. The rebels seemed torn between continuing the resistance—she spotted all sorts of strongpoints, being hastily manned as the steamroller ground its way into the city—and evacuating as quickly as they could. She grimaced as she found a place to peer into the harbour, watching boats casting off and heading out to sea. The navy was unlikely to be able to stop them, not if they made their way around the island instead of trying to get out to sea. The last report insisted the fleet was under constant attack, from speedboats, drones and even a makeshift submarine. Rachel had to admire the enemy's persistence, even though their attacks were more of a nuisance than anything else. They were certainly keeping the fleet from doing much of anything to intervene.

She shook her head, again, as she passed a pub. There were dozens of men, drinking so heavily she was mildly surprised they hadn't poisoned themselves. She wondered why the rebel leadership hadn't knocked some sense into them, then realised the rebels had too many other things to do. The drunkards weren't going to be much of a problem, not until they sobered up. By the look of things, that wasn't going to be until the city had fallen to the government. Her lips twitched. She'd once heard of a retreating force leaving crates of booze behind, in hopes the advancing enemy would get good and drunk. She couldn't remember if it had actually worked.

"Hey, you!" Rachel tensed as she looked up, spotting a heavyset man waving at her. "Why aren't you in your gunpoint?"

Rachel tried to look contrite, as she prepared to spring. She hadn't had time to interrogate the sniper—and besides, she was fairly sure the poor girl hadn't known anything about the city's defences. If there were a set of signs and countersigns, her infiltration was about to come to a violent end. If...

"I was told to get out," she said, bracing herself. "I ran out of bullets."

The man snorted. "Go help the work parties," he snapped, jabbing a finger towards the docks. "Now."

"Yes, sir," Rachel said. She'd been in tighter spots. "I'll go there now."

She turned and hurried off, feeling his gaze on her. Was he suspicious? It wouldn't have been *that* hard for a capable interrogator to tear her cover to shreds, yet...perhaps he'd just seen a pair of hands and roped her into his service, rather than let her board a boat and flee the city. Her lips quirked as she reported for duty, helping a pair of burly men to pick up a crate and carry it onto the docks. They were bigger than she'd thought, from the map, but they looked odd, as if the activity was nothing more than a sham. She frowned, despite herself, as she spotted the wires someone had strung over the dockyards. The enemy was clearly preparing to destroy the docks.

"Get a move on," a man snapped. "We don't have all day."

Rachel nodded and helped them carry the crate onto a small boat, then deposit it in the hold. Her eyes swept the docks as they emerged, noting how the rebels were trying to coordinate the evacuation. A line of rebels, mostly young men and a smattering of women, were boarding the boats, watched by armed guards. They looked tired and wary, glancing constantly towards the advancing battleline. The eastern side of the city was wreathed in smoke, both sides hidden under the haze. Rachel shuddered. She'd seen war before, time and time again, but here...

A hand grabbed her rear as she reached the gangplank. She looked up, pretending to be shocked. "I can get you onto a boat, sweet cheeks," a guard said. "All you have to do is be a little accommodating..."

Rachel's escorts gasped in outrage. Rachel didn't give them time to react. She stumbled against the groper, shoving him off the gangplank and into the sea, the impact carrying her into the water too. Someone shouted in horror, an instant before she hit the water and dived underneath. The groper struggled to the surface, even as Rachel dove deeper... she was tempted, very tempted, to simply snap his neck, but she didn't have time. There were so many ships coming and going, so many eddies running through the water, that it was just possible they'd assume she'd gone all the way down and drowned. The groper would probably be beaten to death by his peers. If not...she shook her head, mentally, as she swam under a light freighter, relying on her enhancements to draw oxygen from the water. She'd been through worse.

She kept going, staying underwater until she reached the cranes. They were unmoving, the demolition charges clearly visible. The work looked decidedly amateurish, something that worried her. She was an expert, and she knew what other experts would do, but amateurs could be dangerously unpredictable. There might be too much explosive or too little, there might be no sensors to keep people from tampering with the bombs or sensors so sensitive they literally couldn't be disarmed...she eyed the wires as she climbed out of the water, keeping out of sight. The shouting was growing louder, but it didn't seem to be aimed at her. It sounded as if the rebels thought she'd drowned and were busy beating the bastard who'd groped her to death.

Good for them, she thought, as she scrambled towards the harbourmaster's office. *By the time they realise they've been tricked, it'll be too late.*

...

"The poor girl," Tamara said. "Where *is* she?"

Her escort, a grim-faced man who seemed in a hurry to get out of the city, shrugged expressively. Tamara shuddered. She'd never liked water—on Earth, the oceans had been polluted to the point of lethality long before Earthfall had turned the entire planet into a dead husk—and the thought of being dragged below the waves was terrifying. The poor girl who'd fallen had probably been weighed down by her clothes, held underwater until she'd drowned...Tamara shuddered, again. It was a fate worse than death.

It did kill her, you idiot, she thought, as she was pushed up the gangplank and onto a small sailing boat. It rocked underneath her, a grim reminder her fate was no longer in her own hands. It depended on the sailors manning the ship...she shook her head, remembering that had been true even before she'd been deported. *At least she's free now.*

The thought was no consolation as a whistle blew, loudly enough to be heard over the fighting. The sailors started to shout at each other, screaming bizarre instructions as they untied the boat and started to steer her away from the pier. Tamara shivered, helplessly, as the boat rocked beneath her, rising and falling even though they were still sheltered within the harbour. What would it be like on the open sea? She wanted to close her eyes, but she didn't quite dare. If the boat tipped over…they were already overloaded, without lifejackets or anything else she'd seen in flicks set in the semi-mythical days of Earth. Hell, she didn't know how to use a lifejacket, either…

She turned her head, taking one last look at the city. It was burning, the flames spreading from house to house. The air seemed to vibrate, an instant before there was a flash of light, followed by a fireball rising into the air. A shell, she guessed, or a missile. Pallas had been spared the bombardment that had hammered much of the island, before the invasion had begun in earnest. She suspected, in hindsight, it had been why the rebel leadership had been so sure the city was about to be attacked. Now…she shook her head. The city couldn't be saved. It was already a pile of ruins.

Her escort nudged her as the boat slipped out of the harbour mouth. "If you want to be sick, don't be sick on me."

Tamara scowled. The rocking was growing worse. She could see the waves advancing towards the boat, each one seemingly large enough to pick the boat out of the water and throw it back to dry land. She knew, intellectually, she was being silly. The sailors wouldn't risk the trip if it was certain suicide. And yet…she forced herself, somehow, to close her eyes. It would all be over soon.

"Thanks," she said, sourly. "I'll do my best not to aim for you."

• • •

Richard stayed low as machine gun bullets rocketed overhead, keeping his head as far down as possible. The enemy strongpoint had been a nasty surprise, tucked away in a seemingly deserted street…so well concealed, he admitted sourly, that the first blast had killed or injured three of his men who hadn't stayed as low as they should. One of the poor bastards was screaming for his mother, clearly all too aware there was no hope of getting him to a medic before he bled to death. The other two were silent. Richard feared the worst.

The radio bleeped, a single note. Richard covered his head as the mortar shells crashed down, silencing the machine gun. He lifted his weapon and darted forward, charging into the strongpoint before the enemy could recover. Four bodies lay in front of him, beyond all hope of survival; two more, badly wounded, were slightly further away. Richard felt a hot flash of rage as they cowered in front of him, understanding—finally—what had driven Angeline Porter to commit a war crime. The bastards had killed or wounded some of his men and they wanted mercy? It wasn't as if they were going to survive the next few hours. One of them was so badly hurt that the only thing keeping him alive was a piece of wreckage, lodged within the wound. If it was removed, he'd bleed to death within moments.

We're supposed to be better than them, Richard told himself. *But why should we waste our resources on men who'll die soon anyway?*

He bit his lip hard, tasting blood. The treacherous thought could not be indulged, not even for a second. It wasn't a bad question…and that, he realised tiredly, was what made it so dangerous. Once he started denying the enemy medical care, it was only a short step to shooting enemy wounded—and then unwounded prisoners. And it would be an utter disaster for the cause. Angeline Porter had been an aberration, one person of madness in an army committed to playing by the rules. If he did it, too…

"Get the medics up here," he ordered, quietly. "And then move the next units into position."

He checked the map, trying to locate his position. He'd always been good with maps—he'd done his best to escape the stigma of being a lieutenant armed with a map—but he'd never visited Pallas and the damaged city bore little resemblance to the paper he'd stuck in his belt before boarding the landing craft. He thought they were close to the harbour, but it was hard to be sure. They should be nearing the harbour wall at any moment.

"We push onwards," he said. If they could secure the harbour, they could isolate the rest of the rebel strongpoints while using the port to bring in the remainder of the invasion force, before pushing into the interior. "Get ready."

• • •

There was a brief, very brief, pause in the storm, so brief that only an experienced soldier would have noticed it before it passed. Rachel heard it as she scrambled up the gutter, up the side wall and onto the rooftop. There were no shouts from below, no cries of alarm or demand for snipers to blow her off the wall before she reached the roof…her lips twisted in grim amusement. It was easy to assume no one could possibly get up a wall and then neglect to guard it, something she'd done herself during basic training. She still flushed whenever she remembered how easy her guardposts had been circumvented by the OPFOR. If that had been a real attack, she wouldn't have lived to reach the Slaughterhouse.

She crawled across the rooftop—there was no point in risking everything by standing up—and found the hatch. It was bolted shut, but her multitool made short work of it. She dropped into the uppermost floor, pistol in hand, and saw nothing, save for a primitive transmitter linked to a set of wires. Her blood ran cold as she realised she'd stumbled across the demolition system. She pulled out the cord, hoping and praying the system wasn't *slightly* more advanced than she thought. The rebels preferred to keep things as simple as possible—Rachel approved, given she'd been taught to do the same—but they might have been a little more careful here. If nothing else, blanket jamming might disrupt the signal or even trigger the detonations ahead of time. Rachel hoped the rebels had taken precautions against *that*.

The interior of the harbourmaster's office was quiet, save for a lone voice from down below. Rachel slipped down the stairs, careful not to make any noise as she swept the upper offices for possible threats. The last thing she needed was an armed rebel behind her, certainly one she didn't know was there until he shot her in the back. The voice grew louder as she reached the bottom of the stairs, the words steadily becoming clearer. It sounded like someone making one last broadcast and reading out the names of people who'd fought and died well, before signing off and leaving to meet their maker. She smiled coldly—she'd clearly located the rebel CO—and kicked the door open. The man inside stared at her, then grabbed for a pistol on the desk.

Rachel lunged at the rebel, flying over the desk and knocking him to the ground. His pistol went flying, clattering somewhere in the semi-darkness. Rachel caught his neck and pressed down, determined to weaken the rebel without killing him. He stared up at her, fighting desperately even with her grip tightening. Rachel was morbidly impressed. There weren't many men who could keep going, not when they were clearly outmatched. His hand flailed at her, as if he was trying to tear out her eyes with his nails. She caught his hand, bending it back…he screamed in pain, thrashing against her. His entire body twisted…

…And she realised, too late, that it had been a diversion.

The rebel smiled as he pressed the wristcom to the floor. Rachel yanked it off his wrist, too late. The signal was sent…she braced herself, half-expecting the world to explode around her. If the explosives upstairs were detonated…the ground heaved, so violently the building threatened to cave in. The sound hit a moment later, a thunderous explosion that she knew—without looking—had been strong enough to take out most of the harbour and its facilities. Another earthquake, a little more distant, followed rapidly. Rachel had no idea what had exploded, but she doubted it was good news.

"It's over," the rebel breathed. His lips were turning blue. Rachel sniffed his breath and cursed under her breath. A suicide capsule. She hadn't seen one of those in years, since she'd been busting terrorist cells back when the universe had made sense. "Bye…"

Rachel let go of him as he died, then stood up. She'd failed. If she'd shot him…she looked at the wristcom and knew it wouldn't have made a difference. The wretched devices were designed to monitor their wearers and react to their physical state. She'd never liked them—she was all too aware how they could be used to spy on someone from a distance, monitoring their every move—but this one could have been reprogrammed to trigger the blast when the wearer died. She shook her head in dismay. If she hadn't disabled the explosives upstairs, she would be dead.

The invasion might have failed, she thought, numbly. *And the rebels now have a chance to push us back into the sea.*

CHAPTER TWENTY-SIX

WINCHESTER ISLAND, NEW DONCASTER

"**THE FAULT WAS MINE,**" Rachel said. She stood in front of him in what had once been the harbourmaster's office, her hands clasped behind her back. "I respectfully submit myself for punishment."

Roland said nothing for a long moment, unsure of quite what she was doing. Another test? Or…or what? It wasn't as if she'd fucked up on purpose. She'd been very lucky she'd been able to deactivate at least one of the demolition charges, saving herself from being blown to atoms along with most of the docks. If her report was accurate, and he had no reason to think it wasn't, there'd been no way to save the docks. The modified wristcom had been a nasty surprise. He wondered, sourly, where the rebels had obtained it. The device was hardly the sort of thing he'd expect the mystery backers to pass to the rebels. It took a devious mind to realise how the wristcom could be turned into a makeshift detonator.

"It wasn't your fault," he said, finally. Their relationship was odd, to say the least. She wasn't precisely his superior, but not exactly his junior either. He had a feeling she had orders to give him enough rope, to see what he'd do with it. Either tie everything up in a neat little bow, he reflected, or simply hang himself. "You did enough to save at least part of the docks."

"Not enough," Rachel said. "The timetable has been slowed down sharply."

Roland couldn't disagree. He'd hoped to secure the docks more or less intact. The rebels had made sure he couldn't. They'd not only taken out the heavy equipment, which he'd expected, but blown up the harbour walls as well as the loading docks. A couple of piers had survived, thanks to Rachel, yet they were nowhere near enough to bring in the volume of supplies he needed. It didn't help, he reflected sourly, that the rebels had evacuated most of the city, including all the former dockyard workers. He hadn't counted on retaining their willing services—he was quite happy to go through a pantomime of threatening their families, to convince the rebels that they'd had no choice—but it was still deeply frustrating. They'd have to bring in more workers from loyalist islands, causing yet more delays.

"It wasn't your fault," he repeated. "No beating yourself up over it. That's an order."

"Yes, sir." Rachel smiled, rather thinly. "How do you intend to proceed?"

"We'll need to bring in additional workers, as well as mobile harbours," Roland said. He glanced at the map, silently assessing the situation. "Putting them in place may prove a trifle problematic."

He scowled. The weather was dangerously unpredictable. The harbour had been designed to be secure, even against the worst storms the planet could produce, but mobile harbours were hellishly vulnerable. The engineers had made it clear, when they'd started churning out the prefabricated units. A single storm might be enough to set the timetable back weeks, if not months. And yet, what choice did he have? There was little hope of striking at another city in hopes of capturing its port. The rebels would make damn sure the remainder of the cities were also rigged for destruction, when his spearheads threatened to punch through the defences.

"We'll build up here, if a little slower than planned," he said. "Our advance units can secure the approaches, making it impossible for the rebels to sneak up on us. Once we're ready, we'll start the offensive towards the factories."

"The rebels will have rigged them for demolition too," Rachel reminded him. "We'll have to be very careful."

Roland nodded, grimly. The planet *needed* the factories, if it didn't want to become hopelessly dependent on interstellar trade. There were already far too many gaps that could only be filled by off-world assistance, assistance that had been in short supply before Earthfall and now would come with heavy strings attached. He doubted anything could be done, if a newly independent star nation sent a squadron to New Doncaster and demanded the government surrender or else. The corps certainly couldn't intervene. Roland and his team would be lucky if they were merely taken off-world and told to get lost.

He stood, trying to brush aside his concerns. He'd expected worse. The rebels might have done more—a lot more—to make the invasion costly, if not impossible. They'd guessed his target—he was sure of it—but they hadn't known precisely where he'd intended to land on the island. If they had…he winced, inwardly. The bombardment had been intense, but a couple of regiments properly dug in would have torn his landing force to pieces before it managed to secure a solid foothold. And, even without advance knowledge, they'd done a great deal of damage. The speedboats and aircraft had exacted a considerable toll on his men.

Rachel followed him, keeping her distance as he strode out of the harbourmaster's office and along the docks. Small teams were swarming over the ruins, looking for unexploded charges while planning how best to dreg the waters and put the harbour back into service. Roland felt his heart sink. The most optimistic estimates were just too long. He tried to tell himself it wouldn't alter the outcome, as he led the way through the gates and into the city itself, but…he shook his head. He had an awful feeling he might be right.

The city looked weird. Some districts had been reduced to rubble, sealed off after the detonations and left for dead; others were intact, to the point it was easy to believe the city hadn't been stormed at all. The houses were empty, abandoned by the rebels; a handful of warehouses had been searched, then turned into makeshift hospitals. Roland shuddered, trying not to feel guilty as he gazed upon the wounded men. He'd been told, back in boot camp, that anything that wasn't immediately fatal could be repaired. The corps had centuries of experience with battlefield medicine. It felt like a sick joke, now, to realise his men wouldn't have access to modern medicine. New Doncaster's advanced medical tech was reserved for the aristocracy, where it existed at all. He spotted a man who'd lost a leg and shuddered, again. The odds were good the poor bastard would never walk normally again.

I knew I could get hurt, he thought, numbly. It was funny how long it had taken for that awareness to penetrate his skull, although—once upon a time—laying hands on him had been punishable by a slow and painful death. *But I didn't realise others would get hurt because of me.*

He tried not to be sick as he moved from bed to bed, speaking to a handful of the wounded in hopes of offering what comfort he could. The air stank of piss and shit and blood and makeshift medicines, the best the planet could produce. He felt his stomach churn as he watched a pair of doctors decide a man's life could not be saved, then inject him with drugs to give him as peaceful a passing as possible. Roland understood—they had very limited supplies, to the point many of the wounded couldn't be treated at all—but it still felt like a very personal failure. Guilt gnawed at his mind. He hadn't even taken the risk of leading his men into combat himself!

You didn't have a choice, he told himself. *You really didn't.*

It was no consolation. He should have led the assault himself. He should have been on the first boats, or buttoned up in the first tanks, or even accompanied Rachel as she sneaked into the city. He owed it to himself, and the men under his command, to share the risks. Hell, if he'd followed a normal career trajectory, it was unlikely he'd have graduated the Slaughterhouse by now, let alone been given a brevet rank. It was going to hurt, he reflected bitterly, when he returned to the corps. He'd have to get used to being just another recruit once again.

A man convulsed, crying for his mother. Roland stepped back, unable to take his eyes off the scene as the doctors fought to save the poor bastard's life. It felt wrong, suddenly, that he didn't even know the man's name. Was he a debtor, serving in the military in exchange for debt forgiveness? Or was he a townie, trading military service for the franchise? Or an aristocrat…there weren't many aristos in the infantry, but there were *some*. Roland winced, painfully, as the man convulsed one final time and lay still. He didn't need the doctors to tell him the man was dead.

He turned and strode outside, unable to take it anymore. "Does it… does it get any easier?"

"It shouldn't," Rachel said, quietly. "But you can't afford the risk of losing your people to render you helpless."

Roland nodded, numbly. He'd studied campaigns—half-assed campaigns, according to the DIs—in which political considerations had been allowed to trump military realities. His instructors had explained that the wars could have been won, fairly quickly, if the politicians had allowed the military to give their all. Instead, they'd played games because they were afraid of being blamed for dead soldiers and wound up paying a far higher price when the gloves finally came off. It was astonishing, he reflected sourly, how many problems could be nipped in the bud by swift decisive action. But it was often hard to realise that until afterwards, when the problem had mushroomed into something that couldn't be handled so quickly.

He felt cold as he walked through the rest of the city, then inspected the makeshift POW camp beyond. The rebels hadn't surrendered easily, from the reports; they'd fought to the last, often trying to take one last soldier with them or—worse—reserving the final bullet for themselves. It chilled him, because he knew why they were so determined to avoid capture and imprisonment. The men behind the wire, watched by MPs, probably expected to be put in front of a wall and shot. Angeline Porter had a lot to answer for.

She might be dead by now, Roland thought. He had some survival skills, but it wouldn't be easy to survive on a deserted island on the edge of a habitable zone. He'd looked at the survey reports. The islands on the rim were barely habitable. *She might have starved to death within a week of her arrival.*

He scowled. It wasn't enough. She should have been openly condemned, then disowned, then finally shot. Her position, and her story, shouldn't have been enough to save her from the firing squad or the gallows or whatever. Instead...he wondered how many of his wounded men had been hurt by rebels determined not to be taken alive, whatever the cost. And how many rebels would die because they feared the worst...

Rachel cleared her throat. "Richard should be waiting for us, along the front lines."

"Then we'd better go meet him," Roland said. He needed to get a feel for the island's terrain before the next offensive began, if it ever did. Bringing in supplies from Kingston and the other bases was going to take weeks, at best. The rebels would have all the time they needed to plan and mount a counterattack. "The rebels won't leave us alone for long."

It wasn't a pleasant thought, but he couldn't avoid it. Standard military doctrine—and there was no evidence the rebels disagreed—insisted that allowing an invasion force to secure the beachhead and bring in more supplies was tantamount to accepting inevitable defeat. Roland knew it was just a matter of time until the rebels collected themselves, then reoriented their forces to slow and perhaps even stop his advance. The terrain would favour them, particularly as they'd had months to consider how best to use it against the advancing army. Roland had hoped for a quick victory, but common sense had suggested otherwise. Now...he suspected it had been right.

Rachel called a jeep, then motioned for him to sit in the back as she drove along a bumpy road to the front lines. Richard had done well, Roland noted; he'd stopped at the crossroads, stationing his forces in position to block any armoured counterattacks. There was no way to keep the rebels from slipping insurgents behind the lines, not when there was no way to secure the entire line, but hopefully such challenges could be limited. It would be much harder for the rebels to get inside the wire. Or so he hoped.

He scowled as he heard a pair of shots in the distance, followed by an explosion. A rebel team, caught in the act of trying to get in or out of the beachhead? Or local farmers, trying to defend their property? There was no way to know. Winchester wasn't just plantations and jungle. It was too large. Roland wondered, idly, which way the island's middle class would jump, then realised it was unlikely they'd side with the government. Even if they didn't regard the aristos with the same fear and loathing felt by the rest of the rebels, they wouldn't be eager to draw rebel attention. Their farms were practically defenceless. The last thing they needed was to convince the rebels they couldn't be trusted.

Richard nodded—salutes were forbidden in combat zones—as Roland clambered out of the jeep. "Sir," he said. "We have secured the line, as per orders."

Roland looked him up and down. Richard looked tired beyond endurance. He should have been given a rest, as soon as the city fell, but there'd been no time. Roland had *needed* a trusted officer in command of the forward spearheads, all too aware of what could happen if they ran into an ambush. They didn't need more atrocities to fan the flames of rebel determination to fight, although…he scowled. The rebels had been pumping out all sorts of horror stories. And one of them was actually true.

"Good," Roland said. "Any contacts?"

"Nothing major," Richard informed him. "Some sniping, up and down the line; a couple of minor ambushes and IED strikes, one of which disabled a tank. I think we punched through their planned defensive line, when we made our landings and struck out."

"I hope so," Roland said. "It'll be a while before we can continue the offensive."

"Yes, sir," Richard said. "I've already given orders to patrol beyond the line, but not to make any further advances."

"Good thinking," Roland said. It wouldn't do to let the rebels think they could operate on the far side with impunity. "Right now, though, you need to get some rest."

Richard smiled, humourlessly. "So do you, sir; so do you."

• • •

"They're digging in, sir," the scout reported. He was out of breath, suggesting he'd run all the way to the bunker. "They don't seem to be attempting to expand the beachhead any further."

Bryce nodded, grateful he'd taken the time to explore the island before the government's invasion force hove into view. The maps were about as good as they got on New Doncaster, but they didn't give him a feel for the terrain. The island was a strange mixture of plantations, fields growing more mundane crops, roads that veered between tarmac and muddy tracks and rivers that could be diverted to turn the landscape into a giant bog. There were plenty of places that could be used as firing positions, giving his men a chance to land a blow, then run before the enemy returned fire. It wouldn't stop the government troops, but it would slow them down. He'd have the time he needed to prepare a proper defensive line.

And to mount a counterattack, he told himself. *They won't have the edge next time.*

"Order the remaining residents to leave," he said, finally. He would have preferred to have had the region evacuated earlier, but the local rebels had been reluctant to issue instructions they feared wouldn't be obeyed. "And then start moving the forward units into ambush positions."

He smiled, remembering the bloody skirmishes on Baraka. He didn't have to commit most of his men to slowing the government down, not when a handful of snipers, mortar teams and IEDs would do the job for him. It wouldn't take more than a handful of explosions to make the government's troops a *lot* more careful about advancing into the unknown and, if their commander tried to push them forward against their better judgement, their morale would sink faster than the government's approval ratings. His lips quirked at the thought. He'd been one of the government's soldiers. He knew how they thought. As the successful landings gave way to a long drawn-out quagmire, and victory receded into the fog of war, they'd start questioning why they were even there.

"And send a courier to the antiaircraft units," he added. "I want them up and ready for when the enemy takes to the skies."

"Yes, sir."

Bryce nodded. There was no denying the enemy had pulled off a successful landing, despite his best efforts. Nor could it be denied they'd overrun Pallas very quickly, although the city's harbours lay in ruins and most of the population had either fled or died in the fighting. General Windsor had good reason to be pleased with himself. But the invasion was far from over. There was no way the government could pull off another landing, forcing them to advance along a very predictable route. Bryce and his men would be waiting, ready to give the government's troops a very hard time.

And even if they win here, he reflected, *they'll win nothing but a desert called peace.*

CHAPTER TWENTY-SEVEN

KINGSTON, NEW DONCASTER

"NOW!"

Angeline braced herself, unhooking a stun grenade from her belt and removing the pin as her subordinate kicked down the door. She tossed the grenade into the room beyond, her skin prickling uncomfortably as blue-white light flashed inside, then led the way into the chamber. A pair of young men were on the ground, twitching helplessly; a young woman, lucky enough to have been partly sheltered from the blast, was staggering out of the room. Angeline darted forward, stabbed the woman in the back with her shockrod and kept going, stepping over her crumpled body as she crashed into the next room. It was empty, but she heard someone in the loft overhead. She took a second grenade, counted down the seconds after removing the pin, then threw it into the loft. Something—someone—hit the ground hard as the stun pulse jangled their nerves. Angeline felt a faint glimmer of sympathy as she scrambled up the ladder. She'd experienced stun grenades during basic training. Even knowing what to expect, they'd still been terrifying.

She reached the top and looked around. The loft was little more than an incomplete room. There was no proper flooring, beyond a pair of wooden planks that had been laid on top of the wooden rafters. The suspect lay on a rafter, on the verge of slipping off and probably crashing through the roof. Angeline zapped him with her shockrod, just to be sure he was helpless, then dragged him back to the hatch. Her comrades were forming up around the ladder, ready for the suspect. She shoved him down, then glanced around the loft one final time. There was nowhere to hide much of anything.

"Clear," she said. "The rest?"

"All five rooms have been cleared," Private Jones assured her. He was an aristocrat, just like her; an aristocrat who didn't seem to know what to make of her. "Seven prisoners in all, stunned and bound."

Angeline nodded as she scrambled down the ladder. She didn't know where Lord Ludlow had found the volunteer prisoners and she didn't much care, although she hoped they were being paid well for their services. It wasn't easy playing the OPFOR, even if you were allowed to fight back. From what she'd been told, the prisoners were meant to be taken by complete surprise. They hadn't known when the attack was coming, or what form it might take, or anything else they could use to plan a response. Their first warning would have come when the squad had inched up to the croft, then burst inside.

"Get the prisoners onto the lorry, then search the croft from top to bottom," she ordered, curtly. "And make absolutely sure you don't miss anything."

She gritted her teeth. Physical exercise and basic combat training was all very well and good—they'd spent the last two months running through an ever-expanding set of drills—but they had their limits. They were meant to be more than *just* soldiers, even if they were armed to the teeth and becoming increasingly proficient in everything from unarmed combat to heavy weapons. She hadn't realised just how serious Lord Ludlow—and his mystery allies—were about the whole affair until she'd discovered he had over five hundred men involved in his little plan. She honestly didn't know how he managed to draft them without setting off alarm bells all over the island. Even for the aristocracy, it would be difficult to hide so many men from the government.

And the Prime Minister doesn't know anything about this, she reflected. *How does Lord Ludlow keep his army off the books?*

She put the thought aside as the prisoners—five men, two women—were roughly searched, then carried to the lorry. They were in no state to walk, let alone fight, but the troops took no chances. The prisoners were shackled, then blindfolded. They wouldn't have the slightest idea where they were going, nor even the faintest chance to escape. It would be a good exercise, she supposed, to hunt an escaped prisoner in the woods, but to do that properly they'd need someone who could give them a run for their money. She made a mental note to look for someone later, when the exercise came to an end. It was just something else they'd have to put together on the fly.

Jones sidled up to her as the lorry rumbled away. "You want to go for a drink afterwards?"

"You want me to cut off your cock?" Angeline found it hard to keep her temper under control. "Or put a knife though the brain you don't have?"

She glared at Jones until he hurried away, then scowled. It hadn't been easy being a woman in basic training, not after spending most of her life as a princess on a plantation, but at least the DIs had cracked down hard on any suggestion of sexual harassment. Here…she cursed under her breath. Six months ago, Jones—the youngest scion of a high-ranked family—would have seemed an ideal husband, someone who could propel *her* family to the very highest ranks even if he brought nothing else to the match. Now…the thought of touching anyone, anyone at all, was revolting. She wondered, sourly, just how much of her story he knew. In her experience, younger sons were so entitled they couldn't be bothered paying attention to anyone, other than themselves.

Sure, her thoughts mocked. *And some of them are so lazy they marry pregnant women.*

The thought haunted her for the rest of the day, as the squad swept the croft from top to bottom, then made its way back to barracks to complete the exercise. Angeline breathed a sigh of relief as she checked the evaluation, noting the squad had taken all the prisoners and found everything concealed within the croft. Lord Ludlow had brought in a pair of police officers to demonstrate where illegal goods might be hidden, although Angeline feared they were nowhere near as capable as they claimed. God knew, the illicit weapons and supplies on the plantation had never been found, despite regular searches, until the uprising had begun. Her stomach churned in hatred. The searches had been carried out by trusted servants, people who'd been so close to their masters they'd practically been treated as family. And look how they'd repaid their benefactors.

A servant caught her eye as she left the barracks. "My Lady, His Lordship would like to see you in his office."

"Thank you," Angeline said, concealing her annoyance. She wanted something to eat, then a few short hours of sleep before going back to work the following day. But there was no point in arguing. "I'll be along in a moment."

The maid curtseyed, then departed. Angeline eyed the girl sourly as she turned away. Was she trustworthy? Or was she reporting back to the Prime Minister or General Windsor or someone—anyone—who might object to the aristocracy building an army of its own? There was no way to know. Lord Ludlow had assured her his family retainers were all trustworthy, but Angeline's father had said the same and look what had happened to him! She'd seen the photographs of his body, so heavily mutilated it had barely been recognisable. She hoped Lord Ludlow was canny enough to watch his back.

Her blood ran cold as she made her way into the hunting lodge. She'd never realised how close her servants had been to her, from birth to the uprising, until it had been turned against her. They'd been part of the furniture, always there…lurking on the edge of her awareness even during her most private moments. She'd had a nanny, then a governess, then… she swallowed hard, remembering how the governess had used to dress her, as if she'd been incapable of doing it for herself. The old woman's fingers had touched her neck…she could have killed Angeline effortlessly, if she'd wished. And then…

Angeline caught herself, taking a moment to centre her thoughts before knocking on the office door. Lord Ludlow came and went as he pleased, leaving the hunting lodge and training centre in the hands of his trusted staff. Angeline knew he was a busy man, and had long since mastered the skill of delegating, but it was still irritating. She would have preferred to know when he was coming, if he wasn't a constant presence on the training field. How could he know what he was building if he wasn't watching it take shape? And…would he understand, deep inside, what his army could do?

"Come!"

She pushed the door open, feeling a hint of the old apprehension. She looked unrecognisable. If her mother had seen her, she wouldn't have *known* her…Angeline wished, suddenly, that her mother had lived, even if it meant putting up with her disapproval. And yet, would her mother have *wanted* to live? Her husband was dead, her plantation was gone, her children dead or unmarriageable…she shook her head, banishing the thought sharply. She couldn't bring the dead back to life. She could only avenge them.

Lord Ludlow looked up, then stood. "Angeline," he said. "Thank you for coming."

"Thank you for inviting me," Angeline said. She knew she hadn't really had a choice, even if her etiquette lessons insisted she had to pretend otherwise. "It's been a busy week."

"And not just for you," Lord Ludlow said. "Have you been following the news from the front?"

"When I've had time, yes," Angeline said. Lord Ludlow had forwarded reports to her and his other trusted staff, but she hadn't had time to do more than skim the documents for anything that stood out. "The invasion appears to be going slowly."

"It may have bogged down," Lord Ludlow said. "General Windsor landed a formidable force, but the rebels denied him a harbour and its proving hard to ship reinforcements to the islands. My contacts suspect the general is deliberately prolonging the war."

Angeline blinked in surprise. "My Lord?"

"The general is an offworlder," Lord Ludlow said, as if he was speaking more to himself than to her. "He has no power base of his own, not here. Even Collier"—he spoke the name as though it was a vile obscenity—"has a greater power base, one he can use to secure and expand his position. General Windsor may find it convenient to keep the war going, allowing him to put his loyalists in positions of power and eventually take over."

He cocked his head. "What do you make of it?"

"The general and I are not friends," Angeline said. The only time she'd spoken to the general had been after she'd shot the rebel traitors, after he and his cronies had made sure she'd face a court-martial and probable execution. The injustice still burned. She was quite prepared to believe the worst of him. "I believe he would prefer to end the war as quickly as possible, but..."

She frowned. General Windsor *was* an offworlder, one who wouldn't have risen so far if there hadn't been a full-scale war underway. It was easy to believe he might want to prolong the war. She had wondered, when she'd joined her old squad, if *she'd* be able to go back to being nothing more than a plantation princess. Could General Windsor feel the same way too? She wasn't sure what he'd been doing, before the insurrection turned into outright war, but he sure as hell hadn't been a general. He was barely older than she was!

"It might be true," she said, carefully. She'd known quite a few young men whose grand plans bore about as much resemblance to reality as rebel propaganda. "He certainly seems reluctant to close with the enemy."

Her thoughts churned. The invasion of Mountebank had been planned to proceed as quickly as possible, yet it had stalled. General Windsor had been unwilling to throw his men into a meatgrinder, or simply bombard the rebel lines into submission. A sensible concern for his men, she asked herself, or a reluctance to win the war too quickly? It was hard to be sure. In her experience, rebels were cowards. They never stood and fought when the odds were even, let alone tilted against them. General Windsor might have chosen to preserve his men so he could keep his eye on an even greater prize.

She scowled, her expression darkening. It was possible. The Empire was gone. No one would come to their aid, if there was a military coup. Hell, certain townie politicians might even *welcome* a coup. Collier and his allies had to know they'd never be allowed to go too far, not to the point they might secure real power for themselves. A military coup, led by an offworld general and backed by local political figures...he might just get away with it. He'd certainly refused to act quickly, when the rebels were on the ropes.

"Right now, the general is requesting we ship more troops to Winchester," Lord Ludlow informed her. "The alpha units will probably be dispatched within the week, followed by the beta and delta units once they have finished working up. General Windsor may also be drawing down the troops on Mountebank, as they're no longer needed on the island. It doesn't bode well."

"No, My Lord," Angeline agreed, shortly. She'd kept an eye on the progress of that particular campaign, in hopes of seeing something that would prove she'd done the right thing. "Mountebank City has not surrendered."

"No." Lord Ludlow looked pensive. "We may have underestimated their ability to feed themselves."

Angeline took a breath. "What do you intend to do, My Lord?"

Lord Ludlow studied her for a long cold moment. "My allies and I have discussed our options carefully," he said. "We cannot rely on the Prime Minister to restrain either General Windsor or the townies. Poor William has been losing his grip on his power base, which weakens his ability to steer the planet's course, while his daughter seems besotted with the general. She has been quite...*protective*...of her grip on him."

"She may have been asked to get close to him," Angeline said. She'd never done it herself, but she'd heard stories of young girls who'd been asked to get close to prospective allies, even at the cost of their maidenheads. Sandra would be in some trouble if General Windsor left the planet, no matter the how and why of their relationship. It would be difficult for her to marry well if she'd been in a relationship that couldn't be denied. "Or he might have courted her instead."

"Being an offworlder, he could hardly be expected to know the proper way to do things," Lord Ludlow said, stiffly. His face darkened, his thoughts clearly heading towards unpleasant conclusions. "Of course, it raises another problem. Does William think he can ally with the townies, or the general, against us?"

Angeline frowned. It smacked of paranoia. And yet, she had to admit it was possible. She found it hard to imagine Sandra Oakley getting so close to an offworlder without her father's consent, not when the relationship could destroy her reputation and weaken her family's position in the marriage market. She'd only met the Prime Minister once and he hadn't struck her as a strong man, hardly the sort of person fit to lead a war. She wondered, suddenly, if *Sandra* was the brains of the whole affair. She might be quietly manipulating her father behind the scenes.

"I don't know, My Lord," she said, finally. She'd never met Sandra. The Prime Minister's daughter hadn't even tried to welcome her, when she'd been shipped to Kingston. It wasn't really a surprise—they were from different islands—but it still grated. "I'm not close to the PM either."

Lord Ludlow smiled, humourlessly. "We have been putting the pieces in place for the last few weeks," he said. "Tell me, is your force ready to fight?"

"We've completed the basics," Angeline said. "It helped that some of the newcomers already had military training, either from the army or the militia. We should be able to carry out the handful of missions we discussed, although we won't *know* until we actually try. Once we go public, we can recruit more openly...but that'll risk diluting our effectiveness until we get the new recruits trained up too."

"There's a limit to how many people we can report dead," Lord Ludlow commented. "The rebels have helped us a little, by sinking transports, but if someone carries out a full audit the deception will be immediately obvious. Thankfully, we can fiddle the figures to some extent shortly before we put the plan into operation…"

He shook his head. "We need to start tightening up the plan now," he added. "When the time comes, we'll need to move fast."

"Yes, My Lord," Angeline said. She couldn't keep a hint of tired waspishness out of her tone, even though it could be dangerous. Her father would certainly have been unamused. "It would help if you told me what you want us to do."

"Would it?" Lord Ludlow met her eyes. She saw a challenge within his dark gaze. "Do you not know?"

"You never told me," Angeline said. She had some guesses, very good guesses, but her life had taught her it was dangerous to let people know how smart she was. Lord Ludlow might have saved her life, and he was committing treason as well as numerous lesser crimes, yet she couldn't let go of her old habits. "What do you want us to do?"

Lord Ludlow met her eyes. "Isn't it obvious?" She couldn't tell if he truly believed she didn't know or if he was merely humouring her. "In order to prevent a coup, we're going to strike first."

After a long pause, he went on. "We're going to mount a coup of our own."

CHAPTER TWENTY-EIGHT

WINCHESTER ISLAND, NEW DONCASTER

"PATIENCE MIGHT BE A VIRTUE," Roland muttered, "but it sure as hell isn't one of mine."

"I had noticed," Rachel agreed. "But you don't need to be patient for much longer."

Roland shot her a sharp look, then nodded reluctantly. The war had practically stalemated over the last four weeks, although both sides had raided the other with weapons and tactics of ever-increasing sophistication. He was uneasily aware, as he landed more troops and moved them into position for the advance, that the enemy was making good use of the time to prepare its own defences. His scouts had reported a growing network of trenches, bunkers and heavy weapons right in front of him, a morass of enemy positions designed to slow his advance and wear down his men. He didn't have a good assessment of just how many enemy forces waited behind their lines, even though he had some very good guesses. The drone he'd risked sending over enemy lines had not come back.

He stared at the map, feeling tired. It was hard to escape the feeling political trouble was brewing back home. The PM was still supportive—he could hardly be anything else—but some of his allies were talking about finding other solutions, ranging from actually talking to the rebels to outright genocide. Roland had promised himself that, if the government decided it wanted to commit mass slaughter, he'd resign on the spot, but he feared it wouldn't be enough if the government got desperate. The offensive appeared to have stalled, which made it all the more important he resume the advance as soon as possible. And, despite his best efforts, the planned date had slipped further and further into the future.

It wasn't a pleasant thought. He'd thought he'd understood the importance of logistics, but—in truth—he hadn't really grasped the concept until he'd had to wrestle with it himself. The rebels knew logistics was his weak point and they were doing everything in their power to cut his supply lines, hurling torpedo boats, missiles and even primitive submarines at his transport ships. The death toll was frightening, even though many of the sailors and soldiers had been rescued before they could drown. Too many men were simply unaccounted for, even after extensive efforts, for him to be sanguine about their fate. It was possible some of them were still alive, on deserted islands, but it struck him as wishful thinking. He didn't fault their families for wanting to think so, yet he couldn't afford to delude himself. The death toll was rising by the day.

He cleared his throat. "Do we have everything in position?"

"I believe so," Rachel said. "The infantry and their armoured support are ready to move on your command. The aircraft and artillery are ready to engage. It's time."

Roland nodded curtly, trying to look confident although he couldn't help feeling unsure of himself. The coming battle was going to be a slugging match, with both sides all too aware of what the other intended to do. Roland would be astonished if they managed to get even tactical surprise. The enemy had probably heard the sound of engines revving, of infantrymen moving forward into jump-off positions. Hell, they probably had observers watching his men from a safe distance. They'd certainly had more than enough time to lay down a whole new network of landlines, then conceal them before the government troops landed. Roland had taken out the official network, but it didn't seem to have made it harder for the enemy to coordinate its operations.

"Give the order," he said, all too aware he was about to lose control once again. "Begin Operation Jackie."

"Yes, sir."

...

Captain Thomas Brooke sat in the turret of his tank and watched, grimly, as artillery shells and rockets flashed over his head and rained down on the distant enemy positions. The operational plan had called for a major bombardment, a creeping barrage that would hopefully disrupt the enemy's plans for a counterattack, but he doubted the hammering would be anything like as effective as promised. He'd spent time himself in the trenches, learning how it felt to be on the receiving end, and it was disconcerting how easy it had been to recover and return to his defensive positions. He snapped a command as the radio crackled once, ordering the tank forward. The rest of the troop fell in behind him, weapons sweeping the air for possible targets. It was just a matter of time.

He felt dangerously exposed as he peered at the surrounding countryside, at the blackened mess that had been prosperous fields only a few short months ago. The rebels had evacuated the region, removing everything they could and burning the rest to the ground. It pained him to think of the families who'd been forced to flee, their lives and livelihoods destroyed in a single catastrophic moment. He hoped the rebels had been kind to them, although he doubted it. They'd probably hated the farmers—the closest the island had produced to townies—as much as their former masters.

The horizon seemed to light up as more shells crashed down. Thomas ignored it as best as he could, focusing on his surroundings. It wasn't safe to have his head so exposed, and a single enemy sniper could pick him off with ease, but he had hardly any vision inside the tank. If he buttoned himself up, a lone enemy soldier could get alarmingly close and hurl an explosive charge—or worse—at the tank, then run for his life. Thomas had watched the exercises, time and time again, until he'd become all too aware of the tank's blind spot. His vehicle was no modern tank, so heavily armed and armoured nothing on the surface could scratch it. The rebels wouldn't need *much* to put the tank out of operation for good.

He snapped commands, ordering the tank to accelerate as they raced towards a small hamlet where three roads met. The scouts insisted it had been abandoned, but the planners had cautioned the rebels would probably turn the buildings into a strongpoint. Thomas suspected they were right. The hamlet wasn't that important, in and of itself, but the attacking force wanted control of the roads. They'd need to secure the crossroads before plunging on to the bridges, further into enemy territory...

Something moved, hidden in the foliage. He snapped out more commands, directing the machine gunner to hose the target down. An antitank position exploded, rebel soldiers running for their lives, trying to find cover before it was too late. Thomas smiled, coldly, as they were wiped out by another burst of machine gun fire. They'd waited too long, either through confidence in their camouflage or a simple desire to make sure they actually hit something when they fired. The rebel-produced antitank rockets were good, Thomas had been cautioned, but not all of them were powerful enough to punch through the forward armour and detonate inside the vehicle. They could have been trying to aim at the tracks instead, in hopes of crippling the tank. Who knew? It might have worked.

He barked a curse as he saw something—a dog—bursting out of the undergrowth. No, five dogs, running straight towards the tanks. He sucked in his breath as he spotted the explosive packs underneath the animals, primed and ready to explode the moment they touched the tank. If they detonated under the tank, they'd blow the tank and its crew to hell. Thomas barked orders, despite a twinge of reluctance to open fire on the dogs. Their explosive packs detonated as the machine guns tore them to bloody chunks. None survived.

"Fuck," the driver breathed.

"Eyes on the road," Thomas snapped, as the tank lurched towards the hamlet. A rocket whistled overhead and exploded somewhere behind him, followed by two more. The enemy had definitely turned the buildings into strongpoints. "High explosive. Fire!"

The main gun barked once, then selected a second target and barked again. Thomas smiled, coldly, as the buildings disintegrated one by one, the high explosive shells blasting them to rubble. It felt like massive overkill, but it was far too dangerous to risk taking the tank into the hamlet itself. A Landshark could knock down an entire building and never know it had been in a fight; his tank would, if he was lucky, grind to a halt and refuse to move again. He ducked down as a bullet pinged off the canopy, slamming the hatch into place as the machine gun returned fire. The enemy sniper hadn't been very well trained, he guessed. The stupid bastard should have held fire for a few more seconds, long enough to get a solid bead on him before pulling the trigger. Now, he was safe as long as the sniper didn't have an antitank missile launcher as well as a rifle.

"Sir, the infantry are taking the lead," the driver said. "They'll be in the hamlet within seconds."

"Cover them," Thomas ordered, curtly. It was hard to make out anything from inside the tank. The driver had a duty to keep him informed, which distracted from his real job. It would be so much easier with modern sensors, allowing them to see in all directions while remaining safely buttoned up, but it would be years before the planet could produce them for itself. "And then prepare to continue the advance."

He peered towards the hamlet, watching the infantry advanced with the squeamish determination of trained but untried troops. They moved in squads; one advancing forward while the other provided cover, then swapping roles to allow the second to advance forward itself. The rebels might have been able to slow them down, if they hadn't been so badly disrupted by the tank bombardment. Instead, the handful of survivors were either fighting to the last or trying to run, in hopes of getting to the next set of defensive lives. The tanks killed most of them before they could get away.

Thomas undogged the hatch, then stuck his head back into the open. The enemy sniper didn't try to kill him again, suggesting the bastard was either dead or in hiding. There was no shortage of cover in the distance, for someone who had the nerve to find a new firing position and prepare for his next target. It didn't matter. He sniffed the air, his stomach clenching at the stench of burnt human flesh, then issued orders. The tank rumbled back into life, heading towards the next target. The rebels were waiting for them.

He heard a flight of aircraft overhead and looked up. They were heading towards enemy lines...friendly, he hoped. No one was entirely sure how many aircraft the enemy had left, but at least the aircraft weren't dropping things on his head. They were probably friendly, he decided, as he looked back at the ground. Hopefully, they'd keep the enemy off balance before the groundpounders reached them. And if they didn't...

We're coming for you, he thought. *And this time we're not going to stop.*

...

"They're advancing on a wide front," the operator said. "We don't know which one is the *real* thrust."

"I suspect it depends on which spearhead accomplishes the most," Bryce told him, dryly. "They'll reinforce the ones that promise to break into our territory and withdraw the ones that can't make any real progress,"

He studied the map, all too aware it was already out of date. The government probably didn't realise it, but their bombardment had cut a handful of landlines that had been laid too close to the surface. He had repair crews already putting the network back together—the sheer primitiveness of the network made it easy to repair, even for untrained men—yet it had cost him dearly. The only proof he had that the government hadn't *meant* to hit the landlines was that the damage had been strikingly limited. They could have made it a great deal worse.

And they will, if they realise what they did, he thought. *Thankfully, our outer defences had orders to act on their own, without waiting for my command.*

He frowned, doing his best to project an air of calm. The operator was correct. General Windsor's men were advancing along a broad front, with no spearhead—armoured or infantry—seeming to have precedence over the others. Bryce suspected, from the way the reports were worded, that the advance was actually a very *light* advance, with heavier forces waiting in the rear to take advantage of any breakthroughs. The government troops were spreading out, in a manner that would be suicidal if they were counting on it. He had a feeling the effect was largely an illusion.

"Sir!" The operator caught his eye. "Captain Dragon is requesting permission to mount a counterattack."

Bryce looked at the map, then shook his head. Captain Dragon—he tried not to roll his eyes at the absurd *nom de guerre*, although he understood why the rebels rarely liked using their real names—had strict orders to hold, give the enemy a hard time and then fall back before his position could be overwhelmed and crushed. Launching a counterattack now, right into the teeth of an advancing army, would get his men crushed for nothing, perhaps even leaving the next set of strongpoints open to attack. No, he had to hold position. Bryce just hoped he was one of the smarter officers. There were too many cell leaders who'd won their posts through popularity or threats, rather than tactical acumen. They rarely regarded orders from higher up the chain as anything more than suggestions.

"Tell him to stay in his post and follow orders," Bryce said, coldly. "I don't want his men killed for nothing."

"Yes, sir."

"Good." Bryce shook his head. "And signal the rocket launchers to be ready to engage on my command."

He studied the map for a long cold moment. He'd spent weeks, back on Baraka, reading every military manual he could download from the library. It was deeply ironic, he reflected, that the sheer primitiveness of the armies—on both sides of the war—meant that a great deal of useful material wasn't classified, let alone removed from the library databanks. If he was right, General Windsor intended to continue pushing forward on a wide front until he absolutely had to narrow his spearhead, then keep going. And when they attacked...

Let them shoot their shot, he told himself. *And then I can shoot mine.*

· · ·

Richard hurled a grenade into an enemy bunker, then darted inside himself the moment after it detonated. The two occupants were dead already, their ruined machine gun lying in pieces on the concrete floor. Richard checked, sweeping the rest of the tiny position for possible threats, then hurried back outside. The noise of distant shellfire was growing louder. It was becoming clear the enemy had long-range guns of its own.

We knew it, he reminded himself. *There's no reason they couldn't have constructed them for themselves.*

He put the thought aside as a line of tanks rumbled forward, spreading out as they charged the enemy position. Two died, the enemy gunners standing their ground long enough to return fire; the remainder kept going, slamming into the enemy and sending them running for their lives. Richard sensed, more than saw, a shell pass overhead and land behind him, fired too late to slow the tanks. The armoured spearhead kept moving, slashing further and further north. Their orders were simple. Keep going until they ran into something so hard they had to stop.

The ground heaved again as Richard collected the rest of his squad, then ran towards the enemy position. It had been devastated. An antitank gun had remained intact—somehow—but the operator hadn't been so lucky. He'd been caught and squashed by a tank, his body torn apart and his remains ground into the dirt. Richard was no stranger to horror, but he still felt sick. He hoped the poor bastard had died quickly, if not cleanly.

A man stumbled into view, staggering so badly it looked as if he was constantly on the verge of falling over. "I...I...I surrender!"

Richard raised his rifle. "Hands where I can see them," he snapped, feeling a shiver running down his spine. The rebels rarely surrendered and, when they did, it was almost always when they were too badly wounded to fight. There hadn't been many exceptions. "Keep your hands where I can see..."

He saw a glint in the man's hand and threw himself to the ground without thinking, an instant before the suicide pack exploded. The shockwave passed over his head, knocking two of his men to the ground. Richard rolled over, raising his rifle even though he was mortally sure the suicide bomber was dead. How could he have survived? It had been sheer dumb luck he hadn't put together a bigger charge, something that would have caught them all in the blast and...Richard swallowed, hard, as he staggered upright and shouted for a medic. One of his men was down, bleeding so badly he might not survive...

Richard felt sick. The rebels rarely used outright suicide tactics, certainly not when they hadn't been pushed into a corner. Who had the bomber *been*? The question tormented him, even though he knew it would never be answered. A plantation slave? A runaway? Or someone who had lashed out at his tormentors and now feared retribution? Who knew? The man had been reduced to atoms, his remains scattered across the battlefield.

God, he thought, as he put as much pressure on the wound as he dared. He was all too aware he might kill his subordinate while trying to save him. *What is this war doing to us?*

CHAPTER TWENTY-NINE

WINCHESTER ISLAND, NEW DONCASTER

"STAY STILL, YOU BASTARD," Flying Officer Chas Parker snapped. "Hold still!"

The fighter plane twisted, gee-forces pulling at Chas as he whipped the aircraft around, trying to draw a bead on the rebel fighter. They'd either copied the aircraft designs the government had recreated and put into mass production, he noted, or simply come up with the idea independently. The combination of modern computer modelling and ancient designs had proved a winning one, for both sides. Chas gritted his teeth as the rebel pilot turned on a dime, trying to bring his own guns to bear. There was a moment of opportunity...

Chas fired. The rebel fighter jerked, as if it had run into a brick wall, and then started to slide out of the air. The pilot slammed open the canopy as his plane fell out of the sky, jumping out of the dying aircraft. Chas watched, just long enough to make sure the pilot's parachute opened, then turned his aircraft away. He didn't have any orders about firing on pilots bailing out of their craft and besides, if he had, he would have quietly ignored them. The pilot wasn't a threat any longer. Besides, it wasn't clear if the parachutes actually worked as advertised. The early trials on Kingston had been inconclusive.

They'll work the bugs out, hopefully before I have to bail out myself, Chas thought. He'd volunteered for aircraft, the moment he'd realised the government was serious about building a dedicated force. He'd expected it would take years to learn to fly, but the instructors—themselves learning the ropes—had cut the course down to two weeks. *And if I land in friendly territory, I'll be up in the air again within a day.*

He grimaced as he pulled the aircraft upwards, eyes scanning the horizon for threats. The rebels were playing it smart, turning on their sensors for a few brief seconds and then shutting them down before the gunners could get a lock on their positions. The spooks hadn't been sure the rebel systems could track the primitive aircraft, but they'd cautioned the pilots to take nothing for granted. The rebels could easily slave a sensor to a battery of machine guns, blasting a passing aircraft to atoms before the pilot even realised he was under attack. Chas had been told there were warning devices that would alert the pilot, if enemy gunners got a lock on his position, but there were none on *his* aircraft. The primitive propeller-driven fighter plane barely had anything, beyond the very basics. He didn't even have any real navigation aids.

The aircraft shook, slightly, as something exploded far below. Chas looked down. It was hard to make out anything with the naked eye, but he could see hints of movement and explosions amongst the smoke. Flashes of tracer flew through the air, blasting from side to side in a manner that left him confused. It was hard to watch a town get torn apart, particularly when the forces involved looked like ants. A missile lanced over the battlefield, heading deeper into enemy territory. There was a bright flash of light, followed by a massive fireball. The shockwave struck his aircraft seconds later, making the airframe shake violently. Chas gripped the stick and held on for dear life, cursing under his breath as another explosion blasted up, too close for comfort. He muttered a quiet prayer for the men on the ground as he steered the aircraft away from the fighting, heading into enemy territory. There was no visible resistance. The rebels on the ground presumably had the same problem telling friend from foe as their government enemies. Chas had already nearly been shot down twice by his own side.

Bastards, he thought, as he kept a sharp eye out for possible targets. The rebels had been withdrawing slowly, refusing to allow the government troops to pin them down and annihilate them. Rumour had it the rebels were flatly refusing to surrender, even when their position was hopeless. *And who can really blame them?*

He smiled, coldly, as he spotted a half-hidden enemy strongpoint. The position would have been impossible to see, at least from the air, if the enemy troops hadn't been clearly flowing into the building. Chas flipped switches on the console, priming the bombs on his racks, then put the aircraft into a steep dive. The screamers activated automatically, producing a terrible racket that would—he'd been assured—strike fear into the hearts of enemy troops. He hoped that was true. His plane was uniquely vulnerable during the dive and, if the enemy stood their ground, he might fly straight into a hail of fire and crash. The only upside, he reflected, was that he'd come down right on top of the enemy position.

The aircraft lurched, dive brakes slowing the fall long enough for him to make sure of his target. He flipped off the safeties, then dropped the bombs before pulling out of the dive and skimming along the treeline. Going too high so close to an enemy position, after proving his hostility beyond doubt, was asking for trouble. The bombs went off behind him, a series of explosions blasting into the sky. Chas hoped he'd hit something important, although there was no way to be sure. The bombs were designed to punch through heavy armour and explode inside their targets, but there were limits. The bunker might have been tough enough to survive.

He flipped the aircraft over, then gunned his engines and raced for friendly territory. The rebels knew he was there now. They'd send their own fighters after him, in a bid to ensure he didn't make it back to safety. He didn't relax until he entered the air corridor around the airfield, then dropped out of the sky and landed neatly on the makeshift runway. The aircraft was designed to take off and land anywhere, even on a bumpy road. He'd been told there were contingency plans to do just that, if the rebels managed to wreck an airfield.

The aircraft taxied to a halt. The ground crew rushed towards him, ready to refuel the tanks and reload the guns while he clambered out of the craft and took a leak. His body felt tired and sore, even though he knew he lived in luxury compared to the soldiers on the front lines. They'd been fighting for days, pushing through the enemy lines one by one. Chas hoped, silently, that he'd never have to join them. He might, if the airfields were overwhelmed and the aircraft were destroyed. His fighter was a great little aircraft, but she didn't have the range to reach friendly territory. The battle could still go either way.

"Incoming," someone shouted. "Incoming!"

Chas glanced at his aircraft, briefly considering trying to get back in the cockpit and take off, before dismissing the idea as crazy. The aircraft was surrounded by loading racks and support vehicles, including a trolley crammed with bombs. It would be suicide. Instead, he turned and ran to the trenches as the antiaircraft guns started to fire, trying to blast the enemy aircraft. He threw himself into the trench as the aircraft roared overhead, guns blazing at everything in sight. Something exploded, not too far away, as the enemy pilot vanished into the distance. Chas tried to convince himself that the aircraft had been hit, that it was trailing smoke and was going to crash a few short miles away, but it was unlikely. The unguided antiaircraft guns were simply not that accurate, even at close range. As long as the pilots stayed relatively low, they were at greater risk of flying into a tree than being shot down by the airfield's defenders.

Luckily, he didn't hit much, Chas reflected, as he stumbled to his feet. Cratering the runway wasn't a bad idea, in modern war, but the airfield was so primitive that repairing the damage was easy, requiring nothing more than a handful of men with shovels. *The air raid won't slow us down for very long at all.*

"This is as close as you're getting," Rachel muttered, as the jeep drove towards the front lines. "You are not going into danger."

Roland nodded, impatiently. The battle had lasted for nearly two days so far, the advance slowing as the lead spearheads tangled with enemy defences, traps, and stay-behind forces intent on weakening his logistics as much as possible. They'd driven past the burnt-out remains of a convoy, one that had walked right into an ambush and been devastated, according to the reports, before the escorts could even *begin* to return fire. There hadn't been much left for his men to recover. The wreckage had simply been abandoned. There was no point in trying to recover the dead hulks until after the war.

He put the thought out of his mind as he surveyed the remnants of yet another town. It had been devastated by the fighting, only a handful of buildings even remotely intact after the settlement had been bombarded, then assaulted. Their walls were covered with bullet marks, bearing grim testament to the sheer intensity of the fighting. Roland scowled as the jeep came to a halt, stopping beside a pair of disabled tanks. The repair crews swarming over them looked optimistic, although one of the tanks was clearly past easy repair. It would probably have to be cannibalised instead.

A troop of modern tanks would be enough to win the battle in an hour, he thought. *The feared Marine Corps Landshark could have crashed its way from one end of the island to the other, ignoring antitank shells and IEDs capable of disabling or destroying its primitive cousins. And if we could call down orbital strikes on enemy positions, we would completely dominate the battlefield.*

He shrugged as he jumped out of the jeep and made his way to the command post. Richard had set up a CP within the town, concealed under netting rather than risk using one of the surviving buildings. They'd all been checked for IEDs, but Roland would bet half his inheritance that the enemy gunners had them marked down for attention, if they thought the government troops had turned them into offices. Richard looked up from the camp table as Roland stepped inside, looking tired. Roland understood, all too well. The mid-ranking officer was leading assaults that, in a better-organised military, would be left to expendable juniors. In hindsight, Roland reflected, New Doncaster should have worked harder to build up a cadre of officers before the planet collapsed into chaos.

And they should have dealt with the resentments before they became impossible to handle peacefully, his thoughts added, sourly. *Right now, the only way the issues will be settled is through force.*

"Sir." Richard nodded, rather than saluting. "The forward units are meeting increasingly stiff resistance."

Roland surveyed the map. The broad front was starting to narrow, despite his best efforts. He didn't like it. There was too great a chance of the enemy hitting his flanks, then getting heavy forces into position to cut off his spearheads from the rest of his army. And yet, he couldn't afford to slow the offensive. The enemy didn't need *more* time to toughen their defences. They'd already taken full advantage of the brief but violent rainstorms.

"We may need to reinforce the spearheads, then thrust into enemy lines," he said. He briefly considered trying to encircle the enemy position instead, but that would just give the enemy more time to tighten their own defences while trying to break the blockade. It was frustrating. The more they advanced, the more exposed they were to insurgent attacks. "Did we learn anything useful from the prisoners?"

"No." Richard shook his head. "The few we took, all wounded, refused to talk."

And trying to make them talk would be a war crime, Roland thought. He had no qualms about forcing pirates, terrorists and other monsters to talk, even if it meant using drugs, direct brain stimulation or even old-fashioned torture. But the rebels hadn't put themselves outside the laws of war. They could still claim their protections. *We could always offer to bribe them.*

He smiled tiredly, then shook his head. It wouldn't work. Probably. "If we reinforce now, then resume the offensive tomorrow…"

Richard spoke quickly. "We may need more time," he cautioned. "The forward units are running short of supplies."

"And we also need to clear the rear area," Rachel added. "There are too many insurgents running around behind the lines."

"Yeah." Roland studied the map crossly. They simply didn't have the manpower to sweep the entire occupied zone for enemy insurgents, not without bringing in more infantry and cancelling the offensive. There was no point, even, in putting guardposts along the roads. The enemy would simply go around the guards or pick them off, one by one. "We may not be able to do it in time."

He understood, in a flicker of grim amusement, why so many paper-perfect offensives he'd been told to study, months ago, had bogged down. The enemy refused to sit still and be battered into surrender. He could take much of the island relatively easily, his tanks thrusting into enemy lines and tearing them to shreds, but the important parts were heavily defended and the blitzkrieg would leave his forces weak and exposed. If the enemy refused to panic...

"We'll ship reinforcements and supplies forward as quickly as possible," he said, as guns boomed in the distance. "And then we'll target the enemy lines and force them to either surrender the factories or stand and fight."

"Yes, sir," Richard said. "We'll be ready."

Roland glanced at Rachel. "Do you think you can get into the enemy lines?"

"Perhaps," Rachel said. "Right now, I suspect it will be very difficult to pass unnoticed."

"Drat." Roland tapped the map thoughtfully. "I think we may have to simply grind them down."

He glanced up as he heard a flight of aircraft heading north. Friendly? He couldn't tell. The rebels had stolen the modified plans, ones he'd put into production, and started churning them out themselves. Clever of them, he acknowledged sourly. They weren't just insurgents any longer, but a formidable army in their own right. He wouldn't be surprised if they had tanks too. Even if those designs had been kept secure—and Roland doubted it—the rebels had access to the Imperial Library. They could easily download a set of plans of their own.

"That will be costly," Richard warned. "I don't know how long support for the war will last, if the death toll gets too high."

"Politics," Roland muttered. "If we don't win quickly, we might not win at all."

...

The road was silent.

Danielle Chang listened carefully, feeling uncomfortably exposed even though she was concealed behind the foliage. She'd seen bullets tear through trees and bushes like hot knives through butter, killing or maiming comrades who'd thought they were safe. The silence worried her, even though it suggested she was alone. The insects should have been making a racket. Why weren't they?

She inched forward, keeping her ears open as she crawled onto the road. It had been tarmac once, but a combination of bombing—by one side or the other—and unprecedented use had torn up the surface, putting a hell of a lot of wear and tear on passing vehicles. Danielle found a broken patch of ground, lifting up pieces of debris to reveal a small pothole, then carefully removed the makeshift IED from her bag and placed it in the hole. The timer clicked when she pressed the switch, cautioning her she had only five minutes to cover the device before it went live. Her hands shook as she pressed the debris back into place, then turned and ran for her life. The IED wasn't very well designed, she'd been warned. It was quite possible the device would explode, triggered by the debris the moment the timer reached zero. It wouldn't be a total loss—the road needed to be torn up as much as possible—but it wouldn't be enough. Danielle had grown up on a plantation. She'd watched, helplessly, as her father and brother were beaten to death for answering back. She wanted revenge.

Her ears twitched as she heard engines in the distance, heading towards her. She'd been warned some military vehicles were practically silent, but that didn't seem to be true. The tanks and trucks she'd watched from a safe distance had been noisy enough to deafen her, although she supposed they were sourced locally. New Doncaster might claim to be an advanced world, but the truth was very different. She smiled at the thought, then leaned forward as the sound got louder. A small convoy of trucks and military vehicles were heading towards the IED, spearheaded by a motorbike. Her heart sank. If the driver triggered the IED, or even spotted something out of place...

The IED detonated. The motorbike was vaporised. The convoy came to a juddering halt, infantrymen dismounting and running forward to check for other IEDs. Danielle smiled as she started to crawl away. There were no other surprises, as far as she knew, and there were no ambushers lying in wait to catch the troops with their pants down. But they didn't know that. They'd have to waste their time, looking for someone who wasn't there. Hopefully, the delay would cost them. They might not reach the front lines before their time ran out.

And one of their bastards is dead, she thought, coldly. She had no idea who she'd killed, but he'd joined the government's military and that made him the bad guy by default, a servant of slavers and rapists and murderers and every other crime her former masters had committed. He'd died quicker and cleaner than he deserved. *It's a good start.*

CHAPTER THIRTY

WINCHESTER ISLAND, NEW DONCASTER

IT WAS ALL, BRYCE REFLECTED, a matter of timing.

The enemy offensive had slowed. Reports from his agents in the field had made it clear General Windsor was taking the time to move supplies forward, then consolidate his forces into a single spearhead. The fighting hadn't stopped entirely—Bryce would have been incredibly suspicious if the enemy had pulled back, abandoning the engagement completely—but it had definitely reduced, becoming a constant series of tiny infantry engagements while aircraft fought it out for dominance overhead. Both sides shot at targets of opportunity, hurling shells over the lines and into rear areas, but the intensive bombardments of earlier days were over. Bryce suspected that meant General Windsor was outrunning his logistics. It was quite possible. Bryce's men had turned a number of supply convoys into flaming wrecks over the last few days.

He took a long breath as he studied the map. Sarah had arranged for him to have a great deal of authority, and the local leaders had reluctantly ceded much of their own authority as it became clear the government forces were playing for keeps, but the plan was still chancy as hell. He dreaded to think of how much he didn't know, of how much he didn't really understand because he'd studied textbooks rather than receiving proper officer training in a military boot camp. How much did General Windsor know? The rebels had studied the biography the general's superiors had given the government, but it had been vague to the point of uselessness. There was almost nothing about his past career, save for a note he'd been recruited on Earth. Sure, the general looked young, but that was meaningless. A man with enough money could have his body rejuvenated, to the point an eighty-year-old could look eighteen. For all Bryce knew, the file was a complete crock of shit and General Windsor was old enough to be Bryce's grandfather, with experience to match.

It may not matter, Bryce reminded himself. *His army is still very much an inexperienced blunt instrument. He had the same problems you did, with the added liability of an officer corps composed of asses and deadweights. Even if he realises what you're doing, he will be hard pressed to respond.*

He checked the timer. It was 0600. Dawn was at 0645, officially, but light would already be glimmering over the battlefield. He took a long breath. There was no *need*, from one point of view, to launch a counteroffensive. He could let the enemy continue to bleed itself, pressing against strongpoints designed to drain their manpower and…no, he shook his head. They couldn't afford to just sit still and let the enemy hit them. They had to hit back, to prove they could beat the government's troops in open battle. And Bryce was sure they could. He'd watched the two sides fighting it out over the last few days, silently assessing their relative fighting power. The government had an edge—it could not be denied—but not a big one, certainly not big enough to make up for their weaknesses. And yet…

Bryce looked at the map. The plan had been too complex at first, too complex to have a hope of being pulled off. He'd slimmed it down considerably as the enemy advance took shape and form, turning the unworkable concept into something that his forces could either pull off or abandon if the fighting didn't go their way. He was entirely sure some parts of the plan would fail completely, or be launched ahead of time, but it shouldn't matter. Even if the enemy went on alert, they wouldn't have time to prepare before it was too late.

If this fails...Bryce shook his head. *It must not fail.*

He picked up the telephone—an outdated communications device, only used on primitive worlds and New Doncaster—dialled a number and spoke a single word. The distant radio transmitter would make a broadcast, a simple update—on the face of it—that wouldn't look out of place. The enemy would hurl shells at the transmitter, of course. They might even take it out. But they wouldn't realise the content of the signal wasn't important. The mere fact the signal had been sent was the order to attack.

It's time, Bryce thought. *And all hell is about to break loose.*

• • •

Richard gritted his teeth as the squad stood to, only a few short moments before dawn. The rebels liked to attack at dawn, trying to take advantage of the defenders being tired and unprepared for a sudden transition from relative peace to war. The gloom was rapidly lifting as the first rays of sunlight peeked over the horizon, birds and insects chattering in the distance as they prepared to greet the day. His NVGs swept the darkened surroundings. They'd deployed sensors as well as infantry patrols, but the enemy insurgents were good. If it hadn't been for the NVGs, the enemy might have gotten through the defences and into attack position before they'd been caught.

His skin prickled, his instincts warning him something was wrong even though he couldn't see anything out of place. Perhaps it was the *lack* of gunfire. The enemy didn't seem inclined to fire blindly, but Richard would have been astonished if they didn't have a rough idea of where the government troops were waiting, preparing themselves to continue the offensive. They'd thrown shells over the lines time and time again, in hopes of disrupting the preparations. Why would they stop now?

A hissing *scream* rent the air. Richard looked up, just in time to see a line of fire lancing towards him. There were more...dozens, perhaps hundreds...all seemingly pointed directly at him. He threw himself to the ground without thinking as the scream grew louder, his mind churning in shock. Rockets. Hundreds of rockets. Where the hell had the rebels gotten them? They shouldn't have been able to produce more than a few dozen, if that. He knew how hard it had been for the government to churn out the missile they'd used to clear the way for the landing force and the rebels had fewer factories under their control, factories they needed for everything from weapons to aircraft...

He covered his ears, desperately, as the scream reached breaking point...an instant before the rockets crashed to the ground. Richard gritted his teeth as the soil heaved underneath him, the shockwaves tearing through the air...the sound blurring together into a single terrifying note that tore at his ears, causing them to pop. He sensed, more than saw, pieces of debris flying through the air. The rockets didn't seem to be very well aimed...he frowned as he realised they were little more than oversized fireworks, primitive missiles without any real aiming mechanism. The rebels would be pleased, he reflected sourly, if the rockets came down somewhere in the right general area. They'd thrown so many rockets in the first barrage that they were *bound* to hit something important.

Richard scrambled to his feet as the bombardment came to an end and looked around. The camp had been devastated. The vehicle pool was an inferno. The tents were on fire, although—thankfully—it looked as though most of his men had been spared. A number of rockets had come down in the jungle beyond, starting a fire. Richard glanced at the sky automatically, praying it would rain. They simply didn't have *time* to deal with a forest fire, as well as everything else.

And this is only the start, he thought, as he heard distant guns begin to boom. The rebels wouldn't have shown their hand so openly unless they intended to take full advantage, which meant an attack was probably already inbound. *The camp is no longer secure.*

He keyed his terminal, hoping the enemy didn't have the tech to detect microbursts. They'd shot at radio transmitters before, damn them. He snapped out a quick report to Roland, gesturing for his officers to get the rest of the men into position to repel attack. Given how badly the camp had been damaged, Richard feared it simply couldn't be held. The rebels had hammered the defences so badly he might have no choice, but to abandon the camp before it was too late. He could already hear shooting—and engines—in the distance. The enemy were on their way.

"Fall back," he ordered. They'd have to get to the tankers and link up with the armoured units before the enemy overran them. They hadn't done anything like enough planning for a major counteroffensive, but they should have time to throw together a rough defence line and give the enemy a taste of their own medicine. "Move it!"

He saw the shock on a handful of faces and groaned under his breath. It hadn't been *that* long ago since he'd watched helplessly as an aristo officer led his men into a trap and got them brutally slaughtered. Standing and fighting was suicide. Retreat didn't sit well with anyone, particularly with men who'd been winning only a few short hours ago, but there was no choice. They'd get to the tanks, then prepare to fight back. It was all they could do.

His mind raced as the sound of engines grew louder. The forward lines would crumble within minutes, if they weren't already broken beyond repair. He saw more streaks of fire crossing the sky, heading deeper into government-held territory. A handful of rockets exploded in midair—it took him a moment to realise they'd collided—but the remainder raced on to their targets. He shuddered, realising they were probably aimed at the tanks. The rockets were very lightweight...were they enough to take out a tank? He didn't know. He'd seen a mortar shell punch through a tank's upper armour, but it had been a matter of luck as much as anything else. He forced himself to keep going, cursing under his breath. His world had shrunk to the squad and a few metres around them. He had no idea what was happening beyond his position, no clue what Roland was doing... for all he knew, the troops were starting to panic. If that happened, the rebels would retake much of the territory they'd lost in a few short hours.

Keep going, he told himself. *You'll find out soon enough.*

Juliet Morison was bored.

Guard duty was always boring, even though they were on the edge of a war zone. The bridge had been taken and secured a couple of days ago, the infantry driving the enemy off the structure before they could finish setting charges and turn the bridge into a pile of debris. Juliet and her squad had been assigned to stand guard, keeping the bridge intact so the tanks could head east after the factories had been taken...or so they'd been told. Juliet's sergeant had muttered, rather sarcastically, that they were really nothing more than a tripwire. Their position, right on the flanks of the spearhead, would be the first to go if the rebels mounted a counterattack.

She tried not to yawn as dawn rose, hoping she'd be able to get a nap once her shift ended. There'd been no sign of rebel activity, no hint they'd even noticed the bridge remained serviceable. Perhaps they hadn't bothered to check...Juliet found it hard to believe, but she had to admit it was possible. She'd been caught up in the chaos that had swept over Kingston when the rebels made their bid for supreme power and there'd been so many crazy rumours, each one madder than the last, that it had taken weeks for everything to be sorted out. Hell, the rumours had lasted longer than the fighting. And...

Her ears pricked up as she heard engines, coming from behind her. She looked back, smiling in relief as she saw a truck driving down the road. Friendly, of course. There were no enemy vehicles in the occupied zone, as far as anyone knew. Perhaps they were being relieved ahead of time. Perhaps...she sucked in her breath as the vehicle picked up speed, a man diving from the cab and vanishing into the undergrowth. Alarm ran through her as the truck smashed into the guardpost and careened to a halt, before exploding in a thunderous blast of light. The world seemed to blink, just for a second. Juliet found herself on the riverbank, staring numbly at the remains of the bridge. The rebels had taken it out? Her head spun in complete confusion. What the hell were they doing? Had they noticed they hadn't taken the bridge out after all? Or...or what? It made no sense?

She tried to move and discovered, to her horror, she couldn't. Her entire body felt numb, numb and cold. How badly had she been hurt, if she wasn't even feeling pain? Her thoughts made no sense. She knew a little battlefield medicine, but not enough...her vision was threatening to fade. She heard engines in the distance, from the wrong side of the river, and shivered helplessly. The rebels were on their way. Her recruiting officer had warned her, in graphic detail, of what the rebels would do if they took her prisoner. They'd be mad too, she thought tiredly. They'd blown their own bridge. They'd shot themselves in the foot. Or...?

Something moved at the edge of her vision, a blocky vehicle that slowly took on shape and form. A tank...? Juliet stared at it numbly. The tank couldn't be real, except it was...and it was making its way towards the river. She realised, in sudden horror, that the tank could simply drive through the waters and onto the far bank. The rebels hadn't shot themselves in the foot after all! It was worse...if her superiors knew the bridge had been blown, they might assume there was no danger from the flanks. And that meant...

Juliet closed her eyes, then fell into darkness.

• • •

"Sir! Thank God!"

Richard nodded, grimly, as he surveyed what remained of the tanker base. It should have been secure, but no one had anticipated such a heavy bombardment. The earthen barriers had provided almost no protection, although—looking at the bombardment pattern—he thought he'd saved many of the crews from certain death. Not that it mattered right now, he supposed. Half the tanks were useless and half of the remainder were too disabled to be moved in a hurry. The only good news was that the new CO had had the wit to get the operational tanks out of their bunkers and onto the field.

"Get those tanks on their way south," Richard ordered. It was frustrating, but right now the enemy were breathing down their necks. "Set up the disabled tanks to slow the enemy for as long as possible. The crews are to fire one or more shots, then bail out and run."

"Yes, sir," the CO said.

Richard hoped he was up to the job—the original CO had been killed in the bombardment, along with many of his subordinates—but there was no time to worry about it. Dozens of men were straggling into the tanker position, men from up and down the front line. The former front line. A handful looked as if they were beginning to panic, as if it would be a long time before they calmed down and realised they weren't on the brink of certain death. Richard sighed, inwardly, as he directed them into position. There was no time to try to calm them, not now. Their lack of experience was a serious weakness.

They only just got their first taste of combat, he thought, as the sound of enemy engines grew louder. *And now it's all gone to hell.*

Sergeant Kraft caught his eye. "Sir," he said. "They're coming."

Richard turned and saw a line of rebel infantrymen, probing their way towards the tanker position. His old forward post had probably already been overrun. He hoped the fires had destroyed everything that couldn't be moved in a hurry, particularly anything the enemy could use to glean intelligence or press into service themselves. The rebels had proven themselves skilled engineers, as well as fighters. He hated to think what they might be able to do, if they got their hands on a bunch of disabled tanks. They might be able to take them apart and produce a couple of working tanks from the wreckage.

The disabled tanks behind him fired, a ragged volley that crashed down amongst the enemy infantry, forcing the survivors to duck and cover. Richard shot at a man who didn't hide quickly enough, honestly unsure—as he moved to the next target—if he'd killed the bastard. His men were firing rapidly, trying to force the enemy to keep their heads down as the tanks fired again. Richard could *feel* their grim determination to hurt the enemy, to hold the line as long as possible. He hated to tell them it was time to leave. But there was no choice.

"Prep the charges, then the tanks," he ordered. They were critically short on everything from ammunition to medical supplies. The forward depots had been overrun or destroyed by now. "And then run to the next defensive position."

He watched the tankers abandon their vehicles, his men looking downcast as they joined the retreat. Richard knew there was no choice. If they were pinned down and encircled, they'd either be killed or forced to surrender. And that meant...he wasn't sure how the rebels would treat prisoners, but he doubted they'd be kind. Angeline Porter had made damn sure of it.

They can't drive us back forever, he thought, as they picked up speed. The battle was going badly, but the war was far from lost. *Right?*

In truth, he wasn't sure.

CHAPTER THIRTY-ONE

WINCHESTER ISLAND, NEW DONCASTER

"THEY HAVE TANKS?"

Roland kicked himself, a second later, for even asking the question. The rebels certainly had the ability to produce tanks for themselves, although he'd been unsure if they'd commit the resources they needed to the project. Clearly, they'd decided it was worth the cost. It was sheer dumb luck their vehicles had been spotted before they got into position to block the retreat, warning him what he faced. A few more hours of ignorance and the battle might have turned into a complete disaster.

As opposed to a slightly less than complete disaster, Roland thought. He'd gone to bed in the certain knowledge his forces were in position to resume the offensive, then awoken to discover the enemy had mounted a major counterattack and his front lines were coming apart at the seams. *I don't even know what's happening in half the fucking outposts.*

He stared at the paper map, as if glaring at it would bring forth the information he needed. The rebels had bombarded the entire front line—he wished *he'd* thought of cheap expendable rockets—and then advanced, while launching simultaneous attacks on both of his flanks in a bid to cut off his spearheads and slaughter his men as they tried to retreat. And yet, there was so little actual *data* he wasn't sure what was really happening.

How many of the forces marked on the map were still intact? How many had been destroyed, or forced to surrender, or simply pinned down and bypassed? He didn't know.

The reports continued to come in, a liturgy of disaster. Bombings, shootings and insurgent raids on airfields. Speedboat attacks on freighters in transit, even a long-range missile attack—fortunately ineffectual—on the mulberry harbours they'd thrown together to replace the destroyed port. Roland felt his blood run cold as he considered the likely outcome, if the rebels got into range to rain missiles on the landing zone. It would mean the end of the campaign, perhaps even the end of the war itself. And possibly the end of Roland's career too.

He looked up. His staff were staring at him, as if they expected Roland to pull a rabbit out of his hat. Roland grimaced inwardly. General Carmichael, the semi-legendary founder of the corps, could probably have won the battle alone, by sheer strength of will. The men who'd battled on Hameau could have turned the situation around, with modern tech and experience Roland's troops couldn't hope to match. But here...Roland scowled, mentally shaking his head. He was the one in command. The buck stopped with him. He could have stepped back from the conflict, when all hell had broken loose, but instead he'd chosen to stay involved. It was his bloody job to issue orders to save what he could.

"We'll fall back to the line here," he said, drawing a pattern on the map. It had been a vague idea, rather than a detailed contingency plan. The advance had proceeded so swiftly he'd never had time to give the concept any thought, let alone pass it to his staff officers for them to fill in the blanks. "Get the troops up from the landing zone, backed up by the next brigades of tanks and assault helicopters. As troops fall back from the front lines, I want them rearmed and integrated into the defence line."

His gaze swept the room. He was sure he knew what they were thinking. The army had paid a high price, in blood and treasure, for territory Roland was abandoning as casually as he might discard a piece of wrapping paper. He hated the idea himself, after working so hard to push the lines as far northwards as possible. But his forces had taken a beating and were now scattered out, over an undefendable patch of land. They had to be withdrawn and concentrated before they were run down and destroyed.

"Recon aircraft are to sweep for enemy rocket launchers," Roland added, without giving anyone a chance to object. "If they find any, zone call the artillery to strike them as hard as possible. The remainder of the air force is to patrol the skies above the defence line. I don't want any of their aircraft getting through our lines. Understand?"

"Yes, sir."

Roland glanced at Rachel, then inclined his head towards the corner. She joined him a moment later, her face so expressionless he knew she was deeply worried. He wished, suddenly, he knew more about her record. She'd told him she'd been deployed on Hameau, as well as a multitude of other worlds he'd never even known existed, but what had she been doing? If she'd commanded an army in battle...

Don't be silly, he told himself. *If she was a high-ranking officer, she wouldn't be here with me.*

"This is not good," he said, which what he hoped was a good impression of his old DI's casual understatement. "Have I missed anything?"

Rachel grimaced. "You need to order the forces beyond the line to retreat," she cautioned, quietly. "Some of them won't have gotten the idea."

"Crap." Roland nodded. "Anything else?"

"No," Rachel said. "But you can't let them get past the line."

"I know," Roland said. "It isn't going to be easy, is it?"

"No," Rachel said. "It never is."

• • •

"We just picked up an open-source radio message," the gunner called. "All forces are to fall back on Pasto and regroup there."

"We'll be on our way shortly," Captain Thomas Brooke told him. "Keep your eyes peeled for the enemy."

He tried to keep his face under tight control, despite the worry gnawing in his belly. The enemy had flushed them out of their encampment, driven them back miles with a single blow...Thomas had known nothing was guaranteed in war, but it was still frustrating to be shoved back so hard after advancing so far. They'd come within seconds of being taken out by a lone rebel with an RPG, an asshole who would have killed all three of them if he'd had the sense to take the shot the moment he saw them. The driver had barely had time to run the bastard over, crushing him below the tank's treads before he could pull the trigger. Thomas knew, all too well, that they'd been luckier than they deserved.

And we're not as well hidden as we might have hoped, he thought. They'd camouflaged the tank as best as they could, when they'd volunteered for the rearguard, but he suspected they hadn't done a good job. The rebels were experts in hiding their positions. The government troops had a lot to learn. He'd seen aircraft high overhead, bombing the retreating forces and—probably—directing ground troops to the stragglers. *If they spot us too early, we're dead.*

Sweat prickled down his back as he waited, watching for the enemy. He could *sense* their presence. He could hear aircraft overhead, and guns booming in the distance, but he couldn't see a thing. Perhaps it would have been wiser to remain with the rest of the force, to pray their tank survived the trip back to Pasto. But the vehicles were notoriously prone to breakdowns, if they were put under heavy pressure. He doubted they'd have been able to get the tank to safety, not when the enemy were nipping at their heels.

Alarm ran through him as the first enemy tank hove into view, a cruder design than he'd expected, but brutally effective against unprepared opponents. Thomas studied it thoughtfully, even as he muttered orders to the gunner. The rebels hadn't copied the government's designs, which had been dug out of the archives, but drawn up something of their own. Thomas guessed the crudity wasn't that much of a disadvantage, not when the rebels needed to rely on smaller and more primitive factories than the government. It wasn't as if either side could produce a truly modern tank.

"Target locked," the gunner muttered.

"Fire on my command," Thomas said, as three more enemy tanks appeared. They moved in a loose formation, backed up by infantry who looked dangerously alert. It would only take one pair of eyes to catch them, to alert the tanks before it was too late. "And then shift targets on my order."

He braced himself. "Fire!"

The main gun boomed, hurling a shell into the lead enemy tank. It exploded into a satisfying fireball, the turret torn from the main body and hurled into the air. The enemy infantry dived for cover, a couple showing the presence of mind to raise their rifles and return fire. Thomas snapped orders, his driver gunning the engine and hurling the tank backwards even as the gunner fired another shot. It narrowly missed the second enemy tank, which returned fire a moment later. Thomas smiled as the shell whistled over his head and exploded somewhere safely distant. He would have preferred it to explode close enough to convince the enemy they'd actually hit the tank, but it couldn't be helped. Besides, the main gun firing a third time was probably enough to convince them his tank was still alive and kicking.

"We'll bail as soon as we get into cover," he said. The enemy weren't advancing any longer, but they were firing shell after shell in their general direction. "Prep the charges for detonation."

The tank fired one final shot, then rumbled behind a hillock and ground to a halt. Thomas scrambled up and jumped to the ground, the side hatch popping open to allow the driver and gunner to escape. The shooting was growing louder…hopefully, the enemy would assume the tank had found another firing position and was lying in wait. They might just be careful enough, as they inched forward in hopes of flushing it out, to give Thomas and his men a chance to escape. Thomas checked his pistol as they started to run, trying to put as much distance between the enemy and themselves as possible. He had no idea what the rebels would do, if they took him prisoner, but he had no intention of finding out.

"We did it," the gunner cheered. "We killed a tank!"

"At least we know they can be killed." The driver sounded much less pleased. "And it came at the price of us being expelled from our tank."

"Concentrate on getting away," Thomas ordered, before the argument could get out of hand. He knew why his men were grumbling. The driver was as fit as the rest of them, but he hadn't signed up to march on the ground. Not that he had a choice. There were few vehicles left within the battlefield, none of which were in eyesight. "We don't want to be caught now."

"Yes, sir."

...

Richard had thought he was used to chaos. He'd grown up in a very chaotic household, then joined an army led by fools who constantly led their men into obvious ambushes, then fought in dozens of battles after the insurgency had turned into all-out war. Hell, he'd taken part in exercises *designed* to be chaotic, to help him develop the skills he needed to cope with unpleasant surprises. And yet, the chaos that greeted him as he reached Pasto was more than he'd ever experienced. The army looked more like a mob than anything else.

He took command, silently relieved he'd managed to keep most of his original squad together and integrate other survivors as he made his way to the defence line. It barely existed, except on paper; he rapidly directed the antitank gunners into position, backed up by tanks and infantrymen from intact units. The unattached infantry were ordered to start digging trenches, save for a handful of scouts who were sent to monitor the approaches and watch for the enemy troops. Richard wasn't blind to the danger. If the rebels drove them all the way back to the sea, they were doomed. There'd be no hope of an evacuation before it was too late.

Aircraft buzzed overhead, patrolling the skies. Richard hoped that meant the enemy aircraft were busy elsewhere, although he feared they were merely gathering their strength before returning to the battlefield. The rebels had used their aircraft to harass troops on the retreat, strafing them from high overhead or dropping bombs on tanks and trucks as they tried to fall back to safety. Richard clenched his teeth in disgust. The rebels wanted a victory, and they'd certainly had a major success, but...

"Tanks!" Richard looked up, sharply, as the cry was raised. "They're coming!"

"Hold your fire," Richard snapped. The tanks—unmistakably enemy tanks—were heading straight towards the defence line, flanked by infantry. They seemed to be having problems keeping up with the tanks, something he'd noted back when the first tanks had rolled off the production line and into service. The rebels clearly hadn't had time to turn whatever paper doctrine they'd found into something workable. "Let them come to us."

He braced himself, silently counting down the seconds. Roland had sent everything forward he could—Richard had been relieved to hear his commander had managed to organise a passable defence—but they'd barely had anything like enough time to set up a proper defence line, let alone prep the men to hold it. A single shot, fired now, would be more than enough to alert the enemy, warning them they were about to blunder into an ambush. Would they keep coming? It was possible. The defence line was the only real barrier between the rebels and Pallas, between a prolonged stalemate and outright victory. In their place, Richard knew *he* would have been very tempted to continue the attack. Who knew what they were thinking?

"Fire," he ordered.

The antitank missiles lanced towards their targets, turning a dozen tanks into billowing fireballs. The remainder kept coming, firing both shells and bullets towards the defence line in hopes of pounding it into scrap. Richard saw rockets—the same disposable rockets the enemy had used to start the offensive—lancing into the sky, their launchers silenced moments later by long-range guns. Richard watched the explosions and smiled to himself. The rockets might be cheap, and their launchers very basic, but their crews were another matter. It would take the rebels some time to reconstitute, time they didn't have. Who knew? They might even discard the rockets altogether.

He glanced back as the handful of rockets landed, breathing a sigh of relief as his men refused to panic. They were dug in, safe from anything less than a direct hit. The antitank gunners kept firing, blasting holes in the enemy line as it advanced. The rebel infantry ducked down, pressing the assault as hard as they could. Roland keyed his terminal, calling in a danger close strike on the enemy troops. The risk was tolerable. If they could convince the enemy the offensive was doomed, they might just call it off before they broke the line...

The ground heaved as the shells came down, converting the field to a bloody nightmare as the enemy offensive was smashed flat. Richard felt sick. He knew they had to weaken the rebels, perhaps even destroy them completely, yet...he hoped—prayed—they'd be smart enough to call off the offensive. He keyed his terminal, ordering his tanks to prepare for a counterattack. If they made one final thrust...if...he shook his head. They had to keep going until it was over, whatever the cost.

And if the other guy feels the same way too, he thought numbly, *this is going to get very bloody indeed.*

• • •

"Tell the advance units to pull back," Bryce ordered. He'd hoped to rush the flimsy defensive line, but it was clear his hopes were futile. "We can no longer hope to rush their lines."

He kept his eyes on the map, thinking hard. He'd broken the enemy offensive. It was too early to be sure, but it looked as though they'd wrecked hundreds of tanks and killed thousands of men, as well as driving the enemy back hard. The government had taken one hell of a pounding, better than he'd dared hope. And yet, they'd managed to throw together a defensive line that had stopped his thrust dead. His instincts told him the line couldn't be as strong as it seemed, that one final thrust would be enough to break the enemy for good. But the cost was already too high.

"We'll probe their defences, then resume the offensive once we find a weak spot," Bryce continued. The government didn't know it, but they'd cost him badly. He'd lost thousands of men himself, as well as dozens of tanks and aircraft. The next offensive would be much more bloody, at least until he could convince Sarah to commit more men and modern tech to the operation. "And we won."

He smirked, projecting confidence. "We won," he repeated. They might not have driven the invaders back into the sea, but they'd chewed them up and spat them out. General Windsor wasn't stupid. He'd know he'd lost. "And now they have to come to terms with their first real defeat."

His smile grew wider. He *knew* the aristos. In victory, they were united; in defeat, each and every one of them would be trying to slip the blame to someone—anyone—else. General Windsor might be sacked, ensuring his aristo successor would be *much* less experienced and far less competent. The government would be scrabbling so hard over what to do that they'd pay no attention to the resumed offensive, or the steady collapse of their position. And by the time they looked up, it would be too late.

Today, we might just have won the war, he thought, as the reports continued to flow into the room. *And the aristos might just have lost for good.*

CHAPTER THIRTY-TWO

KINGSTON, NEW DONCASTER

"JUST HOW BAD WAS IT?" Sandra asked.

Roland said nothing for a long moment. The flight from Winchester had been rough. The rebels had set up an antiaircraft position on an outlying island, coming very close to blowing his transport out of the sky...he shuddered, every time he considered just how near he'd come to certain death. The remainder of the flight had been safer, thankfully, but he was all too aware he hadn't been summoned back to Kingston for a pat on the back. He was surprised Sandra had greeted him at the airport. There was a distinct lack of others welcoming him home.

"It was rough," Roland said, curtly. He'd spent the last three days organising the defence line, conceding—reluctantly—that further offensives were impossible without reinforcements and a certain amount of rethinking. He had to give the rebels credit. They'd given his men a bloody nose, sending their morale plummeting even as rebel morale skyrocketed. The only upside, as far as he could tell, was that they didn't have *many* tanks on the island. "They gave us a very hard time."

Sandra shot him a sharp look as she led the way to her car. Roland wondered, unwilling to ask outright, what she'd heard. The news reports had been bland and utterly uninformative, glossing over the defeat as much as possible, but he'd been cautioned that rebel radio broadcasts and underground newsletters had been putting out a far more accurate version of events. Not, he supposed, that Sandra had to rely on the rebel media. She was her father's trusted assistant, after all. She sat in the corner when he held meetings, keeping her mouth closed and her ears open. Roland suspected she offered her father her insights, when the meetings were over. It was astonishing, Rachel had once told him, what people would say in front of someone they considered to be nothing more than part of the furniture.

"There was a terrorist attack on Yelena Island, two days ago," Sandra commented. She started the engine and steered the car through the checkpoint, then down onto the motorway. "They blew away a recruitment centre, killing at least fifty promising new recruits as well as the staff. Since then"—her fingers tightened on the wheel—"there have been more and more terror threats, all of which have to be taken seriously. It doesn't look good."

"No," Roland agreed. "And with us taking a bloody nose, the terrorists have been encouraged."

He sighed inwardly, wishing he'd been able to get more sleep on the flight. The government was caught in a bind. If it clamped down too hard, it would destroy its economy while provoking resentment that would eventually lead to a second major insurgency. If it didn't clamp down at all, the terrorists would run wild and everyone who was trying to sit on the fence would move to support them out of sheer self-preservation. It would take a very capable government to steer a course between the two extremes and he feared the Prime Minister wasn't up to it. He had too many enemies on both sides of the political divide.

His heart sank as they drove into the capital itself. There were more checkpoints, more troops on the street, more visible evidence of antiterrorist precautions. The strutting militiamen—many of whom had joined the militia to avoid the army—had been replaced by armed and dangerous men, their eyes sweeping constantly for possible threats. Roland scowled as he saw them checking passes, making it clear no excuses or deviations would be tolerated. It was just a matter of time before the security precautions started antagonising civilians, turning them against the government. And then the war would be on the verge of being lost.

"Here we are," Sandra said, as she drove into the underground garage. "Good luck."

Roland composed himself as he clambered out of the car, submitted to a brief search by a pair of guards, then allowed Sandra to lead him up the stairs and into the council chamber. The guards didn't search Sandra, something that suggested half of the security deployment was nothing more than pure theatre. Sandra could cause real trouble for them, if she thought the search was just an excuse to grope her, but they could have called a female officer to do the dirty work. Letting her proceed without a search was asking for trouble.

He put the thought aside as he surveyed the council. There were more MPs, some he didn't know personally, gazing at him with a mixture of indifference and open hostility. Lord Ludlow and his peers sat in a group, Daniel Collier and the remainder of the townies sat on the other side... Roland's lips twitched as he noted Lord Ludlow had brought his own personal secretary with him, a blonde woman young enough to be his daughter. The poor girl kept her head demurely bowed, unwilling to look up even as the PM called the meeting to order. Roland suspected she wasn't born to the aristocracy. She certainly didn't look remotely comfortable in the chamber.

"General Windsor," the PM said. "What, precisely, happened?"

A nicely open-ended question, Roland thought, sourly. He'd made a full report, leaving out nothing of importance. *Are you interested in the truth, or are you trying to give me enough rope to hang myself?*

He felt a flicker of sympathy. The PM had gambled his political future on allying with the townies and appointing Roland general-in-chief. There'd been no choice, something that hadn't stopped his enemies from hacking at his position whenever they got a chance. They weren't the ones in the hot seat... Roland's lips twitched, wondering if the opposition didn't *want* to give the PM a very hard time. If they did too good a job, they might find themselves lumbered with the same tasks—and the same limitations—as their former leader.

"The rebels fell back as we mounted our offensive, then launched a counterattack of their own aimed at isolating and destroying our spearheads," Roland said, curtly. He'd put together a pretty good picture of what had happened in the aftermath, from the intelligence failures to tactical shortcomings that had given the rebels a chance to strike and strike hard. "Their offensive was, at least at first, successful. They drove us back until we were able to set up a defensive line of our own, then bleed them white. They hurt us badly—I cannot deny it—but they failed to pull off a strategic victory."

Lord Ludlow snorted. "The reports made it clear, *General*, that the rebels deployed newer and better weapons systems than ourselves. What do you say to that?"

"I would say, the reports were written by someone who didn't understand what he was talking about," Roland said, bluntly. He supposed he could have been a little more diplomatic, but he was too tired and worn. They could have given him time to take a shower, damn it. "The rebels did not come up with anything revolutionary. They merely chose to produce different weapons and vehicles, which gave them a brief tactical advantage. Their expendable rockets did a considerable amount of damage, for example, but they were of strictly limited value. Once we knew what to expect, we were able to take precautions."

"They also deployed tanks," Lord Ludlow said. Beside him, his assistant shifted uncomfortably. "And they caught us by surprise."

"It should not have been a surprise," Roland admitted, curtly. "We always assumed the rebels would produce an armoured force of their own, but we felt it was unlikely they'd commit the resources to building one so quickly. In that, we were wrong. However—it must be noted—their tanks were actually inferior to our own, suffering from breakdowns even when not advancing on our positions. Their value as a deep-strike force is very limited."

He paused. "In this, we were lucky. If they'd deployed tanks equal to ours, they would have crushed the beachhead and driven us back into the sea."

Daniel Collier leaned forward. "How many of our soldiers were killed or wounded?"

Roland winced. "As of the last report, we lost around five to six thousand men," he said, grimly. A considerable percentage had been wounded in the fighting, then died before the medics could do anything for them. "A number of men remain unaccounted for, which means they may have been killed in the opening stages of the rebel counterattack or taken prisoner. The rebels have not, as of yet, made any attempt to inform us about their prisoners, let alone make arrangements for swaps. We may never know what happened to some of the missing."

They might have fled the battlefield, then deserted rather than return to the ranks, his thoughts added. *The rebels really did a number on our morale.*

The PM tapped his table. "The offensive was a failure..."

"You promised us the offensive would succeed," Lord Ludlow interrupted. "And now, we are staring total disaster in the face."

"The war is not over," the PM said, crossly. "General Windsor, the offensive was a failure, but does it really bode the end of the war?"

"And should we start opening talks with the rebels," Daniel Collier added, "while we still have something to offer in exchange for a negotiated transfer of power?"

"Traitor," Lord Ludlow snapped. "Do you think the rebels will forgive you for serving on the council?"

Roland scowled as the two men argued, their voices rising as the argument got nasty. Lord Ludlow was dead, if the rebels won the war. Daniel Collier wasn't *that* much better off. The rebels might not see him as a hatred aristocrat, even though he was a social climber as well as an MP, but they would probably regard him as a class enemy. The townies should, in their view, have sided with the rebels. Daniel Collier was one of the reasons they'd sided with the government instead, for the moment. If they thought the war was on the verge of being lost, they'd start trying to switch sides before it was too late.

The PM gavelled for silence. "General Windsor," he said, again. "Can we still win the war?"

"Yes." Roland let the word hang in the air for a long cold moment. "Our assessment of the rebel forces is that they shot their bolt, expending most of their arms and ammunition—as well as manpower—in a single desperate counterattack. There are hard limits on just how many men they can deploy against us, particularly trained and experienced men who won't be anything more than cannon fodder, and we think they're reaching those limits. Their tanks, for example, will need to be replaced before they can think about hitting our defence lines again."

"They are not short of manpower," Lord Ludlow said with a sneer.

"Yes and no," Roland countered. "Trained manpower, men who know how to do everything from setting IEDs to driving tanks, is in short supply. We have seen insurgents blow themselves to hell in the process of rigging traps, because they simply don't know what they're doing. It's easy to give a man a short lesson in using a rifle, but harder to teach them how to drive a tank or steer a motorboat or anything else they need to be anything more than a minor nuisance."

"Forgive me," a MP Roland didn't recognise said, "but is it not true the rebels have been training their people from day one?"

"Yes," Roland agreed. "And many of those trainees have been killed."

He paused. "Manpower is not the clincher, however. There are hard limits on just how much military hardware they can produce, or how much civilian gear can be repurposed for military operations. They used their speedboats very effectively, but we have sunk hundreds of them and their effectiveness is dwindling. Their aircraft have the same limitations. They have expended much of their pre-war hardware in the fighting. It simply cannot be replaced in a hurry."

"They do have thousands of speedboats," the MP said.

"But they cannot commit them all to the war," Roland said. "Even if they did, they'd have problems getting them all to Winchester."

The PM raised a hand. "What do you propose we do?"

Roland hesitated. A long, drawn-out campaign was in no one's interests. Whichever side won, finally, would inherit a devastated planet…assuming, of course, that offworlders didn't intervene. His instincts told him he needed to launch a single decisive strike and yet…it wouldn't be easy. He had an idea, but making it work…

"We have cleared most of the shipping lanes to Winchester," Roland said. "I propose deploying heavy reinforcements to Pallas, then resuming the offensive by isolating the rebel factories from the remainder of the island and pinning the rebels in place. We could then wear down the defences or, if it seems impossible to take the factories intact, simply bomb and shell them into rubble. I believe it can be done."

Lord Ludlow made a rude sound. "And why should we listen to you, after your failure?"

Roland felt a hot flash of irritation. "The campaign is not yet over," he said. "I cannot deny we lost a battle. Nor can I deny the enemy has been gifted a chance to undermine our morale, attack our rear area and further weaken us. However, we can continue the offensive, which will repair the damage as quickly as possible, or we can step back, go on the defensive and accept eventual defeat."

He wondered, as the argument began again, if the Grand Senate had ever been so…dysfunctional. He'd studied countless military campaigns, mounted in the final years of the empire, which had been hampered by political considerations that had next to nothing to do with the campaign itself. New Doncaster's politicians were a little smarter than the Grand Senators, who'd been living inside a bubble right up to Earthfall, but they were still bent on ensuring they came out of the fighting with all the advantage they could muster. Lord Ludlow wanted the aristocracy to remain on top, while Daniel Collier wanted a more reasonable division of power...Roland tried not to roll his eyes as the debate went on and on. They had to hang together or the rebels would hang them separately. It still puzzled him, despite everything, that they didn't seem to realise it.

But then, you grew up in a bubble too, Roland reminded himself. *You didn't even know how ignorant you were until Belinda popped the bubble and showed you the world outside.*

The PM caught his eye. "Are you certain you can beat the rebels?"

"Yes, Prime Minister," Roland said. He had no doubt his plans would leak out—or, rather, the plan he'd told them. If the *real* plan worked, all would be forgiven. If it didn't...he put the thought out of his head. If it didn't, he was likely to be too dead to care. "We have a window of opportunity to grind them down, to force them to face us on our terms. And then we can win the war."

"We do need to offer a political solution," Daniel Collier said. "If we offer better terms..."

"Right now, it would be taken as a sign of weakness," Lord Ludlow snapped. "We can't risk offering them anything until we have a clear victory under our belt."

"Agreed." The PM silently assessed the chamber's mood. "General, put together your reinforcements and take them back to Winchester as soon as possible, then win us the war."

"The campaign," Roland corrected, already compiling the list of assets he'd need. Thankfully, most of the preparations were dual-use. The rebels shouldn't see anything odd in a sizable convoy of transports and makeshift warships setting course for Winchester, not until it was far too late. "I will attempt to get the reinforcements on their way within the week."

Which will make it harder for the rebels to realise what we're really doing, he added. He had no faith in the government's ability to keep a secret. The rebels had clearly known Winchester had been his first major target, although they hadn't worked out where he intended to land. *This time, we really need the advantage of surprise.*

"Good luck, General," the PM said. "I'll see you again, before you depart."

Roland nodded, recognising the dismissal. He wasn't blind to the underlying message. His position was shaky, perhaps on the verge of collapse. If there was a second failure, if the rebels managed to stop him in his tracks, he'd be fired. He wondered, idly, what they expected him to do. Wait for a freighter, then take passage to a more developed world? Or return to training duties, leaving the fighting to native officers. It didn't really matter. The Commandant would be unamused if he failed, particularly after exceeding his orders so drastically. He'd had no choice, but that might cut no ice with the inquest if the excession led to utter disaster.

He saluted, then left the chamber. He'd go back to the training base, then discuss the matter with his most trusted staff. He'd have to tell them what he had in mind, although the remainder would be given sealed orders and cautioned not to open them until the right time. He needed them to do a sanity check before he committed himself to a suicidal idea. It wouldn't be the first time he'd come up with something that looked good on paper, only to have a more experienced officer point out the gaping holes in the plan.

If this works, it will be a masterstroke, he thought, as Sandra joined him. He couldn't help a thrill of anticipation. *And if it fails, I'd better make sure I don't come home.*

CHAPTER THIRTY-THREE

BARAKA ISLAND, NEW DONCASTER

SARAH STOOD ON THE BALCONY and stared at the streets below. They were crammed with people, whooping and laughing as they celebrated the great victory. Alcohol was flowing freely, men and women drinking heavily as they danced and sang; she smiled, tiredly, as she spotted rebels from a dozen different factions cheering together, all differences put aside in the wake of the victory. Her lips twisted as she saw what looked like an orgy in the garden, people so lost in pleasure that they were fucking as if there was no tomorrow. It reminded her of some of the parties she'd attended on Earth, but *they* had been strangely depressing no matter how many times she'd woken up naked, surrounded by strangers. And yet, there was something almost wholesome about the scene below. No one, as far as she could tell, had been pushed into taking part.

She shivered, feeling cold despite the heat. She'd never realised how warped Earth's society had become until she'd been sent into exile, until she'd met people who'd grown up on another world. The subtle pressure to conform, to mouth platitudes and pretend to be rebels in a particularly conformist matter; the far less subtle pressure to open her legs for anyone, to be denied the right to pick and choose her lovers as she pleased...she shook her head in disgust. How was it that saying *no* made one a prude? How was it that saying *no* meant there was something wrong with you? And…perhaps it wasn't really a surprise. Rape had been endemic on Earth. If a crime went unpunished, was it even a crime?

The thought gnawed at her as she raised her eyes, watching the fireworks exploding over the harbour. She'd cracked down hard on misbehaviour, although it hadn't been easy. Too many rebel bands were too tight-knit for them to take it calmly, when one of their number was accused of anything from theft to rape. Others…she cursed under her breath. They'd been bandits during the pre-war days, using the rebel cause as an excuse for their behaviour. And she'd needed to deal with them. It hadn't been easy and it had certainly done nothing for her popularity…

She shook her head, taking one last look at the orgy before turning away and giving the participants what privacy she could. It was tame, compared to things she'd seen on Earth, but…it wasn't important. Right now, her people needed to celebrate. They needed to feel victory, to taste it, to believe they had a chance to win the war. The enemy landings on Winchester, and enemy raids on other islands, had been bad for morale. The victory, on the other hand…

As long we don't get victor's disease, she thought. *We may have won a battle, but the war is far from over.*

Sarah padded down the corridor, silently amused by how empty the mansion was. Her staff—and the guards—were on the streets. She hoped they didn't come to regret it. The party would come to an end, and, in the cold morning, they'd have to return to their work. The soldiers would have hangovers as they trained for war, the farmers would feel wretched as they continued uprooting the plantations and replacing them with fields of crops humans could actually *eat*. Sarah wasn't blind to the economic importance of the plantations—she had every intention of making sure the aristos spent their final days slaving in the fields—but she needed to feed her people first. If they started to starve, her government's days would be numbered.

She paused outside a door, then pushed it open. Bryce was waiting, sitting in a comfortable armchair. He'd covered the table with maps and charts. Sarah was torn between a sudden desire to take him in her arms and a reluctance to do anything of the sort, a reluctance spurred by the awareness he might expect it. She told herself she was being silly as she closed the door behind her, then walked to the drinks cabinet and poured them both a drink. She'd found the bottle of expensive—and illicit—liqueur weeks ago and put it away for a rainy day. Now, with Earth nothing more than a desolate wasteland, the bottle was irreplaceable. It was almost a shame to drink it. She had seriously considered trying to sell it. If she was any judge, the senior aristos would part with half their fortunes to get their hands on the bottle.

"Cheers," she said, passing him a glass. "You'll never see the likes of this again."

Bryce took a sip. "I think it's a bit too light for me," he said. "I prefer beer."

Sarah nodded as she sipped her own glass. The lower classes—which meant everyone who wasn't an aristo—drank beer, rather than wine. She'd found it a little odd, when she'd been told about it, but it made a certain kind of sense. Being able to afford the expensive stuff regularly was a sign of wealth, just as designer genetic tweaks and fancy clothes had been on Earth. She recalled a girl who'd had her entire body revamped twice, despite the risk of permanent genetic damage. The poor bitch was probably nothing more than radioactive dust now, unless she'd been sent into exile too. It was possible. Sarah didn't know what had happened to her fellows, when she'd been arrested. She hadn't seen any of them since that fateful day.

"My escorts are on the streets," Bryce said. "It's a madhouse out there."

"They've had very little to celebrate for the last few months," Sarah pointed out. "We might have secured control of the islands, but we didn't win the war in a single blow."

"It was always a gamble," Bryce reminded her. "And now, we've stopped them in their tracks."

Sarah smiled, then turned her attention to the map. It had been risky, asking Bryce to bring them with him, but she needed a proper report. Besides, the government's military was in disarray. The risk of flying from Winchester to Baraka wasn't *that* high—or so she'd been assured. So far, the government hadn't copied her concept of setting up antiaircraft positions on uninhabited islands and banging away at targets of opportunity.

"The enemy seems to be holding its line," she observed. "And now they're going to be shipping in reinforcements."

Bryce frowned. "Is that confirmed?"

"I have sources within the government," Sarah said. "They're trying to keep it on the down low, but they're planning to ship in reinforcements and resume the offensive as quickly as possible. The best figures I have suggest they'll launch the convoy in a week, which means they'll be ready and raring to go in three."

Bryce stroked his chin. "It will be risky, for them," he said. "We've taken the time to reinforce the defence lines, even the ones they broke originally."

"But they cannot afford a complete defeat," Sarah countered. "Even sitting on their asses and holding the line isn't going to look good, not after we drove them back. They need to resume the offensive as quickly as possible."

"I agree, at least in principle," Bryce said. "But they cannot risk a second defeat."

"And we need to give them one," Sarah said. She met his eyes. "I have more weapons, and vehicles, and trained men lined up. If they're shipped to Winchester, could you make use of them?"

Bryce said nothing for a long moment. "The last engagement was the first time we sent the tanks and rocket launchers into battle," he said. "We learnt a great deal about how they performed in combat, at a high cost. Driving straight into the enemy defence line will get us nothing, apart from a number of dead men and destroyed tanks. I'd sooner try to probe the line with infantry, looking for weak spots and then trying to poke through and tear their lines apart from the inside."

"They might launch their offensive first," Sarah pointed out.

"Yes." Bryce drew a line on the map. "On one hand, we'd be dug in and ready for them. On the other, they'd get to choose the time and place of their attack and make it harder for us to seal off any breaches. I'd honestly prefer to fall back a little, at least until we get reinforcements in place, forcing them to tip their hand by moving their forces into attack position. We don't want to give them a chance to cut our forces off, then crush us."

Sarah met his eyes. "I trust you to handle the situation," she said. She knew how to fight and win an insurgency. Conventional war was very different. "Once I get the reinforcements to you, I need you to smash the beachhead as quickly as possible."

"They'll fight to the death," Bryce predicted. "There's no way in hell they can pull out, when we're breaking the lines. They'll be lucky to lift even a few hundred men out of the port before we overwhelm them. And very few government troops want to surrender."

"I know," Sarah said. "They think we're going to kill them."

She scowled in frustration. The government had told its troops that surrender would lead rapidly and inevitably to a rebel firing squad. It wasn't true, not now, but she had to admit that some prisoners, taken during the uprising, had been executed on the spot. She hadn't been able to bring the killers to justice. Hell, she was aware that even *trying* might get her killed. The hatred for the aristos who'd run the plantations was just too strong to be buried or simply ignored. And the men who'd killed the aristos were local heroes.

Bloody inconvenient local heroes, she thought, numbly. *They gave the government all the propaganda it needed to convince its troops not to surrender.*

"I'll see to it you get what you need," she said. "Build up your forces, crush the beachhead and win us a major victory."

"We will," Bryce said. "Have you considered landing on Kingston again?"

Sarah gave him a sharp look. "It was considered," she said. "Right now, the general feeling is that they'd be able to stop us in our tracks, then shove us back into the water."

"We could mount a handful of diversionary attacks," Bryce said. "If we have them pinned down, we can just keep them there and find ways to hit them elsewhere."

"Winchester is too important," Sarah said, slowly. She could see his point, but she hated the idea of dispersing her forces too widely. It was hard enough to convince *all* the rebel factions that they needed to send troops to other islands. Too many of them were solely focused on home defence, or reluctant to aid their fellows. "We can't take the risk of leaving them on the island, not when they're too close to our factories for comfort."

"There's a final option," Bryce added. "Could we get our hands on a nuke?"

Sarah shook her head. "Our backers said they were reluctant to give us anything that could be traced back to them," she said. "Even a simple nuclear demolition charge would be revealing…or so they said. If they gave us one…"

She had a sudden mental image of Kingstown vanishing under a mushroom cloud and shuddered. Nuclear weapons were taboo on planetary surfaces. She'd looked it up once and, in all of recorded history, there'd only been a relative handful of nuclear strikes on enemy targets. If they blew up a major enemy base with a nuke, it would raise the stakes and invite outside interference…she shook her head. The war was bloody enough, without resorting to weapons of mass destruction. The government would certainly try to retaliate in kind.

"I understand the concerns," Bryce said. "But, right now, Pallas is one hell of a target of opportunity."

"We don't have any nukes," Sarah pointed out, dryly. "The whole question is immaterial."

"And no way to produce them," Bryce said. "Right?"

Sarah shrugged. There were fusion cores on Baraka, Winchester and Rolleston—as well as several government-controlled islands—but the majority of power in rebel-held territory came from coal or wind. There was no such thing as a planet-wide distribution network. She wasn't sure of the steps needed to produce a nuke—from what little she'd been told, it was incredibly difficult to put the reactors together—but she was fairly certain it would be the work of years, if not decades. By then, the war would be over, one way or the other. There were better uses for her limited resources.

And the government wants the islands relatively intact, she thought. *They're not going to risk turning them into radioactive hellholes.*

"Right now, we have other problems," she said, sternly. "We have to win the war."

Bryce nodded. "Reinforcements should make it easier to crush their beachhead, particularly if you send newer and better guns," he said. "We may have made a mistake by not churning out heavier rockets and missiles. They can heave heavier warheads than us, even if their accuracy is pretty shitty. Our rockets are cheaper, but their range is considerably lower."

He smiled. "If we can put shells in their beachhead, we'll be within shouting distance of forcing them to come out and fight, or concede defeat and start evacuating the harbour."

Sarah nodded, suddenly feeling very tired. She'd forced herself to keep going, even though the first reports from the war zone had not been encouraging. She was all too aware *she* was the only thing holding the factions together, an offworlder who could be trusted to make decisions because she didn't have any tie to the older rebel fighters. And yet, the position had its downsides. She might have no cluster of long-term enemies, no one who would oppose anything she said just because she said it, but she didn't have a power base of her own either. Her ability to give orders was very limited. Sooner or later, someone would tell her to go to hell and she wouldn't be able to stop them.

I need a break, she thought. She hadn't had a real holiday since she'd become a student. Life had always been busy, even before she'd been sent into exile. *And perhaps a chance to relax.*

Her lips twitched. Her people felt the same. They'd never been safe, not really. Life on the plantations was nasty, brutish and short. It hadn't been much better in the cities, or in the rebel bands. Even the old hands had been jumpy, constantly aware they were living in a dangerous environment, one infested by snakes and scorpions and other poisonous and unrelentingly hostile creatures. And, every time they slipped into position to harass the militia, they were taking their lives in their hands. The party outside—she could hear the singing, even though the walls—was a grim reminder they finally had something to celebrate. She just hoped they didn't think the war had come to an end. The government was far from beaten.

Bryce cleared his throat. "I said, I'll be flying back tomorrow," he told her. "I can't risk leaving a committee in charge for long."

Sarah nodded. Bryce had done well, perhaps too well. His subordinates would be jealous. It wasn't hard to imagine one of them trying to organise an attack while Bryce was gone, hoping to score a victory for himself. Or… the moment victory seemed likely, the various factions would be jostling over who got to claim power over the island. It was all too possible the arguments would turn into gunfights, tearing the island apart and giving the government a chance to launch a second invasion. It had to be stopped.

"I understand," she said. She rather wished she had more like him, but if she had she would have had to send them to other islands that needed leaders. "If you go tomorrow…"

She pulled him into her arms, pressing her lips against his. They made love with savage intensity, both to celebrate the victory and push their fears away. Sarah knew better than to allow herself any illusions about their future—she would probably be pushed aside, when the war was over—but right now it didn't matter. If they didn't win the war, they'd be put in front of a wall and shot. She was, after all, the face of the provisional government. She moaned as Bryce bent her over the table and entered her from behind, fucking her so hard she lost control. She wanted...

Afterwards, the afterglow faded. She'd enjoyed herself. She really had. Bryce was a strong and considerate lover, without the sheer brutality of the men she'd been forced to accept when she'd been sent into exile. It helped that she liked as well as respected him, as a partner as well as a lover. And yet, it hadn't changed anything. How could it? The war was yet to be won. And she couldn't do anything, but issue orders and hope for the best. There was no quick path to victory, no brilliant strike that would save the day. She'd tried that and it had failed and now there was only a grinding path to victory or defeat.

"Good luck," she said, as she looked at Bryce. She'd shower, then go to bed and return to work in the morning. Perhaps she'd be the only sober person at the table. "I'll see you afterwards."

"And you," Bryce said. She wondered if he was going to join the party, then decided she didn't want to know. "Send the reinforcements as quickly as possible. We'll crush the beachhead, drive them back into the water, and then we'll have something to *really* celebrate."

CHAPTER THIRTY-FOUR

KINGSTON, NEW DONCASTER

"IS THIS ROOM SECURE?"

"It was checked ten minutes ago, on your orders," Rachel said. "I did the check myself, then stayed in the chamber until you arrived."

Roland nodded, glancing from Rachel to Master Sergeant (Auxiliary) Brian Wimer. The older man looked back at him, his face a mask that betrayed none of his inner feelings. Roland was sure, with the benefit of hindsight, that Wimer had orders to quietly override anything Roland said, if his lack of experience threatened the success of the mission or the lives of the people under his command. No one, not even the most wary spook, had predicted New Doncaster would explode so quickly, or that Captain Allen and his men would be wiped out before they could secure the spaceport and lend their weight to the civil government. Roland wondered, not for the first time, if it would be wiser to stay on New Doncaster after the war. He had no way to know how the Commandant, and the Major Generals, would react to his actions. He'd twisted his orders so far out of shape they might as well be effortlessly snapped.

"Good," Roland said. "It is vitally important, and I mean *vitally*, that not a single word gets out before things are underway. If the rebels know what we're planning, we're fucked."

"And not in a good way, one assumes," Rachel said, sardonically. "What do you intend to do?"

"The council has agreed to reinforce the beachhead on Winchester, then resume the offensive as soon as practical," Roland said. "I don't think it *will* be practical, not in a hurry. The rebels may be short of tanks and aircraft, but they know the terrain better than us and they don't *need* vehicles to give us a hard time. I'd expect them to brace for the offensive, wear us down and *this* time push all the way to the beachhead when they counterattack. The best we can hope for, if that happens, is a persistent bloody stalemate."

"I can't fault your logic," Wimer said. "I assume you have something else in mind?"

"Recon reports suggest the rebels are shipping more weapons and men to Winchester," Roland continued. "Both by sea and air, the latter relying on transport aircraft they cannot replace in a hurry. They fly too high for our fighters to catch them, but they're very vulnerable when they come in to land, particularly as they can't put them down on bumpy roads and dirt tracks. My general feeling is that the rebels are doing everything they can to reinforce, then either crush us on the beaches or let us hit them and *then* counterattack. They need a victory as much as we do."

Wimer nodded, his face showing a hint of impatience. "Sir...?"

"I plan to take advantage of their distraction," Roland said. He outlined his plan, piece by piece. "If we can pull it off, we'll deal the rebels a crushing blow."

Rachel said nothing for a long moment, then leaned forward. "The men under your command, even the most highly trained and experienced, are not Marine Riflemen or Pathfinders," she said. "The mission would be difficult to pull off even for the best of the best."

"I'm aware." Roland had considered either ditching the idea, or putting it on the back burner until his men gained more experience. "If it works, it works. Even a failed operation would give the enemy a nasty fright, letting us claim a victory even if we knew otherwise."

"You could also get yourself killed," Wimer pointed out. "If something went wrong, you'd be trapped in enemy territory with no hope of escape."

"I'm aware," Roland repeated, sharply. Wimer—and Rachel—didn't *have* to treat him like a child. The bratty prince he'd been was dead and gone, replaced by a professional soldier. He didn't like the idea of death, or even being wounded on a world without proper medical facilities, but he wasn't going to let his fears deter him. "Do you—either of you—have any better ideas?"

Rachel frowned. "It would have the advantage of letting us call the operation off, if it seemed unworkable."

"True," Wimer agreed. "It isn't going to be *decisive*, though."

"No," Roland agreed. The rebels had operated on a cell structure. Now, even as they struggled to put together a provisional government, they were *still* very much a dispersed system. It could be weakened, but not broken. Not completely. "If it works, we'll have weakened the rebels. We'll have bought time to raise more troops ourselves, as well as deterring any outside powers from recognising the rebels as the real planetary government. And if it fails…it'll still deal the rebels a major blow."

"You hope," Rachel said. "If they get one word of what's coming, you're dead."

"I believe I said that," Roland reminded her, dryly. "Us—the three of us, Richard, and a handful of other auxiliaries—will be the only ones who'll know the real plan. Everyone else will be given sealed orders, with strict instructions not to open them before receiving the execute message. Outside this room, we'll be taking reinforcements to Winchester. That will be treated as a secret"—his lips quirked—"which is the easiest way to make sure word reaches rebel ears."

Rachel laughed. "You're getting the hang of this."

"It would be a great deal easier if we were allowed to vet everyone properly," Wimer said, sardonically. "There are too many unvetted people wandering around with open mouths and inactive brains."

"The government is a mess," Roland agreed. "And too many politicians are trying to hedge their bets."

He wondered, suddenly, if he'd get away with taking over the government. He could hardly be worse than the locals. Hell, he'd get a lot of political support if he rounded up the bulk of the aristocracy and confined them to a penal island, while launching a diplomatic campaign to win over the rebel moderates before going after the extremists with all the firepower he could muster. Did he have enough of a power base to get away with it? He considered it for a moment, then shook his head. It would trigger a civil war within the civil war, if he was any judge, and if he survived that he'd face the anger of his superior officers. He was meant to be training the locals to fight, not mounting coups to take power for himself.

There's nothing to be gained and a great deal to be lost by trying, he told himself. *It would cost you everything, for nothing.*

He tapped the table. "Are the reinforcements ready to go as planned?"

"We gave them two days of leave, then orders to muster at Kingsport for transhipment," Wimer informed him. "The freighters and warships are already being loaded. I take it you want to include the helicopter carrier, as well as the rest of the newer ships?"

Rachel cleared her throat. "Do you want to inform Admiral Forest?"

"No." Roland had no reason to suspect the admiral of anything beyond a tendency to be a little self-important, but the secret had to stay in a few hands as possible. Besides, the fact the admiral had been recalled for 'consultations' worried him. The admiral was an aristo who had many aristo patrons. He might feel obliged to share the truth with his backers, bringing the entire plan down in flames. "He doesn't need to know. I'll write him sealed orders, as planned."

"Yes, sir," Rachel said. "And Sandra?"

"I won't breathe a word to her," Roland said, recognising he was being teased. "Like I said, when we're on the outside, we make a big show of concealing the fact we're headed for Winchester. The real plan must remain a secret until it's too late for the rebels to get in our way."

"Yes, sir."

Roland stood. "I'll write the orders now, then give them to the admiral," he said. "And then I need to give Richard a call."

• • •

Angeline had been nervous, very nervous, when Lord Ludlow had informed her that she would be posing as his assistant, when the council grilled General Windsor on the recent defeat. She'd grown up in a world where everyone—everyone who thought they were anyone, at least—had known her name and face. General Windsor had only seen her once, after the incident on Mountebank, but it had been memorable. Lord Ludlow had been dismissive and she had to admit he'd been right. The general had no reason to think she was anywhere near the council chambers. If he thought she was familiar, which was unlikely because of how she'd changed her appearance, he'd probably think it was nothing more than a coincidence. And indeed, he hadn't paid any attention to her at all.

She smiled as she studied the reports from her subordinates. The terror threat had provided all the excuse Lord Ludlow needed to move more troops and militiamen into the city, covertly taking over as many guardposts and command centres as possible. There were so many different units moving around—police and security personnel as well as army and militia—that no one would see through the shell game and realise some of the units didn't have any official existence. It helped, she supposed, that Lord Ludlow had effectively taken command of much of the civil service. By the time they went public, they'd have already won.

Good, she thought. She had no doubt the mission had to be carried out, but she had no desire to kill her fellow aristocrats. They needed a sharp smack, and a reminder the world wasn't a genteel and friendly place, yet—afterwards—they'd have a place in the new order. *If resistance appears futile, they might surrender without a fight and join us.*

Her expression turned cold as she focused her attention on the list of named persons. There were hundreds of others, mainly townies, who would be taken into custody as soon as the balloon went up. Many of them were important, political or military personnel, but others were simply too big for their britches. Reporters, publishers, merchants...they'd be rounded up and told to cooperate or else. She scowled as she spotted a name she recognised, a reporter who had dared to suggest her ordeal had been deserved. He wasn't going to survive, she told herself firmly. Perhaps she'd take her dagger and show him *precisely* what it felt like to have a blade shoved in an intimate spot.

The terminal bleeped. Angeline glanced at the message, then stood and checked her appearance in the mirror. The blonde wig and stuffed bra felt like overkill, although she was very aware that most men wouldn't pay too much attention to her face while they were staring at her chest. It helped she was, at least on paper, Lord Ludlow's aide. The guards wouldn't risk putting their hand down her shirt, not when it would get them in hot water. And yet, if they did, they'd blow her cover clean out of the water.

Slack, she thought. *When we take over, all of that is going to change.*

She walked down the corridor, passing two sets of guards before stepping into Lord Ludlow's city office. It was as secure as the planet's tech—and some offworld tech the aristo had obtained from somewhere—could make it, although Angeline feared it wasn't as secure as he hoped. The Prime Minister was a weak man, but some of his supporters were tough and the townies were determined to maintain their new privilege. In their shoes, Angeline would have done everything in her power to put someone in Lord Ludlow's household. His retainers were old family men and yet... could they be swayed?

"Angel," Lord Ludlow said. The assumed name was close enough to hers for instant recognition, without any particular risk of anyone making the connection between *Angel* and *Angeline*. It wasn't as if either of them were uncommon names. "What did you make of our esteemed general's speech?"

Angeline took a moment to consider her answer. She'd spent all her spare time studying military textbooks, once she'd realised she couldn't wait for someone else to give her the answers, yet she'd barely scratched the surface. Her experience was real, yet very limited. General Windsor couldn't be much older than she was, if at all, and yet he'd seen much more than she had.

"I think he has a point," she said, finally. "The rebels may well have burnt through their stockpiles during the counterattack. They certainly didn't try to break the lines with rockets and other modern weapons."

"Quite," Lord Ludlow agreed. He met her eyes. "It may also interest you to know, Angeline, that he gave secret orders to Admiral Forest and the other captains."

Angeline blinked. "What do they say?"

"I don't know." Lord Ludlow shook his head. "Forest was unwilling to try to open them without orders. If General Windsor caught him, he'd be quite within his rights to shoot Forest on the spot. But why would he need to give sealed orders—*secret* orders—unless he was up to something?"

"I…" Angeline had no answer. There was nothing particularly secret about the planned reinforcement operation. The council was certainly *trying* to keep it secret, but everyone already knew what was happening. Why bother with sealed orders? What needed to be kept secret? The precise sailing timetable? The route the convoy intended to take? It was possible, yet…it didn't seem right. "I don't know."

"There are fifty-one ships in the fleet, including forty transports and a helicopter carrier," Lord Ludlow informed her. "A man with bad intentions could do a great deal of damage with that force. And *dear* General Windsor is already on thin ice."

"Yes." Angeline let out a breath. "A second failure and his career comes to an end."

She shook her head. "Do you want to move now?"

"We'll let General Windsor leave, then start putting the final pieces into place," Lord Ludlow said. "If he thinks we don't suspect him, he might pretend to be following his stated objectives a little longer. If we get lucky…we might just be able to neutralise him completely. If not… he'll be a very long way away for quite some time."

"Yes, My Lord." Angeline met his eyes. "We will not fail."

• • •

Rachel watched, keeping her face under tight control, as the helicopter carrier came into view. It rested in the middle of the convoy, surrounded by troop transports and protected by makeshift warships. The navy had done well, she acknowledged, with the limited time at its disposal. They might not have been able to lay down proper wet-navy warships, the battleships and carriers and cruisers of long-gone days, but they'd done a remarkable job of putting together a formidable force. And yet, she feared the outcome if a single missile slammed into the carrier. The explosion might be enough to turn the entire ship into a death trap.

Be honest, she told herself. *That's not what's really bothering you, is it?*

She shifted, uncomfortably. It would have been a great deal easier if she'd remained with her original team. Or a new one. She wouldn't have to wear so many hats, balance so many contradictory roles…perhaps it would have been easier, a lot easier, if Roland had never seen through the deception. She had no qualms about using her skills to ensure the mission's success—it was her job, for fuck's sake—but her primary concern was Roland's safety. It was her job to protect him, even over his objections. And yet, doing it too openly would make life difficult for both of them. Roland was, despite months of boot camp, still very much an immature brat. If he saw her as authority, as someone to rebel against, their relationship would shatter beyond repair.

And now he wants to risk everything on one throw of the dice, she thought. *If it fails…*

She frowned. She'd done things many civilians would consider impossible. She knew others who'd done things *she* would have considered impossible, if they hadn't been verified by people she trusted. Roland's plan was no madder than some of the other operations she'd studied over the years, although she feared the forces at his disposal were not up to the task. There was no time for enhanced training either. It would be far too revealing.

And he could get himself killed, her mind pointed out. *He's insistent on going himself.*

Rachel felt her mood darken as the helicopter landed neatly on the carrier deck, the ground crew rushing to secure the craft before the passengers could get out. Common sense told her she should carry out her threat to tie Roland to a chair or something—anything—other than let him lead the mission in person. Roland would make one hell of a fuss, she was sure, but the Commandant would back her up. He wouldn't even make a show of pretending to agree with the prince's complaints. The days when he'd had to nod in agreement with well-connected fools were long gone. And yet, Rachel knew that refusing to let Roland go would destroy their relationship. It might even destroy *him*.

A man must become a man, or otherwise remain a boy in the body of a grown man, she reflected. *But what if he doesn't survive long enough to grow into a man?*

She scowled. It didn't help she wasn't sure what the Commandant wanted from the whole affair. Give Roland a chance to prove himself, to live up to his ancestors and then…and then what? It wasn't as if anyone wanted to put him on the throne. The galaxy believed Roland dead. And if they'd known he was alive…so what? The empire was gone.

Keep him alive, let him learn from his mistakes, she told herself. *And let the future take care of itself.*

CHAPTER THIRTY-FIVE

NEAR WINCHESTER ISLAND, NEW DONCASTER

ROLAND HAD STARTED TO HATE TRAVEL BY SEA.

It wasn't that it was uncomfortable, although his cabin on the ship was cramped, smelly, and generally unpleasant. He'd been in worse. He might have grown up in a palace, with his every slightest whim carried out at once—as long as it didn't include *real* power and *real* freedom—but boot camp had toughened him up considerably. The DIs hadn't known who he was and hadn't cared. They certainly hadn't made any allowances for recruits who'd come from privileged backgrounds. His cabin on the makeshift carrier was so vastly superior to the barracks that his DIs, if they saw it, would make snide remarks about Roland living in luxury.

No, it wasn't the lack of comfort that gnawed at him. It was the sense time was ticking away, that it wouldn't be long before he ran out completely...and that there was nothing he could do about it. The fleet was sailing as fast as it could, yet the combination of an evasive course to avoid enemy spies and sheer distance made it impossible to reach their destination quickly enough to suit him. Roland and his staff were doing what they could, to keep the men primed for battle, but the monotony of the voyage was wearing them down. It galled him that they could travel from the primary star to the outermost planet in less time than it took to sail from friendly to rebel-held territory. He understood, now, why so many stories from pre-space days talked about voyages and engagements that had lasted days, if not weeks and months. The idea of a war that lasted over a hundred years was suddenly very believable.

And the fact we're maintaining strict radio silence makes it difficult to know what's happening back on Kingston, Roland thought. *Anything could be happening there, anything at all.*

He rubbed his forehead as he leaned on the railing, staring over the waters. The politics had been threatening to get out of hand, before the convoy had set sail for a classified destination. Victory had many fathers, Roland had been taught, but defeat was an orphan. The government was threatening to split into several factions, all keen to evade the blade for the defeat on Winchester. Sure, it hadn't been a complete disaster—Roland knew it could have been a great deal worse—but it had been quite bad enough. Too many men had died, fighting to capture territory the rebels had recaptured shortly afterwards. A second defeat on such a scale would be the end, for his career and probably for the government too. The townies would split with the aristos, the military would fragment and the rebels would simply pick up the pieces once the former government had finished tearing itself apart. Roland felt cold, every time he considered the enormity of what he was planning to do. If it worked, it would gain the one thing he needed desperately. Time. If it failed...

If it fails, I may as well not go back to Kingston, he thought. *The Commandant won't be very pleased with me.*

The thought mocked him. He knew he'd gone *well* beyond his remit, although there'd been little choice. The government he'd backed had a reasonable hope of implementing political reforms, of salvaging something from looming disaster before the planet collapsed into chaos or a warship entered orbit and conquered the planet in the name of one warlord or another. If the rebels took power...Roland wasn't sanguine about their future. They'd already purged vast numbers of aristos, trustees and collaborators, destroying plantations and redistributing land to their followers. It would be worse, if they won the war. They'd have to build a new government that could actually rule the planet, all the while trying to overcome the hatreds that threatened to tear the planet apart. Roland doubted they could do it. The rebel government was much more likely to slaughter all its enemies, then turn on itself in a bid for ideological purity that would eventually lead to a dictatorship. It had happened before and it would happen again. Building a working government required skills few rebel groups ever had time to develop.

Because it is much easier to point a gun at someone and force them to comply, rather than talking them into doing whatever you want, he reflected. *And once you get into the habit of coercing people, you never get out of it.*

He straightened. Right now, there was no point in worrying about the future. They had no contact with either the government or the rest of the corps, one on the other side of the horizon and the other hundreds of light years away. He could ask for orders, secure in the knowledge they'd never come…he shook his head. It would be cowardly to pass the buck, let alone pass it to someone who didn't know what was going on and couldn't hope to reply in time for their answer to matter. The Commandant would tell him if he disapproved, when contact was re-established. Until then, Roland had to do what he saw fit and hope for the best.

And they haven't even sent a courier boat to find out what happened to us, Roland reminded himself. *Do we not matter?*

Of course not, his thoughts answered. *New Doncaster is a very small world in a very large universe.*

His lips twitched as he made his way through the hatch and down to the CIC. The aristos thought they were important, and that they had immense influence on galactic affairs, but the truth was they were effectively powerless outside the planet's atmosphere. The Empire was gone. The contacts and connections they'd built up over the last few hundred years were meaningless. There was nothing they could do to stop a warlord flying a ship into orbit and taking control of the planet, dropping KEWs on everyone who dared say no. The Marine Corps had done what it could, but it hadn't been much. Roland rather suspected his superiors simply didn't care about New Doncaster. There were far too many fires that needed to be put out, fires that could easily sweep across the settled galaxy. New Doncaster might wind up being little more than a prize for whoever won the post-Earthfall civil wars.

Admiral Forest looked up as Roland entered. "General."

"Admiral," Roland said. "How long until we reach the RV point?"

The admiral looked pained. "We'll be there this afternoon, sir," he said. "I don't know how long we'll be waiting."

Roland frowned, inwardly. The admiral hadn't opened his secret orders yet, but it didn't take a genius to work out that the mission wasn't what he'd been told. It was quite possible the admiral had worked out their real target, or even come up with a theory that was too close—or too far—to the truth for Roland's peace of mind. If he thought Roland intended to do something crazy, like trying to land behind enemy lines on Winchester... Roland wished, suddenly, that he could take the admiral into his confidence. There was certainly no way to keep him from thinking, or drawing his own conclusions. And yet, the more people who knew the truth, the greater the chance of utter disaster. If the rebels had the slightest hint of warning...

"We have time," Roland said. The admiral had been at pains to explain that perfect timetables were barely possible on land, and not at all at sea. The fleet couldn't be *sure* when it could reach the RV point, let alone when it would make contact with the forces on Winchester. "We can wait, well outside the rebel perimeter."

Admiral Forest didn't look convinced. Roland didn't really blame him. On one hand, the sea was vast and the fleet was tiny. The rebels might miss it completely, at least until it sailed up to its target and opened fire. On the other, the rebels had vast fleets of fishing boats patrolling the waves and it would only take one stroke of bad luck for them to spot the fleet when it altered course. They might even mount radar sets on aircraft and do regular sweeps for unexpected ships...Roland had done what he could to ensure that no aircraft that flew close to the fleet would survive long enough to report back, but the fact an aircraft didn't return home would be enough to alert the rebels. Roland didn't dare assume that *they'd* assume the aircraft had simply flown into bad weather and been knocked out of the sky, without even a distress signal. The local pilots were good, used to their environment. They wouldn't fly into a squall unless there was no other choice.

"We have time," Roland repeated. "Is the fleet ready for battle?"

Admiral Forest straightened. "We have made preparations, as per your orders," he said, stiffly. "However, in the absence of specific target data..."

He paused, expectantly. Roland didn't rise to the bait. "As long as we're ready, we should be fine."

"Yes, sir," the admiral said.

Roland understood. Admiral Forest was an *admiral*. To be left out of the loop...Roland shook his head, mentally. He liked to think his soldiers and sailors were completely loyal, and that they'd keep their mouths shut, but he knew better. There'd been no time to vet most of the new recruits and, even if there had been, he suspected most rebel sympathisers would pass a security check with ease. There was certainly no shortage of townies who quietly supported the rebels, either out of ideological conviction or a simple desire to keep a foot in both camps. If one of them found out the truth, a simple radio message would be enough to blow the mission completely. Roland would have to withdraw without a fight. The only upside, as far as he could tell, was that the rebels would never be sure the signal was anything more than a crude deception. They might assume their agent had been turned or was simply mistaken.

And we'd be roundly fucked, he thought. *Any hope of backing off and trying again at a later date would be gone.*

"Right now, the rebels don't know what we're doing," he said. "And as long as they don't know, we might just be able to catch them by surprise."

"Yes, sir."

Roland kept his expression blank as he turned away. There was something in the admiral's voice...Roland hoped, prayed, it was nothing more than wounded vanity. It really *wasn't* easy to be told one didn't have a need to know, even though one should be mature enough to take it in one's stride. Admiral Forest was an aristocrat as well as a high-ranking officer. He would be more than human *not* to resent it, as well as worrying about what might happen if the operation went wrong because he hadn't known what he'd needed to do. Or because Roland—a groundpounder—had missed something obvious to a wet-navy officer. It was quite possible.

But at least he isn't a rebel spy, Roland told himself. *He has no reason to try to alert the enemy or sabotage the mission.*

He scowled as he made his way back to the training suite. It was hard not to feel uncertain of himself, to come up with dozens of reasons why the operation should be unceremoniously cancelled and the troops redirected to Winchester to resume the offensive there. The delay wore at his mind, making it harder to think straight. He knew he'd be fine, when the bullets started flying, yet the waiting was somehow worse. The plan was *his*. If it worked, he'd make his mark on the battlefield and prove he deserved to continue his career. If it failed...

Don't think about it, he told himself. *Just wait. You'll be back in the thick of it soon enough.*

...

Richard hadn't been sure what was going to happen, when he'd been sent a coded message ordering him not to take his overt orders too seriously, but he hadn't expected Rachel to arrive with instructions for Richard to turn his command over to his second, then join her in a speedboat heading out to sea. Richard found it more than a little bizarre. Roland had been coming back to Winchester, hadn't he? There'd been extensive plans to crack the enemy defences once and for all...

He gritted his teeth as the speedboat accelerated, passing the remains of a freighter that had grounded itself after an enemy torpedo had struck it in the stern. The fighting on land had stalemated, with neither side able to take the offensive, but the fighting at sea was still going on. His intelligence reports made it clear the rebels were shipping more and more supplies onto the island, building up their forces to the point they could overwhelm the bridgehead and push his troops into the sea. He feared the worst. The government had put vast resources into the navy, but it had concentrated on troop transports and makeshift warships rather than torpedo boats and submarines. They just didn't have the numbers to keep the rebels from moving troops around as they pleased. Richard was starting to wonder if they should cut their losses and abandon the beachhead before it was too late.

Rachel altered course, slightly, as they left the shoal of islands behind, heading further into the deep blue sea. Richard frowned, watching the horizon. She hadn't been very talkative, even after they were well away from the harbour. Richard understood the need to maintain operational security, but there were limits. And yet…he felt his heart start to race as he saw a handful of ships, holding position well clear of the islands. A trio of transports, a large freighter that had been turned into a helicopter carrier, a set of makeshift warships brimming with missile launchers… it looked as it something big, or desperate, was in the offing. He forced himself to wait as Rachel took the ship towards the helicopter carrier, pulling up beside the rope ladder with practiced ease. Richard scrambled up onto the deck, accepting the offer of a towel gratefully. His clothes were soaked, clinging to his skin.

Roland met him as he stepped into the briefing room, a low rumble running through the vessel as she brought her engines online. "Richard. I'm sorry about the cloak and dagger nonsense."

Richard nodded, curtly. "Rachel told me I wouldn't be going back in a hurry."

"No," Roland agreed. "We're going somewhere else."

"I see." Richard sucked in his breath. He trusted Roland, and he wouldn't normally be so tart with him, but he was wet and cold and tired. "Where—exactly—are we going?"

Roland tapped the map. "The problem, as I see it, is that the offensive on Winchester has bogged down. We failed to deliver a killing blow and now the rebels are rushing supplies into the island, in a bid to land a killing blow of their own. I think you will agree that losing the beachhead, both the troops and the supplies, will be an utter disaster."

"Yes." Richard nodded impatiently. He already knew it. "I assume you have a plan?"

"I think we have an unexpected window of opportunity," Roland said, as Rachel joined them. "The rebels may have given it to us, quite by accident."

He looked at Rachel. "Once this meeting is finished, inform the captains they are to open their secret orders."

"Yes, sir," Rachel said.

Richard studied the map. "Where do you intend to land?"

"Here." Roland tapped an island. "If it works, we get in and hurt the rebels. *Really* hurt them. Even if it fails, we'll give them a nasty fright and tear up a considerable amount of their infrastructure. It won't slow them for long, but it'll buy us time—time we need desperately."

"Yes." Richard said nothing for a long moment. The plan was daring. Roland had worked in a few points where the operation could be called off, without exposing the troops to serious risk, but the deeper they went into enemy territory the greater the losses if they had to abandon the mission. "And you're leading the operation in person?"

"It's my idea," Roland said. "And if it fails, better the government blames me—posthumously—rather than tearing itself apart over the issue of just who is to blame."

Richard glanced at Rachel. She didn't look pleased. Richard wasn't entirely sure what her real job was—he'd worked out there was something odd about her well before discovering she was a special ops commando—but he was reasonably sure part of the reason she was there was to protect Roland. It puzzled him, at times. Why did Roland rate a bodyguard? He might have been named after the Childe Roland, but they were hardly the same person.

"I hope you're right," he said, finally. "How are the politics back home?"

"Nasty." Roland drew a line on the map. "The fleet will be underway shortly. We'll be crossing the enemy shipping lines within hours. If we can locate a suitable target, we'll move in and take it. If not...we'll have to proceed with the operation anyway."

"Yes, sir," Richard said.

"And that's why I wanted you along," Roland said. His voice was grim. "If something happens to me, you'll have to take command in the middle of a firefight."

Richard shivered, helplessly. It would hardly be the first time he'd had to assume command in a tearing hurry, but...this time, the stakes were almost impossibly high. Roland was hardly an incompetent and yet... he could die at any moment, forcing Richard to take command within seconds. And the confusion alone might prove disastrous. His low rank would be worse.

He met Roland's eyes. "Yes, sir," he said. "I won't let you down."

CHAPTER THIRTY-SIX

NEAR WINCHESTER ISLAND, NEW DONCASTER

JEAN MCCOLL WOULD NEVER WIN any beauty prizes. She was no elegant yacht imported from another star system at vast expense, no clipper ship or even one of the small and fast transports the rebel-held shipyards had started churning out, now that the government's rules and regulations were a thing of the past. She was an ugly rusty tramp freighter, who had passed from owner to owner as she made her way around the world, calling in at various islands in hopes of picking up shipping contracts that would pay for her upkeep for a few months more, a difficult task when the government's shipping lines had sewn up most of the harbours. Her master was permanently on the brink of going bankrupt, at least until he'd taken service with the rebels. She delivered a life less ordinary, at the constant risk of one bad voyage leading to utter disaster...

...And yet, Captain Harold loved her.

He stood on her bridge and peered into the darkening skies. He'd had a good war, ever since the aristocratic government had collapsed. There'd been no need, any longer, to go cap-in-hand to loan sharks, when he failed to pick up a shipping contract he desperately needed. The loan sharks themselves were dead, thrown from cliffs or put in front of walls and shot by rebel forces. He had few qualms about accepting the request to deliver troops and supplies to Winchester, even though there was a very real risk of having his ship sunk by government warships. Even an air raid hadn't been enough to put him off. The government had to go, or it would destroy the independent shipping community completely if it regained control of the planet. Harold knew the dangers, but the risks of doing nothing were far higher. The government could not be allowed to win.

And besides, the rebels pay well, he thought. They hadn't haggled—much—over shipping costs. Harold had been granted access to captured warehouses, crammed with tools and supplies he hadn't been able to afford only a few short months ago. *We could run for years on what they're giving us for a few short months of dedicated work.*

The radar pinged. Harold glanced at it. The shipping lane was nearly empty, save for a pair of freighters heading in the opposite direction. There were no convoys, a reflection of both the rebel inability to provide escorts and the government's failure to produce *attackers*. Harold had no doubt that would change—both sides were learning lessons from the other—but for the moment, sailing alone was relatively safe. The government's aircraft never came out after dark—that would change, too—and their ships were occupied elsewhere. Harold had been told the government intended to reinforce their beachhead, then attack again. Perhaps it was true. It wasn't his problem.

He eyed the radar thoughtfully, then shook his head. Radar wasn't a precise science at the best of times. The crappy kits that had been put together on the planet's surface only made a bad situation worse. Hell, he wasn't even keen on turning it *on*, knowing it would lead an enemy hunter right to him. And yet...he shook his head. The shipping lane might be empty now, but that would change. To die because his ship had accidentally rammed another would be...

Something clattered, far too close for comfort. Harold knew every last inch of his freighter. He knew there was *nothing* that should have made that sound. He hit the emergency alarm on instinct, waking his crew. If it was nothing, his family would never let him hear the end of it, but better that than death creeping up on them while they lay in their bunks. He heard the sound of running footsteps and cursed under his breath, one hand grabbing for the pistol at his belt. The only person who should have been awake was the engineer and *he* was right at the other end of the ship. Cold horror shot through him as he realised what was happening. They were being boarded. They were miles from anywhere and yet they were being boarded. It was impossible!

The bridge door crashed open. Harold started to draw his pistol, too late. There was a blinding blue-white flash, followed by a wave of cramp that locked his muscles and sent him crashing to the deck. Strong arms grabbed him, rolled him over and cuffed his hands, then searched his body roughly. Harold wanted to protest, but he couldn't speak. He could barely breathe. His body felt as if it was nothing more than a dead lump.

"The holds are empty," a voice said. "They're not transporting the wounded back to Baraka."

Lucky for them, Harold thought, savagely. He couldn't see clearly, but he thought he could make out at least five different footsteps. *If we'd been taking the wounded back home, would you be tossing them into the sea right now?*

His heart sank as the boarding party searched his ship, capturing the rest of the crew effortlessly. Harold tried not to groan in shame as the crew were piled up on the bridge, cursing himself for not posting watchmen on deck or up in the crow's nest. It might not have been enough—the boarding party clearly had access to modern technology, if they'd managed to find and board his ship in the middle of the night—but at least he would have felt better about himself. He cursed, mentally, as he heard his daughter gasp in pain. What was going to happen to her? She couldn't expect mercy, not from the government's troops. Death? Rape? A life sentence in a brothel? All of the horror stories about what he could expect, if he fell into enemy hands, suddenly seemed very real. His ship had been taken and his life, as he knew it, was at an end.

"Transfer the crew to the hold," a voice ordered. It was hard to be sure, but it sounded female. That wasn't good news. Harold had been told the female aristos were often worse than the males. They had so little control over their own lives that they took it out on their social inferiors, be they maids or shopkeepers or anything. If the stories were true..."Leave the captain here. I'll deal with him."

Harold gritted his teeth as strong hands hoisted him up and plonked him down into a chair. His bridge felt...*wrong*, a nightmarish version of the bridge he knew and loved. It was no longer his...he pushed the thought out of his mind as he surveyed the boarding party, a trio of men in black outfits that seemed to blend with the darkness. The leader didn't look very feminine. Her body was trim, almost mannish. If it hadn't been for her voice, he would have thought she was a man.

"Captain," she said. "What is your name?"

Harold glared at her, torn between defiance and the grim awareness the government troops could do *anything*, to him and his family. He'd heard the stories of what happened to runaway workers who fell into government hands, or smugglers who were caught trying to break the monopoly on trading cartels. He didn't want to talk and yet, he feared what would happen if he tried to keep his mouth shut. The troops could beat him to a pulp...worse, they could beat his family until Harold started talking. His thoughts ran in circles. Perhaps he could make a deal. Perhaps...

"I'll make you a deal," the woman said, as if she'd been reading his thoughts. A chill ran down his spine. He'd heard stories of telepaths, but most of them were just absurd legends from the rim of known space. "I have questions. If you answer them honestly and completely, we'll let you and your family go. We won't bother with a holding camp. As soon as the operation is underway, we'll just let you go. If you refuse to answer, well..."

She cocked her head. "We have ways of making you talk."

Harold didn't doubt it. They could hurt him. He was tough—one didn't become a sailor on New Doncaster without developing a high tolerance for pain and discomfort—but they could just hit him and keep hitting him until he talked. Or they could shoot him full of drugs, or simply turn their attention to his family. And yet, if he talked, the rebels would declare him outlaw. They'd want him dead. His life, and that of his family, would be over.

He swallowed, hard. "Water. Please. Water."

It was a stalling tactic, and he didn't expect them to give him anything, but—somewhat to his surprise—the woman took a bottle from her belt and pressed it against his lips. The water refreshed him, clearing his mind. Perhaps it was a good sign, he thought. Perhaps...

He hated himself for speaking, but he had no choice. His family was at stake.

"If...if I talk, will you protect my family?" His voice sounded weak, even to him. "Will you keep them safe from retribution?"

"We'll make sure no one ever knows the truth," the woman said. It was the *kindness* in her voice that got to him. "We can give you new identities, or even take you off-world. You will be safe."

Harold gritted his teeth. He wanted to believe her. He had no choice, but to believe her. And yet, he felt like a traitor. The rebels would certainly see him as a traitor, as someone who'd betrayed the freedom fighters for vague—and probably soon to be broken—promises from a government stooge. They'd hunt him down like a dog, if—when—the truth got out. He knew they would. He'd seen the rebels do worse to people who had abused their power, when they'd held the whip hand. But he couldn't let his family be tortured. He just couldn't.

"Keep them safe and I'll talk," he said. "What do you want to know?"

• • •

Rachel had few qualms about battlefield interrogations. The prisoners she'd taken, on most of her deployments, had been terrorists, pirates, or criminals trying to take advantage of a lawless environment to build power bases of their own. Any doubts she'd had about forcing terrorists to talk at knifepoint had faded, after she'd seen what they'd been prepared to do in the name of their cause. The men who blew up schools, raped women and children and gloried in their brutality to intimidate those who might stand again them had put themselves well outside the protections of the laws of war. Rachel didn't enjoy forcing them to talk, to spill everything they knew before they got their throats cut and their bodies dumped in mass graves, but she accepted it as necessary. Good people could only sleep soundly in their beds because of hard people doing hard things.

And yet, she couldn't help feeling a twinge of guilt as she tossed question after question at Captain Harold. The man wasn't a terrorist, nor a die-hard rebel. He was a civilian who'd been in the wrong place at the wrong time, a civilian caught between the awareness she could do anything to his family if he refused to talk and the certainty his own people would kill him and his family if he did. Rachel had seen enough civil wars and insurgencies—and studied countless more—to be aware matters were rarely as cut and dried as outsiders claimed. She couldn't blame the rebels for rebelling, given how they'd been treated. And yet, she also knew the rebels had to be stopped. The horror that had given birth to them would be nothing, compared to the horror they'd leave in their wake.

She sighed inwardly as she started to repeat her questions, to make it harder for him to lie or hide something from her. It was difficult to maintain a coherent narrative when one's interrogator was jumping around, asking about *this* and *that* in a manner that suggested the interrogator couldn't focus on a single subject. Rachel had been extensively trained in maintaining her cover story and even *she* would find it difficult, if the local security services brought her in for interrogation. Poor Harold didn't seem to have any training.

And the rebels don't seem to have had time to evolve proper security procedures yet, she thought, numbly. *We might just pull the plan off after all.*

"Very good," she finished. A low *thump* echoed through the tramp freighter as the transport came alongside. Replenishment at sea was evidently difficult, a far cry from the relatively simple operation in interplanetary space. "I'll see to it you and your family are safe."

She helped the captain to his feet, then marched him along to the gangplank. Harold and his family would remain on the transports, at least until the operation came to an end, whereupon they'd be let go. Rachel was sure there'd be some people in government who'd make a fuss about simply letting the family leave, if the rebels didn't know they'd been captured, but she found it hard to care. She'd known too many regular officers who'd reneged on their promises to potential allies. They'd tended to realise, too late, that word got out and no one trusted them again. Even their allies had learned to distrust them...

Roland will understand, she told herself, as the troops flowed down the gangplank. It had been sheer luck the tramp freighter was undermanned, with empty holds. They'd come up with contingency plans to deal with enemy wounded, but she was uneasily aware the plans hadn't been very good. *He'll make sure the poor bastards get their freedom.*

Richard walked down the gangplank to her, snapping a salute as he stepped onto the freighter. "Permission to come aboard?"

"Granted." Rachel allowed herself a tight smile. "If you set your men up, we can get underway."

She considered, just for a moment, asking Captain Harold to remain on the freighter. He'd assured her there were no signs and countersigns, at least on the harbour, but they might need help to deal with any unexpected surprises. She dismissed the thought a moment later—they'd made a deal, after all—and headed to the bridge. The new crew were already taking up positions, readying to get the freighter underway. The rebels shouldn't have noticed anything was wrong, she thought, as she set up her microburst terminal by the command chair. They certainly shouldn't have any warning before the shit hit the fan.

The new helmsman glanced at her. "Ah...Captain, we've embarked the last of the troops," he said. "The gangplank is being withdrawn now."

"Get us underway as soon as the transport is clear," Rachel ordered. "We don't want to be too late, not when the rebels might notice."

She sucked in her breath, bracing herself as the tramp freighter lumbered forward. The vessel felt...*wrong*, somehow. She was sitting low in the water...would the rebels notice? They'd timed their arrival for early evening, when dim light should make it harder for anyone to spot anything out of place, but she feared the mission could still go badly wrong. If they were caught, they were fucked. There was no hope of beating a hasty retreat on a tramp freighter that could probably be outrun by a duckling. The rebels would blow them out of the water and ask questions of the wreckage.

...

Admiral Terrace Forest felt sick.

It wasn't *just* the content of his secret orders, when he'd finally been allowed to read them. Terrace was no fool. He'd assumed they were up to something a little out of the ordinary, although he had to admit General Windsor had come up with something that would either be a brilliant success or a complete disaster. Either way...Terrace swallowed hard. He was no coward, either, but he knew time was running out. He had two sets of secret orders and if he carried them both out...

His heart churned as he stood on the deck, watching the live feed from the stealthed drone high overhead. He was loyal to his family and yet, he was also loyal to the navy. He had no illusions about how he'd reached his rank and post, but he liked to think he'd done well. General Windsor had certainly never hesitated to sack officers who hadn't come up to his exacting standards. Terrace almost wished he *had* been sacked. He'd tried to serve two sets of masters and, now, that was impossible. If he got a certain signal, he would have to choose a side very quickly.

An operator glanced at him. "Sir," he said. "The missile batteries are primed and ready."

Terrace nodded, curtly. "Good," he growled. Time was ticking away, slowly but surely. His chest hurt, a grim reminder of what he was about to do. What he had no choice, but to do. He knew what would happen if he failed. "Have we picked up any signals from Navy HQ?"

"No, Admiral," the operator said. He sounded vaguely surprised by the question. He had standing orders to alert his superior officers if HQ—or the government—attempted to make contact. There was no reason to think he would have ignored them. "They haven't attempted to contact us."

"Good." Terrace almost wished they would, just to get it over with. The feeling in his chest was getting worse. He hadn't felt so bad since he'd been summoned to the headmaster's office to explain his sins, sins that had come far too close to getting him expelled. "Inform me if anything changes."

"Yes, sir."

CHAPTER THIRTY-SEVEN

BARAKA CITY, NEW DONCASTER

THE STEALTHED DRONE, Roland thought numbly, was a great piece of equipment.

He studied the microburst transmissions on his terminal as the flight crews prepped the helicopters for departure. *Jean McColl* was making her slow way towards the harbour, ignored by the rebel defences. The ops crews were already noting the location of enemy defences on outlying islands, marking them down for missile strikes when the balloon went up. It was a shame he couldn't risk flying the drone over the island itself, or even try to get a long-range view of the harbour, but he had no choice. There was no way to be *certain* the rebels could not spot the drone. It wouldn't be the first time an operation had been screwed up because the attackers had underestimated the enemy defences.

And if they realise we're sending one of our handful of irreplaceable drones over the island, he thought, *they'll know we're up to something.*

He felt his stomach twist, painfully. Rachel had fought on Hameau. She'd told him the landing force had been too used to technological superiority, to having drones that couldn't be detected and communications networks that could neither be tracked nor knocked down. And yet, the corprats had had equal technology and given the MEF a very hard time until it had adapted to the new reality. Roland had no way to know, either, if the rebels had been sold something capable of detecting and shooting down a drone. He intended to vector the drone over the city as soon as the missiles started to land, when the rebels would have other problems, but it wouldn't arrive in time to be helpful. They weren't flying *completely* blind, if the intelligence reports were accurate, yet...

Don't worry about it, he told himself. *The die was cast the moment you came up with the plan.*

He studied the young men as they lined up, preparing to board the helicopters. They'd been trained extensively, by local standards, but Roland had been worked harder during his first month at Boot Camp. They were unprepared, despite everything. Roland silently congratulated himself on developing an aerial assault component, an expansion of the force he'd led into battle nine months ago, but they'd never truly been tested. Were they ready to jump? He knew, even if they didn't, what would happen if the operation went spectacularly wrong. They'd be pinned down, then either captured or killed...

Don't worry about it, his thoughts repeated. *Just prepare yourself for combat.*

He took a breath, wondering if he should address the men. Every action flick he'd seen, with impractical weapons and worse tactics and female eye-candy who lost their clothes in giant explosions, had the commander giving his men a rousing speech. Roland couldn't think of anything to say, but he knew he could crib one from a flick or even a play, from the days before electronic media and datanets. No one would notice. The flicks had never spread to New Doncaster. The planet didn't have the datanet for them.

But whatever he said, he feared, would be inauthentic.

"We know what to do," he said, finally. "And we'll do it. Mount up."

Ten minutes later, they were in the air.

Rachel was mildly surprised the rebels weren't trying to search the flow of freighters and other ships as they made their way in and out of the harbour, a handful heading further up the river to ports and settlements deeper inland. Captain Harold had told her that the rebel leadership wanted to keep the independent freighter captains and crews onside, to the point they'd abolished everything from taxes to security sweeps, but it struck her as dangerously lax. The fact she was driving a freighter, loaded to the gunwales with soldiers and their kit, was clear proof there was something wrong with the rebel security precautions. But then, she reflected, they'd taken far more precautions within the harbour itself. They didn't *need* to ensure the freighters were searched before they docked.

She stood in the crow's nest and looked around, her enhanced eyesight peering through the twilight as if it were noon. The city was bigger than she recalled, an ever-growing cluster of apartment blocks, warehouses, barracks and even a tiny handful of shipyards and primitive industrial facilities. Smoke rose in the distance, alarming her until she realised it was another industrial node. New Doncaster had taken a giant leap back in time, she noted, wryly admitting the rebels might have a point. They didn't *need* to produce cutting-edge tech to win the war, merely weapons and equipment they could use. She felt an odd little pang as she saw a barge leaving a small dock, carrying what looked like a giant—and primitive—combine harvester. The rebels were clearly preparing for the next growing season, a sign they felt confident in ultimate victory. Rachel told herself they were wrong.

Her fingers tapped her terminal, logging more and more targets for the missiles. She wouldn't send the signal just yet, not unless it became apparent they'd been rumbled, but she needed to keep it updated. Roland's missile crews would be making the final preparations already, bracing themselves for their role. She took one final look around the harbour, as the tramp freighter slowly glided towards the harbour mouth, then scrambled down the ladder to the bridge. Richard was already there, watching the enemy defences with a wary eye. The guns were primitive, but a single shell would be more than enough to blow the freighter out of the water.

"I've done all I can here," she said, once she'd uploaded her targeting data to his terminal. "Are you ready?"

"Yes." Richard sounded calm, but she had no trouble telling he was nervous. The moment they entered the harbour, they'd be trapped. "See you on the other side."

"You have command." Rachel grinned as she turned to the hatch, then looked back at him. "See you soon."

She felt her smile grow wider as she picked up her pack, scrambled down the ladder to the deck, then pulled on her mask and allowed herself to fall overboard. Her suit wasn't a perfect chameleon, but the combination of suit and twilight—and distance from the shore—should ensure no one realised she'd jumped into the water. Twilight played tricks on the human eye. Rachel kept swimming down, then oriented herself on the river mouth and swam for it. A handful of fish glided past, disturbed by her passage. Rachel hoped no one was watching, although she was sure they'd make nothing of it if they did. There were so many ships coming and going she was surprised the fish hadn't gone elsewhere. Captain Harold had told her the rebels were fishing so frantically they were running the very real risk of driving the shoals to extinction.

Probably not an immediate problem, Rachel thought, as she glided up the river bed. *It is a very big and mostly watery planet, after all.*

Night was falling rapidly when she came ashore, well above the city. Her lips thinned in disapproval—the rebels didn't seem to understand the importance of light discipline—as she checked her surroundings, then stripped off her suit and buried it under the sand. She didn't have time to do a proper job of it, something her instructors would have chewed her out for if they'd seen it, but she doubted it would be found in time to make a difference. Underneath, she was wearing a simple rebel fighter's outfit, complete with authentic armband taken from a soldier who'd died on Winchester. She shouldn't draw too much attention in the darkness, but—as she started to circumvent the city—she stayed low anyway. The last thing she needed was to draw attention, let alone questions she couldn't answer. It would mean the end of her mission.

She walked slowly, feeling dangerously exposed as she moved from camp to camp. The rebel positions were odd, as if they were both disciplined and undisciplined. Their layout was seemingly random, tents and fireplaces scattered as if they'd been thrown around by an angry god, but their guards seemed alert, ready to challenge anyone who tried to get into the camps. It looked slapdash, yet she had to admit there was a certain degree of sense to the design. On one hand, a stranger would be very obvious; on the other, a missile strike wouldn't do as much damage as the planners might hope. It would take a modern weapon, with submunitions, to wipe out the entire camp and vehicle parks. She made note of their location anyway, then headed to the barricades. The rebels looked to be trying to make them even stronger. She doubted she could get across them in time to matter.

Shaking her head, she turned away and keyed her transmitter, pulsing the targeting data to Roland and his men. The missiles would be fired soon, clearing the way for the real attack to begin. She kept walking, all too aware the rebels might be able to detect the transmission even though it had barely lasted a second. Her experience on Hameau had been a grim reminder that, while the Marine Corps had the best hardware as well as the best men, there were others who were almost as good. If they picked up the signal, they'd sound the alert…wouldn't they?

You can't count on them mistaking the signal for a stray radio transmission, she reminded herself. Signals wasn't her speciality, but she knew the basics. The techniques that made microburst transmissions almost impossible to detect or localise for people without the right equipment would make them unmistakable, to those who did. *You have to assume the worst.*

She silently counted down the seconds, bracing herself. The die was cast…

"Admiral," the operator said. "The missile targeting data has arrived."

Admiral Terrace Forest nodded curtly, despite the fear gnawing at his heart. "Forward the data to the missile crews," he ordered. "And tell them to fire when ready."

"Aye, sir."

Terrace nodded, studying the display as the missile targets popped up in front of him. The rebels were determined to keep unwanted visitors out of their harbour, judging by the missile batteries and weapons emplacements along the shoreline. If they hadn't captured a freighter, it was unlikely the fleet could get close enough to do some real damage before the enemy noticed and opened fire. He felt his heart begin to pound as he looked at the clock, wondering just how long it would be before his *real* orders arrived. There would never be a better opportunity. General Windsor and his townie sidekick were deep in enemy territory, unable to withdraw. They were trapped between victory or death.

The ship shuddered as the first missile launched from the tubes. Terrace tapped the screen, watching the live feed as the rest of the fleet opened fire. The missiles weren't as accurate as the navy had hoped—even the latest couldn't be trusted to land *right* on top of the target—but the warheads were large enough to make up for the inaccuracy. If nothing else, he reflected numbly, the rebels were in for a nasty shock. The missile bombardment would strike deep into occupied territory. A handful had even been aimed at bridges and crossroads to make life difficult for anyone who wanted to rush to the city's rescue.

"Sir," the operator said. "All missiles are away. I say again, all missiles are away. The crews are reloading the tubes now."

"Good." Terrace had his orders. The fleet would continue to provide fire support, up to the point it ran out of missiles. Or he received the orders he'd been expecting for days now, although putting them into practice would have been pretty much impossible. "Mr. Bartley, inform HQ that Operation Flower has begun."

"Aye, sir."

Terrace nodded, grimly. There was no point in trying to maintain radio silence now. The rebels would have to be blind and deaf, if not dead, to miss the missiles rocketing towards them. They'd know the fleet was there, watching from a safe distance. He half-hoped the rebels would come out to fight, although it was unlikely. It would provide an excellent excuse for backing into deeper waters, one the general would almost certainly accept.

And now he's in the helicopters, heading into enemy territory, Terrace thought. It was a maddening thought, simply because he didn't know which side he was really on. *Who knows? He might not come back at all.*

• • •

The rebels, Richard decided, hadn't been as foolish as he'd thought. They might have let the freighter into the harbour without a full inspection, but the harbour walls were solid and there were armed guards everywhere. Indeed, the more he looked at it, the surer he became that the designers had simply copied Kingsport. The harbour was effectively separate from the rest of the city, ensuring anyone with bad intentions had to overwhelm the local defences before spreading out, thus giving the defenders a chance to realise they were under attack and take countermeasures. It wasn't ideal, but given their political limitations it would suffice.

His terminal bleeped. He glanced at it, taking a breath as he realised the missiles were inbound at supersonic speeds. The rebel antiaircraft defences were already reacting, firing frantically as if they hoped the barrage would be enough to take the missiles out of the sky before they reached their targets. They weren't. Richard covered his eyes as he saw a blinding white flash outside the harbour, a dull rumble of thunder shaking the air as the shockwave passed overhead. More followed, explosions blasting up around the city as the enemy camps were hammered. He hit the alarm, snapping orders to his men. The missile tubes they'd concealed within the superstructure were suddenly revealed, swinging around to fire on the enemy guardposts. They exploded, one by one.

Richard blew a whistle. The first assault squads came out of hiding, half of them running down the gangplank and the other half throwing new ones into place before they scrambled down them and onto the quay themselves. His snipers moved forward, sweeping the burning harbour for targets. There was no time for mercy. Every enemy soldier within eyesight was shot down before he could run for cover.

The ground shook again. Richard looked north and saw a fireball, climbing into the sky and casting an eerie flickering radiance over the scene. For a moment, it puzzled him. The missile warheads weren't that heavy. A missile must have come down on top of an ammunition dump. He put the thought aside as he heard more shooting and looked over at a nearby ship. The crew seemed to be trying to do something, either mount a resistance or run for their lives. He winced as he saw a man fall from the deck and land in the water. The poor bastard didn't stand a chance. He'd hoped they could keep the death toll low, given how many civilians were trapped within the city, but cold logic told him it was going to be higher than anyone wanted. He could only hope most people would stay inside, out of the way,

"Start the transmission," he ordered, as his men secured the outer gates. He could hear firing in the distance, but he wasn't sure who was doing the shooting or what they were shooting *at*. Rachel? It wasn't impossible. She was meant to be near the barricades, if everything had gone according to plan. Or had they been so badly disrupted they were firing on their own men? "And then signal the helicopters. The harbour is secure."

"Aye, sir."

Richard checked his rifle, then hurried to the gangplank and down onto the pier. The remaining freighter crews seemed to be keeping their heads down, although that would change if they worked up the nerve to either come off the sidelines or try to make it out of the harbour before it was too late. He suspected they'd be in deep shit if they tried. The rebels might assume they were hostile, while the government's navy might fear they intended to sink themselves in the channel and block Richard's escape. It would end very badly.

"Sir." Captain Peabody snapped a salute. "The gates are secure. I've deployed antitank and sniper teams, backed up by mortars and machine guns. So far, no sign of a major counterattack. We spotted a handful of civilians, who were...ah...discouraged from asking any questions."

Richard nodded, recalling the city maps he'd memorised. They were probably out of date, given how many people and supplies the rebels had brought into the city, but they couldn't have changed that much in a mere nine months...could they? He shook his head. The rebel troops were in disarray, their camps bombarded and their radio networks jammed. Their landlines were tougher, but how many of their telephones remained intact and operational? It would take them time to reorganise, time that would enable him to push out and secure the area. Hopefully, the civilians would stay off the streets. The rebels, if the reports were accurate, insisted on everyone being armed. The death toll was going to be horrendous if everyone with a pistol insisted on coming out to fight.

The transmission should discourage them, he told himself. *And if they don't, they'll have only themselves to blame.*

"Get the scouts into position, then ready the follow-up forces," he ordered, finally. Time wasn't on their side. If the rebels got organised, the mission would be over before it had fairly begun. "We need to be ready to move. Quickly."

"Aye, sir."

Richard nodded. In the distance, he could hear the sound of helicopters.

CHAPTER THIRTY-EIGHT

BARAKA ISLAND, NEW DONCASTER

ROLAND COULDN'T HELP HIMSELF. He whooped.

The city was surrounded by explosions, giant fireballs rising into the air and casting a baleful light over the settlement. He knew, deep inside, that each of the explosions had killed innocents, civilians and children who'd been trapped alongside rebel fighters and their vehicles, but from high overhead it was hard to believe. The helicopters swooped over the harbour, now in Richard's hands, and over the city. Behind them, he could see more fires on the outlying island. The defences had been smashed. Admiral Forest could send the fleet into the gulf now, without the risk of being intercepted and sunk.

Good thing they didn't want to risk impeding their own deployments by laying mines across the channel, he thought. *It would be a great deal harder to get the fleet into position if they'd barred the entrance.*

His fingers danced over his terminal, sending orders to the fleet—and the advance forces—as the helicopters closed on their targets. There was no point in being stealthy now. The government helicopters were nowhere near as quiet as the craft the corps used for quick insertions behind the lines and it wouldn't have mattered if they were. Stealth helicopters weren't invisible, and the entire city was lit up, bathed in the light of countless fires. They would be seen. Their only hope of completing the mission was to move with speed.

The tension faded as the helicopters made the final approach, the old government mansion coming into view. It was an odd design, both part of the city and yet isolated from the people below. The original plans had been lost long ago—reading between the lines, Roland thought they'd been taken from the archives by the owners—but he'd managed to find enough people who'd actually visited the mansion, in happier times, to put together a fairly comprehensive floor plan. The assault force wasn't going in completely blind. Besides, it was better they assumed they didn't know everything—and accepted the floor plans might be inaccurate—rather than being blindsided on the assumption they had perfect intelligence. The spooks weren't *that* good. Roland smiled as he checked his rifle, one final time. The die had been thoroughly cast. There was no point in worrying now, no point in fretting over how things would work out. They had to do or die.

"One minute," the pilot called.

Roland grabbed the rope, bracing himself as the helicopter's guns opened fire. A flash of light shot past—a missile, vanishing into the distance before his brain registered its presence—as the guns swept the rest of the enemy defenders off the roof. He didn't really blame the enemy for being caught by surprise, even though he'd mounted an aerial assault against a rebel camp nearly ten months ago. The mansion was surrounded by a friendly city, crammed with rebel fighters. There was a very real risk of being trapped, unable to retreat or even to surrender.

The hatches slammed open, the helicopter lurching to a halt. Roland threw himself forward and out into the open air, rappelling down the rope as quickly as possible. Rachel would be pissed, when she heard he'd gone out first, but it didn't matter. The open air was now safer than the helicopter. If the rebel soldiers weren't already drawing beads on the aircraft, the soldiers were either dead or stupid. He dared not assume they were either. The helicopter guns opened fire again, blasting a nearby building in hopes of suppressing enemy fire. It wasn't enough. Roland sensed, more than saw, bullets snapping through the air as he hit the rooftops. The rest of his men landed beside him, seconds later.

He kept low as he scanned the rooftop. Blood and guts lay everywhere, the remnants of the men who'd tried to fire on the helicopters. A gash in the roof beckoned to him, suggesting a way down that wouldn't be immediately predictable. Roland nodded to the rest of his squad, then led the way forward. The darkness leapt up at him. He snapped his NVGs into place and peered into the hole, then hopped down. It was dark and cold, seemingly abandoned. He was amused to note someone had crammed dozens of pieces of furniture, now battered and broken, into the chamber. It made little sense.

His rifle swept the room, looking for targets. There were none, but he could feel vibrations running through the floors. Intelligence wasn't sure how many rebels actually *lived* in the mansion—they'd be fools to allow their entire leadership to be concentrated in a single location—yet Roland was sure there'd be guards as well as close-protection units. He rather hoped there were a lot of different units. They'd be unsure what was going on and disinclined to trust anyone they didn't know. It was quite possible they'd wind up shooting at each other. Roland wasn't inclined to count on it, but it would be a lucky break if they did.

Keep moving, he told himself, as he kicked out the door and hurled a stun grenade down the corridor. *Don't give them time to react.*

The building shuddered, pieces of dust falling from the ceiling. Roland gritted his teeth as a second missile exploded, too close for comfort. The gunfire was getting louder, rebel rifles and RPGs answered by helicopter-borne machine guns. Every time they passed a door, they hurled a stun grenade into the darkness. It was hellishly wasteful—Roland knew they were going to expend most of their supply in a single short operation—but he dared not risk leaving an enemy force behind him. Even a lone man with a gun, or a radio, could put one hell of a crimp in his plans. And if that person got onto the roof and threw a grenade into the waiting helicopter...

Keep moving, he told himself again, finding the stairwell that led to the conference rooms and heading down. The walls looked as if they'd been stripped, paintings and priceless works of art torn from their mountings and tossed out of the mansion. A statue still stood, in an alcove halfway down the stairs, but someone had taken a hammer to it. *If you're going through hell, keep going!*

...

Sarah had been in bed when the first explosions rocked the city.

She hadn't expected trouble. No one had. There'd been no reason to expect anything more than a handful of probing attacks, enemy aircraft trying to scout the defences and get away before they were shot down by radar-guided machine guns or antiaircraft missiles. She certainly hadn't considered the possibility of the government opening a new front, one even closer to the heart of rebel power. But her reflexes didn't fail her. The moment the mansion started to shake, she rolled out of the sheets and under the bed before the bullets and shrapnel started. Her mind caught up with her moments later. The city was under attack!

Shit, she thought. It was never a good time for the enemy to attack, but this was particularly bad. The rebels had been moving volunteers into the city, loading them onto freighters and transporting them into Winchester. If nothing else, the bombardment would kill hundreds and demoralise thousands more. *Did they time it purposely?*

She let out a sigh of relief as the last of the missile hits faded away, but her heart sank as gunfire echoed through the city. She'd seen enough firefights to *know* the sound wasn't men panicking and firing randomly into the air, in hopes of shooting down missiles that had already reached their targets and exploded. The sound was far too concentrated. She wondered, as she checked the pistol she kept with her at all times, if the government had bribed a rebel faction to move against her. It seemed unlikely the government troops could thrust up the channel and into the harbour without being detected. She'd done it, in her bid to win the war in a single stroke, but she'd had months to prepare and an enemy who didn't take her seriously. The government hadn't had very long at all.

The door shook, then burst open. Sarah braced herself, then breathed a sigh of relief as she saw her guards. She'd gone to some trouble to keep them loyal, although she was uneasily aware they were badly outnumbered by the other rebel forces within the city. They could do the sums themselves and decide to abandon her, if the odds looked too grim. Sarah had no reason to expect anyone to turn on her, certainly not *now*, but she feared the worst. Her personal power base was quite limited. The assets that had convinced the rebels to recognise her as their leader would cripple her when the war was won. Or if they wanted to blame her for when the war was lost.

"Sarah," Patrick said. "The city is under attack!"

Sarah nodded, crawling out from under the bed and inching to the windows. It was risky—there might be enemy snipers already taking aim at the mansion—but she needed to know. The city was brightly lit, fires clearly visible all around the barricades and down towards the harbour. She heard helicopters clattering over the city, heading towards the mansion. The ground shook, repeatedly, as missiles crashed down all around her. She saw a streak of light flash out of the sky and slam into a distant building, just out of eyesight. The explosion shook the ground once again. She cursed under her breath as the gunfire grew louder. This was no mere raid.

"We need to get to the bunker," Patrick said. "Quickly."

"No," Sarah disagreed. "We have to get to the war room."

She grabbed her coat—there was no time to get dressed properly—and led the way into the hallway. The staff were running up and down like frantic chickens, the guards were clutching their weapons as if they expected to be attacked at any moment. Sarah feared they might be right, as she heard the sound of breaking glass. Someone had just strafed the mansion with bullets. A dull thump echoed through the building, suggesting…suggesting what? She forced herself to think as they made their way down the stairs and into the war room. The bunker was secure, at least on paper, but it was a death trap. There were no secret passages, no way to get out without passing through a single bottleneck. If the government forces stormed the building, or simply threw a missile at it from a safe distance, there'd be no way out. She'd be dead or trapped, forced to wait until she was either dug out by the enemy or simply left to starve.

The war room was in chaos. Operators yammered into telephones, trying to draw meaning from what little they could discern and draw it on the map. Someone had had the sense to put a map of the city on the table, but it was completely useless. There were no positions—friendly or enemy—marked on the map, no suggestion of anything she could use to steer the engagement. She cursed under her breath as an operator slammed down a phone so hard it broke. Her communications and coordination staff had never really been tested. They'd never had the time.

She met the operator's eyes, holding him with all the command presence she could muster. "Report!"

The operator blanched. "I...the city is under attack."

"Yes." Sarah felt a hot flash of irritation, mingled with impatience. "Tell me something I don't know."

"I..." The operator swallowed and started again. "The harbour has been stormed. I was able to speak briefly to an operator on the docks, who told me armed men had burst out of a dozen ships and were rushing towards her. The line went dead moments later. I tried to contact several other posts within the walls, but the lines were either dead or the telephones rang uselessly. An operator outside the walls reported more armed men on the gates and told me he was going to attempt to determine enemy positions, numbers and intentions. He hasn't reported back since."

Sarah looked at the map. A *dozen* ships, crammed with government troops? She didn't believe it. It might be a political headache, searching ships before they were docked, but the harbour was designed to stagger entry and exit to make life difficult for anyone planning a repeat of *her* trick. She doubted the government had commandeered more than three ships at the most and even that might be giving them too much credit.

No, it might be no more than one enemy-controlled ship. It didn't make things much better. The enemy could have landed thousands of troops in a single trojan horse.

The operator cleared his throat. "We have lost contact with the camps, the garrisons and almost everywhere outside the city," he continued. "I think the landlines have been cut by enemy fire."

"I see." Sarah forced herself to be calm. It wasn't easy. If the enemy had captured the harbour, it was only a matter of time before they started advancing into the city itself. They wouldn't want to risk giving her time to get her troops into position, to force them to fight building by building. They knew how badly it would cost them, if she did. Their advantages—and she was honest enough to admit they existed—would be minimised if they were drawn into urban combat. "Contact the troops you can, get them into position blocking advances from the harbour."

"Got it."

Sarah watched the operator go to work, then looked at the map. The enemy had nicely isolated her—it was frustrating to admit, yet it was true—and they'd done a great deal of damage. The repercussions, both political and military, would be profound. She was tempted to wonder if they'd pull out now, quitting while they were ahead. Why bother risking getting sucked into a bloodbath when they could just leave, secure in the knowledge they'd hit the rebels hard? If nothing else, it would be difficult to keep shipping reinforcements to Winchester after Baraka had been attacked. The local rebel factions would all assume *they'd* be the ones targeted next and refuse to send their defenders away...

Not that it matters, she told herself. *If anything happens to me, someone else will take control or the rebel factions will split up and continue the war separately.*

The ground heaved again. She cursed under her breath as the operators looked around, as if they expected to be attacked at any moment. She was starting to think it would be wiser to evacuate the mansion. They were losing control—no, they'd *lost* control—and there was little to be gained sitting around doing nothing. The enemy would certainly target the mansion shortly, if they weren't already. In hindsight, it might have been better not to move operations into the captured building. She should have stood firm against it when the suggestion had been made.

An operator looked up. "We just got a message from the Winter District," she said. "The enemy troops are advancing."

Sarah blinked. The Winter District was on the other side of the city, nowhere near either the harbour or the mansion. It was little more than residential complexes, mostly abandoned during the uprising and then parcelled out to rebels and civilians who'd moved into the city. She couldn't imagine any reason for the government to attack the district—it wasn't that important—and even if they did, they'd have to pass through several other districts first. The report had to be false. Someone had seen friendly troops, maybe rebel militia or even men running to the docks, and panicked. It just couldn't be real.

Unless they landed troops behind the lines, she thought. She'd heard helicopters over the city. The antiaircraft defences were in ruins. The enemy could have landed anywhere they wished, if they thought it worth the risk. *But why would they bother?*

"Ask for confirmation," she ordered, tartly. The sound of shooting was getting louder again. She couldn't tell who was doing the firing, but it sounded as though it was getting closer. The enemy might have dispatched men and vehicles on a thunder run into the city. "And then start preparing to evacuate the building."

She dismissed objections as she directed the preparations. They'd slip out of the mansion and make their way to the barricades, setting fire to the building as they left. Her men were already laying charges. She'd done what she could to ensure her forces kept as few records as possible, but the ones she did have would be utterly disastrous if they fell into enemy hands. She dared not let that happen. She silently breathed a prayer of relief she'd thought to destroy the debtor files, the records of who was so deeply in debt they had no hope of escape. If nothing else, the government would have trouble forcing the debtors to pay their debts if they didn't know who owed what. Who knew? The former debtors might just have a chance to avoid falling back into the mire and being trapped once again.

The building shook, violently. Sarah looked up. That had been too close…

A man ran into the chamber, screaming. "They're here!"

CHAPTER THIRTY-NINE

BARAKA ISLAND, NEW DONCASTER

RACHEL KEPT HER HEAD DOWN as the missiles slammed home, giant explosions reducing the enemy camps to rubble. She keyed her terminal once she saw the enemy barricades, heedless of her safety, sending targeting coordinates back to the fleet. The missiles screamed through the air moments later, coming down hard. The barricades shattered, men and vehicles tossed in all directions. There was so much confusion that Rachel had no trouble getting through the remains of the barricades and into the city, heading straight towards the mansion. No one tried to bar her way.

The city was disintegrating, chaos spreading rapidly as law and order—such as it had been under the rebels—broke down. She saw more barricades being thrown up, seemingly at random; she saw fighters desert their units and run into the streets, either heading to their families or trying to desert after the first taste of combat. She wondered, idly, how the rebels would react. It was never easy to predict how someone would behave, when they came face to face with the harsh realities of war. The Marine Corps had had thousands of years of experience in screening recruits, and drilling them in combat before they fired a single shot in anger, and yet even the corps had its problems. The rebels would have to crack down hard, yet even trying...

She kept moving. There didn't seem to be anyone trying to organise defences, let alone a counterattack, although it was hard to be sure. There were districts that seemed quite heavily defended—and well-organised, with fire-fighters being sent to tackle the blazes—but in others, it was every man for himself. It looked as if some rebels were simply looting too, or worse. She spotted a rebel soldier pushing a woman against the wall, clearly planning to rape her. Rachel came up behind him, bashed him over the head and retreated as quickly as she'd come. She didn't know what his would-be victim would do—scream, faint, run, kill her tormentor—and she didn't much care. Right now, she had other problems. Her old instructors would have chewed her out for stopping to help, no matter how much the poor girl needed it. The mission came first.

Her lips thinned as she neared the mansion, trying not to scowl as she spotted improvised defences being thrown into place. The helicopters were orbiting the mansion, raining death on any enemy soldier foolish enough to show himself, but Rachel knew it was only a matter of time before they ran out of ammunition. The rebel CO seemed to know it too. He was organising his men carefully, getting them into position to either drive the helicopters away or block Richard's men if they managed to fight their way up from the docks. Rachel drew her pistol as the CO stepped into view, shot him neatly through the head and ran for her life, keying her terminal to call down more fire from above. It was unlikely the fleet would aim missiles so close to the helicopters—it would be the height of irony if a missile accidentally took out both Roland *and* the enemy leader—but the helicopters should be able to provide covering fire. She heard a pair of machine guns chattering as she ran, then scrambled up a ladder to hide as the mob came after her. It was unlikely they'd realise she'd gone up. To a normal person, it would look as if she'd trapped herself.

She heard more explosions as she scrambled onto the roof and looked around. The city was surrounded by fires, the camps around the city burning brightly. It didn't look as if anyone was having much luck fighting the fires. The enemy could no longer coordinate their forces. She checked her terminal and smiled, grimly, as all radio channels were blanketed by the message. It was unclear who, if anyone, was listening, but telling the city's population to remain indoors and out of the line of fire was secondary. The important thing was to keep the rebels from communicating. They still had the numbers. If they got organised, the operation was doomed.

And we have to keep them from getting organised as long as possible, she thought, keying her terminal. *The more time we have, the better.*

• • •

Roland was almost relieved, despite everything, when they ran into the first ambush. A hail of bullets came within bare inches of striking him. He fired back, throwing a stun grenade after the bullets in hopes of knocking the enemy troops out. They kept firing, seemingly untroubled. Roland cursed as he unhooked a HE grenade from his belt, pulled the pin and hurled it down the corridor. He'd hoped the enemy below could be kept in ignorance of his presence as long as possible, although cold logic had told him that was little more than wishful thinking. He certainly hadn't dared count on it.

The grenade exploded. The enemy fire abruptly stopped. Roland glanced at his men, then led the way forward. Four torn and broken bodies lay on the battered floor, all dead. A fifth man was dying, too badly wounded to be saved by anything less than a modern hospital…a hospital that simply didn't exist on New Doncaster. He gritted his teeth, then shot the man through the head. It was a mercy kill, and not the first he'd made during his short career, but it still didn't sit well. If he could have saved the rebel…

He led the way further downstairs, wishing they had better intelligence. The original builders might have stuck a bunker under the mansion—or a panic room, somewhere within the walls—but he had no idea where the entrance had been hidden. The handful of prisoners they'd taken had been unable or unwilling to shed any light on the question, save for a man who'd bragged so openly it had been impossible to take him seriously. The spooks had said he'd been trying to mislead them, and Roland agreed. He'd read the report anyway, just to be sure, but it was clear—now—it was a pack of lies from start to finish.

And we're not allowed to hit him for trying to mislead us, Roland thought, sourly. *It would set a terrible precedent.*

His mind raced as they reached another stairwell, only to be greeted with a hail of fire. The enemy CO was thinking fast, Roland thought. He'd thrown an ambush together in a tearing hurry, trying to buy time for the senior leadership to escape. Roland hoped the helicopters were enough to deter their bodyguards from escorting their principals above ground—no close-protection team worthy of the name would take such a risk—but there was no way to be sure. Was there a secret tunnel, perhaps leading to a mistress's apartment, somewhere underground? The people he'd consulted hadn't known. If there was, it would have been a very well-kept secret. It might even have been left off the original—now missing—plans.

"Set charges," he snapped. The stairwell might as well have been *designed* to ambush people coming from above. There was no way to hurl grenades down without running the risk of the weapons being caught in the middle, detonating uselessly. He didn't have the grenades to spare. "Quickly."

His men hurried forward, slapping the demolition charges into place. Roland glanced at the walls, silently calculating how much they could take. How strong *was* the mansion? He didn't know. The spooks had calculated the building had been designed to be a fortress, but the rebels had overwhelmed it so quickly Roland suspected the spooks were wrong. Setting off so many charges within the building was asking for trouble, if the walls were weaker than they thought. He didn't want to accidentally bring the entire mansion down on his head. It would be an embarrassing way to die.

"Charges set," Corporal Salter said.

"Take cover," Roland ordered. He took the detonator and braced himself. "Three…two…one…"

The charges detonated. The floor ahead of him dropped, falling onto the enemy position like the hammer of God. Roland felt the entire building shake, once again, and looked up. The ceiling seemed unsteady, but—thankfully—the walls seemed to have directed the blast downwards. He snapped orders, rappelling into the hole and landing on the bottom, weapon sweeping for targets. The enemy position had been shattered. He breathed a sigh of relief, then ordered his men onwards. The enemy leaders would be trying to escape. It could not be allowed.

...

"This way," Patrick urged. "Quickly!"

Sarah followed him, feeling numb. It was hardly the first time she'd been in danger, but there was something about *this* threat that made it hard to think. The government troops had landed right on top of the mansion and come crashing through the roof, trying to find her...it galled her that she'd let herself be targeted, that she'd let herself be talked into moving into a place the enemy knew as well as herself. They'd probably already found the plans in the government offices on Kingston, then used them to target their attack perfectly...

An explosion, so close she thought the mansion had been hit, shook the building so violently it threw her to her knees. She struggled to her feet, dust and pieces of plaster falling from the ceiling and landing in her hair. Behind her, she heard people panicking. The operators were meant to be shutting everything down, wiping computer files and destroying telephones before they could fall into enemy hands, but she feared they were on the verge of breaking. The sound of gunfire, just outside the mansion, grew louder. The enemy were dominating the surrounding streets...

Patrick caught her arm. "We need a diversion!"

Sarah tried to think of something, but nothing came to mind. There were no underground tunnels, at least as far as she knew. The bunker was a death trap. The last reports had made it clear the enemy was advancing, to the point they might get to the mansion to support the commando force before her people could organise a counterattack. She doubted they could hold the city for long, not when the rebels still ruled the island, but whatever happened wouldn't come in time to save her. She reached for the pistol at her belt as they hurried down a flight of stairs, passing a row of fighters heading up. Sarah hoped they'd slow down the invaders, perhaps even stop them. She feared it wouldn't be anything like enough.

The ground heaved. She heard windows shattering, pieces of glass and debris crashing to the ground. Someone was shouting...she stumbled along the corridor, clutching her pistol as she heard creaking and groaning echoing through the mansion. A handful of servants were already gathered near the doors, peering out onto a scene from hell. The buildings on the far side of the walls had been devastated. Half were missing, knocked into piles of rubble; the remainder were badly damaged, covered in bullet scars or burning. Another explosion thundered in the distance, a fireball rising into the sky. Sarah felt a sudden twinge of an emotion she didn't care to look at too closely. She'd unleashed something similar, when she'd sought to take control of Kingston. And now the government was doing the same to her.

Patrick swung around, raising his gun with one hand and shoving her down with the other. Sarah barely had a second to spot the dark-clad men coming out of the shadows before their guns barked, sending Patrick's body to the ground. She raised her own pistol, only to have one of the attackers stomp on her hand hard enough to force her to let go. The gun went off, the bullet cracking into the distance. Sarah grunted in pain as a man landed on top of her, wrenching her arms behind her back and wrapping a plastic tie around her wrists before searching her roughly. Her mind churned as the rest of the servants received the same treatment. She didn't look *that* much like Wilde, the rebel leader and spokesperson. Perhaps if she pretended to be dumb, they'd send her to a POW camp instead of shooting her out of hand. It wasn't much, but it was all she had. It would have to do.

"That's her," one of the men said. "She had a bodyguard. It has to be her." Sarah's heart sank. *Shit.*

...

Roland had been told, once, that some of the most dangerous people in the known universe had looked harmless.

He believed it. Belinda could easily have been taken for a dumb blonde by someone who looked at her tits and not at her eyes, while Rachel was short and wiry and hardly the kind of person who would be put on a recruitment poster. There was a certain safety in being underestimated, although his instructors had pointed out that looking ready and able to fight could deter someone from actually trying their luck. And yet, looking at the rebel leader, part of him was tempted to wonder if he'd caught the wrong person. Sarah Wilde didn't *look* very impressive. She was clearly hardened by life, but she didn't have the same attitude as a professional soldier. If she hadn't had a bodyguard with her, he would have been sure he'd made a mistake.

"Get her upstairs," he ordered, as he checked his terminal. The mansion's defenders were running now, abandoning their posts instead of fighting to the last. He didn't blame them. Richard's men were cutting their way through the streets, opening a path he could use to either secure the city or withdraw before the rebels counterattacked. "And then see what you can get from the records."

"Yes, sir."

Roland nodded, trying to ignore the sudden wave of fatigue. It wasn't *that* late, but he felt as if he'd been fighting for hours. His men half-carried Sarah Wilde upstairs, leaving the rest of her escorts for later processing. Roland hoped they'd talk, although he feared their knowledge would be out of date very quickly. The rebels would have been wiped out long ago, if their organisation was too fragile to survive losing a handful of key personnel. The government had had few qualms about authorising torture to force prisoners to talk.

His terminal bleeped. The advance units were nearing the mansion. The rebel forces were breaking up and withdrawing, heading for the barricades and the open lands beyond. Roland issued orders, directing the fleet to drop missiles on the retreating units. It didn't sit well with him, but a retreating force was one that could rearm, then turn around and come right back. Better to crush it now then give it time to come back. He sighed, then looked up as Rachel stepped into the room. She looked as tired as he felt.

"Parts of the city are still in enemy hands," she said, flatly. "They'll cause trouble tomorrow morning."

Roland nodded. The rest of the force should be landing now, ensuring he could keep the city secure, but it wouldn't be easy. Controlling an entire city never was, particularly when the inhabitants feared they'd be kicked out of their new homes, or enslaved, or simply executed without trial. It would take time, time he feared he didn't have, to convince the citizens the government had no intention of going back to the bad old days. He knew they wouldn't believe him. Deep inside, he feared he wouldn't be telling the truth.

"When Richard arrives, tell him to clear and hold a corridor, but to leave the rest of the city alone," he ordered. Gunfire sputtered in the distance, then died out before he could feel more than a flicker of alarm. "We'll try to hold, at least long enough to draw what intelligence we can from the mansion before we have to leave."

"Yes, sir," Rachel said. "And what were you thinking, jumping out of the helicopter first?"

Roland blinked, unsure who'd ratted him out. Most of his men didn't think Rachel was anything more than his assistant. The ones who didn't know about Sandra assumed Roland and Rachel were sleeping together, even though it was a serious breach of regulations. They wouldn't tell her. Why should they? He realised, too late, she *hadn't* known. But his reaction had told her everything she needed to know.

"I owed it to myself to take the risk," he said, finally. Now the operation was a success—he certainly hadn't planned to stay in the city, covering himself if he needed to withdraw—he was suddenly very aware of just how much could've gone wrong. "If the operation had failed, my career would have failed with it. I wanted—I needed—to be on the ground."

"You did well," Rachel agreed. She met his eyes. "And just remember, this isn't the end of the war."

Roland nodded. The rebels had taken a beating, and it had cost them dearly, but they were still a very capable force. Baraka was hardly a *small* island. The rebels would have all the time they needed to reform, appoint a new leader and resume the offensive. And yet, he knew the rebels had been badly shocked. Who knew? Perhaps they'd be more inclined to negotiate, now the government had proved it could hit them where it hurt. They might just see reason after all.

And we won time, he thought. *That's what we need most of all.*

CHAPTER FORTY

KINGSTON, NEW DONCASTER

ANGELINE WOULD NOT HAVE ADMITTED IT, not to anyone, but she'd been hellishly nervous as her force took up guard duties across the city.

Lord Ludlow had been dismissive, and she'd understood the reason for his confidence, but it still worried her. The militiamen were, on paper, a perfectly legitimate part of the military. Lord Ludlow and his clients had fiddled with the paperwork, to the point that—as far as anyone could tell—there was no way to tell they owed loyalty to their lord and his backers. But in the real world...there weren't *many* female militiamen, certainly not women in uniform, and Angeline was all too aware *she* was the most notorious of them all. It seemed too likely, as her unit crossed paths with other units, that she'd draw too much attention. But she was needed. The operation could not be left to men with even less experience than herself.

She sucked in her breath as she led her men down the corridor. The security emergency—and the constant barrage of terror threats—made it easier to move trustworthy troops into position, while putting unreliable or untrustworthy men well away from locations that simply *had* to be secured. They could stay on the sidelines for the moment, where they couldn't influence events one way or the other. Afterwards, if things went according to plan, they could be rounded up and dealt with at leisure. If the plan went wrong...

Her lips twitched, remembering something Lord Ludlow had told her. *Why does treason never prosper? Because if it does, none dare call it treason.*

Her radio bleeped, once. New Doncaster might lack the communications datanets of other, more advanced, worlds, but what it had was quite enough. Lord Ludlow's squads were making their moves, some targeting communications hubs, command posts and other strategic and tactical points, others fanning out to capture people of interest, from townie leaders to aristocrats who simply couldn't be trusted to take care of their own best interest. Angeline suspected Lord Ludlow had added some names of people he disliked to the list, but she found it hard to care. The new government would be eggshell-fragile for the first few days, while it struggled to take full control. They dared not risk someone getting loose and causing trouble. It was bad enough laying down plans for General Windsor and *he* was a very long way away.

She glanced at her men, then pushed open the door to the PM's office. The antechamber was empty, save for a female secretary who gaped at the soldiers as if they were creatures from another world. Angeline jabbed her pistol into the woman's face, motioning for her to rise. The dumb bitch would be loyal to the PM—she wouldn't have been allowed to remain so close to him if he had the slightest doubt of her—and she couldn't be allowed to go free, not until it was too late for her to make a difference. The woman looked unsteady on her feet as she stumbled up, as if she were on the verge of fainting. Angeline didn't bother to hide her contempt as she cuffed, searched and shoved the woman into a corner. The woman reminded her too much of the person she'd been, nearly a year ago.

The PM's door was closed. Angeline lifted her hand, counting down the seconds before the point man kicked down the door. She'd wanted to hurl a stun grenade into the room, to jangle the nerves of everyone inside, but the PM was old as well as set in his ways. The medics had cautioned she might accidentally kill him, even though—on paper—stun grenades were harmless. She crashed into the chamber, eyes snapping from face to face as the rest of her team piled in behind him. The PM, his bitch of a daughter…and Daniel Collier, MP for some godforsaken townie shithole. A surge of anger, mixed with relief, ran through her as she pointed her gun at them. Daniel Collier was on the list of people to be arrested, yet they hadn't known he was visiting the PM. The meeting had been so hush-hush Lord Ludlow's sources hadn't known it was taking place…

The PM stared at them. "What is the meaning of this?"

"Hands in the air," Angeline snapped. She was disappointed the PM hadn't recognised her, although she looked nothing like the girl he'd visited in the hospital, after she'd been shipped to Kingston from Baraka. "Get your fucking hands in the air right fucking now!"

The PM stared at her, then complied. He seemed more shocked by her language than the rifle in her hand, something that amused her even as it made her blood boil. How *dare* he? He was the man who should have taken precautions against rebel attacks, he was the man who should have made sure everyone—particularly the women—were armed at all times, he was the man who'd appointed a foreign gigolo to command the planet's armies instead of someone who actually knew how to fight and win a war. Angeline's finger tightened on the trigger. Lord Ludlow wanted the PM alive, but she was quite prepared to shoot him if he gave her any trouble. He deserved to die for his treason against his own homeworld.

"This is a coup," Daniel Collier said. He sounded as if he'd expected it, although Angeline was sure that couldn't possibly be true. They'd have recalled General Windsor if they'd thought Lord Ludlow's plans were about to go into action. "Are you mad…?"

Angeline jabbed her gun at him. "If you cooperate," she snarled, "you will live. All of you. If you refuse"—she allowed her finger to tighten again, for a second time—"you will be hurt and hurt badly until you do. Seize them."

Her men hurried forward, grabbing the politicians and searching them roughly. Angeline took care of Sandra, discovering—to her surprise—that the PM's daughter was carrying a pistol within her skirt. A flash of naked rage ran through her. It wasn't *proper* for a young woman to carry a gun, or even to touch one, which was why Angeline hadn't had one before her world had gone to hell. But the PM's daughter was carrying…she was tempted almost to shoot the bitch, just to make the PM feel what Angeline had felt, when she'd realised she was suddenly helpless and defenceless and completely at someone else's mercy. Lord Ludlow wouldn't be happy, but…Angeline sighed and bound the brat's hands, then shoved her aside for later. There was no way to know, just yet, if General Windsor had been dealt with as planned. Sandra might, if nothing else, serve as a valuable hostage.

Daniel Collier scowled at her. "Do you think you'll get away with this?"

Angeline glanced at her radio. The updates were coming in thick and fast now. Government House had been secured. The Military HQ—and the civil service buildings—had been secured. Kingsport and the army training grounds had been secured. And, outside the government, hardly anyone knew anything had happened. Lord Ludlow had taken over the government, with barely a shot being fired. No one, friend or foe, had died. Not yet.

There will be a purge, she thought. The townie leadership would be eliminated. So too would the rebel sympathisers. *And then we will deal with the rebels themselves.*

She didn't bother to answer the question. "Take Collier down to the cells, then make sure he's secure and kept isolated," she ordered two men. "The other two can stay here."

The PM looked at her, tiredly. "What do you want with us?"

"You are going to order the rest of your loyalists to stand down and submit," Angeline told him. Lord Ludlow was already on his way, ready to be sworn in as PM in front of a much-reduced government. "If you do, you will be safe. If not"—she eyed Sandra, who was staring at her defiantly—"your daughter will be raped, right in front of you."

"You…" The PM's eyes went wide. He'd recognised her. Finally.

"You...you *wouldn't*."

"I would." Angeline felt her fingers tighten again. "If you refuse to cooperate, your daughter will pay the price."

Hatred rushed through her. Sandra was...everything she'd been, before her world had been ripped apart and she'd been violated, then left to die. Sandra was...the thought of tearing her down, of showing her how the world really worked, was almost intoxicating. She knew, deep inside, that she had become a monster, but she didn't really care. Sandra had betrayed her people. She deserved to suffer before she died.

The PM bowed his head. "Whatever you want," he said. "Just don't hurt her."

Angeline nodded, curtly. The coup was nearly complete. The previous government had been overwhelmed. General Windsor was stranded, caught between the rebels and the deep blue sea. Lord Ludlow had planned well, she decided, as he stepped into the office. The operation had been a complete success.

She allowed herself a tight smile as the staff prepared to make the broadcast. The islands would be secured. The traitors would be purged. The rebels would burn...

...And then, finally, she would have her revenge.

EPILOGUE

BARAKA ISLAND, NEW DONCASTER

THE CHAIR WAS UNCOMFORTABLE.

Sarah shifted against her bonds, trying to keep the blood flowing. They'd shackled her hands and feet, making it impossible to move, commit suicide or even try to seduce one of the guards. Sarah thought it was just a softening up tactic, one designed to weaken her resolve to resist when the pain *really* began, although she'd been through enough hell in her life to hold out for quite some time. Besides, who knew? She was probably still on Baraka. It was just possible her former subordinates would put together a counterattack and rescue her—or kill her—before she could be made to talk.

The door opened. She thought about pretending to be asleep, then decided it was pointless and looked up. General Windsor stood in the doorway, studying her. Sarah studied him back. He was oddly handsome, although there was a cast to his features that set her teeth on edge. It was the first time they'd met properly—second, if one counted her capture—and yet, there was something weirdly familiar about him. She couldn't say what. She'd seen photographs and government propaganda, crap pulled out of a PR specialist's butthole and then cleaned up by a committee of aristocrats who'd been sidelined from the important roles, but she thought she'd seen him before her exile. Had he been on Earth? It was rare for Imperial University students to go into the military—anyone who expressed pro-military views had been shunned, back in those days—but it was possible. Perhaps someone she'd known had been given the choice between life on a penal colony or military service. Perhaps...

"We need to talk," General Windsor said. His accent was weak, but she was sure she detected traces of Earth. "Now."

Sarah snorted. "Do you think that capturing me has won you the war?"

"No." General Windsor stepped into the room and closed the door. "Things have changed."

"Really?" Sarah snorted, again. "Are you here to try to bribe me? Or to beat me into submission with your bare hands?"

General Windsor squatted in front of her. "Last night, at roughly the same time as you were taken into custody, reactionary forces on Kingston mounted a coup. The operation was very well planned. Admiral Forest and the rest of the navy squadron withdrew overnight, without so much as a single word of warning to us. If we hadn't set up a pair of drones to establish a communications link back to Kingston, we wouldn't have known what was going on for quite some time."

Sarah blinked. "What?"

"We've been stranded," General Windsor said. "They've abandoned the troops completely."

"Oh." Sarah tried not to giggle. It was impossible. "They royally fucked you, didn't they?"

She didn't need him to answer. She already knew. The landing force was stranded in hostile territory, surrounded by rebels capable of maintaining a steady pressure until the invaders ran out of ammunition and surrendered. And then...Sarah allowed herself to dream, just for a moment, of an aristocratic civil war that would tear them apart, allowing the rebels to walk in and take over. She might not live to see it, but...it would be a world worth fighting for.

"Yes." General Windsor didn't try to hide it. "The army is mostly townie. And now it is stranded, while the new government takes control."

Sarah shrugged. "And your point is?"

General Windsor sighed. "My orders from my superiors were to stabilise the planet in hopes it would neither collapse into chaos, nor fall into the hands of unfriendly powers. New Doncaster is of relatively little importance, on a galactic scale, but if it were to collapse it may take others with it. My superiors believed it was worth some slight attempt to prevent chaos."

"Your superiors sided with a reactionary force bent on keeping the entire planet trapped in a nightmare," Sarah said, bluntly. "This world's wealth is built on a mountain of dead bodies and destroyed lives."

"My superiors believed that a working army, based on townies, would inevitably lead to liberalisation and eventual reform," General Windsor said. "But that is no longer important."

"Because the aristos have screwed you," Sarah taunted. "How long do you think you can hold out here?"

"Not long." General Windsor met her eyes. She saw youth—he wasn't that much older than she was, if at all—and cold determination. "I propose an alliance."

Sarah felt her world tip upside down. "You really think we can work together? What would your superiors think of *that*?"

"I told you." General Windsor looked grim. "My superiors want the world stabilised, in a manner that will allow for gradual reform rather than either stasis or anarchy. Beyond that, they are not too concerned with just *who* is in charge. We could work together, destroy the new government and build something better. Or you could do nothing and, eventually, inherit the ruins. What do you intend to do, after you win the war? How do you intend to move from an insurgency to a proper government? We can help you build a world that actually works."

He took a breath. "The offer is genuine," he said, as he started to undo her shackles. "You can take it to your people, to convince them to join us. Or you can watch us die and throw the opportunity out the airlock.

Whoever wins—eventually—is going to win a broken world, unless your offworld allies take over instead."

Sarah said nothing for a long moment. "If you're telling the truth..."

General Windsor smiled. "I dare say your sources will confirm it."

"Quite." Sarah stood, rubbing her wrists. "I'll check with them."

Her mind raced. If this was a trick...she couldn't see what he hoped to gain. She'd been a prisoner. The rebel leadership would be wary of her, at least for a while. If they didn't know what was happening on Kingston ... she met his eyes. It was hard to be sure, but he looked desperate. His army was trapped and his mission on the brink of total failure. And if they worked together, perhaps they could both get what they wanted.

"If it checks out, I will push for an alliance," she said. She held out a hand. "And then we will see."

General Windsor smiled, then shook her hand.

• • •

END OF BOOK TWENTY

Prince Roland's story will conclude in:
The Prince's Alliance
COMING SOON

AFTERWORD

WHY DID THE UNITED STATES lose the Afghan War?

In the weeks and months since the withdrawal from Kabul, which has left the people of Afghanistan (and, as of writing, an unknown number of Americans and other westerners) in the hands of the Taliban, a great many fingers have been pointed at President Joe Biden. It is clear that a number of extremely poor decisions were made, in the run-up to the withdrawal, and while Biden's allies have been trying to blame the affair on former President Donald Trump the fact remains that Biden was the man in the White House when the withdrawal took place and therefore bears the ultimate blame for the disaster. One can argue, and Biden's more reasonable allies do, that the war was already lost and needed to be brought to an end as quickly as possible, no matter how painful it was for the United States.

But why was the war lost?

In 1949, after the Chinese Communists defeated the Nationalists and unleashed a reign of terror, Americans asked 'who lost China?' It seemed difficult to believe that the vast amount of treasure expended on the Nationalists could have led to defeat, rather than victory. And yet, the answer was relatively simple. The United States didn't lose China because the United States literally never *had* China. It's ability to influence events on the ground was extremely limited, despite how much money and weapons were directed to the Nationalist Chinese. The US was unable to push the Nationalists to reform – it took decades for Taiwan to develop into an economic powerhouse, well *after* the government received a salutary lesson in the importance of political and economic reform – and they enjoyed very little support from the Chinese population. The issue was decided based on factors on the ground, not in Washington. And Washington did not realise this until it was far too late. Indeed, there is a case to be made that Washington never recognised it at all.

This is a problem that has bedevilled the United States since 1945. The US became one of two global superpowers in 1945 and, after the collapse of the Soviet Union, found itself the sole hyperpower. This has bred a degree of dangerous overconfidence, mingled with a lack of strategic focus. The US enjoyed the great good fortune of not needing to care about many regional issues, yet found itself involved in places that were of little interest to the US or – worse – caught between two parties, both of which expected the US to take their side. This lack of focus made it hard for the US to commit itself to anything long-term, creating a world in which the US is in the rather odd position of permanently being a transient power. The US's allies, therefore, see US involvement as temporary and are therefore reluctant to commit themselves wholeheartedly to supporting the US, on the grounds the US will eventually put out and leave them holding the bag.

From the US point of view, this is not wholly a bad thing. The US can pick and choose its engagements at will, as most local issues simply do not threaten the US's existence. How can they? But this leads to a major problem, in that Washington is often unaware of the facts on the ground, dismissive of local concerns and unwilling to either invest in the region sufficiently to have long-term influence or to abandon it completely. The US, from everyone else's point of view, neither hot nor cold. America's enemies have been quick to point out that, when the going gets tough, the US gets going. There is enough truth in the charge to ensure every single US ally had one eye on the exit, ready to bail if the US starts trying to slip out of the area. This fatally undermines American positions right across the world.

The Afghan War, however, was extremely difficult to fight right from the start. The US did not, as far as I can tell, do any serious thinking about how the occupation would go, nor did it make the commitments it needed to both invest in the war *and* convince both the locals and American allies that the US was serious. Worse, the US found itself trying to tackle a series of problems that could not be easily solved, even with the political will to do so (which was often lacking).

First, Afghanistan is an extremely difficult place for the United States to even reach, not without support from neighbouring powers. The logistics made it impossible to support a major force within the country, let alone the sort of effort required to evict the Taliban and then build a working state that would, eventually, win hearts and minds and ensure the eventual US withdrawal wouldn't be followed by a rapid and inevitable return to Taliban rule.

Second, the US's understanding of local politics and culture was extremely limited and its willingness to understand the realities facing its allies was, at least at first, non-existent. The average local warlord was unwilling to send his men into meatgrinders on American behest, as losing his troops would reduce his power and eventually get him killed (particularly if his men blamed him for the deaths). Nor was the average farmer willing to give up growing poppies – for drugs – when all the alternatives would simply make him poorer. Worse, there was a flourishing culture of nepotism and corruption that was appalling to American eyes, but – as far as the locals were concerned, the only way to get ahead. This bred frustration and resentment on both sides, making it difficult for the country to be stabilised and creating openings for the Taliban to exploit.

Third, Afghanistan's neighbours were reluctant to support the US for domestic policy reasons and/or suspicious of America's long-term intentions. This limited their willingness to provide meaningful assistance, particularly as it became clear the US was slowly sinking into a quagmire.

The US didn't have many options for dealing with the neighbours, nor did it have much to offer them. This created situations in which, for example, Pakistan would side with the US, but also offer the Taliban sanctuary within Pakistan. The US saw this as treacherous. The Pakistanis, all too aware that their country was constantly on the brink of collapse, felt they had no choice. They could not destroy the Taliban, so they had to find a way to live with it. It is quite possible Pakistan was unaware Osama Bin Laden was hiding in Pakistan, but – given his location – it is also possible Pakistan was quietly ignoring him in the hopes he would serve as a bargaining chip, if they needed one.

Fourth, there was no solid long-term plan for stabilising the country and creating a flourishing rule of law. There was little appetite for accepting the political and cultural realities of Afghanistan, particularly corruption and the treatment of women, but – at the same time – attempts to change the culture ran aground on local realities, ranging from simple unwillingness to accept western ideas to the inability to remove American allies who committed crimes against the local population. Indeed, American soldiers who blew the whistle on such crimes were punished by the American government, ensuring a colossal lack of faith in the government and a belief it was just a matter of time until the war was effectively abandoned.

Fifth, and perhaps worst of all, there was no honest assessment of these failings, nor was there a willingness to do what needed to be done. No American President was willing to tell the American people that there would have to be sacrifice, that the US would need to either commit itself to Afghanistan for a very long time – and that progress would be very slow, at least at first – let alone acknowledge the US's mistakes and missteps. Both Obama and Trump inherited wars they couldn't bring to a close, at least partly because senior military officers refused to admit defeat and tried to sell them both on 'war-winning' strategies that were nothing of the sort. It was clear to everyone, save Washington, that the US was in deep trouble long before the final denouncement in 2021. This did not do wonders for American credibility.

The result of all these failings, and others, led to a steady collapse of the American-backed government. Local troops saw no reason to fight and die in a hopeless war, not when they could turn their coats – a long-standing tradition in the region – and find themselves on the winning side. Nor were local farmers and other civilians prepared to die for the government, when the government had repeatedly failed to deliver even the simplest of its promises. The Taliban only got into power, in the first place, because post-Soviet Afghanistan was a lawless nightmare. The Taliban might have been bad in the eyes of the average local, but they at least *tried* to produce law and order. It is easy, if one lives in a reasonably civilised country governed by the rule of law, to condemn people who join extremist groups and support them. If one is not so lucky, it is harder to reject the extremists when the only other option is death and destruction.

What choice would *you* make?

Fighting and winning an insurgency requires several things. First, you must be honest about the *reasons* for the insurgency (insurgents don't pick up arms for no reason). Second, you must seek a political solution that tackles the root causes of the insurgency, as well as isolating the insurgents who want to fight to the bitter end (or you'll be refighting the war again and again until you do). Third, you must make it clear that you are willing to commit yourself to fight (to show you have something to bargain with). And fourth, you must acknowledge there *will* be setbacks and try to learn from them (rather than telling lies everyone involved *knows* are lies). None of this is easy, but it has to be done.

In one sense, the US defeat in the Afghan War is unlikely to cause any real long-term problems for America. The Taliban are not going to cross the ocean and invade the United States. The building blocks of US power remain intact. America's major enemies are still unable to produce more than a limited challenge, one that – win or lose – will not threaten the US itself. In another, US credibility has taken a body blow. US allies will shy away, openly or covertly planning for the time the US backs away, leaving them isolated and staring at their enemies. It will not be long before

China starts eying Taiwan, and Russia starts eying Ukraine and Eastern Europe, and pointing out the US cannot be relied upon to come to their aid. And, historically speaking, they may well be right.

Again, this can be blamed on Joe Biden. But it will linger long after he leaves office.

And now you've read this far, I have a request to make.

It's growing harder to make a living through self-published writing these days. If you liked this book, please leave a review where you found it, share the link, let your friends know (etc, etc). Every little helps (particularly reviews).

Thank you.
Christopher G. Nuttall
Edinburgh, 2021

HOW TO FOLLOW

Basic Mailing List—http://orion.crucis.net/mailman/listinfo/chrishanger-list
Nothing, but announcements of new books.

Newsletter—https://gmail.us1.list-manage.com/subscribe?u=c8f9f7391e5bfa369a9b1e76c&id=55fc83a213
New books releases, new audio releases, maybe a handful of other things of interest.

Blog—https://chrishanger.wordpress.com/
Everything from new books to reviews, commentary on things that interest me, etc.

Facebook Fan Page—https://www.facebook.com/ChristopherGNuttall
New books releases, new audio releases, maybe a handful of other things of interest.

Website—http://chrishanger.net/
New books releases, new audio releases, free samples (plus some older books free to anyone who wants a quick read)

Forums—https://authornuttall.com
Book discussions—new, but I hope to expand.

Amazon Author Page—https://www.amazon.com/Christopher-G-Nuttall/e/B008L9Q4ES
My books on Amazon.

Books2Read—https://books2read.com/author/christopher-g-nuttall/subscribe/19723/
Notifications of new books (normally on Amazon too, but not included in B2R notifications.

Twitter—@chrisgnuttall
New books releases, new audio releases—definitely nothing beyond (no politics or culture war stuff).

Printed in Great Britain
by Amazon